Immigrant

PATRIOT

One Family's Struggle For Freedom And Faith In A World Gone Mad

CRAIG MATTHEWS

Craig Matthews Media

Permissions for quotations or use may be sent to:
Craig Matthews Media
P.O. Box 611235
Port Huron, Michigan 48061-1235

Visit www.CraigMatthewsMedia.com for news and information on this and other exciting titles.
ISBN: 978-1-7355017-0-3
eISBN: 978-1-7355017-1-0
General Editor: Mr. Lawrence Giroux the Word-Smith
Cover Design: Marc David Creations
Embedded font: Caslon LT Std Antique

To my Nea and Bepaw;

Your lives forever changed my world.

To my grand children;

That you may know their story.

And for my brother Jeffery Cameron,

you insisted on being first to meet Jesus.

My Motivation

One of my earliest memories of my maternal grandparents is playing in their gravel driveway in Royal Oak, Michigan. It was a sunny summer day and I was wearing jeans and a short sleeve shirt. I was creating a city for my matchbox cars in the part of the drive that was used less and had patches of thick grass. I asked my grandmother for a spoon so I could dig roads for my cars. The bare places I used as parking spaces, pretending they were stores and homes and parks. A spoon was required to excavate roads between destinations.

'Nea,' my brother Mark's longtime name for her, complied and I retrieved a serving spoon from the kitchen drawer. Shortly thereafter, my grandfather entered the house. He complained to her, just loud enough for me to overhear the discussion, through the open window. I never heard him be disagreeable before and a bolt of fear danced momentarily in my heart.

"Leave him alone," she responded, "he is just playing with his cars."

"Bepaw" exited their old brick house and asked me not to dig my holes too deep. He walked away to his white garage to busy himself on one of his many projects. As I watched him leave, his work boots clunked past me on the narrow sidewalk, I wondered who he was? Where did he come from? Where had he been? Then, like any five or six year old, I went back to building my city in the gravel while those inquisitive thoughts vanished like a mist in the wind.

I have vivid memories of Nea and Bepaw. Seasons came and went, when I would consider their story in depth. This book testifies to those efforts. Their deaths interrupted that discovery process. I have longed to know more of their history. The limited information I had was passed down to me, including many assumptions. Research has been an arduous process taking me virtually across the globe. Thank God, for the internet enabling that electronic journey.

As a grandparent, considering my own grandparents, I subscribe to the notion that we only know three generations. Our parents, ourselves and our children. That is it. I desire to make my grandparents known to my grandchildren. Giving them a sense of the world that they lived through and handed down. Searching to contextualize their lives in history, I discovered a richness that compelled me to consider a myriad of people that would benefit. I knew that I wanted to share their incredible tale to bless my family.

My motivation morphed as their universe was unveiled. Lives are much more complicated than we suspect. I believe this is a universal truth. Digging through my family's history has revealed surprises. Connecting their life choices within a more complete story diminishes the shocking nature of their secrets. In the end, their place on a pedestal of my heart will not be shaken.

Nea and Bepaw lived an amazing life in a frantic world. Nations preoccupied with destroying their neighbors using modern weapons, a world-wide pandemic killing sixty five million and religious persecutions that ravaged freedom. Alone, each of these traumatic events could usher in change, but as they combined they unleashed a global hurricane of societal upheaval. Life forever changed.

I pray that you will be as blessed by my quest as I have been in uncovering it.

Craig Matthews.
August 13, 2020.

Thank You!

Thank you for reading this story. I appreciate your investment of precious time. Many people have enabled this book to move from an idea onto a page.

Connie Jean you push me, almost always in the right direction.

BoTa you encourage me upward each day.

Larry G, my word-smith, has hammered crude ramblings into comprehension.

My parents that I have exhausted through my shenanigans for decades.

Siblings, well - you know where we have wandered.

Three great kids that married and gave us three more.

Plus seven precious grand kids.

I am blessed beyond all measure.

Contents.

I.

'On To Zion'

Long before the sun was to rise Joseph Jacobucci slept deeply in his cramped Army cot in the middle of a row of twenty men. He had always possessed the gift of sleep, able to settle down wherever he was and catch a few winks. Most of the men around him had spent that night cloaked in anxiety over the task that lay before them. While they tossed and turned, he snored loud and long, with his face buried in his picky wool blanket.

Then the thunder began in earnest, rolling from the northwest to the southeast, whistling overhead. The thunder was only heard in the twenty-four year old man's dreams. The sounds triggered a distant dreamlike memory in an instant for the private. He was unexpectedly whisked back almost twenty years to his home in south central Italy. A strong storm had pushed in from the sea fifty miles to the west, crashing across the peninsula with a distinct violence. As the lightning cracked and thunder roared, young Joseph covered his ears with his hands and a bolt of fear shot straight through his defenseless heart. His large brown eyes looked around the darkened room for his mother, Maria. She had been there before the storm, when he had laid down for a nap, but now, was nowhere to be seen.

"Momma!" The young Giuseppe cried out in terror.

"Momma!" Louder, he cried.

"She will be right back," said the calming male voice, to his brother.

Joseph cowered beneath his blanket as his older sibling John, came to his side. John was born five years before his kid brother, and had been left in charge until his mother returned from the Post Office.

"Momma must have got caught in the storm and is staying at the Post Office, until it clears," he explained to the frightened mass of blanket that contained the little guy.

"Why did she have to go to the Post Office, Johnny?" Asked the muffled little voice.

"To see if we got a letter today, maybe from Papa," John explained, knowing that the outpost of Spinete only received mail about once a month via horseback, up from Compobasso.

The blankets were immediately thrown back from the young boy, revealing his tear stained face.

"Papa wrote a letter again?"

A suddenly happy Joe inquired, with a big smile. Hoping to hear from the mysterious figure that everyone called his Padre.

Just then Maria pushed through the family's front door holding it tightly against the blowing wind and rain.

"Wow! It is really storming out there," she said shaking the water off her hands, now completely drenched.

Maria was a beautiful woman with long black hair, a petite figure and a natural glow about her. However, in those years, she had rapidly aged. Caring for her two boys was her priority, like any Italian mother, but her beloved husband was literally half a world away.

She had not seen him for almost six years, waiting patiently month after month, to get word for the family to join him. Any, and every communication from him was treated like a precious jewel, cherished above everything else. On the second Monday of the month a letter would magically find its way across the vast North American continent, sailing the Atlantic Ocean in a ship to Naples, Italy. From there it made it inland to Compobasso by train and up the winding road to her village on the back of a mule. It always amazed her that they could talk to each other in such a manner and considered it a minor miracle. Benny, as she called her beloved Barbato, would write the most exquisite letters that she treasured for weeks, reading them over and over again to hear the whisper of his voice.

"Oh Benny I miss you, my love."

On 'mail' Mondays, Maria always had a letter to Benny ready for the Postman to take back down to Compobasso. She prayed that the piece of her heart, she sent with the correspondence, would make it back around the world to find her lover and remind him of her undying affection. She was so proud of him, for his willingness to do whatever it took to provide for her, and waited patiently to join him. It was becoming harder to remain patient.

She stuffed the highly anticipated parcel down her blouse before exiting the tiny Post Office, just two blocks through the town square from her home. She paused for a few moments, while the heavens opened up to wash the earth, inside the musty and cramped old building. Watching through the small window, she noticed a slight lessening of the rain and made a break for her house in full sprint. Just ten steps into her race she was completely soaked by the cold rain and was praying that the letter would be protected in her shirt. She held on to it as her feet sloshed through the growing puddles on the cobblestone. Violent lightning cracked and made her let out a frantic cry as she reached for her door, a few seconds later.

Removing the letter from her shirt, she reached for a clean towel to dry the damp envelope before it was ruined.

"Momma, you are all wet!" Smiled the youngest, as he shot out of his bed clinging to her side.

"Is it from Papa?" Asked John inquisitively.

"It is," she said, padding the white paper before the ink could smudge.

"See honey?" Showing him the letter.

"I want to read it, Momma," said little Joseph excitedly.

"Maria Iacobucci," John read the first address line out loud.

"Hey!" Little Joey protested.

"All right you two, I will read it out loud to both of you," Maria said.

"Do you see what it says up in the corner?" She asked and they looked intently.

"Barbato Iacobucci Bingham Junction, Utah, U.S.A." She guided them through the unfamiliar English words on the envelope.

"Sant'Antonio! Papa!" Joseph said and jumped with glee.

"Yes it is tuo Padre, Giuseppe!" Maria smiled with growing anticipation.

After carefully prying the well sealed envelope with a knife from the kitchen, she opened the letter and some bills fluttered to the floor, causing the boys to lunge with excitement toward the odd looking money.

Maria seized her mouth when she saw the amount that he had mailed.

"Benny, why would you take such a chance mailing money halfway around the world?" She asked out loud still trying to read the long handed script.

"What does it say?" The excited boys wanted to know.

"Well, Uncle Tony and Aunt Andrea arrived last week, he says!"

"Yeah, they made it to America!" John exclaimed while holding up two of the three crisp green bills.

"What about Carlo?" Joseph wondered, hanging on to his new treasure.

"Yes Carlo too, my little one. Tuo Padre says he misses you both very much," Maria said, while still reading ahead in the letter.

"What is this green paper, Momma?" Joseph asked, turning it over studying it closely. She howled!

"Boys, we are going to the States to see your dad! Madre di Dio! We are moving to America! It is really going to happen! The tickets have already been paid for and we leave in February! Oh, Grazie Gesu!"

Thunder boomed and the cot shook beneath the resting soldier, destroying the pleasant memory of the distant dream. He missed his mother, while he tried to shake the sleep from his mind. Drool had wet the side of his face. He opened his eyes, as he dried his cheek with a numb right hand.

"Come on Bushy, wake up, we gotta move out," whispered the soldier standing above him, while he tugged on his clean khaki trousers.

The sight of his buddy getting dressed right there in front of him brought Joe to attention, and he jumped out of the cot. The entire tent was in motion; he was the final doughboy out of his rack, which was not unusual. The scene struck him as odd. The soldiers rushed to quickly ready themselves. There was no one speaking, just focused activity. The severity of the moment fell on him like a lead anvil. Today, we go fight the Huns.

•

"Oh my, the mountains here are so beautiful in the early morning light," said the young farmer's apprentice.

"That they are, my boy, that they are," replied the older man, while the pair walked toward the large red barn. They were both astonished at the beauty of God's creation, as the water vapor from their breath formed long trailing lines of fog in the cold spring morning.

"It never grows old," whispered the grateful farmer under his breath.

"Those are the Bannock Mountains son, and the tallest one is Scout Mountain," the forty-two year old said.

"And Bonneville Peak is the big one behind you."

Then came a few moments of reverent silence.

"This is such an amazing place to have a home and with the river just down the hill, it's like living in a painting," he paused with a look of enchantment, as if he had been transported to the celestial heaven itself.

"What's the name of the river again?"

"That's the Portneuf."

"Legend says that it got its weird name, which means ninth harbor, from a French-Canadian fur trapper who was killed up here almost a hundred years ago," he continued, while walking.

"How long have you lived here, Uncle?" Inquired the younger.

"Well, back when you were about ten, I guess, the federal government opened up over four hundred thousand acres for settlement in this part of the state," replied Uncle Christian.

"So, you have built this entire farm in only eight years?" Questioned Neils, with a sense of fascination.

"It has been a lot of hard work to get to this point, Neils," said Christian, proudly.

"And there is still so much to do."

"Well, I am so glad that you had a place for me to come and work, Uncle, I won't let you down, Sir," he promised.

"I know you won't, son. You're a Skeem and we keep our word."

"Yes sir, we do!"

"Alright, I am going to let your younger cousin Chris walk you through the morning chores that we have to accomplish before breakfast everyday, except on the Sabbath, of course."

"Whatever you need, sir."

"Well Neils, we are glad to have you here son, welcome aboard," he reached out and shook the young man's soft hands and smiled. He knew that, if his nephew was going to make it as a farmer, his hands would have to quickly change both in strength and in condition. Neils seemed eager enough though, and Christian Skeem thought that eager was a good place to begin.

"Chris!"

"In here Pa,"

Over the next few weeks young Neils became acquainted with farm life through a baptism by fire. He was so sore, every muscle ached and even the muscles he never knew he had screamed for attention. Mornings were the worst. Facing the weather before breakfast for a few hours, before the sun even bothered to bathe the beautiful mountains in light, took some getting used to. All of the stacking, shoveling and carrying of heavy things wore him down. His hands bled as blisters formed on top of blisters so gloves became his best friend and a highly prized commodity. Calluses would form where the blisters had ruled while he stacked, cleaned, planted and shoveled. All of that was before they even got to eat!

Aunt Gin, short for Virginia, was an amazing cook and she put out a generous spread at every meal. Eggs, bacon, biscuits, hash, toast and her cinnamon rolls were to die for. The food was fit for a king and he soon knew that if it was not for the meals he would have found an excuse to go back home to the family store in Nephi. His primary reason for leaving the family business was the adventure, not the money. Second of all, he treasured the experience of sitting at the feet of his legendary Uncle Christian. Finally, he loved the notion of becoming a first rate farmer and ranch hand. He had jumped at the opportunity when asked.

The young Neils had never traveled far from his birthplace of Nephi, Utah. A couple of trips to Salt Lake City to visit the Temple and extended family, but not often. The railway had not come to town, until about two years ago, and travel by stagecoach was arduous. When the trains arrived, in 1910, the family's general store began to grow rapidly and vacationing was no longer a priority. They were extremely busy trying to keep the mercantile filled with durable goods from across the country. Working from sun-up to sunset, Neils busied himself with keeping proper records, stocking shelves, sweeping floors and loading wagons. He recognized that talking to customers was necessary, but that was his father's area of expertise and for the most part he kept to himself. At night, during those moments just before sleep, he would dream of exploits of building his own farm, but he fell asleep believing it was just a fantasy. For the most part, he had resigned himself to being a store clerk for the rest of his days. It could be worse, he reckoned.

Then his big break happened last year when his oldest sister Shelly, married John Clegg. His brother-in-law became a big part of the family business, which took pressure off of Neils. That, along with his younger brothers coming of age to help, allowed the possibility for him to make the dream of being a ranch hand become a reality. With his father's blessing he took the train two hundred miles north to Pocatello where his dad's older brother welcomed him. Loading his one bag, he and his uncle departed with a team of horses hauling them on the twenty mile trip southeast, into the glorious valley.

Just south of the little town of Inkom at a curious bend in the Portneuf, lay the large picturesque ranch. Nearly surrounded by mountains on all sides, the farm occupied over a hundred and twenty acres of rolling farmland and woods. All of it had been cut out of the rugged Idaho wilderness, in eight short years. To say that Uncle Christian was a hero to Neils, would have been the understatement of the century. He was god-like to the young man, possessing every quality he deeply yearned to possess.

As months on the farm passed, the young man from central Utah moved into his role of ranch hand without a hitch. Becoming familiar with his responsibilities and physically growing in strength and stamina, allowed him to step up and begin to learn other areas of farm life. He gained twenty pounds, converted every bit of store clerk fat into hardened muscle, along with growing an inch taller. He chalked it all up to living right.

The small community of believers had welcomed Neils into their midst, with open arms. The tight knit congregation became the center of communal life outside the ranch and Sunday meetings were a highlight for the growing young man. Most of the people of that church close to his age, were already married and settled down with their own responsibilities, including children. The congregation had few female prospects for Neils to consider. Aside from that, he was focused on learning everything that he could, so one day he could have a ranch of his own. That was his goal, romance could wait. Figuring that he was only eighteen, he didn't see the need to rush into something that was certain to happen anyway. He would work hard and the rest would fall into a place of its own, he reasoned.

Seasons turned. The busy harvest came and went and the progressive Democrat Woodrow Wilson was elected President, in November. Neils, having voted for the first time, cast his ballot for one of the two Republicans running, former President Teddy Roosevelt.

After the election he took a brief, end-of-the-year trip home, for the holidays. His former town of Nephi, was growing exponentially, transitioning away from just being a small community of farmers into something different. He could hardly believe the number of automobiles scurrying down the roads and the pace of life. Everyone was in a hurry to get somewhere apparently important. This made Neils somewhat sad for the change, and, at the same time, his sister was bursting at the seams pregnant, soon to bring another life into the world, which would make him an uncle for the first time. She was radiant and happy in her married life. They stayed up late talking about life on the ranch and his dreams to build his own place one day. It was good to catch up with everyone. It had been over nine months since he had left.

On returning to the Pocatello ranch, he noticed for the first time that the rhythms of farm life had become normal to him and it felt right. This is what he was meant to do, what he was born to do, his destiny. Living in the middle of that rugged beauty, embraced with that sense of purpose and peace made the next couple of years fly by.

•

"Johnetta!" Yelled the tall rugged dirt laced farmer who was possessed by a smoldering indignation that he was struggling to keep veiled.
The young woman's head snapped around in a startled recognition of the angry voice. His jeering face was cloaked in dark shadows by the bright early morning sun.
"Johnetta, you bumbling idiot, you left the coop gate open and the chickens are wandering all over the back yard just waiting to become a meal for the coyotes!"

He was angry again, she knew from the tone and the slapping of his brown hat against his thigh, like he was banging dirt out of a brand new hat dropped into the dust. She knew that there was absolutely nothing clean about where they lived in Idaho. As beautiful as Inkom was, it certainly had been a filthy place to try to start a ranch.

"Do you hear me girl, or have you gone off somewhere in your thick little head again?"
He was much closer to her now and quite visible.

"Ye-yes, sir," she stumbled in reply, with her sullen face pointed into the ground.

"This isn't fantasy-land! Get your sister Mary and get them birds back where they belong,
right now!" If Walter was red-faced by this point of the early morning, she knew that the
rest of the day would be filled with all manner of frustrations.

"Good grief girl, you are almost fifteen, start acting like it."

"Johnetta, dae as Walter says, please," said Margret, quickly interjecting herself and her
heavy Scottish Brogue from just outside the door of the farmhouse. Margret jumped into
this conversation before it got any more heated. It was not the first time that she had to
protect one of the girls from her ill-tempered husband.

Over the last five years, she had learned to step into conflicts sooner rather than later,
both to protect her girls, and to ease the tensions in their crowded home. He was getting
better about controlling his anger, but she knew that she needed to be vigilant and wise in
dealing with his short-tempered ways. These kinds of conflicts could drive her last two
Cameron daughters out of the home. Margret knew that day was coming soon enough
and was well aware of the pain it would bestow. It would rend her heart again, just as it
had when the oldest two left. They got married, in part, so they would not have to put up
with Mister Walter Adamson.

Back in 1911, Margret's oldest daughter, Maggie, got married to Robbie Sagers just ten
weeks after her younger sister Annie married Robbie's cousin Les. If that was not enough,
in between those two weddings, Margret, got remarried, to Walter. Neither of the two
older girls ever had the distinct thrill of living with the old bachelor. He had been a single
man for so many years, because he did not have many of the social skills needed for
marriage and became easily frustrated when things did not go his way. To curb his vast
and confusing feelings of insecurity, he over compensated with anger, yelling and
drinking, when he could afford the alcohol, which wasn't too often.

Upon hearing her mother's direct request, Johnetta hastily dropped the well worn hoe in the dirt of the vegetable garden. She turned and made her way to the rear of the house, away from the presence of that man, while he glared at her with a renewed agitation until she disappeared around the corner.

Walter threw up his hands in frustration toward his wife Margret, exasperated with one of her daughter's, again. He turned back toward his mule team and the lonely plow, and muttered something to himself about the curse of teenage girls.

The trip to the back yard for Johnetta was not a long one because the house was a pile of dirt with the middle dug out, and some old boards covered in canvas for a roof. The front door barely opened, but the stone fireplace worked well. This mud pile had been his castle for the last few years as Walter, or Walty, as she condescendingly referred to him in her mind, had moved them all out to the middle of nowhere to start working on his dream of owning a ranch. Inside, she did not feel much like a ranch hand, but more like a slave that always had to answer to a whip-cracking owner.

"He is such an old mule, I will never understand what she sees in him," Johnetta often pondered.

"There is no wonder he had been alone for thirty five years!" She would determine.

As Johnetta made her way, she tugged up on her old worn-out pants because her rope for a belt had slipped its knot again. Her britches were baggier this spring after the long lean winter months and her ankles were more exposed to the wind due to a recent, final adolescent growth spurt. If it had not been for the church dropping off food a few times they may well have starved. Now, another humiliating trip was required to the Bishop's Storehouse for needy families after Sunday's meeting, to see if anyone had donated pants in her new budding size. Feelings of unworthiness, along with anger, swirled inside of her heart again, but she knew that she dare not let it show. That had to remain a secret. She was stuck here in this never ending effort to forge out a life from this unforgiving ground, at least for now.

"This isn't my damn dream," Johnetta whispered under her breath, turning the second
corner, looking for Mary.

Mary Robina Cameron was not a pretty girl by any measure. She looked much more like
her rugged father than vivacious mother. For being almost eighteen years old, there were
few features that made her attractive to the opposite sex, at least as of yet. Some might
say that her curves were in all the wrong places and her facial features were rather homely.
No boys had ever been interested in sharing her company when they lived in Salt Lake.
Now, so far removed from everyone, the only hope of contacting prospective husbands
would be on Sundays after church service. The congregation in Inkom was so small the
prospects were few and far between. By being forced to move so far from civilization,
Mary felt as if she had been tethered to a post in the middle of the plains and no one
would be coming for her.

Her father had seemed to abandon her the minute he got off the train in Utah, which was
almost six years ago. For her, God was buried the same day her father was put in the
ground. She didn't understand why they had come to this country, to this place where
death and deception ruled the day. It was destroying her. Confused and challenged by all
of this over the years, she held on to hope. She described herself as a realist, not an
optimist with their head in the clouds, and certainly not a pessimist that could not see
beyond her own navel. Life had dealt her a crummy hand and it was up to her to work her
way out of it. Work she did. Mary was tireless and Walter loathed her for it. He was, by
nature, a lazy man and she did not possess a slothful bone in her body. His dream was
having a ranch to call his own, not the work that it took to make it happen. Mary liked to
work. It made her feel useful and a part of things that mattered. Work infused her with
the idea that she did have meaning, that life had a purpose.

Because Mary was the nearest daughter in age to Johnetta, there was a close bond between
the girls, especially since their dad had passed away. Now, here in the middle of Idaho,
living in Walter's dream, the two had become inseparable and found that they shared a

common disdain for their mother's husband. They used every opportunity to deride the man, but only in each other's company. They held their secret close and sought out ways to bolster their collective indignation. Opportunities did abound for comedic relief from such stark circumstances. He was under constant scrutiny.

Johnetta rounded the final corner into the backyard where she called out for Mary, who was busy hanging up some laundry on the line stretched between two pathetic cottonwood trees.

"Are you done in the garden already?" Mary asked her younger sister, as she approached.

"No," she said while finishing tightening the knot around her waist. Johnetta moved in close, so as to not be overheard.

"Walty was yelling at me because the chickens got out of the broken down coop again," she said while making the exaggerated look toward Mary. The special look that only the two of them understood.

Mary rolled her eyes and smiled acknowledging the slight.

"Was he beating his hat on his leg again?" She asked with a broad smile that revealed her crooked teeth. Johnetta was one of the only people that Mary felt comfortable enough around to let her guard down to smile.

Johnetta laughed out loud.

"So, did you hear the news about the lumber?" Mary said quietly, while stretching out a shirt on the sagging clothesline.

"No, I must have been out collecting eggs."

"It seems that some of the cowboys from the Skeem ranch will be here to drop it off later this afternoon," Mary said, and watched for Johnetta's response, trying to see if there was any change to her facial expressions.

"Oh yeah?" Johnetta deadpanned, without any outward reaction. She knew what her sister was up to.

"Aren't ye excited, young lassie?" Asked Mary in a thick Scottish brogue, for effect.

"Yes I am very excited that we are going to finally have the lumber to build a real house on this God-forsaken ranch," she replied in clear American English. Knowing that she was avoiding Mary's real unspoken question.

"What about the ranch hands?" Mary taunted her younger sibling with her elbow.

"Not having a dirt floor is way more exciting than any boy could ever be," Johnetta said.

"Tis nae th' wee jimmies a'm talkin aboot Johnetta, tis that jimmy wha mak's enn at ye ilka Sunday in kirk. Whit's his name?" Mary prodded and pried.

"The man making eyes at me in church on Sunday?" Slowly said a hesitant Johnetta, clarifying the translation to be correct.

"Aye," Mary responded with a mischievous smile.

"Neils. His name is Neils, Mary." Johnetta held back a smirk.

"He is older than me, he shuid be making een at ye Mary," she returned the old language back to her silly sister.

Mary wished that were true on some level. Not necessarily Neils Skeem, the nephew of Christian Skeem, who owned the big ranch down the road, but someone. Anyone. She didn't want to brood about it now and yet it did weigh on her heart more with each passing year.

"He is a handsome man, Mary," Johnetta admitted sheepishly while hanging the final wet shirt for her sister.

"Or mibbie, "He is a braw jimmie tae be sure," she replied in jest, as they both giggled.

"Girls!" Mother was calling for them to stop socializing and get back to work before Walter really came apart at the seams.

While they were walking away arm in arm toward the chicken coop, Margret smiled in admiration of her 'cinn bheaga hens.' They had been through so much and it did not destroy them. They were hard workers who never complained about their meager lifestyle. Even though she knew that they missed their calm, even tempered and strong father. They had pitched in to make the farm viable over the last two very tough years. Margret still missed Dugald terribly. Life was hard here. Harder than it needed to be, she reckoned.

Looking past the girls, Walter was out in the field, kicking up a little brown dust cloud in his wake, while he raked the last of their ten acre homestead. She was proud of him as he guided the old mules forward in the morning sun. He was beginning to see his dream become a reality and that was good. They had turned the corner in more ways than one. After the crops were all planted he was going to start building a genuine house for them. Getting off of the dirt floor would be good for her aching feet. Ethel, her and Walter's four year old daughter, would not always be so dirty and sickly. She was desperate for a real house.

•

The thunder Joseph had heard in his dream was the beginning of the artillery barrage to soften up the German defenses before the attack. He knew that barrage would commence at 0100 and they were to 'jump off' about five hours later in a massive assault. Almost a quarter a million Doughboys and Marines supported by one hundred thousand 'Frogs' of the French Fourth Army on the flanks, as the American Expeditionary Forces, or AEF, mounted its first truly American campaign of the war.

The new American Army had proven themselves in recent battles, but it was under French authority and French Command. General "Black Jack" Pershing finally insisted in a bitter fracas with French General Foch, that the AEF was an independent fighting force and would only fight as the American army for the rest of the war. The summer battles at Cantigny, Belleau Wood and Chateau-Therry had proven the tenacity of the Doughboy and now by September, it was time to command their own campaign. Over a million American soldiers were now in France, ready to fight with three hundred thousand more arriving each month.

America entered this war relatively late, about two and a half years after it had begun, preferring not to get involved in Europe's mess. The United States had remained neutral, until April 1917, in the global conflict. The country was pushed over the edge when the German high command announced it would return to unrestricted U-Boat activity in the Atlantic; meaning that all shipping to and from the United States would be open to attack from their menacing fleet of underwater destroyers. That, coupled with the release of the Zimmerman telegram was enough to convince President Wilson and Congress to formally declare war against the Central Powers of Europe.

Zimmerman was the Secretary of State from Germany who had tried to convince Mexico to come into the conflict. All of southwestern United States would revert to Mexico, in return for helping to defeat the Americans. Along with the property promises, the Germans said that they would give money and arms to our southern neighbor.

General Pershing had led an expeditionary force deep into Mexican territory in 1916 to hunt down the notorious Pancho Villa. The legendary Mexican revolutionary had attacked Columbus, New Mexico in a March cross-border raid. He burned and pillaged part of the town, killing seventeen Americans in the attack. The Germans were hoping to capitalize on the difficult relationship that had resulted from Pershing's year long unsuccessful hunt of the popular Villa.

Joseph's unit, the 101st Infantry of the 26th Yankee Division arrived in June. By August they had been called into battle, but on that day, it ended up only being in a reserve role. They were now to assault the northern section of the line in the second wave. Joe was grateful to be a part of the second wave. The unfortunate soldiers of the first wave had to spend the night out in the trenches of the front lines and were drenched in a cold driving rain. His 101st division was given the blessing of a hot meal and a dry cot for the evening, but all that comfort was about to be exchanged for the hell of trench warfare.

Outside the tent, the rain was lightly falling as the men sloshed through thick mud on their way to the front. The small road leading away from the Army encampment was clogged with men and equipment trudging in a hushed dirge. The disciplined march was often interrupted by French built light tanks, manned by United States Army soldiers, affectionately called "tankers." The small armored vehicles were manned by a driver and a gunner. On that road, before the fight commenced, many tankers were both peering out of the noisy contraption with the top driver door and hatch flung open to the night sky. Having it open during driving allowed them to avoid inhaling exhaust fumes that often hampered them during battle.

As company D pushed forward everyone wrestled with the thought of death. Was this to be their last day on earth? The young Italian-American murmured a familiar prayer for protection as he bit off a piece of dried tobacco plug to chew, stuffing the remains back in his pants pocket. He never had been a morbid man and was not one to wallow in self pity or doubt. But this pressure was unlike any he had ever experienced. His left eye began to twitch in response to the stress.

The Army had been a grand adventure for him ever since being drafted just over five months ago in Utah. It was a half a world away from the muddy rain-soaked French countryside he now found himself marching through. His pack straps dug at his shoulders and his gas mask bounced against his chest with each step. At least the helmet kept the rain out of his eyes, while his chin strap clung snugly to his face.

With his Springfield slung over his right shoulder he held onto the leather strap of the ten pound rifle while trying not to lose his footing. The march would be about two miles up this bleak road, then through a stretch of woods, before they entered the feeder trenches that led to the front lines. Those feeder trenches were how men and supplies moved forward to the fight. The front line trenches were a series of parallel fortifications that stretched across the battlefield for miles. The entire western front, which ran from the English Channel to the Swiss Alps, some six hundred miles, had opposing trenches. The Germans called their side of the front the Hindenburg line, so named for their famous General. The section of the front that was being attacked today was about a fifteen mile bulge held by the Germans near the French town of San Mihiel. The bulge was known to the army as the Salient.

For the last month the operation had been carefully planned by Pershing and his general staff. Knowing that any bulges in the front lines opened up opportunities for flanking maneuvers by the enemy. This is what the Americans were seeking to exploit. The major obstacle was that part of the line had been held by the Germans for the entirety of the war. They were well entrenched with complicated defensive systems in place, including overlapping fields of fire. The machine gun nests firing positions allowed them to overlap with other nearby machine gun nests. This made for a formidable defense against infantry.

They were, however, a war weary army. The energy that the Americans were bringing to bear in the war caused the Germans great fear. Before the bombing commenced the German high command began a limited withdrawal from the Salient. The relentless shelling from the American lines caused a certain level of panic among the Hun forces. Of course, the average doughboy did not know this, as they pressed forward into the night.

Worry was written over most of the men's faces, while they moved through the early morning darkness and the pace of the shelling increased. Occasional German artillery rounds would whistle close overhead and the men would scramble for cover.
"Don't worry Lads, the one that kills you ... well, you won't hear a thing," announced some Sergeant of obvious Scottish descent.
"Thanks for the encouragement, Sarge!" Someone yelled in reply, to a chorus of nervous laughter.

Over the course of the next hour, the men of the 101st forged their way to the front, as the thunderous roar of thousands of artillery rounds pounded the German positions a half a mile to the southeast. Even the dark water that stood in the puddles, gave testimony to the raging fight. As the ground rumbled and shook with each explosion the water shimmered in response, causing a paleness and a spirit of dread to fall over the soldiers who anxiously waited. The army division in the trenches immediately in front of the 101st was the 102nd and they were tasked to jump off to lead the charge, followed by Joe and his brothers in arms. Many that stood against the muddy walls of the trenches in the rear of the line prayed. Some smoked a final cigarette, others cursed out loud as the pounding guns came to a vicious crescendo.

•

As Margret stood and glanced at her husband out in the field, she was also looking back in time. She knew that she had been vulnerable during those early months and Walter had promised her many wonderful things during their brief courtship. That time together was arranged through the church's network that encouraged the unmarried widows not to remain that way for too long. They needed people to populate Zion after all, so being a widow was discouraged. 'Mourn for a short time, then just get on with life, have more babies,' was the plain teaching of the Bishop of the Latter-day Saints, in that ward.

Considering Walter, the man, it was easy to look upon him as a path away from her pain. A way out from beneath the heavy burden of mourning her first, best, and frankly, the only love of her life, Dugald. At that deep, dark time, Walter was a means to an end of loneliness and insecurity. He was a way out from the frightening madness that had enveloped her just a few weeks after arriving in Utah. Dugald had only been working at the smelter for four days when he took ill. Initially thinking the sickness was a reaction to the stifling heat, here in the promised land, he ended up in the local hospital in Tooele, undergoing a surgery for a mastoid and never recovered. Her lover was gone by July the Sixth and her dream of being together in this new blessed land, lay ravaged.

Margret was devastated and disillusioned by everything around her, including the Missionaries who had promised so many wonderful things in this land flowing with milk and honey, as they had said, while visiting their home near Edinburgh, Scotland starting early in 1907. During the next three years they had convinced them all to sell everything and immigrate to the United States. Margret bought the vision. She was hooked and enthusiastically went to every meeting offered by the 'Godly Men,' as she called them. The new and exciting religion that was building a genuine promised land was like a breath of fresh air in an otherwise rote and stagnant Presbyterian world.

The first to leave was Maggie, the day after her eighteenth birthday, taking a job as a teacher just outside of Salt Lake City in Lincoln, Utah. Then, the second oldest daughter, Annie, left for Zion eight months later and worked as a caregiver in a private home near her sister. Six months after Annie's departure, the rest of the family boarded the S.S. "Canada" and sailed west out of Liverpool. In just three short weeks they were settling into their exciting new life along with many other Scots who had made the crossing during those years. Then the tragedy of Dugald struck like lightning out of a clear sky, and her perfect, holy bubble burst.

The church was enthusiastically behind the new marriage to Walter which would solve a couple of issues for them in taking care of her family. Just a few months after her Dugald was placed in the ground, a Bishop with the last name of Miller, had advised her to not remain alone for too long. Even though they were living with Maggie, who was a teacher and able to provide for their immediate needs, the Bishop, a wee little man, on more than one occasion, made it known that Margret needed to move on with life. Somewhat reluctantly, she had agreed to be Walter's wife.

Standing in the temple in Salt Lake City that April day, just nine months removed from Dugald's demise, Margret knew that she had little romantic interest in the man before her, but hoped those feelings would be born over the passing months and years. She truly hoped that the overwhelming melancholy that had settled in her heart would be given chase, and life would return to her.

Margret had always been optimistic and upbeat, but that seemed like a long distant memory, particularly on her wedding day in that demeaning temple. She would marry him and be sealed to him, but out of an obligation to care for the rest of her family, not because some little Bishop had commanded her to do it.

The humiliation of the marriage ceremony was a harbinger of things to come. Forced to disrobe, five strange women washed her from head to toe in the secret ritual. It was the beginning of the end of her trust in her new found religion.

Dugald Jr, her son, was off working at a ranch south of Salt Lake and was already providing for himself, but Mary and Johnetta were too young for that sort of thing. That is why, in the end, she had endured the traumatic torture and said 'yes' to the question from Bishop Miller that day.

Then, during those difficult first few years, she was not certain that the relationship would last for any length of time. Amidst those long days, she lost substantial hope in the dream that she had placed on Walter's shoulders. Of course, putting those demands on anyone was not fair, but she had not been thinking clearly.

Having already married the love of her life when she was nineteen, they had set out to raise a happy and healthy family in her beloved homeland of Scotland. Dugald was a herdsman by trade and had developed a good reputation in his field as an honest hard working man. He cared for the cattle that had been placed in his care, and for many years received better offers to serve on different farms in south central Scotland. That is why all of their children had been born in different towns across the country. As his reputation grew, so did their status and rank in the communities in which they lived. On the "Tryst," which was always May 28th and November 28th of each year, the land owners would make it known how many workers they needed for the next six months. The workers themselves could put in requests to other farms as well and receive offers of employment.

That was the way the Scots had determined to staff the ranches in the country. Dugald, being a quality, hard working dairy farmer, often received offers that gave opportunity for more income, or for a higher quality work environment. Moving about the countryside was a normal, yet adventurous, part of their early life.

•

"Hey Bushy, I sure wouldn't want to be a Hun on the receiving end of that volley," said the skinny, nervous private standing next to him. Leaning back into the side of the eerily dark sand-bagged trench he drew deeply on his cigarette causing it to glow an intense red. His head was tilted to the side as he inhaled and one of his deep-set eyes half closed against the stinging smoke. This thin man ended up with the unfortunate nickname 'Weasel', because his last name was Wetzel. He was of German descent, so no one trusted him. 'Bush' was the nickname gift that the stout little Italian received from a belligerent drill Sergeant who had struggled to pronounce Jacobucci and shortened it to 'Bush' after screaming at him during a training exercise, one day in June. The rest of the guys in his unit stepped in and adopted the name without hesitation, except they added a friendly "y" at the end.

Many other men in company D ended up with nicknames. It was just what bored soldiers did. There was 'Big,' Freddy Smith, who was 6'3." 'Cookie', was originally from Salt Lake City with the last name Cook. 'Tool' was a soldier from Idaho named James O'Toole. 'Fingers' was Bob Johnson. 'Mule' was the stubborn Robert Clark. 'Frenchy' was played by Danny Marquette. 'Biscuit' Lee Hamilton. 'Guns' Jesse James Holiday, and on and on and on it went. Everyone understood that if you got a nickname you had graduated into acceptance, and if you didn't have an Army name, you were under suspicion until you did something noteworthy enough for ridicule. Otherwise, you were generally shunned and expected to shut up unless asked a direct question. This basic warrior code was enforced by everyone who was already on the inside of the unit, meaning, everyone who had a name.

Because Joseph Jacobucci knew three languages, Italian, English and enough French to navigate, he became the unofficial, official unit translator, which caused him to get the strangest requests at all hours of the day and night.

"Bushy, how do you say bread?"

"Bushy, how do you say coffee?"

"Bushy, how do you say smoke?"

Along with inquisitions for translations for every female organ, and one particular male organ. The demands were relentless from the men and serious from the Sergeant. He could have fought the designation, but it became a sort of badge of honor.

It was also valuable to his side job. Bushy had purchased a small barber kit from a Frog on their march from the sea. Not really a march, but a series of train rides through countless French towns and hamlets. They were joined by soldiers making their way to the front, a number of creative entrepreneurial French villagers marketing different supplies, even certain illegal commodities, to the vast quantities of foreigners who had infiltrated their noble nation. In one particular stop, a pathetic looking young French boy approached Bushy wanting to sell him the kit and Joe took the leap. He had tried cutting hair in his youth and put it to use to make some extra money. By the time of the Salient, he had pocketed quite a bit of cash, from his fellow soldiers. Being so well known by his nick-name, made it certain that he would get referrals from other men seeking to look good for important activities, such as a three day pass into Paris. Those guys paid Bushy very, very well.

"Fix Bayonets!" Came the order down the entire line.

•

II.

'The Hard Row'

As the day's light was fading into tomorrow Johnetta placed a couple of small logs on the fire, which sent excited sparks dancing into the cool evening sky. She was waiting for Mary to come outside and join her for their evening chat before bed. The two of them would often retreat to the fire pit on the back side of the house to escape the evening tension that always began building after suppertime. That was usually when Walty dug out his special bottle of forbidden libations to 'relax'.

"This is how men relax in private, and it isn't the business of anyone else to know," he would insist, making them complicit in keeping his ritual silent from the unsuspecting world.

Johnetta knew that it was just another of a long line of self deception to which the old bachelor clung. Despising the man was easier every day that she lived with him. In a few minutes, right on signal, her mom and Walty commenced their shrill fight. Sometimes, little Ethel would run outside to escape. Mary usually made it out to the fireside before the evening fireworks began in earnest.

Thoughts of her father filled Johnetta's head, while the imposter ranted in the background.
The man whom she considered her hero was gone now, and that staggering memory consumed her straightaway with an overwhelming melancholy. She was so much like him. She ached for his strong hands and calm demeanor, that would reassure her that everything was going to be alright. Johnetta wrapped herself in her own arms, subconsciously seeking that long lost, long yearned for, security of her daddy's touch. He did not have to say anything in particular, just his presence would be enough through

those younger years. She had been calmed by him, carried by his strength and secure in his arms.

Remembering is all she had left of him and she was determined to keep those memories alive, to keep him alive. Loneliness bit at her with a sustained rawness, like the cool mountain breeze pushing down the back of her neck, making her shudder. The fake dad's tirade rang in the background over the crackle of the fire in front of her. The feeling of hatred welled up inside her again and she knew that loathing the man in her midst was not the answer to her loneliness. She had to forgive the fake dad, but she would never trust him.

The cup of steaming hot tea warmed her dirt sheathed hands and her insides. As she sipped the weak concoction, the hypnotic orange, yellow and blue flames danced her right back in time to another fire on the other side of the ocean. A simpler fire in a simpler time. She was young then, almost nine, and had crept out of the house during the fare-thee-well party, just before they departed for America. Remembering back into that time, she had wanted to escape the loud party just to be near her dad. He was talking by the fire with Uncle Angus in somewhat hushed tones. It had seemed like they were having an important conversation, so she hid by the stack of wood and positioned herself to hear from the shadows while they spoke.

"You know Dugald what they say about this Smith, the man who started the whole Latter-day Saints thing, don't cha?" Asked Angus.
"What do they say, Angus?" Dugald was interested to hear what his younger brother had found out about the Mormons.
"They say he was a quack. That he and his family used to hunt in the hills of upstate New York for hidden treasure. Constantly digging for buried gold. They would use divination stones to guide them to where they should dig and then spend weeks digging up the ground. The holes are still there to this day. Then, when they came up empty, and they always came up empty Dugald, they would make an excuse to go dig somewhere else."

"If they used divination to tell them where to dig and they always missed the mark, why would they believe the divining stones anymore, it makes no sense?"

"I know. What's worse, is when he started this religious thing, it began with this joker saying that he had dug up secret golden plates that only he could read with special golden glasses. No one has ever seen these plates or the glasses," Angus said with passion.

"Well, even the missionaries explained that to us, well to Margret. She seemed convinced that what they were telling her was real," Dugald retorted.
"Some of the crazy things that these plates 'supposedly said,' was that they were going to build another promised land, this time in America. Zion. First it was in Illinois, then Missouri, and finally now in Utah. The truth is Dugald, they got run out of those other places, because Joe Smith claimed he was better than Jesus himself," Angus insisted.
"The people in his hometown signed an affidavit swearing that the Smith's were a family of dubious character and couldn't be trusted."
"Really?"
"After Smith was 'martyred in Missouri,' as they purport, Brigham Young picked up right where Joe left off but as the second prophet, and marched the lot of them to Utah."

"Angus, they would say that Jesus himself was rejected by his own people," Dugald replied.
"But Jesus said that He was the way and the truth and the life, not Joseph Smith."
"Jesus died on the cross and rose to life again, Smith is still dead."
"Listen, Angus I have many questions about what they teach."
"Do you know that they are polygamists, Dugald?"
"What?"
"Yes, only if you are high enough up in the Mormon way of things, but you could have as many wives as you could support. It is even encouraged, like you are earning a better place

in the 'celestial heavens', as they call it."

"I didn't know that," he said looking into the flames.

"One wife is all I can handle."

"I am afraid for both of the girls, Dugald. Like those missionaries came here to recruit women for their sex cult or something. Maggie and Annie are in Utah right now and I am afraid for them," he was being genuine.

"Well Angus, we have gotten many letters back and they seem to be doing quite well," Dugald said with appreciation. He could not deny his brother's love for him or his family.

"I hope you are right, Dugald."

"Listen, brother, I appreciate your concern and I want you to know that I am suspicious of all of their rose colored claims, too."

"The devil's boots don't creak, Dugald."

"That old saying is true brother and that is why I need to go and see for myself. It's my girls living halfway around the world and I need to be there to protect them."

"So why did you get baptized?"

"Simple Angus, no baptism, no travel. You can't go to the promised land without it."

"Aye."

"I have to go, Angus. Go and see for myself. I can't help them from here. If it is all a ruse we will move to another part of the country or get back home somehow," he insisted.

"I think it would be better to avoid the Mormon mess altogether, brother."

"Too late for that Angus. I am afraid that we have let our feet run faster than our shoes."

It was nearly six years removed and Johnetta remembered every detail about that night. She has discussed it many times with Mary but never with Maggie or Annie. They were the true believers in the family, while Johnetta remained a skeptic, just like her daddy. Uncle Angus was right about the Mormon mess, especially when it came to Walter. The man had always looked down on her mom, like she was a frail butterfly, until she found her footing again and began to fight back. Margret Cameron was no pushover and Walter Adamson was getting his nightly lesson in that truth.

"Go Mom, go," she whispered into her tea as the shouting came to a crescendo from within the mud hut.

"Hey, do you have any room left in your head for your sister to join your big adventure?" Mary quipped, taking a seat on the log next to Johnetta, the flickering light revealing her sarcastic smile.

"Lots of room in my head," Johnetta smiled in return.

"Where is Ethel?" Johnetta asked.

"She is out like a candle," Mary responded.

"Getting used to that shouting, aye?."

"But if you think about it, Johnetta, this is Ethel's normal. Our dad was our normal."

"You got that right, nothing like that man," she sat up to make the point and stir the fire with a stick sending a thousand little lights into the sky.

"Ethel will be alright, Mother won't let anything happen to her."

"Right. Mother is a ferocious woman, to be sure. I don't know how she does it. I guess i'm not like her at all," Johnetta said.

"Nonsense, Johnetta. You aren't a screamer, but you love deeply like Mother does. You are strong and you are a thinker like Father was. You're a Cameron and you cannot escape it, Luv."

Johnetta's reassuring sister helped to keep her sane and gave her strength to push through to another day, much like what her dad had done for her.

"What did you think about those cowboys, today?"

"They were a sight to see, sister."

"And everyone of them as strong as an ox,"

Now the evening laughing session began in earnest. They craved the laughter that naturally happened when they were together. It transported them far away from their troubles and into a place of lighthearted rest. Many times their mother would join them by the fire for a time after her husband had fallen asleep and it would take them back to the old, carefree days. From the sounds of it, Mother would not be joining them this evening. Apparently, Walter's wounded soul still had some shouting trapped inside of it that needed to escape.

•

While Neils was out riding a fence line in the south pasture, a spring snow squall blew through the area depositing chilled shivers down the back of his bare neck. The fence had been installed the previous fall and overall the herd had not done any significant damage. He found one large mountain spruce in the southwest corner that had been forced over in a sudden gust, snapping the wire and breaking two posts. The branches of the fallen tree hid the gap in the fence and the herd had yet to notice the break, but he was sure the wolves would find it soon enough.

Neils spent most of the morning fixing the mess and was cleaning up the fallen brush he had cut from the tree, when he noticed a man waving at him with both hands. This was not the 'hello' kind of wave, but a 'look at me,' 'do you see me here,' or even a 'help me', desperate kind of wave. Standing up, Neils jumped the wire fence to meet the man who was running towards him.

"Hey," said the man through heavy panting. He had been moving at a quick pace and was too out of breath to speak for a moment.

The young rancher thought about his rifle that was attached to the saddle of his horse, some fifty yards away.

"Hey, could you help me, son?"

"What do you need, sir?" Asked Neils, a little hesitant.

"I am sorry, my name is Walter Adamson and I am your new neighbor, south about a mile," he said extending his hand.

"Welcome to the neighborhood, I am Neils Skeem, pleasure to meet you, sir," he returned the gesture.

"My mule team is stuck, well actually the plow is stuck, in some rocks and the mules are lodged in the mud and I need some extra help getting them free before they hurt themselves," he explained, with his hat in his hand.

"My wife and daughters are not quite strong enough."

"Sure thing, Mr Adamson, I can go hitch a team and meet you back at your place if you want."

"I really appreciate that son," said the humbled man.

"I will be right along sir," Neils said and wanted to turn.

"Tell your folks how much I am indebted to them," Adamson said.

"I will pass along your gratitude to my aunt and uncle, Mr. Adamson," he said as he left.

After that day, the Adamson clan began attending the small LDS congregation along with the Skeem's. Appreciation for the help was imparted to Christian and Gin.

A shared meal, to welcome Walter and his family into the tight knit community was produced and delivered within the week. The two Cameron girls were unable to attend due to unfortunate female things that needed to be looked after. The two families became fast friends, at least Gin and Margret. Whereas, Christian did not connect with Walter except on a surface level. Walter was jealous of Christian and all that he had accomplished on his ranch, and how well organized it was compared to the mud hut and broken down chicken coop just down the road. Walter Adamson was outclassed and embarrassed. He was a proud and stubborn man determined to figure things out on his own. He did not need a Christian Skeem to show him the ropes or give him charity of any kind, he would earn his way through this life or he would starve trying.

And starve they did, that first winter. It got so bad that Margret whispered to Gin in church one Sunday morning that they had not eaten much of anything for nearly a week, which opened the floodgates of anonymous help, from all over the valley. Much of that help was initially rejected at the front door by Walter, then duly accepted with gratitude at the back door by Margret. Word quickly got out that Walter Adamson did not want help and was willing to starve his family to prove his stubborn point, but Margret was more than willing to accept the gifts from her neighbors and the Bishop's Storehouse at the church in Inkom to feed her family, often promising to repay the help in the near future.

Later in the evening Margret would scold the man, shame him in front of all three of the children, trying to shake free his insolent pride. The thorough tongue lashings would last as long as she deemed necessary. Even longer, if he dared to dig into his 'bottle of relaxing'. She was brutal in those days, desperately trying to save her children from starving to death from his inertia.

•

"Fix bayonets!"

Muscle memory took over as a shock wave flashed through them and they instantly reached for their bayonets to affix them to the barrel of their Springfield rifles. The men of the 101st had done this maneuver at least a thousand times in training, but this was for real. They were going to be charging out into the darkened landscape to kill someone they didn't know hopefully before getting killed. Hearts were pounding out of chests. Prayers were desperately reaching up for heaven.

Bushy's mind was filled with a thick fog as he tried to prepare himself for the attack. Then, quite unexpectedly, his mother's angelic voice whispered to him from a near distant place in his memory. His Momma always had a great faith, often praying out loud when they were younger, in particular while dad was away for all of those years. Momma used to say that it was God that had walked her through those lonely times, and she had taught both her boys to pray as well. There was a Psalm that Momma would say to them from memory whenever they were feeling afraid and insecure. There in the soggy trenches of northern France it miraculously came back to his lips like a long forgotten song, rushing up from the depths of his heart.

"I lift up my eyes to the hills, from where does my help come?
My help comes from the Lord, who made heaven and earth.
He will not let your foot be moved; he who keeps you will not slumber.
Behold, he who keeps Israel will neither slumber nor sleep.

The Lord is your keeper; the Lord is your shade on your right hand.

The sun shall not strike you by day, nor the moon by night.

The Lord will keep you from all evil; he will keep your life.

The Lord will keep your going out and your coming in from this time forth and

forevermore."

He made the sign of the cross and whispered his "Amen."

Weasel and Mule, on each side of him, made the same sign.

The early morning sky hung low, with stifling foreboding clouds, and was suddenly

illuminated with bright red flares. Hundreds of flares shot so high they pierced the

darkness causing the sky to give off an eerie red glow for miles in each direction. It

looked as if the men would be marching straight into hell. With that visual signal,

sergeants up and down the line began yelling for the men to jump off.

"Move, Move, Move, Move!!!" Rang out from every quarter.

The soldiers in the forward trenches began clamoring up the ladders into no-mans-land

with a scream. As the number of men going over the top increased the roar gained

volume while they fiercely charged into the eery red darkness. With the mass of soldiers

pressing forward, the artillery began its rolling barrage. Two hundred yards out in front of

the surging men, shells began hitting the ground with a deafening rumble, throwing mud,

metal, and human remnants into the sky. The barrage was designed to expand out in front

of the charging men and force the German machine gun crews to take cover during the

attack.

The first teams forward had the dangerous job of cutting through the wire with hand

snips, making them more vulnerable to rifle and machine gun fire. Artillery shells had

little effect on the coils of barbed wire strewn across the battlefield. The wire was used by

both sides in the war to impede progress of attacking armies. The enemy had to be killed

in no-man's-land, or in your own trenches.

There should have been ample early morning air cover for the battle. 1,600 planes had been assigned for the assault, but the heavy cloud cover forced the bi-planes to remain grounded. The famous American Hat in the Ring Squadron, led by Ace Eddie Richenbacker, was expected to patrol the skies above the Yankee Division, on the north side of the salient, but it never happened.

As soon as the first troopers arrived at the wire, guns opened fire at them from concealed positions. Enemy infantrymen began sticking their heads out of trenches to fire rounds into the early morning darkness at the Americans. Limited German artillery began launching high explosive shells into the charging mass of men with dramatic effect. Men were simply vaporized, others mangled, limbs discarded in helter-skelter turbulence. Modern warfare raged in all its ghastly glory.

The sky began to brighten as the tremendous noise of the battle erupted. Men continued to pour out of the Allied trenches and many entered their crossing with a primal scream directed toward the unseen enemy. Weaving through the littered landscape they rushed forward, compelled and pushed. The artillery pounded out in front of them, then savagely exploding with frequent secondary blasts. The wiz of bullets passing closely by, the thud, thud, thud of rounds impacting the mud all around their feet. The ping, ping, ping of bullets ricochet off of metal. The screams of the wounded and calls for medics. The roar of hundreds of rifles returning fire into the smoke filled scene. Sergeants yelling commands and obscenities at their soldiers to push harder. Men screaming in pure unadulterated terror. Renault Tanks rumbling by sporadically firing off thunderous rounds, while their cold steel tracks crushed whatever they encountered. The incessant clack, clack, clack, clack of water-cooled machine guns. The smoke, flying dirt and debris, along with hundreds of thousands of bullets all causing a palpable thickening of the air. The putrid stink that permeated everything in the battle zone was unbearable. Mud, sweat, blood, cordite, gasoline, steel, grease, death, feces, urine, fungus, a cacophony of mixed body odors, wet leather, burnt skin, singed hair, torched clothes, melting rubber, vomit, rotting plants, burning wood.

There was no wonder so many died. The real surprise, the genuine miracle, was that anyone could live through it. Death was not just knocking at the door of these brave soldiers, it kicked the whole wall in and shamelessly grabbed men by the hundreds.

From the reserve position in the lines that company D occupied, it sounded like the gates of hell had been blown open and a vast demonic horde was pressing in. Men urinated themselves, while others vomited, as most placed at least one hand up to an ear to block off some of the bitterness of the fight that they would soon occupy. Bushy and his compatriots knew that the true meaning of the word 'pandemonium' had just been unleashed upon them.

Sergeant Mulholland, or Molly as he was known, gathered the men of Company D in close, now that they were in the final forward trench waiting for the command to jump off in the second wave.

"Listen up, men," he shouted over the roar of battle with impressive confidence.

"I know that this sounds like hell. It is, but it is in these moments, right now, that this battle will be defined. We are bringing a lot of hurt down on the Huns and how you respond under this pressure will determine the outcome. We press forward men. We press forward and finally take the fight to these bastards for once. We win today, men. We win today! That's how we get home. We win today!"

Focus and determination returned to soldiers' countenances with those confident words.

"Remember you have friendlies out in front of you, so no firing your rifles into the smoke. Pick your target only by sight, no suppressive fire until we catch up with the 102nd."

"You got that Weasel?" Molly wanted to get the attention of the frenzied private.

"Yes, Sergeant!"

"Listen for the gas alarm, the Krauts are famous for waiting until your butt is out of the trench and then pour down the chlorine on our heads. If you hear the alarm, drop down, get your mask on then get back in the fight. Remember, the gas won't kill you, just make you so miserable. If they use the Mustard, that yellow cross will burn your skin, eyes, anything it touches and it remains potent for at least 48 hours, so stay away from everything with a yellow haze. Let's give them hell, boys! Show them what an American Army can do!"

The red flares were calling again. The second wave of men was needed to bolster the attack before the confidence of the young army waned.

"I lift up my eyes to the hills, from where does my help come?
My help comes from the Lord, who made heaven and earth..."

•

Neils was very nervous riding south on the River Road. His horse, 'Ranger,' carried the young ranch hand down the stony path that split the sunny meadow. Portneuf was surging through a small rapid off to his right. The gurgling water and the clap, clap, clapping of Rangers hoofs would normally have been a hypnotic tonic to quiet one's soul, but not on this day. He was anxious. Neils had been waiting for this moment for almost a year, dreaming about it. The first meeting, a year ago, did not go the way that he had hoped that it would. Instead, he discovered the wrath of a Scottish woman.

It was an innocent enough encounter, after church he had asked to speak privately with Mr. Adamson. His intention was to ask permission to court one of his daughters. It was the right thing to do before an interested man went calling on a young woman. Mr. Adamson was enjoying the encounter with the nervous young Skeem, as Neils stumbled over his words multiple times. Confusion entered the discussion and Mr. Adamson assumed that Neils was asking to formally court the older daughter, Mary, who would reach seventeen years in July, a little less than a month away. It was not unheard of that a twenty year old man, who would turn twenty-one in October would be interested in a vivacious seventeen year old woman. It was at this point that Margret became involved. What began with smiles and friendly banter, turned tense, quicker than the rope cinching down on an angry bull's flank, sending it wildly bucking out of rodeo starting gates.

Neils resolved that he was not asking to court Mary Robina, but he was asking to court Johnetta.

"Johnetta?" Margret responded with a sudden fire in her eyes like a Momma bear protecting one of her young cubs.

"Yes ma'am, Johnetta," Neils stumbled, feeling his Sunday school confidence wain.

"Why, she is barely fourteen years old!" Said Margret in a loud enough voice to be heard by others gathered near them.

"And just how old are ye, Mr. Skeem?" Margret insisted.

"Twenty, Ma'am," he replied sheepishly with his hat in his hands.

"Margret, maybe we should listen to him," was Walter's miscalculation and the real trigger that heated up Margret's Scottish dander. She glared at her insolent husband.

"These are MY girls Walter, and I will not have you or any other man giving them away!" Turning back to Neils.

"Mr Skeem," she stared into his eyes.

"You, Sir, are going to be twenty one years old this October, is that right?" Her finger was probing into his chest now.

People were watching from all around them and the Bishop was even taking notice, as he had completed the after service hand-shaking ritual.

"Johnetta just turned fourteen a week ago, barely a woman and you want to court her, do ye?"

"That, that was my plan, ma'am," replied the clearly outmatched young Neils.

"I will not let that happen, out of the question," and she was done with him.

"Margret, Neils is a fine young man and has taken notice of Johnetta," Walter reasoned.

"Well, Walter, would you be so reasonable if he had taken a fancy of Ethel?" Margret demanded.

At that moment you could hear an audible gasp rise from the abruptly scandalized people, gathered near the contentious scene.

"We will be taking our leave, Walter," insisted Margret, who did not wait for him but just turned and left. As Margret Whitelaw Cameron Adamson left, she shot a shaft through the tender young heart of Mr. Neils Skeem. That look he would not forget for the rest of his life.

"Girls!" Margret called her three daughters to her side and stomped off before Walter knew what had happened. None of the girls had apparently heard any of the conversation while they were playing with Ethel on the swing at the side of the church.

A small shudder of remembrance made its way all the way through Neils, from his scuffed brown leather cowboy boots, through his dark wide brimmed hat. A bead of nervous sweat gathered on his forehead. He calmed himself by remembering the follow up events of the last year. How his copious, prolific apologies to Mrs. Adamson for overstepping his bounds. The flowers he had delivered to their home as well as the anonymous gifts he left at church for the family. The thing that had finally coerced Margret's forgiveness was the visit Uncle Christian had paid to the Adamson ranch to plead for the virtue of his nephew. He in essence made a pledge to his nephew's character, insisting that he was a man of hard work, honesty and integrity.

That discussion paved the way for a visit on this beautiful final day of June. He would formally ask for permission to court the just turned fifteen year old Johnetta, whom he held in such high regard. His desire was to marry this young woman one day and to start a ranch and a family, in that order, with her help. He was not sure if those feelings were mutual. His disquiet was based in the unknown heart of a fifteen year old girl. Would she reject him and decline to be courted? Would he find her overly immature and then decide that she was not the one for him to complete all of his grand plans? So many uncertainties in life and so many more in love. While Neils was confident that he could provide for her he was uncertain about her needs. Johnetta seemed so shy and withdrawn to him, of course that was only watching her from a distance. What was she like up close?

Around the final bend and the Adamson farm lay on the left of the road, away from the river. It was a fine plot of ground and in two years they had accomplished much. He and his cousins had dropped off the load of lumber about six week previously, so seeing the progress impressed him. He was hopeful that Mr. Adamson had been busy building the family home, so Mrs Adamson would be less prone to contentiousness.

He noticed that the fields were a healthy green with wheat, corn and potato, as he proceeded out a patch of woods.

"Wow," whispered a surprised Neils. Mr. Adamson had been busy indeed. The new home was standing with walls, roof, covered porch, windows and doors. Walter was on a ladder finishing up with some trim work near the peak as Ranger sauntered in.

"Greetings, neighbor!" Neils proclaimed, lifting his hat in salute.

"Greetings, Mr. Skeem!" Said a happy Walter, in return.

"I bring you a house warming gift from my Aunt and Uncle," he announced with pleasure.

"Along with their warmest wishes."

"Well, that is certainly unnecessary, but we appreciate the thought, Neils," said the descending man.

Neils dismounted from Ranger as Margret came out on the front porch with a broad smile.

"Mr. Skeem, it is a pleasure to see you today," Margret said with genuine affection.

"Mrs. Adamson, the pleasure is all mine," while he reached to shake hands.

"It certainly is a beautiful day ma'am."

"Indeed these are the days we long for in the deep winter."

"Your home is looking so lovely!"

"Thank you, Neils," Walter said proudly.

"You have gotten so much accomplished in a short time," Neils was being honest.

"Everyone worked very hard to make this dream come true," Margret said with all sincerity.

"I believe that to be true, ma'am."

Turning back to his horse, Neils untied a small potato sack and handed it to Mr. Adamson.

"Just a little something from your neighbors, sir."

"We thank you, son," Walter said while taking the bag. He handed it to Margret.

"Honey, why don't you open this thoughtful gift?"

"Oh, my! Look, Walter it is a new set of kitchen knives," Margret was impressed.

"I had my father order them through his store down in Nephi, and my Uncle paid for them," he said.

"Well thank you, that was very thoughtful," she said.

"Yes, thank you, son. Make sure you pass our appreciation along," Walter said, while he reached out and shook the young man's strong calloused hands.

There was an awkward silence for a few brief seconds.

"There is another matter ma'am, that I would like to speak to you about," Neils said with all the confidence he could muster.

"Why yes, Mr Skeem, whatever could it be?" She was toying with the poor lad.

"It is about asking permission to court your daughter Johnetta, ma'am."

"You would like to court my daughter Johnetta, now would ye?" She said with a sparkle in her blue eyes.

"Ye, yes, ma'am," he stuttered and cringed.

"Well, this is the first that I am hearing about this, young man."

"We never said anything to the girls last year," Walter leaned in and whispered.

Margret rolled her eyes and Neils knew that she was playing.

"Johnetta! Come out here, there is a young man who would like to make your acquaintance," she hollered over her shoulder and through the door.

"The girls ran inside giggling when they spotted your horse coming through the woods," Walter whispered with a goofy smile on his face.

"Thank you," blushed the ranch hand.

"You best have honorable intentions with my youngest Cameron daughter, Neils,"

Margret was staring at him with those soul piercing eyes again. It made his back stiffen. "Yes, honorable. All-always honorable ma'am," was the only thing his mouth could manage to say.

The door opened slowly and Johnetta stepped through. She had on a yellow summer dress that hung just below her knees and smelled of lilac and roses. Her black hair hung past her shoulders with long relaxed curls that shimmered in the sun as she stepped off the porch. There was a single daisy suspended above her ear. Walter met her at the steps and helped her down with an extended hand, like she was royalty.

"Mr. Neils Skeem, I would like to formally introduce you to our daughter Johnetta Whitelaw Cameron. Johnetta, this is Neils Skeem, who has asked permission to court you beginning this beautiful day," said Walter. The fake dad was doing a remarkable job with this introduction, thought the shy Johnetta.

Neils heart melted with wonder. Johnetta's face blushed from the attention.

"I thought that you were coming to call on my sister Mary," Johnetta replied.

"No Johnetta, he has asked permission to court you," Margret said.

"Oh," was the only word the quiet girl could say.

"Miss Cameron, I invite you to take a walk with me for a short time," Neils managed to say clearly.

"Mother?" Johnetta inquired.

"That's fine Neils, just stay where we can see you," she said in reply with just enough authority.

Inside the new home Mary was combing long strokes through Ethel's fine hair and watching the scene unfold through a front window. She too had on a summer dress and had in fact taken a bath, yesterday. Her hair was done up with small white flowers decorating her deep red curls. Upon hearing all of the formality that had been apportioned to her younger sister, tears ran down her cheeks. She had been skipped over. She had been left behind. She was supposed to marry next, it was the natural order of things. Mary Robina's heart broke again on that beautiful summer day.

"Was there no one that would love me in this world?" She wondered.

"I love you Mary," said Sarah Ethel's four year voice.

"I love you more kiddo," Mary said, grabbing her little step sister from behind.

•

"Go! Go! Go! Go! Let's move, move, move gentlemen. Come on, up the ladders," shouted Molly.

Time had mutated in Bushy's mind; seconds became minutes. He went up the ladder and over the top of the trench. The sun was up, why had he not noticed sooner? Its light was still shrouded with heavy cloud cover, sprinkling a fine mist into his face. The scene was surreal; all vegetation had been eliminated from this land between the armies, not even a blade of grass remained. The ground was pockmarked with craters of various depths, much like he imagined the surface of the moon would be. The landscape had taken on a pale gray hue with the daylight being bent by clouds and tainted with smoke. In addition to the craters was the vast amount of wrecked equipment, broken pieces of wood and twisted metal strewn about with chaotic resolve. The mud, rocks and debris of every kind imaginable made running almost impossible.

A couple hundred yards out, with his heart pounding and chest heaving, the holes became deeper and more frequent and so did the bloodied bodies. Many of the men and horses he came across in these first few eternal moments were certainly dead, a fact revealed by their mangled positions and missing body parts. Too many wounded soldiers had dragged themselves into shell craters, often leaving a bloody streak for an ominous trail. Their moans, cries, and the neighing of horses were not what he had expected. Neither was the rancid smell. He had to fight the urge to vomit over the stench.

"Just keep moving," he thought as his boots splashed through thick muddy puddles, his feet tripped and caught on various objects, like rifles and helmets, and an arm without a body.

"I lift up my eyes to the hills, from where does my help come?

My help comes from the Lord, who made heaven and earth." Bushy was concentrating on the soothing words of the Psalm as he made his way across no man's land. It was his mother's heart calling out to him in this frantic moment.

Clack, clack, clack, clack. Thud, thunder, wiz, ping, ping, thud, wiz, thud, thud. A machine gunner was targeting the group of running soldiers of company D. Then, it wasn't, like he had run out of ammo.

"Behind the tank!" Screamed Big, who was holding his helmet down tight with his free hand, galloping toward the cover of the steel beast, while he clutched his rifle with a death grip. In any other setting it would have made for a hilarious scene as uncoordinated long arms and legs high-stepped over the rough terrain, backpack flailing, his loose gas mask bag smacking his face with every stride.

"He will not let your foot be moved; he who keeps you will not slumber.

Behold, he who keeps Israel will neither slumber nor sleep." Bushy continued striving for the protection of the tank. Ting, ting, ting, thud, thud, thud. Dirt rain.

The gasoline fumes hung heavy behind the little tank and was the first thing that greeted the men of company D. The steel tracks of the Renault were screeching and crawling forward over a coil of barbed wire toward a trench with at least twenty men trying to take cover in its shadow.

"The Lord is your keeper; the Lord is your shade on your right hand.

The sun shall not strike you by day, nor the moon by night."

Thunderous explosion off to the right by fifty yards sent several howling men airborne, flinging wildly away from the impact, then the spray of putrid dirt slapped Bushy in the face.

Clack, clack, clack, clack. Thud, wiz, ping, zing, ping, thud, wiz, thud, thud, thud.

"The Lord will keep you from all evil; he will keep your life.

The Lord will keep your going out and your coming in from this time forth and forevermore."

As Bushy finished breathing out the agonizing prayer the second time, he looked to his left just when Weasel's face exploded, while the rest of his body was launched backward.

Suddenly, Bushy was flying through the air, although he wasn't conscious of that fact, the only thing that resonated was the ringing in his head. The swirling turmoil was forthwith snuffed from his life.

Upon impact, Joseph was walking up the long grey gangplank to board the huge black ship. It was a cool, cloudy and breezy day in the shipyard at Naples and the ship was docked with many ropes securing it, like long tentacles gripping the shore for dear life. The gangplank ran right into the middle of the hull, the steep walkway had taunt thick ropes for rails and some white sand had been cast for traction on the wet wood. Giovanni 14, was walking in front of the seven and a half year old Joseph, while their Momma was behind them, encouraging them to keep moving. Momma's cousin, Nicolino Cacavelli was in front of Johnny leading the way forward.

Nicolino had come with them on the trip to America to help protect them on the long voyage. He was a big man with strong hands who would not put up with anyone trying to take advantage of this traveling family. Plus, he enjoyed playing with the boys, since his wife, Katarina, had given him three beautiful girls for children. Nicolino and Katarina had done much to help Maria's family over the last ten years during Benny's absence. They would be moving into Benny and Maria's house in Spinete when Nicolino returned home, after three months.

But first, Nicolino had to act as a bodyguard and escort for the family. He would also be playing the role of husband during this part of the voyage. To any outsider, he was going to be the man of the house, who would do anything to protect his family. Which he would do for them anyway, still Benny was paying him well to deliver his family safely to Utah.

The complex and extensive journey began with a twelve day sail on the Furst Bismark, a German boat that was making the trip to Ellis Island, New York. It was a large modern ship, just a couple of years old, on which Benny had secured a mid-level suite for the four of them. He had to work extra shifts and it took an additional year to save the money to get the four of them across the Atlantic in that level of luxury. He did not want the kids traveling in the poor man's class located deep in the hull and locked below deck for the duration of the voyage, since he had experienced being packed in like cattle in the past. Being in the mid-level gave them privacy and the ability to be up walking around the ship, which would help the travel seem more like the adventure that it was, especially for his boys.

Benny had originally come over to America when a company out of Utah had sent a paid recruiter out into the Italian countryside in the spring of 1890. The recruiter carried a satchel full of fancy colored flyers printed with the information that the United States Smelter and Refining Company was looking for workers to move to a place in western America called Utah. The bright new facility promised good wages, company housing and free travel for any qualified man. The money promised was more than triple what he had made over the last ten years being a farmer in his south central Italian village of Spinete. Triple the money meant that he could live in Utah and send twice as much money back to his wife than she had in the past. He figured that within five years they could all live together in Utah and become wealthier than anyone in the whole of Italy, except the Pope, that is.

Benny went to Naples to meet the company officials and get his physical examination. Everything progressed quickly and the company offered Barbato Jacobucci the job of laborer at their new Bingham Junction, Utah smelter. The copper smelter was one of the largest of its kind in the world and he would be trained in several 'critical' jobs, they said. He would have a place to stay at the new company housing complex just as soon as they were completed. He accepted the job on the spot and rushed the ninety miles home with the news. Giovanni, his son, was a little over two years old and his beautiful wife Maria, would be excited for the new adventure. He was to leave after Christmas, early in 1891.

The work was hard and the several critical jobs for which he was trained all involved a shovel and a wheel barrel. The cost of living was higher in Utah and the company housing was several large flop houses. It was fine for what he needed, living as a single man, but he would never have his family live in that situation. He worked long and hard to save and send home as much money as he could.

By the middle of 1893, Benny had become so lonely he thought that he would die. He asked for an unpaid vacation to visit his 'sick' mother back in Italy. He made the long journey back home to surprise Maria in the middle of September of '93. What a reunion it was! Like the conquering Roman heroes of old had returned home from the battlefield complete with the spoils of war, gifts and money for everyone. Those two weeks revitalized Benny's soul and impregnated Maria. He returned to Utah with a renewed sense of purpose, a desire to work hard to bring his family with him and his cousin Leonardo tagged along for a job.

Almost nine and a half years later Benny had worked himself to the bone to bring his family over from Italy. Leonardo had only lasted a couple of years and went back home, but Benny got ready for his family's reunification. He rented a home beginning the first of the year, about a mile upwind from the smelter. He was so nervous and excited to finally fulfill his promise to Maria and to his boys.

He received a telegram from Nicolino confirming they were in Naples and boarding the ship the next day. A cold front moved in and that January became frigid. All the mountains were snow covered. The snow on the ground in the city was coated with a sooty black and yellow haze that fell from the smelter's gigantic smokestacks. There were two smelters in the valley with plans for four more.

Of course that was the year Benny came down with the flu, while he waited for his family to make the mid-winter crossing of the Atlantic. He knew that he should have waited until spring for them to make the trip, but he could not stand the separation any longer. He had not met his youngest boy Giuseppe and only had a fading photograph of Maria and Giovanni that was several years old. Yes, the monthly letters kept him going, but he was so close. They were so close. The nearer the departure date got, the more he was hopelessly homesick and that disease would only be cured by their arrival. So he made all of the arrangements that he could from his end and he knew that his family would depart Spinete January 23rd, 1902, just as Benny began to feel better and returned to work.

Giovanni took ill the first day of the voyage and Joseph remembered his mother praying frantically for most of the outrageous trip. The Chaplin on the Furst Bismark even stopped in to offer intercession. The ship heaved and rolled in the heavy north Atlantic seas causing many to take ill. Joseph was fine, unaffected by the constant motion, and with all of the sea sick passengers on board that left plenty of food for the little guy and Nicolino to eat. Since the weather was bad everyday but one, exercise was rare, so the two eaters got fat, while everyone else lost significant weight. By the time they were about to arrive at their destination, Giovanni broke out of his illness and was up on deck breathing the fresh air in time to see the awe-inspiring Statue of Liberty come into view in the early morning light of February 7th. Electricity was flowing through everyone on board, even though it was a bitterly cold New York morning that greeted them.

After waiting on the ship almost an entire day for their medical clearance, they were allowed to disembark onto Ellis Island and go through the immigration interview. The officer was kind to the family, especially the excited boys and filled out his paperwork in the big book.

He asked where they were off to and young Joseph shouted "America!" At that point he did not know much English, but had heard that question often enough on the ship to pick it up. The Immigration Official quietly gave Nicolino some advice on places to avoid while they made their way to Grand Central Depot in New York City. They were hoping to get on a train to Chicago that night. Unfortunately the station was a mess due to a consequential train collision, only a month before their arrival, and workers were still clearing wreckage in one of the tunnels. This caused a delay of a few days and another telegram from Nicolino.

Little Joey, as Nicolino called him, wanted to see everything in his new country. The hustle and bustle of the busy New York streets seemed to be just as alive after the sun had set as during the daytime. The extreme cold gave them all fits on their journey. The trip to Chicago, the wind, and snow drove them all to huddle together in their frozen train car, while whiteout conditions repeatedly greeted them while crossing the great plains. Joey wanted to know how the train engineer could see his way to drive the huge smoking beast. One day when he woke, he wondered if they had gotten lost on their way to find "Dad".

Finally, on February 24th their ice-encrusted train crept down the steep mountain side into the Salt Lake Valley. The plan was for them to switch trains and catch a local commuter tram south the twenty miles to the Bingham Junction station. The troupe had been traveling for thirty one days and were exhausted. They disembarked in Salt Lake City and asked for directions from a local vendor, who happened to be from Salerno,

Italy. Off to the left of the little stand stood Benny with a small hand written sign in Italian, the local dialect that only those from Spinete could truly understand. Maria, glancing around, noticed the handsome man with the sign in her peripheral vision. When she looked again, she thought he was a phantom. As she blinked, the truth penetrated her dream-like mind. Maria screamed a joyous tone and yelled "Grazie Mio Dio" over and over while running the entire twenty yards into his arms. They melted into one person and embraced, never wanting to stop.

"Benny, let me look at you!" Cried the travel weary woman.

"Maria, my beautiful you are finally here!" Tears flowed freely down both of their cheeks. Little Joey was hiding behind Uncle Nicci, his new favorite father figure, trying to get a look at the man everyone said was his 'dad.'

"Giovanni! Come and see your Papa. Look how big you are! You are almost a man, my son!" Benny enveloped his oldest boy with his powerful arms and lifted him off of the ground, slathering him with kisses.

"I have missed you terribly, my boy!"

Looking with deep appreciation at Nicolino, Benny hugged the man in a full embrace.

"Thank you, my brother! Thank you so very much."

"It's good to be here Benny," more tears all around.

Benny knew that Joseph was hiding behind Uncle Nicci. And not wanting to frighten the shy boy he got down on one knee and peeked his head around Maria's cousin's leg.

"Giuseppe, sai chi sono?" Benny asked with a smile.

"Si, tu sei mio padre," the boy reached out and touched his father's face with both of his tiny hands, making sure that the man in front of him wasn't just another sad dream.

"Si, Mio figlio," Cried the man, and he picked up his boy for the first time in his life. Benny held him away from his body for a brief moment, to get a good look at his son and then enveloped him in his arms.

"Si, si, si."

The weary Maria and Nicolino both melted at the sight.

"Mio Padre, Mio Padre, Mio Padre," little Joey whispered into his father's ear, as they madly swung around in circles.

"No, Bushy, I am not your Padre," yelled the concerned Sergeant over the melee. "Are you alright? I didn't see any blood." He offered his hand to help his dazed translator to his feet.

Thud, thud, thud, ping, wiz, ting, thud.

"Come on kid, snap out of it, you almost got blown up. Now on your feet. You can't kill Germans sitting on your ass! Let's go soldier!" Molly yanked Bushy up to his wobbly, but attached feet, and hell came back into focus.

Clack, clack, clack. Thud, wiz, ping.

•

Neils drove Ranger hard across the open field, cracking his long leather reins on the horses backside to push the beast harder. He had not forced the horse to go this fast in a good long while and it felt exhilarating. He was in a hurry to try to catch Mary and Johnetta's evening fireside chat that he had heard so much about over the last several months. He used the field to avoid some of the twists and turns of the river road. It was a faster way to get to the Adamson's place before it was totally dark. Of course, he was taking a risk that he would be found out by Johnetta's fierce mother, Margret, because he had not gotten permission for the encounter on their property. Neils was living on the edge to be near Johnetta again. He drove Ranger over the wire fence with a long exhilarating leap.

The flickering light from the campfire was bouncing shadows off of the barn. He dismounted Ranger and tied him to the fence in a grassy spot, then quietly jumped over. Making his way through the tall underbrush behind the house he was assaulted with yelling. The hair on the back of his neck stood up with a shot of fear for Johnetta. He rushed forward to see both Mary and Johnetta sharing a log next to the dancing flames of the fire when he paused. The yelling and cursing was coming from inside the house. He realized that if he could hear it, then the two bundled young women not a hundred feet behind the home could hear it as well. The scene puzzled Neils. Like there was an invisible wall separating the two different worlds. This fighting must have been a frequent experience for the both of them to sit through it without reacting.

The girls had their backs to him as he approached. Trigger, their Collie, must have been inside the house or he would have announced Neils arrival, long before he was so close. He did not want the girls to scream and attract attention to the backyard of the homestead, so he tossed a couple of small stones near the chatting sisters. They quickly stood and whirled around. Mary shouldered a double barrelled shotgun in his direction.

"Whoa, easy girls - it's Neils!" He whispered, showing his hands.

"Neils, what are you doing?" Johnetta said with far too much volume.

"Crashing your fireside chat, if you don't kill me first," he said with a forced broad smile. Mary lowered the shotgun.

"Mr Skeem. You are lucky I didn't fill your arse with buckshot before I looked to see who it was, we have been having issues with Coyotes," Mary said half in jest.

"Thank You?" He said, with his eyes bouncing between the sisters.

Johnetta scurried to his side with the look of young love in her gaze. The next moment was awkward for the both of them and Neils settled on taking her by the hand and making their way back to the crackling fire.

"What brings you out on such a beautiful spring evening, Neils," Mary asked without hesitation.

"I mean other than holding a beautiful young girl's hand," she pointed and meant it to embarrass him.

"What is with all the yelling?" He asked, taking a place between the sisters on the well worn log.

"What, you don't have this sort of nightly relaxation party going on at Uncle Christian's place?" Mary quipped.

"Almost never hear a cross word between them."

"Well ever since our proud mother married Walter, this sort of evening has been a normal part of our life," Johnetta explained.

"I don't understand," said Neils.

"Mr. Adamson is a blootert," Mary said in a rich Scottish brogue.

Neils was lost.

"Walter is a bit of a drunk," Mary translated.

"Although, since the house has been built he has been much better," Johnetta chimed in while she gripped Neils hand tighter. Her heart was pounding slightly faster since their hands had clasp together.

"You are right, Johnetta, it is only two or three times a week that the screaming man makes his appearance."

They both laughed out loud, while Neils was flabbergasted. He knew something was amiss with Mr. Adamson from the beginning, but he had never spent any time with someone that could be called a drunk. Sure, he had witnessed people being drunk from time to time but no one that he really knew would break the church's teaching against the consumption of alcohol.

"Does the Bishop know?" He asked the two.

"I don't know, Neils," said Johnetta, as a crash of glass came from the house.

"Another plate sacrificed on the altar of good old Walty's ego," Johnetta sneared.

"Walty made us all promise never to tell anyone about his bottle of relaxing sauce," said Mary.

Neils shook his head, he did not know what to do with the information. Maybe, he should tell the Bishop. Anger was settling in his heart, that someone he loved would be exposed to this type of harassment every night, from a man with an obvious weak will. His demeanor changed sitting by that fire that night. He needed to act sooner when it came to his plans with Johnetta. He was going to rescue her from this insanity. He wanted to protect her, but felt helpless to act in that moment.

"I should probably go, Johnetta," Neils said.

"You just got here Neils," Johnetta replied with disappointed eyes.

"Find out a little bit of dirty laundry and you're gonna leave in a hurry, Mr. Skeem?"

Said Mary while poking the fire.

Neils did not know how to respond to Johnetta's older sibling's forward manner.

"I don't want your mother to see me out here without her permission," he replied.

"Aye, she is scary wifle, fur sure young jimmy," Mary poked more than the fire now.

"Mairi pat awa' th' brogue fur noo," Johnetta poked back and they both had a good laugh at Neils' expense. He had absolutely no idea what they were talking about.

"Where are you two from?" He asked, now very confused.

On the way back to his ranch that night Neils the thinker took over while he and Ranger walked along. He was weighing his options and decided that when Johnetta reached her sixteenth birthday in two months, he was going to seek her hand in marriage. He knew that he could get a better paying job being a farmer up in Pocatello with American Bean. They could find a place together away from here, so she would be safe from the hypocrite Walter. Then they could begin to live out his dream of having his own ranch and a family. That was what he was going to do.

"Evening Neils," was his uncle's greeting upon entering the homestead.

"Good evening, Uncle," smiled the young man in return.

Looking closer, his Uncle had a grim look about him.

"Did you hear the news today, Son?"

"No sir, what news would that be?"

"Congress declared war on Germany," he said.

Neils eyes fell to the floor, his heart sank and his brain kicked into high gear.

"The newspaper article says that every male eighteen to thirty five in the country has to register for a draft beginning next week."

"You mean that rat Wilson didn't keep his promise to stay out of the war?" Answered the angry Skeem.

"You can hardly blame him if the Krauts are sinking our ships in the Atlantic, Neils."

"That, and the whole Zimmerman telegram to the Mexicans."

"It's a crying shame, Neils," said Aunt Gin who was up and offering a conciliatory hug.

"From what I read the war is going pretty bad for the Allies now, maybe it will be over before we even get an Army together, Son," the man was grasping for a positive side to the news.

"The article also said the Germans were mounting a huge offensive all across the western front in a hope to end the war before an American army can arrive in Europe," said Aunt Gin with a hopeful tone, standing with her hand on his shoulder.

"Well Uncle, there is something that I need to talk to you about."

"What's that Neils?"

"I think that I am going to be taking a job up in Pocatello with American Bean."

•

III.

'Pocatello Pete'

"Why Neils," said the Bishop in a flattering greeting.

"Greetings, Bishop Andersen," replied the smiling young man.

"What brings you into Pocatello on a beautiful spring day like today?" The older man smiled.

"I can't believe Uncle Christian doesn't have you men out planting today."

"I am sure that he does have the men out planting, but I...," he hesitated.

"I just took a new job with American Bean north of town." he said, while looking into the man's eyes.

"Oh, I see."

"It is a good opportunity to earn more money than my uncle can't afford to pay," Neils explained.

"Well that is a blessing for you, young man."

"I feel bad about leaving my uncle's ranch, but we both knew the day would come."

"He will miss you in more ways than one, Neils."

"How's that?" Neils inquired.

"I think that you have become more than just a nephew to Christian. He thinks of you more like a son."

"They have been very kind to me over these last five years Bishop, I can't deny that," Neils said.

"We also have talked openly about my desire to have my own ranch, so this day has been on the horizon for a very long time."

"Yes, he has mentioned it to me, as well," the Bishop replied.

"So, what of this new job? What will you be doing at American Bean?"

"I will start out as a farmer, learning the way they do things and I can advance from there," he explained.

"I will make five times the money, for essentially the same job."

"We'll that is excellent, Neils, and you already know what you are going to be doing with the money, I suppose." the little man smiled broadly like he had inside information that he was storing just below the surface.

"Yes sir, I do," Neils paused.

"Could you pass along a message for me, sir?"

"Certainly, Neils," he said, and then drew a little closer, feeling important.

"Could you tell Johnetta that I have to start this job today, or they will hire someone else. I won't be able to see her again until the spring planting is done, in June sometime."

"You mean Johnetta Adamson?"

"Well, she goes by her birth name of Johnetta Cameron," Neils said.

"I wonder what Walter thinks about that?" Mused the holy man aloud.

"I don't imagine what Walter thinks would bother her at all, sir."

"Mr. Adamson is providing for that family, Neils." Pausing for effect.

"It is always hard to marry someone that already has children."

"Yes, Sir, I believe that is true," he paused, not wanting to delve any further into the matter of Walter Adamson.

"As far as what you told me about Walter's issues," he said, lowering his voice and glancing around. Soon we will be working with the man to change his wayward heart." Neils was uncomfortable about the whole matter. When he had initially approached the Bishop about Walter, he felt like he had betrayed the man in some way, but reasoned that he was doing it for his good. In reality, it was for Johnetta's good, which meant it was indirectly for Neils benefit too.

"Good," Neils said shortly.

"I will pass along your wishes to Johnetta and Mary," said the divisive little man, intentionally mentioning the older Mary.

"Thank you. Good day, Bishop Andersen," Neils said, tipping his dark brown hat and walking away.

"Blessings on your new effort," said the Bishop.

He had no intention of passing along the news to little miss Johnetta Cameron. The Bishop considered that mother of hers, Margret, to be an arrogant and insolent woman who didn't know her place in this world, or the church for that matter. She had a real problem with authority in her life, which was a sure sign of pride, damnable pride. However, his own daughter Joanna would benefit from the news about the strapping young farmer's glowing future. He would let it slip at supper this evening.

•

"Dugald!" Johnetta and Mary squealed their brother's name at the same time and rushed to the door, vying for position.

"Hey girls," embracing them with great warmth, Dugald entered the home on the Adamson ranch for the first time.

"Hi Pearl," said Mary while giving her pretty sister-in-law a warm hug.

"Mother!" Dugald said as she ran to him and smothered him with a hug and a kiss on each cheek.

"Mah son, a'm sae blessed tae see ye again," Margret said in brogue while tearing up.

"'N' his bonny guidwife, Pearl!" More hugs and greetings for everyone.

Pearl had no clue as to what her mother-in-law just said but flashed her a full-mouthed smile in reply.

"Whaur is ma bonny grand daughter?" Margret whispered while peeping at the seven month old baby under the blanket on Pearl's shoulder.

"She is sleeping like a rock," she replied, trying to show her infant's face to the four enchanted women gathered around her.

"She is a bonnie!"

The "oh's" and "awe's" reverberated from all of the females, as they ardently looked upon their tiny new bit of family.

Dugald picked up Sarah Ethel and swung her around in a circle until she giggled with glee.

"You just had a birthday young lady!"

"How old are you now?" He was playing.

"Dugald, you're my brother, you know that I am five years old!" She said with her extra sassy voice.

"You are right again, Ethel! And you are sounding more and more like your sister Mary!" Dugald said as he placed her down to shake Walter's hand in a warm greeting for his mother's husband.

"The house looks amazing Walter," Dugald was serious.

"Thank you, son. It was a lot of work," he said with a broad smile, clearly proud of the accomplishment.

"Well it looks like the whole clan has been working hard. The ranch looks really good," he said to the older man.

Dugald and Walter were both tall men. The younger man was lanky, with short brown hair and sparkling blue eyes. Clean shaven, he looked a youth, almost too young to have a wife, daughter and a new automobile.

"When did you get the new wheels, Dugald?" Johnetta asked.

"Last week. We wanted to try it out on a trip, so here we are!"

"I, for one, am so glad that you did, son. It is so good to see you! We are going to make dinner soon and you will be staying the night." Margret was not asking.

"Yes mother, you read my mind!"

"Again. You almost forgot the "again" part," Margret was so happy to see her son. She hugged him for a second time with a good, long, grateful squeeze.

It had been a lengthy separation that required hours of discussion around the table. Then, continuing in the living room and later out at the fireside chat with his two Cameron sisters.

"So girls, how is life on the ranch these days?"

"Isolated," said Mary.

"Unless you are Johnetta, of course. Life for her is suddenly amazing and full of unlimited possibilities," Mary said with exaggerated expressions of flailing arms and delighted voice.

"Shut up Mary Robina," Johnetta said with her tongue planted firmly in her cheek.

"Who is this man that is courting my sister?" Dugald pressed.

"Well, Deacon Cameron, he is a man of fine standing in the Church, if that is what you are asking," said Mary to her brother, three years her elder.

"Well that is a good thing sister," Dugald replied knowing his sister's history of doubt in their church.

"Why is your face all red, Johnetta?" He said grabbing and tickling his younger sibling.

The next morning the family gathered around the table for breakfast, after the morning chores were finished. Dugald, Pearl and the baby would be leaving before long.

"Dugald, how is work at the old smelter in Bingham Junction?" Asked Walter while passing a bowl of scrambled eggs to his wife.

"It's not Bingham Junction anymore Walter, they changed the name to Midvale, but work at the smelter is going well. I am in the lab now making sure that we are producing a quality product," he said and took a bite of some crispy bacon.

"Midvale, that's very un-Mormon-like of them," said Mary with a sarcastic smirk.

"So, who do you work with in the lab?" Walter pressed through Mary's attempt at humor.

"It's a team that I run, really, and many of the men are from Italy."

"Well there are thousands of Italians in the Salt Lake area, aren't there?"

"Yes, but not as many after the five smelters closed ten years ago," Dugald said.

"I remember that well, the farmers in the valley were getting killed by all of the soot. Couldn't grow a thing." Walter said as he ate.

"Yes, a judge ordered the smelters closed, a few years before we came over."

"I wonder if the land is doing any better now, for growing, I mean?"

"So much has changed. There aren't as many farms in that area anymore, but the ranches that are around seem to be doing well,"

"Somebody's here and they have an 'Auto-go-bile' like Dugald!" said an excited Ethel, pointing out the window.

"Walter, who is that?" Margret wanted to know, as the little black Model T came to a stop in the driveway.

"Two. There are two Auto-go-biles now!"

All laughed at little Ethel's description of the contraptions that were everywhere those days. Walter left the talkative breakfast table to make his way outside. Greeting the familiar man from the porch with a hesitant wave, while he still sat in his rickety old Ford.

"Pete? Pete, what are you doing here?" Asked a peeved Walter in a low voice, as he quickly made his way across the yard.

"Hey Walt! How are you doing today?" The man ignored Walter's irritation.

"You can't just show up unannounced, Pete!" Walter was at the man's door.

"Walter, I have your delivery," the man said coyly, nodding to the floorboard that held two clay gallon jugs.

"You never come in the driveway, Pete, and you never deliver in the daylight."

"I just want to look around at the new place, Walter."

"Margret's gonna get suspicious!"

"Ha, ha, ha, that's funny, Walter. She is well aware of your indiscretions, sir!"

"You owe me a good sum of money and I am here to collect on that debt." Pete said with a sudden firmness of a man in control, while exiting his vehicle.

"I know that I owe you that money, Pete, and I am going to pay you, but today is a bad time. A very bad time. We have got family from out of town visiting." Walter knew that he was in a predicament.

"Well maybe they will trade me that fancy Oldsmobile for my Flivver here and we could call it even Walt?"

"You ain't gettin' that fancy car, Pete. It ain't even mine to give," Walter said emphatically.

"Well it sure looks like you finally have turned things around for yourself Walter. New house, new barn, livestock and green fields growing, rich relatives with fancy cars," Pete said looking around.

"All this new stuff and no respect for an old friend," he glared in Walt's eyes.

"You owe me a lot of money, Walter Adamson, and I aim to collect," Pete said, putting his hand on his hip revealing his shinny Colt.

"Pete, we've been friends for a long time," said nervous Walter motioning him to slow down.

"Well, our friendship should have compelled you to pay me for the moonshine, a long time ago Walter!" Said the large ruddy man.

Pete was from Pocatello and had driven the twenty miles to the ranch to notify one of his most prolific customers that it was time to pay up on the credit he had extended to his childhood friend. Pocatello Pete, as he was called, was a man of his word when it came to the money that was owed him. He was going to collect one way or another, and Walter was well aware of the embarrassing dilemma he had gotten himself into.

"Pete, do you still own that place on Elm Street, down by the school house?"
"Yes."
"How about we set up a trade, Pete?"
"Go on."

•

With one explosion roaring into the battlefield, the German machine gun nest was vaporized. American soldiers surged toward the enemy trenches 'en masse'. Some men jumped right down into the muddy bottom, as others of Company D scanned for immediate threats, rifles at the ready. The noise of the battle had momentarily waned with the death of the three man Maxim crew.

Bushy made his way into the unfamiliar trench with a few others and began searching for Huns. It appeared that the Germans had fallen back under the rabid artillery fire to another parallel trench system, but they would have to spend the time to flush out each and every dugout. The trenches were constructed to survive heavy bombing with large buried vertical four by four beams holding back wooden planks that kept the dirt in place. The portion of the underground fortress in which they had entered the trench was muddy, because part of the wall had been blown in by a shell. The rest of the system had wooden planks for walkways and even some poured concrete embankments. The system of wires for the communications lines was neat and orderly, tucked along the back wall with four or six wires each separately hung on miniature poles that poked out of the bank. Sand bags were perfectly stacked on both sides. Everyone looked covetously at the conditions that the Germans had enjoyed in this place for the last three years. No conflict had touched this sector since the Huns occupied it in the initial surge of the war.

The dugout that Bushy and three others charged into was abandoned, but well kept. Even in retreat, it appeared that the Germans did not want to desecrate their wartime creation. "We need a flashlight in here," Cookie shouted back through the sandbagged opening. "They were living like kings!" Tool said, pointing at the bunks that lined the back wall. "I don't understand why they would just leave all this behind," Bushy said while gazing around.

Someone switched on the light which caused some six or eight large rats to scurry for cover.
"They still got rats in their trench just like we do," Cookie pointed out.
"There are twenty bunks in this one dugout alone," Tool said in amazement.
"You guys gonna take a nap in here?" Molly barked at his four soldiers.
"Come on boys we got a war to fight."
The real danger for the men now would be in clearing the dugouts and connector trenches. Those trenches would either be already blown, wired or mined to slow the progress of the Americans. Sometimes the Huns would set up kill zones in those shorter connector trenches, waiting for the line to fill with men before unleashing on them.
"In the trench men," Sergeant Molly cried back and forth down the line.
"Picuuuu, Picuuu," Big and another soldier shot through an already downed dead German's helmet.

The now familiar rapid clack, clack, clack, clack of a dreaded German Maxim began to fire, impacting the bank behind the doughboys, causing them all to take cover.

"They got a MG with elevation, Sarge!"

"Did anyone see their gun?" Yelled Molly at his men.

"Is this the front line, Sarge?" Asked a confused soldier.

"Yeah, welcome to France boys," he shot back.

"We have got to get some cover fire, speedy little Frenchy here can go get the tankers attention," Molly announced.

"Ahhhhhh," screamed three enraged and charging Germans, as they launched themselves toward the trench now occupied by company D.

Seven bullets pierced the charging Huns within a second, sending them into a dead heap at the edge of the trench, so close that they were all stuck several times with a bayonet just to make sure of their demise.

"Cookie, you and Mule use those Kraut bodies as cover and get some rounds on the MG position, NOW!" Screamed the red-faced Sergeant.

More men poured into the former German trenches and Molly sent Frenchy scurrying off to the tank which was forty yards away on their right. Two small squads of Germans were trying to flank the men and enter the trenches on both sides of company D. They were met with a blistering salvo of rounds from the doughboys and a rush of adrenaline caused the outnumbered Germans to be stabbed relentlessly before they took one prisoner.

"Search him and take him into the dugout," Molly said to Guns while pointing the way.

The thud, thud, thud of a hundred rounds impacting the upper edge of the trench got everyone's attention. Just as Frenchy arrived at the tank he and the entire Renault exploded from a direct hit of a high explosive round from a 76mm German mine thrower.

"Frenchy got hit! He's down, he's down!" O'Toole screeched down to the rest of the troopers in the trench from his perch that was allowing him cover to look to the rear. The news took the air out of the men. It was like a gut punch to the Sergeant who had just sent the man to his death.

"We got to flank that Maxim!" Big yelled out to try and get the men back from the dark distraction.

"Bushy, you and Fingers with his Browning go down to the next dugout and get a firing position against that MG. Then both of the positions will pour it on 'em." Molly said, trying to regroup.

He had been trained to put aside personal feelings of loss until after the battle. Then and only then, do you grieve the departed. That's all well and good, but Frenchy was a guy who he had played cards with, Molly knew his story. Danny Marquette was from Boston, his wife and two kids were anxiously waiting for him to get this war over with and return home. Now he was dead because of the command Molly had given him to get to the tank.

"Damn this war to Hell," he whispered to himself. His men needed him and this type of thinking would have to wait.

"Where is the 102nd Sarge?" Biscuit asked Molly, shaking the man from his doldrums. "I think a few of them were laying out in no-man's land, son."

Bushy and Fingers got down to the next dugout and shots rang out from inside. Five doughboys sent ten rounds inside the dark shadows.

"Grenade!" Bushy and Fingers each tossed one inside, as the men scrambled away with their guns at the ready. Seconds later, both of the charges thundered, shaking the ground and expelling a spray out through the opening. More rounds were sent in the dust filled hole, then a flare was shot in for illumination. That flare had embedded into a recently dead German and fried the body crisp from the inside out. Bushy and Fingers hopped up to a shielded observation deck two feet above the dirt covered wooden walkway. The sandbags were arranged in such a way that would allow them to see downrange.

The firing from the two teams commenced on the German MG 08 position and soon took on a bizarre rhythm in which one side would fire then duck and then the other would do the same. Back and forth. The German gunner was trying to pick up on their cadence when the rest of the company concentrated fire on the nest from the middle of the line.

Fingers noticed a spray of blood right before the gun went quiet.

Thunderous explosions raked behind the enemy lines as an artillery barrage commenced from well behind the American position.

"Where are those bloody tanks?" Molly asked aloud, while German defenders fired a volley from their trench that was only fifty yards away.

Then a strafing line of bullets impacted in front of the new American trench and a red German biplane raced across the battlefield a hundred feet above the ground.

"Fokkers!" Someone yelled and pointed up at the swift impending aircraft. Many of the soldiers' eyes had not even bothered to look up since the beginning of fighting, six or seven hours earlier. They had failed to notice the swooping, shooting, ballet happening above them, with hundreds of aircraft now involved in the battle, as the thick clouds had receded up to higher places in the gray sky.

"I need a runner," Molly yelled and a young kid that had only been with the unit for a couple of days volunteered.

"Go back to command and update them on our progress. 101St stalled in forward German trenches. Communications cut, need Tankers, artillery, water for the men and reinforcements to break through to objective. Sgt Mulholland. Give them these coordinates," he pointed to his map and sent the kid back to the CP.

More men piled into the trenches with company D as bullets wiz just overhead.

"Clay's hit!" Cookie yelled.

"He needs a medic, Sarge!

"Medic!"

•

"I don't know, Mary," Johnetta replied.

"Well he couldn't have just fallen off the edge of the world, Johnetta," Mary suggested while holding her sister's hand. They were resting by their log on a beautiful June evening. The usual fire was alive in front of them begging to entertain weary souls with its hypnotic dance, as if its only job was to soothe unsettled hearts.

"He wasn't at church again for the third week in a row, which just isn't like him at all," Johnetta lamented.

"That tells me that something is amiss," Mary reasoned.

"Perhaps, he has taken ill," Johnetta theorized.

"Don't you think the Skeem's would have said something? Or the Bishop mentioning him in the prayers today?"

"Well, they have been avoiding me like I have the plague," Johnetta pointed out. "They refused even to make eye contact, today."

"Johnetta, then we will have to confront them. I will help you next Sunday!" Mary promised with her back straightened in rigid defiance.

Evening at home was quiet. No yelling, crashing or cursing to be heard. Suddenly, the springs on the rear screen door stretched out with a wail of opposition and Margret stepped through, gently closing the inside door behind her. Not wanting the screen door to slam, she set it in its place and made her way to the fire pit with her girls.

"Howfur ur mah precious wee girls," she said while sitting down, wiggling her hips down between them.

"It's a bonny forenicht Mither," Mary said, and Johnetta just gazed into the flames unresponsive.

Margret placed her arms around her girls and in that brief moment was in her maternal glory.

"What is eating at you, young Johnetta?" She asked while giving her shoulder a little squeeze.

"She is worried about her Neils," Mary chimed in.

"He has been absent for over three weeks without a word." She continued for her silent despondent sister.

"Has it been three weeks?" Margret asked Johnetta.

"Yes," she said, as a single tear dropped off of her lower eyelid, splashing on the sleeve of her shirt.

"And the Skeem's won't even look at her for the last couple of weeks in church," Mary informed her mom.

"Well, Johnetta, I will go with you and we can talk to them and clear this all up. Neils is a good man and I am certain there is a logical explanation for his disappearance," Margret tried to restore her daughter.

"You don't think that he has gotten drafted do you?" Johnetta asked them from her fog.

"That would have been made plain at church today, my darling."

"He could just have been lent out to one of his uncle's farming buddies and is working those long spring hours," Mary guessed.

"We have another matter to discuss girls."

They both turned to look at their mother's fire enhanced face.

"Walter has sold the ranch."

"What?"

"You have got to be joking!"

"No, I am not joking."

"Why would he do such a thing?" Mary was indignant.

"We have killed ourselves here for over three years." Johnetta said, sitting up straight, with the fog quickly evaporating.

"He has not actually sold the ranch, but traded it for a house in Pocatello," Margret explained.

As the news seeped into the consciousness of the two young women, their heads were spinning, trying to weigh the consequences of Walter's sudden dream change and what that meant to them.

"We are moving into the city?" Mary asked for clarification.

"What made him do this?" Johnetta was incredulous.

"It appears that he has gotten himself a job with the railroad," Margret said.

"But he is trading away all of our blood, sweat and tears without saying a word to us?" Said Mary.

"We have all killed ourselves over this dream of his," Johnetta said angrily.

"Listen, these last three years have been the hardest of our lives, girls. Moving into the city, and I have thought about this, believe me, I think our lives will become more normal and easier."

The initial wave of indignation was beginning to wane with the thought of new possibilities.

"There will be more people around, Johnetta," Mary said to her irate sister.

"No more cleaning out barns!"

"Walter said that we may even be able to get one of those fancy 'Auto-go-biles', like Dugald has." Margret announced, repeating Ethel's cute little phrase.

Slowly a glimmer of hope washed over the three ladies like a rising tide. They sat arm in arm gazing into the enchanting dance of the fire, wondering what life had in store for their next chapter.

Six short days later the family was loading up the wagon with the final items from the house. There was an air of excitement circling about them. The many hard days at the ranch they had built had come to an official end. Mary and Johnetta were in the back yard giving it one last look.

"So many memories here, Mary," Johnetta said, while they looked into the past.

"Most of the good ones for me, were sitting around that campfire with you, sister," Mary reached over and hugged her.

"I was thinking exactly the same thing."

Just as she replied, they heard a car charging into their drive around front.

"I wonder who is in such a hurry?" Mary said and they both jumped to race each other around the house.

"NEILS!" Johnetta cried while running to his arms, as he stepped out of his uncle's blue truck.

She nearly knocked him over in the exchange.

"She's been missing you, Neils Skeem," Mary shot.

"Oh, Johnetta, I have missed you terribly." Neils said, backing away from their first full embrace.

"Where have you been Neils, I have been worried sick," Johnetta said, tears flooding her cheeks.

"You didn't get my message?"

"What message?"

"I told," he stopped himself short, before he said that it was Bishop Andersen.

"I told someone I trusted, to tell you that I had taken a job with American Bean, up north of Pocatello," he insisted.

"No one told me anything, Neils," Johnetta said.

"Not a very trustworthy fellow." Mary interjected and then, biting her lip, turned away knowing she had crossed an unspoken boundary.

Now Neils was beginning to take notice of the scene into which he had driven. The wagon was hitched and stacked with every sort of belonging from inside the Adamson home. The whole family was gathered around the young couple.

"What is going on here?"

"Were a movin!" exclaimed Ethel proudly.

"Yep, were getting off this damn ranch!" she said with all of the innocence, sincerity and tenacity that a five year old could muster.

"Sarah Ethel Adamson!" Margret Cameron was not going to allow her daughter to sound like a vagrant and promptly swatted the girl's behind, which landed with a loud crack. The resulting five year old yelp followed on cue and the scene was completed by the accompanying red-faced embarrassment of Ethel's father, Walter. The older two girls covered their faces and turned away to cloak their laughter. Neils didn't know what to do with the strange scene.

"You are moving, Johnetta?" Neils asked.

"Moving into Pocatello, Neils," Walter responded before his step daughter could.

"Walter got a new job with the railroad," Johnetta turned back to explain to her handsome and concerned boyfriend, rolling her eyes at Walty's exuberance in the process.

"We are going to be living on Elm Street, right near the school house," she explained, so he would know where to find her.

"Oh." Neils was processing the information.

"That would have been much closer to my new job," he said aloud.

"Would have been?" Johnetta questioned, picking up on the distinction. She looked at him intently, as Neils removed his hat.

"I've been drafted, Johnetta."

For a moment, no one inhaled.

"When? When do you leave?" Said the shocked girlfriend.

"Monday morning."

•

IV.

'Bells 'N Boots'

Dear Johnetta,

I have arrived safely at Camp Lewis. The training is very physical and I am really sore all
of the time. They are teaching us many good things about soldiering and making us run a
lot every day, sometimes twice a day. We march in formation everywhere we went and
today we got to actually fire rifles. We get plenty to eat, so much in fact that I think that I
am gaining weight, muscle of course. All the men in my unit are pleasant to be around
and we work hard. There is construction happening all over the base and more men are
arriving everyday. My unit isn't attached to most of the men here. I am in the IVy or 4th
Division and will be based out of North Carolina, but we are training here for now. It's
confusing to me as well.

I sure miss seeing your pretty face each Sunday. How is the new house in Pocatello?
What are you spending your time with, since you don't have all of the ranch work to do
anymore?
The drill instructor said that we might be able to get a three day pass to go home after
Boot Camp is completed, but we may have to ship out to France right away too. I hope I
get to see you before we take that long train ride east. We should be done training in
early August. I have to go now, time for lights out.
I miss you terribly,
Yours,
Neils

"Awww! He really is sweet on you, Johnetta," Mary said with a chuckle, while leaving the
room, crossing the hallway and entering her room, all six steps.
Johnetta grabbed the letter out of Mary's departing hand, so she could read it again, for

the seventh time, or eighth.

"When's that boyfriend coming back around, Jo Jo?" Ethel asked, using her special name for her sister.

"Don't know, Ethel," said a melancholy Johnetta.

"He's learnin' how to be soldiering?" She said, sitting on Johnetta's bed.

"Yep, he is learning how to be a soldier."

"Why in the world would he want to do that for?"

"Well, he got drafted, Ethel."

"What does drafted mean, anyway?"

Johnetta took a deep breath searching for the words to translate the reality to her five year old sister.

"It means that the government needs help keeping bad guys away," Johnetta said while playing with Ethel's long hair.

After considering that for a moment Ethel asked,

"We don't have any bad guys around here, do we?"

"No sunshine, we don't have any bad guys."

"Well, Mommy said that Pocatello Pete fella might be a bad guy, what do you think, Jo Jo?"

"The man living out on the ranch?"

"Yeah. Pocatello Pete!" She smiled revealing her missing front tooth.

"Who came up with that name?"

"I dunno, that is just what we call him," she explained, shrugging her little shoulders.

"Well who calls him that?"

"Me and Mary," she said with a finger in her mouth.

"It figures," Johnetta said with a smile.

"Come on kiddo, we have to go outside and weed that garden before it gets overgrown."

"It took three days of nothing but diggin and diggin and diggin to get the back yard ready for the dang garden and now more weeds are gonna keep growin up?" Ethel was incredulous.

"I am afraid that is how it works, Sunshine," Johnetta said and they walked out of their bedroom.

The new old Pocatello house had two tiny bedrooms upstairs, one that Mary was in while Johnetta and Ethel shared the other. The third bedroom, the large one on the second floor, in the front of the house, was used by Margret and Walter. The narrow staircase descended and emptied out at the back of the house, into the kitchen. You had to side-step around the end of the cabinet that protruded a little too much out into the stairwell, to get off the dark staircase. The kitchen was small but it had running cold water in the sink on the back wall, with a window that peered out into the yard, to the north. The wood burning stove that could use coal as well, was in-between the kitchen and dining room, it was used to heat the entire house. That informal dining room had a single window looking out onto the front porch. It also had their rickety rectangle table with six wooden chairs surrounding it. It had been one of the few heirlooms that Walter received from his mother.

Off the front door, that went onto the porch was the sitting room. It had two windows, one looking south out onto the porch like the dining area and the other looked east out into the side yard, with the old white school house, a hundred feet off in the distance. There were two doors on the back wall of the taupe sitting room. The darker brown door on the left, led to the water closet which even had its own bath tub. You had to watch your head when taking a bath because the bottom side of the stairs came through, just above the cast iron tub. A puny sink and a toilet rounded out the space.

This was the very first house they had ever lived in with its own water closet and all of the girls were especially excited to make use of it. When they first moved in the plumbing was leaking, in a few places, and Walter worked to replace the worn-out parts. He also fixed sections of the roof that had leaked for sometime over their bedroom.

The other door off the sitting room, the one on the right, led to a small storage area that

Margret called her mud room. In the middle of the back wall in that mud room, a door opened to the large back yard, where they had planted a formidable vegetable garden. Overall, the house was a real worn out dump, but the family did not notice and never complained. Living on a dirt pile for three years had made them quite resilient. Margret wondered about the arrangement with Pete, knowing that they had been on the short end of the trade, giving the ranch away and all of the work that it took to build it.

The back mud room screen door banged shut as Johnetta and little Ethel went to the garden to start the morning's work.

"Mother, they have gone, open the letter!" Mary said from the kitchen sink to Margret who was at the dining room table. She held a white envelope in her hands. The postman had just dropped it off a few minutes earlier. It was a curious piece of mail, to be sure, for it said, "For your eyes only: Mrs. Margret Cameron Adamson," and it had a Washington state return address.

Sliding the contrived letter-opening butter knife along the thick envelope's upper edge, Margret was a bit uncertain as to what it contained and Mary was almost beside herself with excitement.

"Oh, my!" Margret said, holding the letter up to the light and one hand to her heart.

"What is it mother?"

"Oh, my!" Now tears dropped over the edge of her eyelids onto her blouse.

"Mother?!"

"Sorry, honey," she paused knowing that her next few words would cause Mary some heartache.

"What is it?" Mary wanted to yank the letter and read it for herself, but she knew better.

"The letter is from Neils Skeem. It seems that he is asking my permission to marry Johnetta," Margret overcome, for a brief moment, with happiness for her youngest Cameron daughter.

"She's only sixteen, Mother," Mary's jealousy slipped out.

"Mary, my sweet Mary. You must be happy for your sister, Neils is a fine young man," Margret said while gently touching Mary's arm.

"He is almost seven years older than,..." Mary stopped herself. She knew she sounded childish and petty.

"You are right, Mother. Neils is a fine young man, and I am truly happy for Johnetta. I am."

"Where does he want the wedding?" Mary was redirecting the conversation away from her pain.

"Umm, it looks like he is hoping to get a three day pass in early August," she was reading aloud now, "and wants the wedding in Inkom with Bishop Andersen presiding."

"We have known Bishop for four years or more. I just don't like him." Mary confessed.

"He is a bit of an odd duck." Margret conceded about the Bishop. She could also see the underlying pain and fear in Mary's heart.

"There is a man out there for you Mary." Margret said, touching her daughter's arm.

"There seems to be quite a few eligible young men at the church here in Pocatello." She hoped for Mary, knowing that she was going to be nineteen in a couple weeks and still had plenty of time.

"I know, I am still young is what you want to say to me... There are far more potential suitors than in Inkom,... I have dishes to tend to." She said and quickly turned back into the kitchen. Mary was both happy for Johnetta and sad at her own dismal prospects.

Neils included a letter to Johnetta inside the letter to Margret. She could not resist having to peek at its contents. Neils would make a good husband to Johnetta, Margret thought. With that, she began to worry for her future son in law, with the war looming. More and more young men were being drafted every week. She could not imagine what it would be like for them and hoped that the fighting would be over before Neils had to go and take part in the brutality. War can change a man, she knew the saying well.

•

"Listen Reeves, go back and scavenge all the canteens and ammo that you can find from our dead comrades," Sergeant Molly was serious. The young private swallowed hard knowing that getting out of the protection of the trench put you in danger from enemy snipers.

"Take four guys with you and wait for the flares to fade," Molly was back in teaching mode with both of his hands on the soldier to command attention from the tired kid. "Do you hear me?"

"Yes, Sarge."

"I know this is a crappy assignment but we have to have the water. Carry as much as you can, as fast as you can and get your butt back here!"

"What about the wounded?"

"Report directly to me and we will get them help."

"Now move it!"

The private hurried off, down the trench to recruit four unsuspecting guys for the inglorious duty of snaking around dead bodies for supplies.

"Mule, front and center," Molly barked into the fading light of the former German trench.

"Here, Sarge," Mule was trying to finish eating some canned bully beef out of his rations.

"Robert Clark," said Sergeant Mulholland.

"Yes?" He was confused, he stood in front of the man.

"I am promoting you to Corporal," Molly said with all seriousness.

"Okay. Why now, Sarge?"

"I need you to set a watch schedule on both flanks. Two men each end. Have them set up a barrier with sandbags. Two hour watches, rotate them all through. Another watch set on the line, share the glasses. Wait until darkness sets in and fortify a position on top of the dugout. The rest of the men, half at a time, I want to bed down in the dugouts and get some shut eye."

"Copy that," Mule did not like the field promotion already.

"I got the skinny kid, Reeves, taking four others to gather water from the dead in the rear, so don't shoot them when they come back in the trench."

"Hey, any word on the Signal Corps getting us a working field telephone?"

"Not that I am aware of, Sarge. I'll check."

The brilliant white luminary flares popping over the new no-man's-land were slowly descending. The odd shadows they cast made the area seem like it was shaking. Joseph waited for the flare to fade so he could resume stacking the German sandbags that were lifted up to him. He crouched low on top of the dugout, able to see up and down the trench they now occupied. Most of the guys tried to eat something in the pause in fighting. Off in the distance, artillery continued to rumble away. Their sector became quiet as evening turned to dark. Bushy and Fingers worked to finish an observation post on top of the old German dugout without getting their heads blown off. He knew that there were Kraut snipers working the line, trying to take any advantage.
"Ten more bags should do it," Fingers whispered down.

Within five minutes, the task was complete. Guns and Holes drew the short straw and first watch. Bushy went to find a place to sit and eat, just as it started raining again, sending a shiver down his sweaty spine. He would have to settle in against the wall and put his rain poncho back on. Hoping to get something in his empty and aching stomach.

Bushy ate some dried bread surrounded in the isolated quiet beneath his rain gear and he dug out some bully beef, one of the canned field rations from his pack. Sitting still is when he began seeing Weasel's face explode, all over again. A couple of tears rolled down his hidden face, while his rain gear covered his head. He didn't really like Weasel all that much, but they had spent their entire army experience in the same platoon, almost six months, he figured. He was sad.

He remembered the kid winning a bet with two or three of the guys in the unit. The bet was whether or not Springfield, the makers of their 1903 rifles, was paying the Mauser brothers from Germany royalties on every rifle the American Army used in the war because they had stolen the design from the Germans and lost a court case. The look on those three guys' faces was priceless when Major Legge confirmed Weasel's assertions.

As for the sandbags on which he was perched, he did not mind them being soaked, too much, because he could let go of the ferocity of war for a moment. He was filthy, but his legs were taking the brunt of the driving rain, washing the mud off and making his soaked feet even colder. His body stank and the smell was trapped beneath his rain gear, but he was too tired to care. The occasional artillery shell going off or a flare that would pop to life over the German lines, became white noise behind his closing eyes, while he finished eating.

He went back in time as he dozed off, events swirling in his mind.

His father was looking more gray every day. First his skin had gone flush and then ashen, as he lay in his bed. Joseph's mother, Maria, was doing everything she could to hold herself together, by tending to her dying husband.

Early April 1911, in the middle of the day, Barbato Jacobucci had walked to the old house behind the church in Spinete. Maria and Giuseppi were finishing up their midday meal, together, when a knock came to the door. Joseph was clearing his plate off of the table. He was nearest to the creaky wooden portal, so he opened it without knowing who was calling.

"Padre?!"

"Joseph, my son!" Barbato grabbed his boy tightly.

Maria looked up and let out a hoot from the place she occupied at the table. She came running over to her Benny, plunging him in an embrace, followed by kisses from his face to his hands and back.

"Benny, what has happened? Why are you here?"

"Padre, I thought you were going to send for us again to come back to Utah?" Asked the confused sixteen year old.

"Can I come into my house please?" Benny asked the questioning pair, with half a smile.

"Yes. Of course, my darling, come in, come in," Maria's heart sank inside her. She knew that something was dreadfully wrong just by the look in her Benny's eyes. He seemed frail and weak to her as he walked past. This was not the energetic, powerful, determined man that had left for America fourteen months ago.

Watching him pass, she thought back to the telegram from the smelter that wanted Benny to return to work. They were no longer cooking copper and sending the poisons into the air, but had switched to smelting lead, which supposedly was cleaner when melting. She knew nothing about that factory, but remembered how sad Benny was when he had to leave.

They had become American citizens in 1904, but then a judge issued an order closing the smelters in the valley because of the damage the soot was causing to the crops of the neighboring farms, who had sued for the injunction. They all packed up and made the long, painful journey home in 1907. Returning to their roots, they knew that they would be poor, better to be poor at home.

"Benny, I have food for you, sit down at the table, please." She smiled at him with her warm, affectionate eyes, and made her way to the stove.

"Okay," said the tired traveller.

"Padre, what has brought you home?" Joseph wanted to know. His heart was set on returning to America the second that they had left. To him, it was his real home and his real hope.

"Please go call your brother and his wife, Joseph, so I can tell the story to all of you," Barbato said to his confused son.

"I will go right away," he said and left immediately.

"Maria, Maria, it is so good to see you my darling. I have been dreaming about this moment for over a year. The older I get the harder it is to be away from you, my love."

She came to his side and kissed his mouth, while he remained sitting at the table.

"Benny, what is wrong?" She touched his face with her hands, resting them on his unshaven stubble.

"I am sick my dear," he said and when he began to cry, he placed his head on her shoulder.

She knew in that instant that he was going to leave her again, to never return.

"I wanted to die in my home. Sleeping in our bed, next to my beautiful wife and not alone in Utah in the company flop house," he could barely get the words out.

Maria's heart was severed in half and she sobbed, holding onto her husband with both arms around his head. He remained in the kitchen chair with his head resting on her chest. He knew that God had answered his prayer to get back to his Maria before he died. The doctor in Utah had said that he would not be able to survive the difficult voyage. Benny had prayed over and over and over again. Pleading with God to give him the strength to see her once more. He knew that it was God that had given him this beautiful gift that he now beheld. That realization, and the guilt from the many years that he had spent away from his family, were driving the river of tears that now ran down his precious wife's blouse.

"You are a good man Barbato Jacobucci, and I will always love you!" She squeezed even more.

"I am sorry that I was away from you all of those years," he confessed through a gravel voice.

"You were away, Benny, because you loved us. You have always loved us," she whispered to him.

"I always have loved you," he cried freely, even as those words fell from his lips.

"I always knew that you were sacrificing for us, my love. You have no reason for shame."

"Oh Maria, my precious Maria. God has answered my prayers and has let me see you before I go to him."

"What is important is that we are together now," she said to the top of his pale bald head, kissing it ever so gently.

Then another coughing fit got started and Benny went into his bed, hacking up black Phlegm from deep within his lungs. Maria lay next to him praying, crying and caressing his back.

Two weeks later on a cool and cloudy day, the family was gathered around Barbato Jacobucci's graveside, weeping and remembering. The priest proclaimed a somber blessing over the casket of the departed, punctuated by the sign of the cross over the Pall. Maria, dressed in black, complete with a hat and laced veil, was surrounded by her two loving sons, but most of her heart was buried that day with her Benny. A few moments later Goivanni, the eldest son, pulled down on the heavy rope, causing the bell in the church tower to toll with an ominous tone. Two, then three rings, announcing to the rolling hills that another son of Spinete had departed for his home on the other side of this life.

•

To: Private Skeem, Neils #2264197

IV Infantry - 58th Infantry Division F Company

Camp Lewis, Tacoma, Washington 98433

From: Johnetta Whitelaw Cameron

413 Elm Street Pocatello, Idaho 83201

Message: "Yes!!!"

•

"Mother!" Cried the confident voice of the vivacious twenty-six year old Maggie, while she called in through the old screen door on the front porch of 413 Elm Street.

"Mommie, is Gram Gram not home?" Asked five year old Dorothy.

Ethel came charging out into the front yard wondering if their guests had finally arrived.

When she saw the group standing on the porch, she got so excited she ran full out into the backyard yelling at the top of her lungs.

"They're here! They're here! They're here!" With her arms flailing.

Johnetta left the garden, dropping her familiar old wooden hoe once again and sprinted toward the front yard, looking for her sister.

"Maggie!"

"There is the beautiful bride to be!" Maggie responded, as she navigated the five steps on the porch to embrace her little sister, for the first time in over a year.

Robbie and the three children followed Maggie down the steps.

"Oh my! Look at these little Angels!" Johnetta exclaimed.

Margret and Ethel joined the group to cheers and hugs.

"Auntie Jo Jo!" Cried the adorable red-headed Dorothy, as she lunged for Johnetta.

"Dorothy, you have grown like a weed!" Johnetta blurted out to her five year old niece, lifting her up with sweaty hands.

"Maggie, my dear, it is so good to see you my Bonnie Lass," She was hugging her eldest.

"I am sorry we didn't know when you would be in town and I am a stinky mess," Margret apologized.

"You know the old saying Mother, He who smells the least, smells the best!" Maggie said with her huge voice booming and echoing off of the house.

They all had a good laugh with the old Scottish saying.

"Verne come here and give old Aunt Jo Jo a hug!" Johnetta was chasing the little three year old around the yard.

"Look who is walking around! Ella!" Said Margret to her 18 month old blonde headed granddaughter.

Ella was hanging onto her Daddy's leg trying to hide from all of the commotion that had the neighbors across the street watching.

"Ella, give your Gram Gram a hug," said Robbie to his youngest child.

Robert Bruce Sagers was a tall stoic man, who carried himself with the confidence greater than his twenty eight years should allow. He had served as a missionary and was now serving as a counselor to the Ward Bishopric of the L.D.S. Being even-tempered and soft spoken had served him well. Many people that knew him considered him wise beyond his years. Working at the Midvale Smelter, he was a leader in almost everything that he did. Over six feet tall and slender built, even his gate spoke to his character.

He was the exact opposite of Walter. The two men did not get along but had never had a confrontation, because the younger man exercised restraint many times. However, conflict seemed to remain simmering just below the surface of their relationship. Tolerant, at best, would describe the feelings that each of them held for the other. It was the main reason that Margret and her daughter Maggie did not get together very often, their husbands had nothing in common.

"Johnetta, are you ready for your big day tomorrow?" Maggie asked her sixteen year old sister.

"I am!" she replied, while tickling little Verne.

"So what is he like, this Neils?" Maggie came alongside her sibling.

"He is kind, quiet and strong, Maggie. His demeanor actually reminds me of our father," Johnetta said.

The statement took both Margret and Maggie by surprise.

"Really? Your father?" Margret said, puzzled.

"Think about him as a person mom, not as the one marrying your youngest daughter," Johnetta explained.

"I guess that you are right, actually, I know that you are."

"Wow. High praise from the matriarch!" Maggie said.

"When do we get to finally meet him?"

"He should be on the early train tomorrow," Johnetta said.

"Ohhhh, cutting it close for the big day!" Maggie was playing in the way Maggie always liked to play. Johnetta wanted to impress her older sister, and get her approval. She had spent so many years looking up to her. Especially when Maggie was eighteen and charging off on the grand adventure of travelling halfway around the world to teach in, what she thought at the time, was an exotic place called 'Utah.' Her ten year advantage had always intimidated the young Johnetta and it was important to her to receive Maggie's blessing on her marriage to Neils.

"He can only be away for three days and we wanted to have one full day together before he returns."

"I understand my wee sister, I just hope you haven't rushed into something that you will later regret," Maggie affected the mother role.

"I know Neils and he is a good man!"

"But he's going off to war, girl."

"I know, and I am afraid for him."

"Why are you not getting married and sealed down in our glorious temple in Salt Lake, Johnetta?"

"Because we don't have the time, Maggie," the discussion had heated up a notch.

"But it's an important part of our faith," Maggie insisted.

"Things don't always work out the way you want it to, Sister." Johnetta pushed back for the first time in her young life, surprising even herself.

"Alright you two, lets get some lunch made," Margret took command, as usual, and Maggie acquiesced by biting her lower lip, per Robbie's instructions in the car on the way up.

Dorothy and her Aunt Ethel, born three days apart, were walking arm in arm across the lawn, below the large oak tree, toward the lonely tire swing and patch of worn out grass.

"Girls, be careful," Robbie said, taking a seat alone on one of the four weathered chairs on the old front porch.

"Hey, Mary," Robbie said to his sister-in-law, a half hour later, when she and Annie walked up on the porch.

"Hey Robbie! It is good to see you."

"I see that you brought your sister with you!"

"Very funny Robbie. What, did you want her to leave me stranded after I got my hair cut in bustling downtown Pocatello?" Annie said.

"She got to ride on our fine private streetcar," Said Mary.

"Streetcar?"

"In Pocatello 'streetcar' is just a fancy name for a truck with seats," Mary retorted.

"Dropped us only a block away," Annie was impressed.

"Maggie inside?" She asked, already moving toward the door.

"Yes," Robbie was enjoying a little solitude during what he knew was going to be a busy weekend.

"Aunt Mary is home too!" said a very excited Dorothy.

"Not too loud Dorthy, Ella is taking a nap upstairs." Maggie corrected her bouncing daughter.

"And Mary brought my long-lost sister Annie with her!" Johnetta said with a smile, as they hugged.

"I love the new hair!"

"Thanks!"

Mary and Maggie embraced briefly, getting over old hurts is sometimes painful. They had been instructed to remember why they had all come and to avoid the battle.

"Wid ye keek at that, a' mah girls th'gither at lest!" Margret's emotions got the better of her, she just bubbled over with her native brogue for the very special occasion. All the while holding onto her second daughter Annie for a few extra moments. Annie looked tired, worn out, really. The divorce was wearing her down and Margret could see that she looked older than her twenty four years.

"Howfur is ma lassie?" Margret whispered in her ear, as she held on, rocking her a bit.

"Aye standing," was about all that Annie could muster and still keep her emotions intact.

•

"Bushy, we're jumping off," whispered Fingers to his friend, as he shook him with his boot. Bushy was sleeping on the dirt floor of the dugout. He had found a spot after his watch duty and engaged his super sleeping powers, rats and all.

"I'm up," replied the groggy Italian.

"Ten minutes ladies, pass it down, ten minutes," said Corporal Mule, while sticking his head into the dark dugout.

"Who does he think he is, Black Jack's newest General?" Tools quipped.

"Ammo," a carrier slid a wooden crate of 30-06 ammunition into the dugout.

"Have they been rationing the stuff?"

"This is war after all, we may need some more of that!" One soldier called out after the carrier.

"Maybe the Huns will loan us some of theirs," someone else cracked and got a few laughs in return.

"No, seriously, there has been a huge snarl with supply trucks, horses and troops all trying to get up to the front at the same time down the same narrow road. We just got some water delivered an hour ago." Biscuit said, as he had just come off watch.

"Listen up men. Change of strategy today. The Huns will believe that they are in for hours of artillery, but we are jumping off with the barrage. There will be no signal flares this morning. We are all pushing over in a massive concentrated attack at the center of their line with both the 1st and 2nd Battalions. When we break through, and we will break through, we drive and divide their forces. The 3rd and 4th Battalions will charge with a frontal assault into their lines. 3Rd on the north and 4th on the south of the break out. We have to be quick today. Speed and tenacity will win this fight. The 88th Aero Squadron has given us good reconnaissance, the German lines are the weakest right out in front of our position here. It appears that the Huns were already beginning a staged withdrawal from the salient before our attack yesterday. We have them on the run. We will have air cover all day today. We go at 05:15 with the artillery gentlemen, we hit them hard and we end this today!"

Major Legge called for the Chaplin to lead the men in prayer. After the collective "Amen!" The Major went down the line encouraging his soldiers bravery and thanking them for their sacrifice.

The battle became known as the St. Mihiel offensive and was the only fight in the Great War that was led entirely by the Americans. After the initial slow grind of the first day of the attack, the American forces of the 26th 'Yankee' Infantry Division broke through, moving southeast over six miles and met up with the 42nd 'Rainbow' Infantry Division on the outskirts of Hattonchatel, thus closing off the salient. Two days later the battle was considered over when it was apparent that the Huns could not mount a sustained counterattack. Over two thousand Germans were killed with fifteen hundred captured, along with four hundred forty artillery pieces and seven hundred fifty machine guns.

Tragically, the victory had a steep price. The Americans lost almost seven thousand lives to win the fight. The new Army still had much to learn and they needed to learn it quickly, because in less than two weeks, 1.2 million U.S. soldiers would regroup to jump off into the largest single battle in American history.

•

Christian Skeem checked his watch again, the fourth time in the last ten minutes. The number 288 train from Seattle was not running ahead of schedule today. You could usually set your watch by the combination freight and passenger train rolling into the Pocatello station at noon. Christian was hoping it would have been a little early today. Picking up his nephew for his wedding on the afternoon of the ceremony was easy enough. But that was not all, Christian's family was hosting the reception at his ranch. With many tasks yet to complete and only a couple of hours of leeway, he knew this day could prove tricky.

The stress of the day dramatically increased when Bishop Andersen called just before Christian walked out the door to inform him that he had important pressing matters to tend to, that would not allow him to perform today's wedding service for Neils and Johnetta. The church service was set for 2:00 pm in Inkom, with the reception immediately following. Picking up Neils from the station and now Bishop Walters, who lived west of Pocatello, was going to make getting to the church on time for the groom to get ready difficult. He knew all along that Bishop Andersen did not approve of the marriage, but he could not understand why. It caused a smoldering resentment to build, deep down inside his heart. It was one that very well may cause him to begin to attend the church in Pocatello instead of Inkom. The train whistle brought him back to reality. It was 12:02.

The young man who stepped off of the train that day was not the same person who had departed just two months prior. This Neils was broader, thicker, taller and had a much more confident glint in his eye and spring in his step. His spine was straight as a board, shoulders pulled back and his chest pronounced, with his confident head held high. He looked remarkable in his olive green dress uniform. The top of his left arm proudly displayed the four sided patch of little green leaves, the insignia of the Ivy Division that, along with the shiny black boots gave Neils a professional aura. He looked the part of a genuine soldier and his Uncle beamed with pride.

"Uncle!" he said, a little surprised.

"Neils! You look terrific, Son! What kind of fertilizer have they been feeding you up there?" quipped the old rancher.

"You are a sight for sore eyes." Neils hugged his hero.

"We have to get going, Son, we have another passenger to pick up." Christian went to grab Neils light duffel bag from his hand, as they walked along, but the young man was not letting go, with a slight smirk of defiance that almost dared the man to try and wrestle it away from him.

"Who is our passenger?" Neils inquired.

Pulling into the little church in Inkom, Neils felt home stir inside of him. He was anxious for the day's events and even more excited to see his young bride. He put aside the disappointment of Bishop Andersen's sudden unavailability and wondered if it might be because he had rebuffed the suggestion that he court his daughter a year ago. Bishop Walters seemed like a cordial fellow, and he was more than willing to step in for

Andersen.

The rest of the day was a blur of activity for Neils, with the single exception of Johnetta walking up the aisle way toward him, hanging onto both Walter and Margret's arms. Those two minutes played out with such clarity in his mind, as his heart melted by her simple, pure beauty. The broad smile almost split Neils face in half, tears gathered in the corner of his eyes, as he followed her every step toward him. This moment was the grandest of his entire life. His strident plan for his future was not working out in accordance to his will. He was supposed to already have his ranch up and running, then getting married was to be step three. The war had interfered with his intentions, but this unforeseen turn of events was being remedied by the reality of the blessing that Johnetta was to him.

Johnetta held on tightly to her mother's arm and lightly onto Walter's. This had been the first time in her life that she had touched the man, and it was out of obligation. She desperately wished that it was her real father walking her down this aisle. When the three of them came through the doors into the meeting hall, Johnetta was taken aback by the amount of people gathered for her wedding day and she began to tear up in appreciation. Her white dress was modest and precisely what she had hoped to wear that momentous day. Looking to the front for the first time, her gaze was held by the mountain of a man standing next to Bishop Walters.

"Was that really Neils?" she questioned herself. It had been a couple of months, after all. She had been fighting a persistent fear that he would choose not to be there. That he had met another, prettier, more sophisticated woman up in Washington state, with whom he would run away, never to be seen again. All of those authentic fears of abandonment, gently washed away into the soon forgotten river of welling emotions.

Yet, Neils did look different to her. He looked to be chiseled from granite in that instant. As if he was a more developed, more confident man. While Johnetta felt like a little girl clutching onto her mother's arm on the one side, while racing away from the ugly fake man on the other. Questions of sincerity bounced inside her, while they came close to the front of the familiar church. Was this an attempt to run away from her father's death and mother's choices? Maybe. And, at the same time, Neils was standing right in front of her. Choosing her. In that moment, at that very second, her heart began to mend the seven year old tear. The wounded bond with her father that Johnetta held so tightly, was being wrapped by another caring, strong and loving, male hand.

"Daddy, I still love you," Johnetta whispered to the wind, and reached for Neils outstretched arm.

•

Later that evening, thirty five miles north of the wedding celebration, a lone Ford Model T chugged along a winding dirt road up the side of a mountain. Pete was focused on getting to his destination and a faster car sped up behind him. Moving in closer the hulking pilot slammed the driver side rear bumper of the Ford hard enough to send it into a spin. Pete was shaken as his head hit the inside window when his Flivver came skidding to a violent sideways stop. The boxes of gallon jugs of moonshine tipped and spilled in the commotion, some of them burst their bonds splashing the clear liquid on his seat and floor.

Before he realized what happened a steel object knocked on his window. The barrel of the revolver was pointed at his head and the door opened. A hand grabbed the back of his neck and drug him out of the car, while another kept a gun leveled at his face.

"What? What do you want from me?" Pete nearly wet his pants.

"Pete," said a third man with the headlights of the car behind him he remained hidden from view.

"Just take the shine." Pete said, nervously.

"It's a gift, more than enough to clear up this misunderstanding, I'm sure."

"We don't want your libations Peter." The jugs of illegal moonshine were being broken on the ground to prove the point.

"Peter, you are an apostate. A reprobate who is beyond redemption. The Ward Bishopric has written a decree, that in order to save your soul a blood atonement is required."

"A... Are, Are you kidding me?" Pete hoped this was all a bad joke.

"This is certainly not a matter of amusement Peter." said the dark voice.

Pete swallowed hard as his head spun. He had to get out of this, so he began to fight the grip on his neck only to hear the gun cock, then the cold steel was pressed against the back of his lowered head.

"Don't make this any more difficult than it has to be Peter."

"I don't know what the hell you are talking about!"

"The charges against you are as follows: Adultery. Fornication. Drunkenness. Producing the means of drunkenness for others. Revelry. A general disregard for your own soul."

"Yeah, so-so what?"

"It means that you have moved beyond the blood of Jesus being able to cover your grave and serious sins."

"I don't believe that shit anymore." Pete exclaimed in defiance.

A firm smack from the butt of the gun caught Pete on the side of the head with a dull thud.

"Man you better hope that I don't get up and stuff that thing down your throat," Pete threatened his assailants from the ground.

"Shut up, dirt bag," said the one still holding the gun.

"Easy Bennie, we are going to do this the proper way, there is no need to rough him up."

"We know you don't believe Peter, and we are going to help you finally get your life right tonight."

"How's that?"

"You are going to offer your blood on the altar of sacrifice and the steam of your life will hopefully be seen as an obedient prayer, rising to appease God's wrath for those whose sin is so grievous," announced the man.

Pete began to shake with the realization that he was going to be offered as a ritual sacrifice. He had heard rumors of the practice, but down in Utah, not up here in Idaho.

"You can't do this, I, I have rights!" Demanded Pete.

"We are offering you a final, genuine salvation of your worthless life," said the dark one. The leader nodded toward a fourth man dressed in a white robe. The silent executioner walked over to Pete, grabbed his head from behind by the hair and in one motion slit his throat from ear to ear. Making sure to continue to hold his head up, the blood of the writhing man known as Pocatello Pete pumped from his open neck, drenching the dry ground.

"This one does not deserve a burial, his customers need to be aware of the danger of such rebellion."

Bishop Andersen had been chosen by lots for the ugly, but necessary duty of watching over the flock. He left the grotesque ritualistic scene convinced he had done the man an eternal favor and himself an earthly one. The Ward Bishopric would long remember Andersen's distressing sacrifice of that day.

Back at the wedding reception, a couple of hours later, an anonymous note was handed to Walter Adamson which simply read:

"Your source of libations has quite literally dried up. Be warned. You are close to the same fate."

It was signed with a few drops of blood of a human sacrifice.

Walter knew it was Pete's blood. His own drained from his face.

•

V.
'Hell Of War'

"I will send you many letters, my love," Neils tenderly whispered into Johnetta's ear.

"I will miss you, Neils."

"Get away from that fake Dad, go to Nephi. My parents would love to have you there with them," he told her, during their long embrace.

"I will go," she said.

The whistle to depart sounded twice, announcing that the train to Seattle was preparing to exit the station, and the newlyweds still did not want to separate.

"All Aboard!" The blue capped man cried, looking directly at the soldier and his bride. He had seen it twenty times over the last few months. Soldiers coming home on leave, getting married and not wanting to let go of their new, crying brides.

"Come on son, we have to depart," he said to the soldier.

"You come back to me Neils," Johnetta cried.

"I will," he said, as he ever so slowly, let go. With a final tear soaked smile, Neils turned and hopped aboard, snuck past the conductor and into the front of the final commuter car.

Johnetta watched her husband through the small windows, while Neils made his way back to a seat in the rear of the car. She caught his eye and waved. The train chugged large plumes of black smoke and lurched away from the humble outdoor terminal.

Dread washed over Johnetta, while images of dissolution assaulted her heart.

"Was that the last time I will ever see him?" That was the haunting question.

The thought would disturb her nights during the early part of the war.

"Come on Johnetta, let's go to the five and dime and get a soda," Mary said, while grabbing onto her younger sister's arm.

"What about Mother and, ... him," she asked. They looked over at the automobile where the two were engaged in an all out brawl of a shouting match, behind the glass. Walter was being pummelled at the moment with a full frontal assault by the female Scottish army of one. Both sisters looked at each other and could not help but laugh out loud, following the spectacle of trepidation on the man's face.

"Poor Walty," Mary said.

"He is definitely outmatched in this one," Johnetta said, wiping tears away from her face.

They walked right past the car, toward downtown.

"He doesn't have any of his courage," Mary said.

"Of the liquid variety, you mean?"

"Exactly. When he is sober he doesn't have a chance against her."

"Mom has a quick wit and a faster tongue," Johnetta said.

"Apparently she has had a bone to pick with him all weekend," Mary guessed.

"Really?"

"Like you would have noticed at all!"

"The only thing that you could see this weekend was Neils, Neils, Neils," Mary poked fun at her little sister.

"'N' he is something tae see, Mary! His muscles have gotten so big since boot camp," Johnetta was smiling, like only a new bride can.

"Ahhhhhhh, I don't want to know!" Mary said in jest, while covering her ears.

"But really, tell me everything that happened!"

They both fell into a loud burst of laughter walking arm in arm down the city street.

The disagreement began when Margret returned to the table where she and Walter had eaten dinner during the reception. Something caught her eye on the dark floor while sitting back down. Walter was nowhere to be seen. Reaching down to pick a folded piece of paper up from beneath the chair, she read the contents and wanted to throw up. Margret found the blood stained note on that floor. The implications were enormous. Her rage was instantaneous. Walter would be held to account. Margret wanted to grab him by the collar and force him to explain himself, but, with so many people around, this ridiculous discussion would have to wait. She tucked the note into her bra and went on celebrating Johnetta's and Neils wedding, trying not to think about what she had discovered.

When Margret pulled away from her new son-in-law's departing embrace, she took Walter gently by the hand and guided him back to the privacy of their car. She had waited long enough. For three days, she held in all of her anger and fears. For three long days, her smoldering heart burned. Knowing that they would have several minutes before the train departed, the invasion began.

"What is this Walter?" She removed the note from her brassiere and threw it into his unsuspecting lap.

He knew right away what it was, of course. He had not been able to sleep all weekend long worrying about its implications.

"It.., it just showed up on my plate at dinner," he tried to reduce the importance of the note through deflection.

"Okay, but what does it mean, Walter?" There was three days worth of angst seeking to be released from Margret's aching heart.

"Whit th' hell hae ye dane?" Margret somehow felt better swearing in brogue, like she was throwing everything she had at the man, now through clenched teeth.

"What does that mean?"

"The note says that you are officially warned Walter," her eyes blazed through him.

"I don't know, I..."

"You know. You know exactly what is going on here," she countered, forcefully, thrusting her finger in the side of his arm.

"I guess. I think... Pete got himself into some kind of trouble with the church, or something."

"Literally. Dried. Up!!! It says, dried up, Walt!"

"Sounds to me like Pocatello Pete is dead." Margret said.

"Well... Yeah... That's what I thought it meant too."

"Ye son o' a boot! You have put our family, my girls, in harm's way. Now these killers are watching us all because you can't stop your damn drinking, Walter!" She was beside herself now, furious with the man sitting next to her. Sickened, in fact. The old fear from

Dugald's death flooded right into her heart anew, and sparked all of the underlying insecurities that came along with it.

"I would never have agreed to marry a man like you if you hadn't hidden the truth of your depravities from me. And to think that I gave you the right over my eternal life, to call me into glory by my special name!"

"Margret you know that I would never hold that against you," he said with all seriousness. "A'm sic an gowk fur trusting ye!"

Silence followed, while both of them considered the brutal ramifications.

"Is this what I think it is, Walter?" Said a calmer Margret, who was trying to understand what they were up against.

"I think that it was a ritual killing, Margret," Walter said.

"They are sending a message to everyone one in the church who was connected to Pete through his moonshine. An article is in the Sunday paper about a man found dead with his throat slit." Walter paused.

"You know that if the church doesn't want people to know, it wouldn't be in the paper. It would just disappear as another unfortunate event."

"Do they have that much power?" Margret whispered, as if someone could be listening.

"Are you kidding? The church runs everything out here. Everything."

"Church? Church? They are acting like a Cult!"

"I know."

"If you don't do things their way, you don't have anything. No job. No home. No police. Nothing."

"We have got to get away from this Walter," Margret was showing real fear in her face now.

"Where are you going to run, Margret?"

"I don't know... Somewhere. Anywhere."

"Listen, you take Ethel and go visit Maggie or Annie for a few weeks, if anyone asks I will say that I sent you away."

"Closer to Salt Lake City?" She wondered about his advice.

"No one will suspect a thing Margret and you'd be away from me and the danger I have brought on us."

She thoughtfully considered what he was saying.

"Johnetta is moving in a couple of days, to Nephi," Margret admitted to him for the first time.

"What?..." Walter was saddened by the news.

"I guess I don't have to ask why," he said, lowering his head ashamed. The two had never gotten along.

"She's looking for a new start to her life, Walter. Besides, her husband told her that she needed to go."

"Yeah, I get it," Walter said, as a single tear dropped from his cheek.

Margret slid over to him and placed her head on his shoulder.

"I am going to quit the drink'in for good, Margret."

"You must really be worried," Margret said.

"I am sorry for being such a miserable man all these years," Walter was broken.

"Oh Walter, you haven't been fighting against me, you have been beating yourself."

He wrapped his arm around her, as tears washed down his face.

"Let's give this a few weeks and it will all blow over. I quit drinking. We go to church. It all goes away." Walter was hopeful his plan could work.

Margret felt she had little choice in the matter at this point. She would have to trust him in this moment of grave uncertainty.

•

"Two man teams. Dig your foxholes and keep your heads down!" Molly was speaking forcefully. He had instructed the men in his squad to spread out to whispering distance between holes and get dug in. It was dark in the cool French countryside and the company was being peppered by German machine gun fire. The Huns were shooting at sounds during the dark and dreary night.

"Spread the dirt around," Pops was going hole to hole telling the men to keep from piling the dirt up in front of their foxhole because it would become a target after the sun rose for the German MG crews on the other side of the ravine.

"Boom! Crack!" The thunder-like roar caused all the men to hit the dirt, as a German artillery round exploded seventy yards west, blowing a tree to toothpicks.

"Come on, Ladies, no time to dawdle," the aged Sergeant Pops, urged.

Bushy was digging like a madman into the soft French soil. His partner in the adventure was a fellow Italian American, Giovani Garufi, along with his undignified Army name of 'Wop' in tow. Wop was busy throwing the dirt Bushy had dug up, around the area as quietly as he could. The pair was chatting away in hushed Italian while they worked reminiscing about the old country, comparing their villages, which seemed almost identical. The chatting was just at whisper level, so they wouldn't be heard by the enemy. It was their strategy to deal with the stress of the situation. Never ending chatter.

"Boom! Boom! Boom!" Three successive veiled attempts by a German artillery unit to blindly kill some doughboys. It made the digging go a little faster in the forward area. The 250 men of Company D spread out in two successive lines across five hundred yards of blood and rain soaked countryside, with Company A to their right and Company C behind them by a couple hundred yards. Digging silently, except for the occasional entrenching tool striking rock. Little did they know, they would spend the next three gloomy days in these foxholes; floundering in the worst that war had to offer, being denied the ability to attack because of a lack of logistical support. The French roads couldn't handle the tremendous Allied push to the front and the massive attack stalled.

In the morning the German spotters directed artillery in their general direction, trying to flush out their exact positions. After ten, the loud wooden rattle of gas alarms sounded across the American lines. This warning was for Mustard gas and the dreaded munitions rained down their yellow clouds of malaise throughout the area. The exposed men in the holes only had a few seconds to don their masks to avoid being burnt or blinded by the vicious blistering weapon. This torment was followed by more artillery pummeling the terrain, along with relentless sprays of machine gun fire, so intense, that it disintegrated trees all across the battlefield.

The assault, known as the Meuse Argonne Offensive, stalled with heavy fighting in this area. The 35th Infantry Division initially had jumped off on the offensive early September 26. Within three days of horrific combat they were so decimated by losses they were declared to be an ineffective fighting force and had to be replaced by the 1st Divisions four infantry regiments, the 16th, 18th, 28th and Bushy's 26th.

The men of the 26th marched through the black of night, over unfamiliar territory, trying to find the most forward position that the 35th had occupied. They knew that the veteran German 52nd Division was content to let the doughboys advance on their well defended positions. The Germans mowed down thousands of men of the 35th Division and were resupplying and waiting to exact as much butchery on the next line of men sent into the fray.

The weather was cold, cloudy with just enough light rain to push the men near to hypothermia. These endless days entombed in their foxholes would become known as the 'bitter days'. The men hung suspended between attacks. The stench of rotting horses wafted along with the breeze combined with the rest of the rancid smells of war. The doughboys were commanded out of their four foot deep foxholes at night to exercise in the cover of darkness in order to stave off immobility. The officers were trying to keep their troopers morale up in the withering conditions.

"First Platoon, lock and load, prepare for a scouting mission, we leave in thirty," was passed down the line at 04:00. Wop shook Bushy awake to give him the news of the mission upon which they were about to embark.

•

"Come in Johnetta, we are so glad that you are here with us!" Martina said with her full electric smile.

"Thank you," Johnetta was feeling uneasy with the new living arrangements, wondering if she had made a terrible mistake.

"Please make yourself at home," Martina knew that her young daughter-in-law was nervous. Who would not be, moving in with complete strangers two hundred miles away from home?

"We are so glad that you have come, dear."

"Thank you for having me," she said, somewhat awkwardly.

"How was the train?"

"It was fine. It got really crowded in Salt Lake," she added.

"Andy is closing up the store in just a bit, then we will have dinner. If you want to freshen up there is a bathroom down the hall, feel free." Martina was a little nervous herself.

"Thank you, Mrs Skeem," she said.

"Johnetta, you can call me Martina," trying to ease some of the tension.

"So did Neils make the train to Seattle in time on Sunday?"

"Yes, my mother and Walter dropped us with plenty of time," she explained.

"I bet he didn't want to leave you at all!"

"No, the conductor had to bark at us to stop hugging because the train was going to leave without him."

Martina came to Johnetta's side when she saw the tears begin to cascade down the poor girl's cheeks.

"I am sorry. It is so hard. I wish you two could have had a proper honeymoon."

"It's not even having a honeymoon, I just miss him and..." she did not continue.

Martina kept her hand on Johnetta's back to reassure her, but resisted saying anything more.

"I worry that he won't come back to me," she said, giving in to the sickening thought.

"Yes, dear, I do too," and both women had a good cry.

An hour later the three Skeem gathered around the kitchen table for the evening's meal, trying to make Johnetta feel welcome.

"So did you know that Gordon, Neils oldest brother, is up in Inkom working with Uncle Christian now?" Andy asked.

"Yes, Neils told me that he was just going to stay on after our wedding day."

"It was a lovely wedding dear," Martina was trying to encourage the young bride.

"It was so nice," Johnetta said.

"Neils looked so good in his Army uniform. I was very proud," Andy said.

"I almost didn't recognize him when we were walking down the aisle. I hadn't laid eyes on him in over two months and he had gotten so big," Johnetta was smiling at the fond memory.

"I couldn't believe it either!" Martina admitted.

"They are training them boys pretty hard," Andy pipped in.

"It was almost like he was made out of granite."

They all had a good laugh for a minute that was followed by a few moments of each of them quietly remembering their Neils.

"So Johnetta, if you're up to it, I can show you around the store tomorrow. Then we will walk over to the restaurant and you can decide where you want to work," Andy said, breaking the somber mood that had settled over the meal.

"We really do need the help, Johnetta," Martina sincerely interjected.

"That sounds great Mr. Skeem!" she said.

"You can call me Andy, Johnetta."

"We're not very formal around here," he said with a smile.

"Okay. Andy. Yes, I am looking forward to seeing both your store and the new restaurant," Johnetta said.

"Great!"

"I need something to do to keep my mind occupied."

"Well, there is plenty to do around here!" Martina laughed.

•

14-9-17

Dear Johnetta Skeem,

I still smile whenever I write your new name. I miss you darling, so much. Training is over for us on this side of the Atlantic. We are leaving Camp Lewis at first light. The next

letter may take awhile in arriving since it will be coming all the way from France! I am

excited for the adventure and some men are saying that the Germans are sure to surrender

when they see the great hordes of American doughboys marching at them! Wish me luck!

I hope your time at my parents restaurant is keeping you busy and that you're making

good tips!

All my love,

Neils.

•

"All right men, we are going to patrol out ahead of the lines to find where the German

positions are being held. We need the intelligence for our artillery batteries. Once the big

guns get in position, their barrage will be key in leading us in the full attack." Second

Lieutenant Thomas Amory was an intense young man when he prepared a battle plan. He

was thorough in his explanations and willing to listen to the concerns of the men he led.

As one of the lead officers in Company D he took charge of this probing mission to

ensure accurate gathering of intelligence. Lieutenant Meeker was going to assist in the

predawn action, as the seventy five man force moved out at 05:40, with one Platoon from

D company and four squads from A company.

Bushy and Wop were in the second line of the advance, about 50 feet behind the first

line, with two officers between.

A hundred yards beyond the forward line, the special task force made its way past the two

lookout positions who hunkered down in their deep foxholes. Another fifteen nerve

racking minutes, then the pitch dark woods exploded with Maxim fire, raking across the

formation. Everyone went scrambling for cover. Lt. Amory shouted and led the men

racing to a ravine ahead of them, but off to the right. The ravine was about 120 feet deep,

two hundred yards across, with a small creek at the bottom. That small river, called the

Mayache, connected with the larger Exerment River 500 yards to the north. Scurrying

down the dark embankment and up the next, the doughboys were now being fired on from three directions. Bullets whizzing across their heads, impacting all around their feet as they clambered up the side of the ravine, as the sky began to brighten to the east.

With hand signals relayed down the line to Lt. Meeker, Amory split the group to attack the two closest machine gun nests with separate, vicious assaults. Moving into flanking positions, they eliminated both German crews with several grenades and concentrated fire. Charging into those positions they turned the guns on the next closest nest, until the ammo dried up.

"We will take this next nest, or die trying," Amory rallied his half of the men on to the next attack, despite the heavy casualties being sustained. Even more Germans opened fire, Lt. Armory was shot in the head and died instantly. The Americans of the 26th were being devastated, with men dropping all over the area. Wop died, with several shots through the chest, while Bushy took cover a few feet away from the twitching corpse.

Lt. Meeker rallied the remaining men, to inspire hope of getting anyone back to the lines alive. They fought ferociously through the hail of bullets that peppered them from across the Exerment River for over an hour; crossing the ravine, crawling from rock to rock for cover. They made their way back, going up toward the ridge where they had entered.

Just as the remaining men were about to make the move to get out of the valley of death, a rescue Platoon from the First Battalion arrived to provide covering fire for the retreating men. The blistering fire forced the German guns into silence, allowing the remaining men to clear the ravine and back into the relative safety of the woods. Seventy five doughboys had left out on the mission and two hours later, just twenty men returned. It proved to be a high price to pay for confirmation of previously known intelligence. Some titled it an exercise in futility.

A half hour later, Bushy dragged himself back to his unoccupied hole in the ground. He was spent from the intense battle. He bowed his head, clasp his shaking hands together and thanked God that his life had been spared. Tears streamed down his face in the privacy of his foxhole. Another brother was lost to this insane war. Joe was still breathing while so many were no longer.

"Hey!" Fingers rolled uninvited into the hole with Joseph.

"What happened out there, Bushy?"

"We charged into this ravine and were taking heavy fire from three sides. Guys were getting mowed down like, like wheat all around. We cleaned out a couple of nests. Amory got clipped in the head."

"Lt. Armor is dead? I thought that guy was invincible."

"Wop had his chest blown apart a couple of seconds later."

"It was brutal, Fingers," now looking right at the man.

"I am sorry to hear about the Wop."

"I don't know how I survived. There were so many machine gun nests I couldn't even count them."

"Grace of God, Buddy. The grace of God," he said patting his friend on the shoulder.

"GAS! GAS! GAS!" The wooden alarm was sounding off again.

•

13-6-18

Dear Johnetta

I received your letters, three of them on the very same day, in fact. The letter with the picture included is my absolute favorite gift that I have received in a long time. Thank you. I miss you terribly! The picture is in my pocket over my heart, where it and you shall remain until this war is done.

I cannot hardly believe that over ten months has passed since our beautiful wedding day. I miss our time together and cannot wait to see you again. The men are hoping that we can end this war and be home by Christmas. That is what I am fighting for, to get home to you, my love.

We have been doing so much training since we arrived in the country, most of it you will be very glad to know, has been far from the action. We are moving again and will be occupying a quiet sector of the line here in a couple of weeks, so the scuttlebutt goes.

I hope living with my parents hasn't put too much strain on you. They are loving but can be very driven people. Pass along my love and know that I love you.
Always Yours,
Neils.

•

Around noon Tinsel dropped into Bushy's foxhole, startling the resting soldier.
"Tinsel you scared the crap out of me!"
"Sorry Bush-man," he said through his bulky green gas mask.
"I got kicked out of my hole by a couple of replacement guys."
"No-names?"
"Yeah."
"Sorry to hear about the Wop. I gave him a lot of crap over the last few months, but he was a good guy."
"Thanks, Tinsel," Bushy smiled inside his gas mask.
"I hear you had a rough morning," Tinsel was sympathetic.
"Yeah, we got our butt kicked."
"Get some shut eye, I'll keep watch over the hole," he said.

It did not take long for the sleep to return.
A dream took him back to a vivid Utah scene.
"Joseph, is that you?"
"Hey Joe, you're back!"
"Everyone! Joe Jacobucci is back from the old country!"

It should have been a happy time in Joseph's life. He was able to leave his grieving Mother's side after his older brother John had gotten married to Lucia Botino in April 1913. Mom had prevented Joseph from returning to America for over two years after his father passed away. She was afraid that her youngest boy would suffer from the black lung if he went to work in the smelter again. Just like her dearly departed Benny.

"You look me in the eye and promise me that you will not go back to that dirty place to work," she insisted with her pointing finger to his chest.

"OK, Momma. I won't take a job in that dirty place where Papa worked. But I am going back to America."

"I know you are my son," She said to him, now patting his chest.

"You are a man now Giuseppe and you need to follow your dreams. I want you to follow them."

"Thank you Momma. I have been waiting to get your blessing to return," he said.

"I know. Now, with Giovanni married and staying here in Spinete, you have my blessing."

"Thank you Momma. I will always love you and I will send money home to help you," he promised further.

"Tell me why you want to go, Giuseppe," she asked.

"Momma, here in the old country, I will always be a farmer like my father before me and his father before him. A farmer is good work when the crops grow and the prices for grain are high. But in America, I don't have to be a farmer! I can do whatever I want and make more than enough money to help you. In America, I am a free man, Momma," he proclaimed his dream with pride.

"I can live wherever I want. It is a wild, beautiful country, where I will live and raise a family who will have all the freedom to do whatever they want in life!"

"You sound just like your Padre."

"I will miss you, my son. Please come back to visit me," she said with tears in anticipation of his departure.

"Of course I will, Momma."

He was back in Utah, with his friends gathering around him he was happy to see them, so happy to be reunited with his childhood compatriots. Yet, saddened by his inability to remember how to speak English. His brain and his tongue were stuck. The last six years of his life he had spent in the old country, and school, work, and family was all spoken in his native tongue. The English had abandoned him like his childhood.

He wandered home defeated, to where his cousins had a place in Midvale, and he cried like a baby because he had forgotten the language of his new nation, his new home. He felt lost and isolated, laying on his bed that day. Nothing like a nineteen year old should feel, he reasoned. He never wanted to feel that way again and made a vow to learn the language so well he wouldn't even have an accent.

"Bush-man, are you alright?" Tinsel was watching him twist and turn in the pile of dirt at the bottom of the hole, while he tried to sleep off the trauma and loss of the morning.

•

The row of trucks stretched on for miles, as the Fourth Infantry Division made its way toward the front. The ominous low rumble of distant artillery brought home reality to the otherwise jovial ride east. The cloth tarps on the transports were tied up in the late afternoon sun. The July heatwave that was promised by the divisional headquarters had arrived in earnest. The sweltering heat caused the quartermaster unit to issue, to the men of the Ivy Forth, an additional canteen to carry into battle, along with added ammunition. The men were thankful for the extra ration but not the weight.

This was the first time that the Ivy was being called to the front. Early on a couple of battalions had seen some action north of the area from where they were headed. Those men told horrific stories of the brutality of modern warfare, so much so, that most of the men had to walk away from those stories and not think about what they heard.

"Hey, Skimmer, where did you say that we were headed again?"

"To the front!" It was his deadpan attempt at humor. He was ridiculed by the rest of the weary men in the truck.

"Come on," said the dark skinned doughboy, they all called the Greek.

"I overheard an officer say that we were heading to the front to lead a counterattack near Chateau Thierry," Skimmer said.

"Where the hell is that?" Someone from the front shouted back, over the truck engine noise.

"It's about thirty miles east of Chantilly," Neils explained.

"We are going to war boys!"

"Time to kill some Huns and get out of France!"

"Amen to that," another said in support.

"Been here nine months and I am sick of it already," said the Greek.

"All that we do is training exercises!"

"Not after today!"

The men of the Fourth Infantry Division marched the final three miles to the edge of the battlefield during darkness, so they would not be spotted by the ever present German Balloon Corps. The plan was for a mass engagement on the fifty mile wide salient the Germans had created in the line over the last couple of months. The Hun push was a continuation of their spring 1918 'Micheal Offensive' that was designed to end the war before the Americans could get enough men across the Atlantic to make a difference in the war. This was to be the second battle near the Marne River. A direct frontal assault on German lines to drive them back to where they had begun in the spring Offensive.

Skimmers Platoon was near the front of the push toward the old French town of Chateau Theirry. The men were anxious to get the fight going. They were supported by a thousand allied planes, hundreds of artillery and a few hundred light tanks. With the opening barrage beginning at 04:30, Thursday July 18th 1918, the men were set to jump off only an hour into the bombardment, expecting the Huns not to have dug in, in just a few short weeks. But they had dug in well, especially the dreaded Maxims, with hundreds of interlocking networks throughout the battlefield. The unsuspecting Americans marched into a buzz saw.

The Allied Aero Squadrons mercilessly bombed and strafed the German lines all morning long. Artillery unleashed volleys of devastation into the Hun trenches, along with thousands of rounds of gas early in the day, when the wind was favorable. The final push to break through was achieved on the backs of bayonet clad doughboys, following Renault tanks into the maelstrom. The main breakthrough came about 10:30 as the 58th Infantry Division poured through a new gap in the line. Thinking that they had achieved a final breakthrough, a group of unsuspecting men charged out into the open and were savagely mowed down, by an out of commission Maxim MG that had been resupplied.

In the heat of the day, at the sound of the Maxim, Private Neils Skeem was sent running hard for cover behind a small garden wall, when the hidden MG discharged a burst into his chest from close range. He was shot clean through the heart and dropped dead on the spot. His blood spilled through and soaked the pierced picture of his pretty young wife, still in the pocket over his hushed heart. Neils' war was done.

Three days later his body was recovered and laid in a long line of American dead. All of the deceased soldiers' dog tags would be processed and recorded in official Army records. Neils would soon be laid to rest in the soil of the foreign country where his life ended, far from his beloved homeland.

•

"Bush-man, we got hot grub," Tinsel was nudging him to life.
"I think the Major feels bad for us sitting in these little graves for two days," he said with his mask off.
Bushy released the straps of his mask and took a quick sniff of the moldy, rotten,

stinking burning battlefield air and much to his surprise it was a lot better than the stinky breath smell of his mask.

"What did they cook up for us, Tins?"

"Trench stew!"

"The corned beef soup?"

"Yes and two biscuits per man," he was excited.

"I bet Biscuit is thrilled," he quipped.

"I am," came the whisper from the next hole over.

They all laughed at the big kid from Colorado.

"Did someone drop this off for us?" Joe asked.

"The Scott-man did."

"Barney?" Joe questioned.

"Yeah, I think that is his name, I just know him as The Scott."

"His brogue is so thick I can hardly understand him sometimes," Tins said, then slurped.

"He reminds me of someone I work with back home," Joe said, while looking off into the dark side of the hole, while the rising steam from his soup warmed his face.

"Oh yeah, where is home?"

"Utah. Midvale, Utah," he said, coming back to reality.

"What did you do back home, at work, I mean?"

"I worked at a smelter in the lab," Joe said between the warming spoonfuls.

"Oh yeah? I worked as a machine mechanic at a stamping plant near Detroit."

"Really?"

More eating and thinking ensued. Like they were a couple of guys enjoying a lunch break and talking about their lives, instead of two soldiers on the front lines of the worst war in history.

"I hear that there are a lot of jobs in Detroit, is that true?" Joe wondered aloud.

"They can't get enough people to fill them, and they are good paying jobs, Bushy."

"No kidding?"

"What about the Scott you work with?"

"Oh, yeah, he is right from Scotland and if you can get him upset he will go on a rant that no one in the shop can understand. It is so funny to watch. I used to ask him where his dress was," he repressed a laugh in that memory.

"Dress?"

"Yeah, the Highlanders in Scotland wear these traditional dresses that they call 'Kilts."

"Oh, I think that I saw some Canadian troops dressed up in those not too long ago."

"Yes they were trying to go past us on a cross road a few days ago and everything was clogged up."

"Well those Canadians didn't take very well to a bunch of doughboys laughing at their skirts," Tinsel said with a smile.

"Sounds just like Dugald," Joe said.

"Who?"

"Dugald Cameron."

•

Telegram.

K. War Department, Washington, D.C.

July 18th 1918.

Private Neils Skeem of Inkom, Utah.

KIA near Chateau Thierry France.

Inform next of kin, wife Johnetta Skeem Nephi, Utah. Stop.

Remains to stay in France. Stop. End.

The western Union man with his bulging bag of telegrams entered the gloomy War Department building in downtown Washington D.C. There were three drop boxes for the war telegrams. One slot for the 'K' indications, another for the 'M' Letters and a third slot for the 'P' telegrams. He had been servicing the war department run for Western Union for over a year now and he had never seen so many K cards. Hundreds of K cards, three M cards, and zero P cards.

He knew that all of the 'K' were notifications that someone had been Killed In Action in the war in Europe. What he did not know was if anyone had emptied the box on the other side of the wall, since he could hear the telegrams falling to the floor out of the overfilled bin. It seems that the War department did not have anyone handling the notices and passing them along to unsuspecting families across the country. He considered the magnitude of the lack of oversight as he stuffed the K slot. He imagined that one person had this boring job a few months ago and was now swamped by the thousands of letters coming in every month. Or maybe, the job was vacant and no one cared. He felt compelled to inquire, and sought out those responsible. If these notifications were for his loved ones, he would want to hear the news sooner, rather than later.

"Excuse me, is there anyone in charge of the Telegrams?" He asked an unsuspecting receptionist.

·

"Little Annie Oakley? Are you home?" Johnetta called through the open window to her sister.

"Come on Annie, open up already!" Now Mary was knocking on the door.

"These are your sisters calling," Johnetta said with her hands cupped in front of her mouth to project her voice louder into the house.

"Annie, can you come out and play?"

"Go away, Annie's not here right now," said Annie's voice, from inside her bedroom.

"Come on we want you to open up, so we can go get some ice cream!"

"Please Annie, save me with the ice cream!" Mary was being goofy.

"Boy oh boy, you two are relentless!" Annie opened her door and was mobbed by her two younger Cameron sisters.

"Come on get dressed, we are going out!" Mary announced.

"We can certainly tell who the newlywed is, can't we?" Johnetta said with a smile.

"What has it been two weeks since September 4th and she is still all happy, Johnetta?" Annie quipped.

"It appears so."

"Well you guys are just jealous because I get to fool around all I want!" Mary said laughing.

"HA!" Annie said.

"Yeah, no more sneaking around for her," Johnetta quipped.

They all laughed together. Johnetta and Mary had hoped levity would make Annie's heart lighter. She was still stuck in depression after being divorced from Leslie and they were determined to bring her up out of the muck.

"I need to use your restroom, Annie," Johnetta said.

"In the back and be glad that I updated this apartment from the common Lu, that I was going to rent."

"What a great way to meet new people," Mary threw out there.

"No thank you," Johnetta said, and she left for the toilet.

Annie and Mary continued with small talk about their lives. A minute after Johnetta walked away, Mary's face went pale, like a switch had flipped on inside of her. Annie noticed immediately.

"What is it, Mary?"

"I think something just happened to Neils." It was as if she had been given a terrible gift, in that instant, to know something that no one else on this side of the planet should know.

"What do you mean?"

"Oh my God! I think Neils was just killed in France."

•

VI.

'Bombs Away'

The view from the yard was always spectacular. On that warm breezy September Saturday, it was no different. The house, nestled in a small neighborhood, with five homes flanking each side and another ten on the opposite side of the road. The street, called Sycamore, runs due east for just one long block. The addresses all said Tooele, Utah, but few people know where it is and less can pronounce its name. 'Twilla,' as the natives call it, is about twenty miles south-west of Salt Lake City, as the crow flies. The remote crossroad sits surrounded by mountain peaks. Sycamore Street is east of the village central by a country mile or so. All of the small two bedroom homes sit on one acre lots and have fantastic views of mountain vistas. The view from Robbie and Maggie's place is the best from the grassy backyard, as it looks out over the entire valley.

East of that backyard stands Lone Peak, at over 11,000 feet. It is universally regarded as the most impressive mountain view. Just north of Lone Peak stands the even taller Twin Peaks. North of the Twins is Mount Olympus. If you look southeast, the row of Traverse Mountains wall off that line of sight. Further south, the peak aptly named South Mountain, along with the larger Flat Top Mountain, stand guard over the valley entrance.

The rugged beauty of the valley was a sight to see. Sitting and watching the mood of the mountains change throughout the day, as the sun marched its way across the sky, was one of Maggie and Robert's favorite perks in their modest home. The panorama provided years of solace. The only interruption in the scene was the massive smelter complex with it's three tall smokestacks, like fingers reaching for the stars, albeit soot billowing fingers. Maggie had always been impressed with the sight of the industry in the valley and held an overarching willingness to see it more for its economic contributions than it's smudge on the canvas of the valley's beautiful picture.

On a perfect September day, Maggie and Robbie hosted an unofficial 'Cameron' barbecue picnic, with all of the siblings in attendance. It was unofficial because Maggie had just given birth to baby Glenn a few days prior to the party. With the birth, and everyone being eager to see the little guy, the day's picnic kind of planned itself. Johnetta along with Annie made the short trip from Midvale, riding with Mary and her husband John Decker. Johnetta arrived the previous day on the train up from Nephi and the three of the sisters spent the afternoon together.

Dugald and Pearl, with two year old Emily and four month old Thelma, made their way over from Union. Margret and the young step-sister Ethel made the long trip down from Pocatello a couple of days before, missing Glenn's birth by just a few hours.

As the warm afternoon sun drove many out of the house, Johnetta played with four of her nieces and a nephew out on the lawn. A small splashing pool of water was at the center of the excitement for all the kids. Ethel and Dorothy were both six and in charge of the two little buckets, while Verne, Ella and Emily chased each other and piled on top of Aunt Jo Jo, whenever they caught her. The scene was loud and filled with children's laughter, as many of the others looked on, amused by the antics.

Maggie, Margret and Pearl were inside the home resting and visiting in the front room, when a knock came to the door.

"Go, good Afternoon," stuttered the confused looking young man.
"Beg, begging your pardon Ma'am," said the boy in the blue uniform. He was holding his hat in his hand as he spoke with a look of fear in his eyes.
"How can I help you?" Maggie asked, wondering briefly about the strange look on his face.
"Ma'am I have a telegram," he said, lowering his eyes.

"Yes?" Maggie responded to his hesitation.

"Umm, I, I, I am new at this job," he stumbled.

"It's alright son, what do you need?" Maggie was hanging onto the door frame. The delivery of Glenn had taken its toll on her and the hot air flowing in the door was almost too much.

"Another man who works with me said that you would know what to do with this telegram, Ma'am," he held it out in front of him.

"Apparently, it is a couple of months old," he said in a panic.

"Who is it for, young man?" She asked, without the energy or patience for any nonsense. He read slowly,

"Mrs. Johnetta Whitelaw Skeem," he said.

Maggie knew what the telegram was about and her heart sank in her chest.

"But the address is all wrong and I don't know why he sent me with one of these to, to the wrong address," he was nervously rambling.

"I will take it, Johnetta is my sister," Maggie said, tears welling in her eyes.

Just as the fearful young man handed the dingy yellow envelope over, Margret came to see what was holding Maggie's attention at the front door, startling her eldest daughter.

"Oh Mother," she could barely say those words, while shutting off the incoming flow of afternoon heat, without regard for the delivery man, who turned and left, just as confused as when he showed up.

"What is it Maggie?" Demanded the horrified mother.

"It's Neils," she whispered, holding up the envelope to the horror of her Mother.

"No! No, no, no, no, no!" Margret shook her head and backed away from the yellow letter of death.

"What is it?" Pearl wondered aloud from the davenport, shocked by what was unfolding in front of her.

"From the War Department," Maggie said through a wave of grief.

"Oh No!"

"Where's Johnetta?" Margret asked, after a few moments of raw panic.

"Mother, how are we going to tell her?" Maggie wondered.

"Should we even tell her today?" Asked Pearl, now crying from her place.

"Let's ask Robbie what to do, Mom," Maggie suggested.

"Okay. I will get him to come inside."

As Margret went to turn she was dizzy and nearly fell over.

"Mother!" Maggie reached and grabbed an arm.

"You sit right down on that chair," she insisted.

"I will get Robbie and Dugald to come in for a minute," Pearl stood, wiped her face and walked through the kitchen to the back door. She paused to compose herself for a moment.

"Robbie and Dugald, could you come in here and settle an argument for me please?" Pearl feigned.

The two men looked a little unsure as to what they were being asked to do, but the rest of the guests did not think another thing about it. It was normal for the two Margret's to disagree about almost everything, through the years. Mary sensed something. She got up with the two men and walked behind them and in through the back door.

"What are you two disagreeing about now?" Dugald made a joke in what he thought was another typical Cameron dispute.

"Dugald a telegram has come," Pearl whispered in hushed tones, as the rear door latched behind them.

Dugald noticed that his wife had been crying.

Robbie's attention was grabbed by the state of his wife and his mother-in-law's plight, in the chair next to her.

"What is going on here?" Robbie calmly asked.

"A Western Union telegram has come for Johnetta Whitelaw Skeem," Maggie said.

"Well that isn't necessarily what you are thinking," Dugald said and stepped forward to take the note from his sister's hand.

"Oh No!" He said as soon as he noticed.

"There is a 'K' designation on the top of the envelope." He shook his head from side to side.

"K-I-A?" Robbie clarified.

"That's what someone at work explained to me."

"Kia?" Pearl asked.

"Killed In Action," Mary said, from the rear of the group, just inside the kitchen archway. "It means that letter is going to tell Johnetta that her husband was killed in France," Mary explained.

Tears followed by embraces left the cognizant few, wrestling with what to do. They all understood what they had to do, the obvious question was, when did it have to be done? Did this otherwise perfect day have to be the day that Johnetta's life was crushed again? Or could they wait for some other, less glorious moment of family bliss?

Outside, the scene was the antithesis of the emotions inside the house. All the Cameron grandchildren were gleefully jumping on their happy Aunt Jo Jo, with joyous shouts of rapture rising from angelic voices, echoing throughout the cozy neighborhood and further down into the sun filled valley.

•

Just east of the insignificant French village of Exermont a vicious battle was raging in all its barbarism. This sector belonged to the men of the 26th Yankee Division and they pressed forward through a low hanging morning fog. American artillery honed in on German positions, while German artillery counterattacked the advancing American lines. The Huns occupied this area of France, since the very beginning of the war and had planned for it's defense in intricate detail. Maxim and MG 08's were placed in reinforced concrete nests of five to ten guns each. This defensive design provided a virtual wall of lead being sent downrange, senselessly destroying everything in its path. The dozens of MG nests in this sector were placed in such a way as to be able to cover for each other. Many lay on top of a ridge shooting down into the valley of death, over the top of other well placed Maxims. The greatest obstacle the German defenders had to overcome was the constant need for ammunition in these positions.

On the other side of the ridge, the feared doughboys outnumbered their German adversaries. The officer Corps knew that they would have to attack simultaneously with all contrivances of warfare, in order to break the juggernaut that lay in front of their men. Artillery attacks would have to be coordinated with each unit to suppress the withering fire from individual nests, so soldiers could then attack with grenades, Stokes mortars, rocket propelled grenades from the flanks, working in conjunction with the regimental machine gun companies. Then, finishing individual nests off with a fierce bayonet charge to silence the enemy one by one, when necessary. All of these intricate actions had to happen while enduring the blistering assault by a determined, rested, veteran, entrenched enemy.

This fight was much more intense than the battle at St. Mihiel a couple of weeks previous. The Germans now had their backs against the wall and were willing to fight to the very last man, if necessary. The outcome of the four year struggle was hanging in the balance. The dug-in Hun divisions felt as if they were safeguarding their homeland from foreign invaders and they were the last line of that defense.

One major difficulty with the Americans' battle plan was to be able to communicate each component of the complicated attack in precise ways that allowed all of the moving pieces to work aggressively together. The most vulnerable component was the field telephones, which required direct wire to wire connections to be strung between each phone. These long stretches of wire from the front lines back to the PC got destroyed or damaged in each melee. To counter this, General Pershing's staff ordered Signal Corps soldiers to stand guard over telephone lines. They would race in to repair damaged areas and even fend off German teams sent in to disrupt those precious wires, when necessary.

1st battalion led the assault against the Germans followed by the 2nd at 200 yards to the rear. The NCO's began making the rounds to the individual foxholes at 0400 to rouse the men. The gas attack had continued throughout that night, and few were able to sleep, anyway. The plan called for the battalion to move forward out of their foxholes in the darkness before the launch of the American artillery barrage, so as not to get caught in their dugouts during the German artillery counter attack.

"Bushy, time to kill some Huns," Pops whispered into the hole.

"On it, Sarge," Tinsel responded.

"Bush man, you alive?"

"Yes, I am here," said the semi-sleeping man from behind his mask.

"Gas alarm is cancelled," Tinsel said.

"Is food on the way?" Bushy asked, as he removed the sweaty mask and stowed it at the ready.

"Yes, then we can get the hell out of this hole," Tins frustration spoke clearly.

Within an hour, the four companies of the 1st Battalion were in forward positions, with companies B and C in the lead and A and D following. Each company had units from the regimental machine gun company inserted among them, which was a key missing element in the probing raid of two days earlier, the raid that had such a high casualty rate. Also in tow was a 37mm gunner unit, used to provide close artillery support for each company.

The skies roared to life at 05:40 with an impressive artillery barrage, slamming into the German lines about 200 yards ahead of the American formations, concentrating primarily on the northern ridge of the Exermont. Red star shells rose from the Hun ranks signaling to their artillerymen that an attack had commenced, which quickly brought the big 75mm German guns to life. Within the first salvo at least two U.S. artillery pieces were destroyed along with their nine man crews.

The men jumped off into the fog and darkness of the early morning and were met with blistering fire across the battlefield.

"Cover, cover, cover," yelled those who could, and the men went prone in the dirt.

"Keep your head, men," shouted Molly as the screams of the wounded began to rise from the ground.

"Telephone! I need a Signal Corpsman," Pops was screaming into the chaos.

Company D was forced into cover positions with their faces in the gas soaked dirt. Bullets zipped over their heads pinging off of entrenching tools that were strapped on their backs. Trees splintered all around, raining down tiny wood fragments like snow. Shells exploded to the rear of the men as they crawled forward, praying on their bellies.

A distinct rumble of two tanks off to their left brought some hope, as the Renault's fired into concentrated positions in the German lines. Their targets were identified from the yellow tracers launching out of the fog. That fire drew immediate attention from the Huns, which allowed the Hotchkins machine gun crews to get set up and begin returning fire across the ravine. The water cooled British guns that the Americans deployed were an effective tool in suppressing enemy fire, so infantry could move into more advantageous attack positions.

As Bushy went over the edge of the ravine, visions from the scouting mission came rushing back and fear soared. He dove for a rock to hide behind.

"Thud, thud, thud," hit right next to his head as he readjusted his helmet. He still had not discharged his weapon, knowing that his company was following C Company. At this point he tried to get to a place where he could begin to see enemy positions.

"Forward men, press forward," Pops called back to his troopers.

Those were his last words on earth, as he was ripped through by several rounds, dropping him.

"Pops is down," Tinsel shouted over to Bushy from behind his rock, pointing to the dead Sergeant. That proved to be a grave mistake, as Tinsel's hand exploded from the impact of several bullets. He screamed and rolled over in agony. He horribly rolled away from cover and a round penetrated the top of his helmet, killing him instantly.

"AHHHHHHH!" A primal rage surged from not only Joseph, but so many others up and down the line in response to the carnage. They needed better cover, so they left their dead brothers and crawled forward. Upon reaching a larger rock Bushy had to roll a bloated body to the side in order to have space to work. The dead doughboy must have been left from the 35th's assault five days earlier. He wretched out his breakfast on the spot as he turned the man over. He knelt behind the rock and brought his rifle up to his shoulder and began to send rounds down range as fast as he could rack his bolt. Soon, other men joined him at the rock firing, concentrating even more rounds into German lines some thirty yards in front and below them.

"Grenade!" Two doughboys tossed them toward the Germans, while the others ducked. One fell short and the other hit its mark, silencing that part of the line. The men were rapidly using up ammo in the assault. Another man whom Bushy did not recognize was killed next to him, being hit in the face. The Maxims up on the ridge were still active despite being the target of artillery.

"Alright, I want three men to push forward, probing toward their lines," Lt. Meeker had come up from behind the little group at Bushy's rock.
"You, you and you," Meeker pointed at three others, from C company. They left the cover of the rock moving quickly as the sky brightened enough to run.
"You three, flank out to the right and give them some covering fire, now!" Meeker shouted over the raging battle noise.

Not thinking, Bushy was up and running first, with a death grip on his rifle, searching for cover as bullets whizzed by, impacting at his feet and behind him. He slid in behind a tree stump like Ty Cobb stealing second base and he brought his rifle up to his shoulder. He was alone. The other two men had been forced from this life and into the next in twenty seconds. He noticed the three other soldiers that he was flanking, dropping into a German trench with rifles blazing away. Bushy was up and ten seconds later in the trench with the three men, who were picking over the dead German bodies, looking for trophies. Other doughboys joined the four in the trench, including Cookie and Tool.

"Bushy!"

"Hey, Cookie, Tool," he nodded, slightly smiling.

"Beautiful day for a war, don't you think, Bush?" Tool was wearing a crooked sarcastic smile under his muddy helmet.

"You three on the right flank, You three on the left," Meeker was crouching above the men while rounds impacted near him. He was pointing for the men to have their attention focused on the trench that they were occupying, not knowing how far the line ran.

"Spread out, more men are on the way," Meeker barked, turned and waved more doughboys forward.

Stepping over two dead Huns, the three men from company D went right, rifles at the ready. In just a few steps, the trench turned away from the front at a ninety degree angle. Tool was first around the corner and was run through by a German bayonet and slumped over with a groan, both Bushy and Cookie fired into the attacker, killing him. Just as another man came around the corner with a trench knife drawn. He lunged his blade at Bushy with wild eyes, which he deflected with the stock of his gun, as Cookie drove his bayonet through the man's heart. Bushy racked his rifle, turned and fired through the man's head at point blank range, splattering his brains on the dirt wall. A third attacker rounded the corner grabbing the stock of Cookie's gun. Bushy slammed his shoulder into the German's side, knocking him over the top of his dead compatriot. Tool managed to shoot him through the back from his slumped position. The German attacker released his grip on the Springfield and Cookie finished him off with the rifle's bayonet to his throat.

The next instant, Tool's body was racked with gun fire as he sat in the corner of the fortification. Cookie reached for a grenade, popped the pin and lobbed it blindly around the corner into the bottom of the muddy trench. The close explosion was very loud and startled the two doughboys. It killed three waiting German attackers. More Americans arrived in the trench behind the two shaken men of Company D and went around them to push further into the Hun fortress.

"Come on, boys, reload. You can deal with that later," Sergeant Molly said to the mud covered Cookie and Bushy. He was nodding toward Tool with his head.
"Let's keep pushing."

•

"Johnetta, could you come in here please?" It was Pearl summoning from the back porch. The group of Cameron's had all gathered inside the small house and decided that sooner was better than waiting, to break the sobering news to their youngest sister.
After a few moments, Johnetta walked into the room thick with anxiety, unaware and dripping wet from the final assault from the children.
"Could ye sit down, my Lassie?" Margret summoned her to the couch, patting the colorful cushion, as the rest looked on.
Johnetta instantly knew in the pit of her stomach that something awful had happened to someone.
"Johnetta," Maggie said from across the room stuffed with family.
"Johnetta, there is no easy way to say this to you,...."
"Neils has been killed in France."
"What?" She was confused.
"What do you mean?"
"We got a telegram," Maggie's shaking hand held out the opened dingy yellow envelope. Johnetta's heart broke at the sight. After a moment, she grabbed it away from her sister, needing to see for herself if the information was true, or just some cruel joke.
She read the words once, then again.
"It says that he was killed back in July!"

"It says that he was killed all the way back in July! He was dead and I didn't know anything!"

"How could you have known, Johnetta?" Margret asked with somber concern.

Annie looked at Mary and they locked eyes, remembering back to summer, as the hair on the back of their necks stood straight up in recognition of the gift given to Mary, on that day.

The rest of that dreadful afternoon Johnetta lay in her mother's arms on Maggie's couch, sobbing. Her heart spiralled back to the absolute lowest moment in her life, her father's sudden death. A wave of chilling pain ushered her right back down to that horrid event. She felt like the little ten year old girl who was abandoned, all over again. First her father left her and now Neils. He was the one who had chosen her, he was gone. It was too much to bear for a tender seventeen year old heart.

Through the torrent, she strained to remember his embrace at the train station that day more than a year ago. That was the last time she would ever touch him. Johnetta longed to feel his all-encompassing hug. His strong arms holding her tight. In that moment it felt like he had infused her with his own strength, with his confidence, with his very presence. She couldn't feel that any more. Her arms were empty again. Her heart ached anew.

Everything that had been so perfect just moments before, out on the back lawn, now lie shattered in a thousand pieces. Her internal pain brought moans to her quivering words. The afternoon barbecue lunch twirled and rumbled in her sickened stomach. Her head ached through her eyes to her temples.

Someone placed a large towel on her shoulders, as the breakers of grief washed over her.

"Now what will I do?" she asked God.

"Who am I without him?" she cried in the quiet of her heart.

Peels of thunder shook her. Depressions' storms were threatening its full fury to engulf her once again. The gravitational pull of the darkness was enormous.

"My family is kind to me," she thought in response and decided having them close was a God send.

"I am so sorry, Johnetta," Mary whispered through her matted, wet hair.
Grabbing at Mary's arm that was around her, she just sobbed her response.

"I luv a Lassie, a bonnie, bonnie Lassie. If you'd see her you'd fancy her yourself. She as sweet as the heather, the bonnie, bonnie heather, Johnetta my Scottish gettle." Margret was whispering the familiar Scottish song into Johnetta's ear, while Mary held her tightly, hoping to give her some comfort in her distress.

Margret felt hopeless. She had not been easy on Neils, especially in the beginning. Yet, she had grown to trust him enough to have her daughter's hand in marriage. His death has torn open her own wounds. As she sat on the couch crying for her little girl, she was also mourning her Dugald.

"Life is so hard," she whispered, while stroking Johnetta's long black hair between her own fingers.

•

"We are going to push up to that ridge," said Molly into his weary soldier's ears.
"We are jumping off with the artillery, with the artillery," he yelled across the group of about forty.
The ridge above them burst open as shells impacted across its face and over its top. This was not the ridge across the Exermont River. This was the high ground that jutted out

into the union of the Mayache creek and the Exermont river, south of the Exermont ridge. The plan was to take the high ground to gain advantage for the forces that would be charging up the opposing ridge just as soon as Molly's unit's objective was secured. Removal of the MG's on Molly's ridge would make the going much less dangerous for the doughboys ascending north of the river.

Bushy was worn from the hours of constant combat and took a short breather refilling his ammo belt, clipping on a couple more grenades and swigging the last of his water into his parched and gritty mouth. The bullets were still flying all around their naturally defended position, as he gathered some strength for another charge out into the withering chaos.

"Go, go, go, go!" Molly shouted like a mad man on a mission when the artillery began to pound away.

The forty khaki clad men jumped up from their covered position and raced up the rest of the ridge, while that position was casting dirt and debris down on them, from their own exploding artillery shells. A nest across the convergence of rivers noticed the movement and sprang into life, honing in on the climbing souls. Peppering the Yanks with wild shots, the German gunners sought to thin the ranks of rushing men. Men fell back and crumpled down the slope while others reached the summit with a roar. Gunshots rang out from the charging Americans directed at some terrorized German soldiers who were stumbling forth from bombed out entrenchments. Strafing Allied airplanes raced through the scene overhead, causing panic and additional carnage.

Bushy and Big left cover at the same moment running for their lives up the embankment side by side. They flopped over the top, rolling upright and bringing their rifles to the ready. Wide eyes searched back and forth for cover, trying to comprehend the scene before them. "Thud, thud, thud, clack, clack, clack, clack, wiz, wiz, ping."

Other men crested the small ridge and Sergeant Mulholland was among them.

"Come on ladies, keep moving!"

"Where Sarge?" Big asked, as he was shot and fell backward on the ground, dead.

"Move right, Bushy," Molly screamed and grabbed the soldier by the pack, almost dragging him out of harm's way behind an overturned tree stump.

"NO! Not Big!" Joseph shouted into the wind as the insanity crept in. He felt that he was at his breaking point. So many men died today, he thought, but he knew that he had to suck up the growing uncertainty, into a place deep inside of him. Big was a good man and now he was a good dead man. "Move along, nothing to see here," he told himself to get through the moment.

Of the forty men in the hastily assembled squad, Molly looked around to assess how many made it to the top. It only appeared to be about half, maybe a few more than that. He knew that he needed every man to get together and put some lead downrange, if they were to have any chance in their exposed position. They were taking fire from two sides again and needed to eliminate the enemy on the top of this ridge, so they could concentrate across to the northern ridge.

"Shep, get some grenades on that nest NOW," Molly called and the corporal went to his knees and loaded his rifle fired grenade launcher. Resting the butt on the ground he lobbed a live round toward the Hun nest. It landed beyond the target, but drew their attention.

"A.B. You, Shep, Mags and Bushy work the left flank on that nest," he directed, while pointing.

"Arty, Bull, Ding you're with me," he snipped.

"The rest of you guys put some frontal fire into that Maxim," he commanded and scampered off with his new impromptu squad. Molly was in his glory. It was what he was born to do, leading men into combat for a righteous cause.

•

21-9-18 Salt Lake City Desert News:

"Nephi boy gives his life for the cause of Country. Word has been received here from the War Department that Neils Skeem has given his life for his country's cause on the battlefield in France. July 18, 1918. Mr. Neils Skeem joined the Colors last year and was sent to Camp Lewis where he remained until September 19, 1917, when he was sent overseas. He was married August 3, 1917, and his wife survives him, along with his mother, father and siblings. Memorial Services will be held Sunday in the Stake Tabernacle in Nephi at 4:00 pm."

"Are ye ready, mae Lassie?" Margret's head was poking in the door of Johnetta's room at the Skeem house in Nephi.

"Almost," she sadly replied. Her eyes tired and blurry from all of the crying of the last several days.

"I will wait downstairs for you," Margret did not want to press her youngest for promptness on a day like today. She closed the bedroom door and went back to the sitting room where everyone else had gathered.

"How is she?" Martina asked Margret with genuine concern, worried for the young widow's welfare.

"Really quiet. I think she is a bit lost right now," Margret said while looking into Martina's swollen eyes. She knew that was true for Martina, too.

Walter and Andy were making small talk in the corner while Ethel was coloring a picture of their old Inkom ranch, complete with chicken coop and fire pit, to cheer up her grieving big sister.

"Mother, when is the funeral?" Ethel asked again.

"Soon, my little Lassie," Margret managed to produce a smile for her baby girl.

"Wait, it's not a funeral, because why, again?" Ethel could not remember what her mother said to her, earlier in the day.

"It is a Memorial Service because there is not a body to see," Mother patiently explained to her daughter.

"Oh yeah," she said, as the image clicked.

"So where is Neils' body?"

"It is,... He is staying in France, dear one."

"Why?"

"Well because it is far too expensive to bring him back here."

"Oh. So what happened to him?"

"The Army had a funeral for Neils," Margret explained, as Martina listened to the innocent exchange.

"They did?"

"Yes."

"Well, who went to that funeral?"

"I don't know."

Ethel looked puzzled over the thought.

"Probably his soldier friends went to his funeral, right, Mother?"

"Yes, I am sure they did," Margret said.

Martina wept for her son.

The whole room had gone silent in observation of an innocent child's heart processing the unknown.

Closure may be helped by a memorial service for a lost loved one, but it is not the same as having a body to place in God's hands. Witnessing your dearly departed lying in estate does close the future doors of doubt that roam into random night time thoughts. Johnetta would have no such closure for Neils.

•

The nest was flanked by both teams, after some time, with only one casualty. Bull had been shot through his right elbow, which left the rest of his arm dangling like a limp rope. He was wrestled to the ground and his belt was used to stop the spray from the bleeding artery. It saved his life and ended his war. He would return to his hometown of Winchester, Virginia an amputee. Another living testimony to the carnage of the great war.

After the ridge was cleared of the enemy, the ragtag unit began reclaiming the earthworks for their own purpose. Setting up their machine guns to fire from cover across the ravine at the German positions. More men from the 3rd Battalion came forward to finish the work. A couple of 37mm guns were brought to bear against the nests on the opposite side of the Exermont River. This allowed the rest of the Yankee 26th to rush up the embankment and capture those enemy positions. It was not an easy task, as numerous men were killed and wounded in the effort.

Then the Germans threw more men into the area with effective counter attacks throughout the rest of the day. Back and forth the battle lurched. Brutal hand to hand engagements were happening up and down the line. Men ran out of ammunition and resorted to bludgeoning each other to death with rifle butts, helmets, knives and whatever else they could find. The American supply line was being choked behind the lines by the terrible conditions of the war-torn French roads.

Bushy and the remaining members of Company D, weighed down with ammo, rushed across the 'valley of death,' as they called it. It was early in the evening and they made their way through the littered landscape, past so many fallen comrades, to strengthen the new forward position in the lines. Along the way the men paused to fill their long dry canteens with dirty, bloody water from the knee deep Exermont River. This desperate action would cost many of the men bad cases of diarrhea over the next several days, adding to the overall thrills of their little French vacation.

When the fight of that day waned with the darkness, the 1st battalion of the 26th Yankee

Division had almost half of their force either killed or wounded, in order to win that narrow stretch of land. They lost almost every officer in their haggard ranks. The 2nd battalion had not fared any better, except its officer Corps was largely intact. The two units would be melded together until more replacement troops could be brought up from the rear to reinforce each battalion.

To add to the overall agony, no hot food made it to the front lines for several days. The men relied on their meager rations of hard bread, canned meat and tainted water. Then abruptly the gas alarm sounded and the shelling began anew. It was a long, arduous fight.

•

"Do you think that this is what I want, Mother?" Johnetta's eyes flashed her anger.
"Johnetta, I know you are grieving, but you need to come home for a while and then you can figure out what to do next," Margret presented her well reasoned case.
"I don't want to go back to Pocatello," she explained.
"What else will you do?"
"Nothing!"

Margret knew that her daughter was so deep in pain that she could not even think straight. Margret turned and looked to Annie for some help in getting Johnetta to be sensible.

"Hey, listen. Go with mom and let her take care of you for a while. If Walter is being an ass, you can come and live with me whenever you want."
"Really?" Johnetta questioned her sister by looking up at her eyes.
"Mary and John don't have the room, Maggie has the new baby. Dugald has two young kids. Stay with Mom for now and come to visit me to get away from the fake dad." Annie whispered.
"I just don't know how long I will be able to put up with him," she said.

"I know, but mom needs you as much as you need your mom."

"Why?"

"You remember when dad died how lost she was?"

"Sure we all were."

"Yes, but she had you and Mary around to comfort her for those early years."

"Yeah," she said, remembering back to the painful time.

"Now let mom take care of you for a while, it will do you both some good."

With a heavy breath she relented.

"What time does the train depart?"

•

VII.

'Headlong'

The intense fighting for the 26th continued over the next week through thick woods and across open farm land. The constant shelling, gas alarms, machine gun fire, strafing biplanes, mortars, counter attacks, night time raids into enemy positions, defensive posturing and digging in was wearing the men out. Kitchens were located too far from the front and almost none of the food was surviving the trip forward while under constant barrage. The mules pulling the carts were often easy targets for MG 08's watching the beasts lumber across the lines pulling carts of rations. Food was being confiscated from the corpses strewn across the battlefield. Fresh clean water was scarce. The best source often being found on expired comrades and dead Germans.

The constant flow of German prisoners became an issue for the depleted battalions, often stripping them of weapons and rations, then sending them to the rear, guarded only by wounded men who needed medical attention, or other POWs, who were sent under the careful watch of couriers and inter-battalion liaison personnel. Germans were even forced to carry wounded American doughboys to the field hospitals located behind the lines. The German prisoners were interrogated for information on enemy positions and divisional strength before being shipped out to the various POW camps in France.

The greatest demoralization for the common soldier, was ground taken in the morning through blood and toil, being given up in the evening. This was done to protect soldiers from blistering night time fire from hilltop artillery and Maxims that would rake the unprotected men lying out in the open. To protect them, they were ordered back and the Germans would fill in those unoccupied places with reserves, in darkness. It became a major point of frustration for the men.

The Argonne Forest contained many French farms that had been taken over by the Huns and built into defensive fortresses, with interconnected concrete bunkers and machine gun nests providing protected fire positions. Some of the bunkers were completed with electricity, heat and running water. While the attacking doughboy slept out under the stars, which were rarely seen during the entire length of the battle. Cold autumn rain soaked the region for most of October and November driving up the cases of bronchitis and pneumonia among the beleaguered, exposed troops.

The Argonne had many patches of heavily treed woods that were an effective means of hiding artillery and machine guns. Hun forces would often wait until unsuspecting doughboys walked into range before opening up. The thick forest was also a place of many hills and vantage points that provided the Germans dominance. These high places were loaded with weapons of war and were effective in slowing down the advancing host of Americans.

Each reinforced location would have to be systematically destroyed by hard relentless troops. The normal strategy was to out-flank an enemy position and attack in force, from the rear. Most forward defensive locations were directed toward the enemy advance and were most vulnerable in the rear. Attacking units provided overwhelming suppressive fire from multiple locations across the front, and other units simultaneously worked around the flanks.

This was done at a great cost, since the best defensive positions were elevated providing a distinct tactical advantage to the defender. From those places, the Germans were able to rain down machine gun and artillery fire driving American casualty rates through the roof.

The 26th fought to gain about a thousand yards across their section of the battlefield. The men advanced at the same pace as the 28th which was operating on their left flank. That group fought up through their section of the ravine and then through the well defended French village of Exermont.

The 32nd Division, which operated on the right flank of the 26th, got bogged down and lagged behind the other two divisions. This lag caused a weakness in the right flank of the 26th that was susceptible to counter attack from the Germans located in the Bois du Chene, literally the 'Woods of Oak' in English, which was 500 hundred yards east of the 26th. In response, Major Legge had parts of the MG battalion and a company of the third Battalion fall back and guard against that possibility.

D company spent that next day fighting up and over hill 212 along with A company. After taking that high ground, they came under fire from hill 272 that lay to the northwest by 1200 yards. The Germans were well dug in, on that hilltop, and heavily fortified with many artillery pieces and at least twenty machine guns.

•

It had been a long walk out of Pocatello during the frigid evening. Johnetta was determined that she was done living with Walter. She left a note thanking them for all of the care over the last six weeks, but she needed to move forward with her new life and it was not going to be in Pocatello. She put on as many warm clothes as she could and crept out of the house, after midnight.

The road south was lonely at that hour. Her breath froze in the cold air as large and long puffs of steam gathered around her, while she marched along carrying her one bag of provisions. The further she progressed the deeper the realization of just how long a walk this act of freedom was going to be. Her feet were already complaining about the rough road, so her head could not help from thinking of how long the ordeal was going to be, in the middle of October. Clearly, it was her wounded heart that had taken the lead on this foolish decision.

A distant rumble came up from behind her. She glanced back to see two bouncing headlights, making their way south on this road to Inkom. Johnetta was not sure how to ask for a ride and could not decide whether she was that desperate, yet. The back and forth that her brain engaged in, was dizzying.

"Should I try to get a ride?" She mused, as the vehicle closed the gap.

"Would they even stop for me?" She wondered.

The wheels were almost upon her when she turned so the driver would see the reflection of her face in the darkness. The truck whisked past Johnetta and her heart sank. Not that she had done anything to get the man's attention, but she was still hoping that he would have compassion on a lone woman walking in the middle of the night to stop and ask if he could help, somehow.

Then suddenly the brake lights lit up and the truck came to a creaking stop.

"Maybe chivalry still existed," she thought and continued walking on the side of the road. She acted as if she would keep walking past the truck without acknowledging the fact that he had stopped his delivery truck for her.

"Hey," said the bearded man who was standing on the drivers side running board of the black truck. Johnetta turned, a little afraid of what might follow.

"Kinda cold out here tonight?" He asked.

"Yep," she answered and turned to continue her trek.

"Do you want a ride?" He offered.

"I am going all the way to Ogden and I have room, if you want."

Johnetta stopped walking and turned around to face the man.

"You're not given to violence, are you?" It sounded ridiculous just as soon as it left her lips.

"No Ma'am, I am not a violent man. I have a wife and three young children at home." She considered the offer for a brief second and knew that she did not want to go back to Walterville anytime soon.

"Alright. I appreciate you stopping," she half smiled while she opened his passenger door and climbed into the warm cab.

"Hello, I am Johnetta," she offered her hand in greeting.

"Jake," said the big bearded man.

"Welcome aboard the Loretta, Johnetta," he said with a goofy smile.

Inwardly, she groaned a bit, but was put at ease by the man's ridiculous sense of humor.

"Loretta?" She asked.

"My mom's name. She passed on about a year ago, got cancer and only lived about a month after we found out," he was saddened by stating the truth.

"I am sorry to hear that Jake," she looked over at him.

"My dad died about eight years ago," she announced awkwardly.

"That is a hard thing to deal with Johnetta."

"How'd that happen?" He wondered aloud.

"We just had come over from Scotland on the boat and he got sick and died within a few weeks of our arrival in Utah," she explained.

"Come over with the Mormon's outreach?" He inquired.

"You know about that?" she said.

"Many made the same trek," he said.

"Yeah. Yeah we did. My two older sisters had come across a year earlier and we were making our way to Zion to start a new life in the promised land."

"How'd that work out for you, other than losing your dad, I mean?"

"Not very well," she replied.

"Oh?"

"My mom was introduced to some random single guy from the church and was expected to start courting him within a couple of months of dad's departure," she said.

"I thought it was ludicrous. My father's body was still warm in the grave and the Bishop wanted her to move along with her life."

"I have heard that before," he said plainly.

"Have to have more kids so they can fill up the promised land, or something," she said.

"Sounds like you have a problem with that," he said in the dim light of the truck.

"My sister, Maggie, is the true believer in the family. She came over first and married a devout Mormon. Annie, the second oldest, came over next, got married so she wouldn't have to live with Walter, then quickly divorced from Les which is Maggie's husband's cousin. She said he was a creep."

Once the avalanche of words began there was no stopping the flow. It continued pouring from Johnetta's heart. Recalling everything from her mother's arranged marriage to Walter all the way through her marrying Neils.

"Quite the story Johnetta!" Jake said, after listening for almost an hour, along the bumpy road.

"Yes it is," she replied, reaching into her bag for the jar of water she had brought along for the journey.

"So what brings you out alone on the road on a cold October night, if you don't mind me asking?"

"Well, my husband that I was married to for a weekend," she hesitated not knowing if she could say the words.

"I thought you were married over a year ago?" He was confused.

"We were, but it happened while he was away at boot camp. He got a weekend pass and came home for our wedding. Then, he left the next day," Johnetta was able to talk to this guy, for some reason.

"Oh, I understand. What happened next?"

There was a long silent pause in the truck with no sound except the working motor and rattling metal.

"He was killed in action, in July," she admitted as a tear ran down her face.

"I am so sorry, Johnetta," Jake said as he stopped the truck.

"That had to have been so hard for you," he said sincerely.

"What was worse was I didn't find out for two whole months. He was dead and I was living like nothing was wrong in the world." Guilt washed through her again.

"How could you have known?" Jake asked the young crying widow.

"I don't know," she said, slobbering.

Jake handed her his handkerchief, the clean one from his front shirt pocket, not the used one from his pants pocket.

"Thank you, Jake," she said, taking his kind offering.

"It is my pleasure, Johnetta," he replied and let his foot off the brake.

•

"Men, we are going to break out directly north to the farm. The initial preliminary barrage is set to start at 1300 for 30 minutes. At 1330 the rolling barrage begins and we jump off. It doesn't appear that there are many defensive positions across the farmland, so I expect a clear entry into the farm." Major Legge explained to the gathered men.

"You will likely be receiving fire from both flanks at the time of the advance, so you have to be quick. Spread out and double time it across the area. The 28th will be attacking in the area just to the west primarily against the German forces massed below hill 272. After we take the farm, we reform and the 3rd Battalion will pivot ninety degrees west to assist the 28th by assaulting hill 272. Most of the artillery and machine gun fire we are receiving is coming from that hill. After the farm, 1st Battalion will pivot ninety degrees east and apply pressure to the Bois de Moncey and the German forces there. We will push just inside of the woods for cover. 2nd Battalion will secure the perimeter around the farm and serve as reserve for both ongoing assaults."

"Any Questions?"

"How far is the farm, Major?"

"It is about 700 yards all the way to the farm proper, but you will gather at the stone wall just south of the buildings by 50 yards or so,"' Legge explained to his troopers.

"What about the food situation, Sir?" Asked an annoyed doughboy.

"Working on that son. We lost one kitchen to an artillery barrage, so gather rations as you are able,"

Major Legge was concerned that his men had not eaten a hot meal in a day and a half.

"Sir, we need water too. We've been drinking awful water from puddles and streams for a couple of days now," a thirsty soldier almost begged.

"And a bunch of the men got diarrhea, Sir," said another.

"Supply has been a real issue. We are working on it, Soldier." Legge was boiling mad on the inside, knowing that his men needed to eat and drink to have any hope of effectively continuing the battle.

"You men are doing an incredible job out here against a well trained enemy," Major said. "You should be proud of all of your accomplishments. You have sacrificed so much. Our proud division has been assigned the toughest part of the line, but you men are making it happen. I am proud of you. You Yankees are real ass kickers!" The overtly motivational speech was short and to the point.

After an hour of rest and resupply, the artillery came roaring in from behind the American lines and continued unabated for thirty minutes. It was a brief pause, as the guns were realigned to provide close support of a rolling barrage about two hundred yards ahead of the men.

"Ready men!" Molly was standing and waiting for the thunder to be unleashed.

"Remember as fast as you can make it to the stone wall and we reassemble there," he cried out.

"Father, please protect me again," Bushy prayed under his breath. Most of the rest of the men recognized the hand of providence that had guided them, to be standing where they were standing. One bullet out of many millions fired, with just a slightly different trajectory would have ended their lives in an instant. One fragment from one of the thousands of artillery rounds fired taking a different route could have stopped their heart without any extra effort. The only explanation that made any sense was that God himself had protected them thus far.

The Chaplain's prayer five minutes before this moment had confirmed the same thought after reading from the 24th Psalm.

"Lift up your heads, O gates!

And lift them up O Ancient doors,

that the King of glory may come in.

Who is this King of glory?

The Lord, strong and mighty,

the Lord, mighty in battle."

He read from his Bible, and prayed for protection over the men as they faced their enemy.

"Go!"

The men of the 26th poured out beneath the cover of the roaring artillery in a full out run.

Bushy ran with several of his friends in close proximity. Cookie, Fingers and Mule were either next to him by twenty yards or in front of him by the same distance.

German artillery from the top of 272 erupted into action, blindly lobbing shells into the spread out masses of men racing across the field.

When the formation made the halfway point in the run, German machine gunners opened up through the ongoing American rolling barrage. The men ran for their lives across the wide open spaces, praying that the artillery would continue marching ahead of them.

Upon arriving at the field stone wall a couple of minutes later, gasping for air, most of the men fell to the ground behind the wall. They were exhausted trying desperately to catch their breath and hide from enemy bullets, coming from the reinforced farm. The American artillery barrage focused on the farm and more and more on hill 272 to protect the 26th. When the American machine gun crews arrived at the wall, they were set up

with their water cooled guns, firing on the German position within minutes. Rifle
grenades and Stokes mortars flew toward individual nests.

Within ten minutes the 3rd and the 1st Battalions were off on their respective flanking
maneuvers around the sides of the target. Victory at the farm would take most of the day
to accomplish for the Americans. Prying out an enemy willing to fight to the death is
never an easy task. After the final Germans were killed, the 1st Battalion took up
positions 200 yards east just inside of the Moncy Woods and dug in, expecting a Hun
counterattack from inside the thick forest.

"I am so tired," Bushy said to Fingers, his foxhole buddy for the night.
"I feel exhausted," Fingers admitted while choking down some confiscated stale bread.
Both men slept through the night in their gas masks. The counterattack never came as
the Germans on hill 269, in the middle of Moncy Woods, were low on ammunition.

•

The old box truck Loretta continued on its long journey south. Its two passengers
enjoyed each other's company and felt free to talk about almost anything. After a few
miles of silence, Johnetta handed the handkerchief back to her new friend Jake as the sky
in the east began to brighten, with the approaching morning. Venus was low and bright in
the clear moonless sky. It got cold inside the truck as the side windows had iced up from
the condensation from the two breathing people.

"So how old are you, Johnetta, If you don't mind my asking," he was trying to be kind.
"Seventeen," she said.
"Where are you going, young lady?"
"To my sister Annie's house, down in Midvale, until I figure things out," she said looking
out the window into the early morning darkness.
"Well, if there is anything you need please let me know," Jake looked at the road.

"I can get you almost all the way to Midvale," he said.

"I thought you were stopping in Ogden?"

"I am, but I need to go to Salt Lake for my second pick up," he explained further.

"Okay," she replied.

"So has the Bishop been over to arrange a date for you?" It was an effort to bring some levity.

"That is another reason that I wanted to get out. I was worried some old man would want to claim me off the pile of church widows, or something," she said with a certain level of fear, evident in her tone.

"Have you ever heard of L.D.S. Ritual killings?" He was trying to tread lightly, but there was no easy way to breach the subject.

"Heard it and seen it," Johnetta replied coldly.

"Really?"

"Walter's moonshine supplier was offed as a reprobate," she reported.

"Wow. Was that scary for you?" Jake asked.

"I had relocated to Nephi to work for my in-laws, so I wasn't affected," she said.

"But my mom and little sister got out of town for a while," she continued.

"Yeah, I have seen the leadership in the Mormon church get away with some pretty unsavory things over the years," he said frankly.

"So you're a member then?"

"No way, I am a Christian," he claimed.

"Well, so are Mormons, right?" she asked.

"No. Mormons are not Christians in the traditional sense."

"What does that mean?"

"They don't believe the basic teachings of Jesus as presented in the Bible."

"I thought that's what they were all about?"

"Not even close, Johnetta."

"Why?"

"Because as Christians, we believe that Jesus is the only way to God. In Mormonism anybody who is a good enough Mormon can become a 'god' of their own world," he explained to his captive audience.

"In Christ there is freedom. In Mormonism there is slavery to the church."

"Okay," she was trying to follow his train of thought.

"Don't take my word for it, look up what the Bible says."

"The challenge with all cults is that they will often use the same words that Christians use, but those terms have been stripped of their original meaning and rendered useless."

"It sounds like you have been thinking about this for some time," Johnetta replied.

"I have, because I live in Pocatello and am surrounded on all sides by Mormons. Everyday I was forced to consider what I really believed and what I based that belief on."

"I choose to believe what the Bible says about God, rather than what some well-known treasure hunter claimed to read through special glasses he just happened to dig up."

"I have been thinking about that for a long time too," Johnetta admitted.

"The whole Joseph Smith story always seemed outlandish to me," she said further.

"I bet you have, Johnetta, been thinking about that," he replied.

"It's like they have all of the power to control every aspect of your life," she said out loud for the very first time.

"It is very hard to live in Utah and not be part of the tribe," Jake said.

"Southern Idaho isn't much better," she added.

"Neils was a true believer and he was a kind man," she admitted to what she had wondered about for a long time.

"Mormons are good people, no doubt about it. Some of the nicest folks you will ever find, by and large," he said.

"The issue becomes one of motivation. Why are they good people?"

"Why do you think?" She asked him.

"Honestly, I think that they are trying to earn their salvation," he said flatly.

"And why is that a problem?" she probed.

"No one can earn their salvation, Johnetta. Sin is always our fundamental problem."

"Really?"

"Can you ever be so perfect on your own that you would impress God enough to forget all of your mistakes in life?"

"No," she said. She knew that was true on so many levels.

"Right. Exactly why God the Father sent Jesus his son into the world. Jesus came to pay for your sin by dying on a cross, even though he was perfect and without sin. He loved us so much that he willingly died in our place so by faith we could be forgiven."

"So I don't have to be good then?"

"Like I said, it is all based on motivation. As a follower of Jesus, I want to be good because God has already saved me from the power of hell, which I earned through my sin. Mormons hope to make God love them, praying that He will rescue them if they have done enough good in their life." Jake explained.

"Motivation." Johnetta was thinking.

"Jesus gives us peace with God, by faith." He continued.

"To people who are deeply involved in the Mormon mess, it is hard to see the critical distinction," he said.

"The whole Latter Day Saints Church is so confusing and contradicting," she did admit.

"Well, I will be in prayer for you, young Johnetta," he said confidently.

"Well thanks, I have found that hard lately," she admitted.

•

By the fourteenth of October, the 26th Division had engaged in hard combat for ten straight days and were ordered to the rear to rest and regroup about five miles behind the lines. The doughboys had fought up Hill 269 for almost a week to clear out any German resistance. Afterwards, everyone who survived collapsed in excruciating exhaustion.

The men had showers for the first time in two weeks and three hot meals all in the same day. New replacement soldiers were brought in to fill the gaps created by the men lost during the hideous combat. These new recruits were green since most of them had just been drafted, in June and July of that year. It gave the term 'fresh off the boat,' a new meaning. During those five 'rest' days for the 26th the new recruits were put through training by the veterans of the outfit, working to bring them up to combat proficiency as quickly as possible. However, the vets soon became frustrated by the lack of skill possessed by the green troops and settled on teaching the men simply to shoot straight.

The logic being that if you could operate your weapon you could contribute to the cause, even if you didn't know which way to turn. Teaching intricate platoon tactics was an effort in vanity, at this point, since most of the experienced men were hardened through the actual battle, due to the immense pressure to perform. The vets of the 26th overall did not trust the new guys, and none of the new men got an Army name during those five brief training days.

Marching north again, the Division was closing the gap on the front lines by pressing through the area they had fought so hard for, a couple of weeks ago. They walked right through the 'valley of death' on their way to the front and no one shot at them this time. Progress. All the dead had been gathered and buried by that point and even the artillery moved forward. An abundance of American weapons were placed on top of the hills that these men had won with their blood. Using the former German positions to attack north toward the receding Hun lines.

Soon, the rumble of artillery thunder greeted the lines of marching men. The newbies were all walking wide-eyed, consumed with fear and filled with a new sense of panic that often gave itself away by the twitching glances in every direction. The vets, on the other hand, were steely eyed killing machines marching toward the end of their war. Those men did not want the fight, but the fight was the only way home. They just prayed that one of these new guys would not shoot them by mistake.

"I don't know Bushy, I'm not seeing too many names being given out anytime soon," Guns said.

"Not many, yet," Bushy clarified.

"What does that mean, Bushy?" Asked a new kid from somewhere in upstate New York.

"Hey, you don't get to use his Army name. You haven't earned that right," Fingers starred the New Yorker down.

"Usually, you have to do something really special to earn an Army name," Bushy explained calmly.

"By special he means dumb," Guns said, and laughed.

"So you new guys listen up, when we get into this fight today, you shut the hell up and listen to the guys that have been in it," Fingers said.

"Because if you screw up and get one of us vets killed, you will be answering to the rest of us," he continued.

"Who died and left you in charge, Private Johnson?" Quipped a sarcastic new recruit from out of sight.

"A lot of my friends, you dumb ass," Bushy answered for the rest of men, with more than a little irritation.

23-10-18

Company D was at the ready, moving through an uncut field that was littered with shell holes, dead men, broken equipment and bloated horses. The experience of this scene was amplified by a cacophony of familiar sickening smells that all of that morning's bombardment had stirred up fresh. It was only familiar to the men who had previously marched into battle. The morning began with an artillery barrage, then the usual rolling barrage out ahead of the advance. The men met much less resistance than they anticipated. They were working the sector on the left side of the battalion near Molleville farm. They reached the intermediate objective fifteen minutes before Lt. Meeker had planned. He allowed the men to rest at the edge of the wooded area named Le Houppy.

Private Joseph Jacobucci, Bushy, was in the rear of the spread out formation as a rare German bi-plane shot over the top of the woods and strafed the American line of men who were still making their way to the edge of the woods.

At the sight of the Aero Plane the men looked for markings and noticed the wild colors on the fuselage and wings. It was a German Faukker. They scattered and ran, at the sound of the machine gun, as it shrieked to life overhead. Moving as fast as they could toward cover, they were in a full out sprint for the trees of Le Houppy with dirt flying at their feet, from the impacts of the bullets.

"Come on Bushy!" Mule screamed, as a line of fire came into their path.

Someone swiftly swung a hidden sledge hammer and took Bushy's right leg out from beneath him and he fell headlong into the wet French soil. The German plane drifted away, banking east toward home.

"Medic! Bushy needs a Medic NOW!" Mule screamed and went to his friend as blood poured from his leg.

Joe's pale face was covered in thick mud as his right thigh spurt blood through his trousers.

Mule reached down and yanked Bushy's belt off his pants and cinched it around his leg, as tight as he could make it, right on top of the wound.

"Joe. Joe, can you hear me?" Mule asked, and cried louder for the Medic.

•

VIII.

'Over And Out'

"Thank you Jake, it was so nice to meet you," Johnetta knew that she had been blessed by the man's genuine kindness.

"Johnetta, you take care of yourself now," Jake said waving goodbye from the driver's seat of the delivery truck. The traffic in downtown Salt Lake was thick on the cool autumn morning, with a traffic cop working his whistle frantically, out in the middle of the busy intersection.

Despite her mental and physical exhaustion, Johnetta was flabbergasted that a complete stranger could be so nice. He bought her breakfast and even gave her money for the train ride down to Midvale. He actually apologized that he couldn't drive her all the way to Annie's place because he had to get back to Pocatello with the parts he was sent to pickup.

"It was almost as if God had sent me an angel just when I needed it the most," she thought and followed the comforting thought with a grateful smile.

Johnetta's train was not set to depart for half an hour, but she was nervous that if she rested for too long she would fall asleep and miss it. She and Jake talked through the night and then during breakfast in the small diner. He made her think about her life and told her at least three times that he would pray for her. Johnetta knew that he would do just that for her, and it gave her comfort.

"Desert News! Get your paper! Desert News here! Yanks fighting the largest battle of the war in France. Read all about it!"

"Hey lady, do you want a paper?" The paper pushing boy was only about twelve years old and stood on a box to better project his voice across the bustling intersection.

"No Thanks," Johnetta replied. Her eyes were scanning the headlines while she passed his little stand with piles of the Desert News.

"It's already October 23rd?"

Johnetta could hardly believe that much time had passed. Over a month since she heard about Neils. Where had it gone? What had she been doing other than being down in the dumps? How had she lived? It was apparent to her she had not eaten much since her clothes were hanging on her now.

"Desert News! Get your paper! Yanks fighting the largest battle of the war in France. Read all about it!" The young salesman droned on in the distance, while she wandered away with plenty of time to spare. Glancing in a store window and catching a reflection of herself, Johnetta was shocked. She looked haggard, even to her own eyes. Pale, gaunt, and disheveled were the words that came to mind.

"I have got to do something with my hair," while pulling it down into submission with her right hand and clutching her cloth bag with her left. Johnetta was sure she would not be looking at anyone on the train. There would be no more long conversations with complete strangers.

"This whole mourning thing is killing me," she said to no one.

Johnetta turned the corner toward the train station and felt as if she was taking her broken heart for a walk. The deep darkness was summoning her once more. The old familiar feelings of isolation returned to claim a preeminent place over her wounded heart. The frightening part was that those emotions were becoming her home, her security, a comfort even. A kind of unstable stability, like learning to walk with a permanent limp even though none of your limbs are broken. Before long, the limp is normal.

•

Bushy woke while two men carried him on a litter. It was a bouncy ride, as they huffed and puffed their way over the broken battlefield. His own face was covered in thick raunchy mud that he tried to peel away from his nose and eyes with his dirty fingers. He gave up and rubbed a jacket sleeve across his stubbly face ejecting some dried particles onto his filthy shirt. He felt a bit naked without his helmet and overcoat. He noticed his pack was gone as well. The gun that had become his best friend and an extension of his arm was nowhere to be found. It had not been more than an arms length away from him, since his arrival in June. He knew everything about that rifle, each mark had its own significance. It was gone. Part of him was missing.

His right leg screamed for attention, breaking through his thick mental fog with an unmitigated ferociousness, and he moaned at the throbbing pain.

"We gotcha," one of the men carrying him said.

There was no reply.

"Your buddy, Clark, said to take real good care of you."

"His name is Mule," Bushy said through the searing pain.

"Okay, Mule it is," replied the soldier in the back, right above his uncovered head.

"What's your name, soldier?" he asked as they went down and back up out of a small shell crater.

"Bushy," Joseph said through gritted teeth.

"Bushy? Well that's a new one on me," the soldier smiled beneath his helmet while he walked.

"You hear that, Munson?" Apparently, to the man on the front of the stretcher.

"Yeah, that's a new one alright," Mr. Munson said, turning his head to be better heard.

"Why Bushy?" Private Alvarez questioned.

"Had a DI who couldn't pronounce my last name give it to me and it stuck," he said, glad to get his mind off the pain, for a moment.

"What's your last name, Bushy?"

"Jacobucci."

"Ahhh, Munson did you hear that? We are carrying a WOP on this stretcher of ours," Alvarez said trying to be funny.

"I got my papers," Bushy shot back at the slight.

"You will have to excuse my idiot partner Bushy, he didn't mean anything by calling you a WOP."

"Right. I didn't mean to say that you were an ignorant immigrant who illegally barged into our great country," Alvarez said, tongue in cheek.

"Oh I didn't realize that I died and woke up to a comedy routine from two stretcher bearers," Bushy pushed back.

"Alright hero," Alvarez was readying himself with more derogatory remarks but was interrupted by his partner.

"Here we are," said a smiling Munson.

"Aid station?" Bushy asked.

"No, just the truck to take you back to the Aid station."

"Good luck, Bushy," Alvarez said. The men placed his litter on the back of the truck and smacked the tailgate closed.

"You're good to go," Munson shouted to the young driver in the cab. Off the truck went slowly making its way west from the front and away from the fighting. Bushy's head was swirling with pain and intermittent moments of relief from the constant stress of battle. Those thoughts, combined with pangs of guilt over leaving the guys behind to finish the fight without him. He wondered if he would ever see them again. There were still a few men left that he was close to. Mule for sure. Fingers and Gunny. Biscuit was still in the fight. Sergeant Molly. Lt. Meeker. With those thoughts, tears of separation welled into the corner of his eyes. Laying with ten other wounded men on the bed of that truck he had never felt more alone.

He reached down to touch his throbbing leg as the truck bounced along the muddy trail of a road. His pants were drenched with blood and he panicked a bit. This was the first time he was clear headed enough to consider his predicament. There was a belt cinched around the middle of his thigh applying pressure to his wound which drove his pain level up. He did not think that the bullet had hit the artery or he would have never woken up.

The blood that soaked through his pants was cold and thick instead of warm and runny, which could mean that the bleeding had slowed and maybe stopped. His whole leg ached. His feet were cold in his boots. He began to shiver on his narrow stretcher.

Glancing over at the guy right next to him he was shocked to see the paleness of his face. It was ghostlike in appearance. To Bushy, it seemed like he was dead already. The young kid even looked somewhat familiar but he could have been any one of a hundred thousand soldiers that he had laid eyes on during this God forsaken endeavor. Speaking of God, he remembered.

"God, thank you that I am still alive. Please help me through this. I know that you are with me right now. In Jesus' name. Amen," Joe said quietly, while the truck sauntered along its war torn path to the back of the lines.

Men were marching past each side of the truck on their way to the front. They looked so young and so afraid. Their clean new uniforms indicated that today was to be their baptism into the hellfire of modern warfare. Joe felt sorry for them. Their whole world was going to be changed and challenged like never before. Many of them were taking their final walk today. Death would reach out and claim some before the sun set behind the hills. The soil of the French countryside was soaked in the blood of thousands of Americans who were so far from home and some of the men marching past his escape truck would join them this day. War is brutal.

•

"Annie, are you here?" Johnetta knocked on her dark green door, more firmly. The cool breeze snatched more leaves out of the trees around Annie's apartment. Dead leaves of varying shapes and colors pushed along, dancing over the front lawn, and gathering in a pile at the corner of the bricked building.

Johnetta knocked again, this time louder. Standing on the wooden porch Johnetta decided to sit down and rest, from her travels. That posture did not last long because gravity invited her to lie back and enjoy the warming sunshine. Other than the hustling leaves, it was quiet in this neighborhood. Within minutes, she was out cold laying on her back with the cloth traveling bag beneath her head as a pillow.

"Excuse me Miss," the older woman was nudging Johnetta.

"Miss, it's getting dark outside. Are you alright?"

Johnetta came to. Pushing back the veil of darkness into reality she stretched her arms up and arched her back.

"Are you okay?" The persistent woman asked.

"Yes. Yes, I am fine. I was tired from travelling all night, that's all," Johnetta explained.

"You have been out here all day," said the concerned woman.

"This is my sister's place and I was hoping that she was going to be home," Johnetta said.

"Oh you're Annie's sister?"

"Yes. Johnetta," she said and stood up to greet the woman.

"Well, I am just the nosy neighbor, Edna," she smiled.

"Do you know when Annie gets home?"

"She's been working all kinds of different hours at the restaurant," she replied.

"Yeah, I didn't want to bother her at work."

"She usually leaves her door unlocked, like the rest of us," Edna smiled.

"Do you know why she has been working so much lately?" Johnetta asked.

"I think she said it was because they have a couple of waitresses missing. One's having a baby and, well I don't remember what she said about the other," Edna explained.

Johnetta tried the door and it was unlocked, just like Edna suggested.

"Would you look at that!" She was embarrassed.

"I think that I am going to put my bag inside and walk to the restaurant," Johnetta explained.

"Okay," Edna said, now from her adjoining porch, just to the right of Annie's.

"Do you know where her place is?" Johnetta asked.

"Four blocks south on main street. It's called Stella's," she said, while pointing south.

"Thank You, Edna," Johnetta said and left.

"Be careful, Johnetta," Edna replied.

•

"Don't lose this card, soldier," said the seasoned nurse to Joe. She dropped a card on his chest and walked away.

Bushy had fallen asleep through the rest of the ride to the Aid station. His leg felt worse and the toes on his right foot were numb and cold. His entire leg felt as if it had been set on fire. He moaned a little. When he did, he heard other men moaning and calling for the nurse. He heard screams coming from inside the large green tents.

He tried to sit up to see his thigh, which made the pain surge. Bushy managed to get to one elbow and look down past his gas mask at his pants.

It looked as if someone had ripped them open to see the wound, spread some white powder all over then wrapped it with gauze and put the belt in place to hold it all together. Blood had soaked through the bandage. Joe felt that the belt was cinched too tightly and cutting off circulation to his lower leg. He pushed himself up to a sitting position causing pain to shoot up from the wounded leg, and make him feel dizzy. He grabbed for the belt.

"Hey, Soldier, you have to leave that alone," said a white dressed woman from somewhere off to his left.

"I can't feel my toes," Bushy said to her through gritted teeth.

"Lie down I will be right there," she commanded him like a drill instructor.

Lying down was the easy thing to do at that point.

"What do we have here?" The Nurse said to herself as she looked at his leg.

"Hey, you dropped your field medical card soldier!"

Bushy noticed right away that the nurse stared at him with beautiful green eyes causing him to relax in a manner of speaking. Maybe, it was the loss of blood, or the month of combat that was making him delirious. He could not take his eyes off of her.

"Hang on to this," she said pressing the retrieved card into his hand.

"Better yet, let me put it in your front pocket," she said and noticed the look in his eyes.

"What's your name soldier?" She leaned in closer to tuck the card in.

It was as if an angel was looking into his soul and he did not speak. A slight smile crept across his mouth.

"Ahh, Bushy," is what he could come up with in that moment.

"Bushy? Well that was a cruel thing for your parents to name you after a plant!" she chuckled.

"Well that's my Army name Ma'am," he managed to say.

"I am going to release some of the pressure from the belt for a minute to let the blood flow back into your lower leg, but then I have to tighten it up again." She said while removing his boot.

"Oh yeah, your foot is turning blue," she reported.

Then she cautiously released the pressure from the belt while watching the bandage on his leg. Applying pressure to the gauze she felt for a pulse in his cold foot.

"Well the good news is that you have a strong pulse in your foot now," she was smiling at him again with her dazzling green eyes.

"I am going to look for another bandage and maybe we can get rid of the belt," she tightened the makeshift tourniquet, stood and walked away, much to Bushy's dismay.

Within a few minutes, Green Eyes returned with an armful of items.

"Alright, General Bushy, I am gonna get you fixed up until the doc can see you," she said smiling.

She cut his pants off above the wound and down the front, pulling the severed pant leg out from beneath him. She removed the belt and wrapped a clean bandage around the leg without removing the original gauze immediately on the entry of the wound. She felt around the leg for other entry points and damage.

"Do you remember how you were shot?" she asked him.

"It was an airplane," he said now in obvious pain from the exam.

"How do you know that?" She wondered about the chaos of battle.

"The plane was the only thing firing at us as we crossed the field," he said.

Nurse Green Eyes noticed that Bushys gas mask, laying on his stomach, had a bullet hole through it.

"Looks like the bullet got your gas mask before it hit your leg," she said, holding the mask up for him to see the hole through each side.

Joe did not realize the significance of the way he had been shot.

"There is probably some rubber in your leg along with a bullet. The mask may have saved your life," he noticed that her eyes were trained on his.

"What do you mean?" Bushy questioned.

"If the bullet had not struck the mask first it may have done a lot more damage going through your thigh, maybe even breaking your leg or hitting your femoral artery. You would have bled out on the battlefield.

"Really?" His eyes were now wide with the realization.

"Alright, I have a blanket for you. I will come back and check on you in a while. Then we can fill out your card. The docs are really busy with triage, so it is going to be some time. Drink water," she said to him.

"Thank you nurse," Bushy was grateful.

"Someone was looking out for you soldier," she whispered into his ear and set his canteen next to him.

"What's your name?"

"Jones, Renee Jones," she said.

"You rest now and I'll check on you soon," she promised and left.

He never saw her again. Maybe, it had been an angel that had visited him during his trial. His Field Medical card had been filled out and placed back in his pocket. A doctor visited him and ordered him evacuated to Base Hospital 6. He knew this was real because it was written on the inside of his card. He did not know how he got on the train.

He found his canteen next to his right hand. It was full of cool clean water that he gulped at in the darkness of the frigid musty rail car. Joseph wondered about his buddy's fighting on the front, as he heard the distant rumble of artillery.

"Were they all okay, alive even?" He pondered. He ached to be back with them.

Then flashes of battles assaulted him. The earth shattering explosions he had felt reverberated through his bones. The days on end breathing stale air through his gas mask. Memories of the mud and rain soaking and freezing his body, made him grip his wool blanket even tighter. All of the blood he had witnessed ran eerily through his dreams. The awful stench still bit at his nostrils even in his sleep and he retched at the memory. The gnawing thirst. The nagging hunger.

He wondered how many times he had racked the bolt of his gun. How many rounds had he fired? How many men had he killed? Early on, the scenes were still vivid and as time passed by and bodies piled up, his memory became more cloudy.

"Could it have been more than a hundred men?" Bushy's heart grew heavy with guilt at the thought.

"It was war," he told himself.

That statement reminded him that someone along the way in his nearly seven months in uniform had said to him.

"Kill or be killed, Bushy."

Indeed. He had killed many men. Some up close in a trench with his bayonet. Others a hundred yards away across no man's land with his faithful rifle. Would the flashes of all the dead faces ever go away? Weasel's head exploding had not faded. Wop getting shot through the chest, still played over and over. Pops catching one in the face. All the guys dying on the pre-dawn raid. It was too much to handle and he cried in the darkness, as the train rocked him back to sleep.

•

"Good morning, sleepy head!" Annie's bright smile greeted Johnetta on the sunny morning.

"Morning," she managed to say.

"So you know, Marty was serious about you working at the diner?" She said a little too loudly.

"Yeah, I know," Johnetta replied.

"He is a good guy to work for Johnetta," she said.

"How is Stella?" Johnetta wondered while pouring herself some boiling water from the kettle. The steam rose and warmed her hand. She dropped the little basket with the ground tea leaves into the mug.

"Well, Stella is getting old and only works for a few hours a day now. She can be a bit of a grump but most of the time is pretty quiet," Annie said and sipped at her cup.

Johnetta joined her at the little table for two.

"You will fit right in Johnetta and the tips are good most of the time," Annie said.

"Really?" Johnetta asked a little less than thrilled.

"Well you are going to have to learn to leave the sadness here at home."

"What does that mean?"

"You are going to find out real fast that earning good tips is a game."

"A game?"

"Yes."

"I don't understand," Johnetta said, blowing across her steaming mug.

"The people who tip the best are the ones that you connect with." Annie explained.

"Okay."

"That means that you have to be interested in who they are," Annie said.

"What if I just want to bring them their food?" Johnetta wondered if she could remain in her cocoon.

"Then you will get the tip of a delivery man, a truck driver."

"If you care about them and flash them a smile while doing it, the chances for a better tip go up!"

"I worked in the Skeem restaurant and did okay," Johnetta said.

"And sister, you were in a good place then, here I mean," she said pointing to her heart.

"And now?"

"And now? You are grieving," Annie said and touched her sisters hand.

"I know," she said holding back tears again.

"That's why I said you have to play the game Johnetta."

"That is going to be hard to put the grieving behind me."

"Only at work. When you are here, grieve all you need to," she said gripping her hand more tightly now.

"I will even help you!"

"I think that I can do that," Johnetta said with little confidence but no tears.

"I called mom last night," Annie admitted to using the telephone at Stella's.

"Okay?"

"She was glad to hear that you were here with me," Annie said.

"I guess Walter was driving around all day looking for you."

"Why?" Johnetta coldly asked.

"He will never be dad, but I think that he has grown to care about you."

"I just couldn't take all of the looks and questions anymore," Johnetta explained.

"Being there just reminded me of Neils. I was constantly thinking about him and he is dead, Annie! I will never get to see him again. So I can't keep living in a place that reminds me of my dead husband. I have to move on with my life. I had to leave and I didn't want to fight with mother. You know how she gets."

"I do," Annie said.

"Everywhere I turned I was looking for Neils and seeing him. It was driving me crazy because he is not in Pocatello. He isn't anywhere anymore," she said, and with that thought the tears returned.

"I am so sorry, Jo Jo," Annie said.

The long sobs ended up being a cleansing cry. It was important to be heard and Annie had blessed her with that gift this morning. The loneliness faded some, in her sister's loving embrace.

•

"Momma?"

"Momma, what are you doing in France?"

Maria smiled at her youngest boy. She was concerned for him but was proud of him at the same moment.

"It is going to be alright Giuseppi, Momma's here now," She was holding him on her lap and gently rocking him back and forth singing a lullaby while caressing his forehead.

"I got shot by an Aero Plane, Momma," he said while looking into her deep brown eyes.

"It is going to be alright, my boy," she said with her confident smile.

"How are you here with me?"

"I was worried about you," she said.

"You were fighting with your cousin Mario," she said.

"I was?" He was confused.

"Yes dear," she said, and her face exploded from a gunshot, just like Weasels had.

"MOMMA!" Bushy screamed and tried to sit up.

"Easy now soldier," said a calming voice.

"Easy."

Joe opened his eyes to an unfamiliar scene. He was in a bed in a long room with many other beds all filled with men.

"You're in the hospital. You had surgery to remove the bullet from your leg."

"What?"

"You are okay," she was touching his arm.

"It was so real," he said, still confused.

"The vivid dreams are from the anesthetic," the nurse explained.

"They were just dreams."

Bushy had a hard time shaking the image of his mother's head exploding from a Maxim round to the face.

"Here drink some water," the nurse held a glass to his lips and helped him up a bit. With the movement his leg felt like someone hit it with an ax, so he grabbed for it.

"No. You have to keep your hands off of your leg," she said bluntly.

"We can't have any dirty fingers digging around, you will cause an infection."

Bushy laid back in pain.

"Doc said that the surgery went well. They removed the bullet and some rubber from your wound. He expects you to make a full recovery Private." She was smiling now.

Bushy just nodded his head, acknowledging he had heard the report. He wanted to ask if his mother was there to visit but he knew that she was not.

"Lunch is going to be served in a little while and you need to start eating again."

With those words he felt the pain in his stomach rise to the front of his mind.

"How long had it been since he had eaten anything?" He wondered through the mental fog and dozed off again.

•

"How would you like your eggs cooked sir?" Johnetta asked the gentleman sitting alone.

"Scrambled please, Miss."

"Toast and bacon with the eggs?" She asked as she was writing his order down on the notepad.

"Please."

"Is that it then?" Johnetta said flashing her smile.

"Ummm," the man sat up taller in his seat, drawing closer to the waitress.

"Do you have any hot coffee?" He was whispering now.

"Just order the hot cocoa, Joe's way," Johnetta whispered in return. She was looking into his eyes to communicate without words. In Mormon land of zero stimulants, hot coffee only was sold under cover, so as not to offend the Mormon clientele.

"So just the water then?"

"Ahh. No could I have a hot cocoa?"

"A hot cocoa?"

"Yes."

"Okay." Johnetta looked a little disappointed at the middle aged customer.

"Oh, ah, could I get that Joe's way, please?"

"With the bitter cocoa?"

"Ah, Yes?" He was uncertain.

"Sure," she said smiling, nodded, wrote it down and walked away.

Johnetta's morning slipped into the afternoon in the same fashion. Her feet were hurting, she needed some new shoes. With the decent tips that she was making it would not take too long to be able to buy them for herself. She had promised to pay Annie half of the rent to stay with her. Marty was impressed with her work ethic and was willing to give her as many hours as she wanted at the understaffed diner. The business was steady throughout the morning and lunchtime, then came the afternoon lull before the dinner rush began around five.

For Johnetta it was a positive way to spend her time and it was making a difference inside. She had plenty of sad moments after work, whenever she was triggered to think of Neils. Sometimes, it was the strangest things that would set her off. Like the group of boys playing war on her walk home, she lost all composure when they pointed old broomsticks at each other for their pretend guns, and needed to jog away. Even seeing the flag flying over the post office, stirred emotions inside of her.

The fact that she was a real war widow seemed surreal. For Johnetta knowing that her husband had given his life in service to the country did give her a feeling of genuine pride. Neils believed enough in the freedom that our country offers to everyone that he was willing to fight and to die for it. When she could remember that truth, without focusing on her loss, it allowed her to lift her head up from the darkness. It helped her to be thankful for what she had and for who he was.

•

Dear Momma,

I wanted to write again and let you know that I am doing okay. I was shot in the leg during a battle but I am at a good military hospital in France recovering. The wound wasn't too bad because it hit my gas mask before my leg. I won't have to fight anymore and am glad for that. I am hearing that the war is going to be coming to an end soon, I pray that is true. It was the hardest thing that I have ever done. I will go back to Midvale and will send you a telegram when I return.

How are you doing? I miss you and wanted to thank you for all that you did for me when I was growing up. Me and Johnny both. I miss Papa too. I hope to send you a picture of me in my uniform, I know that you would be proud. Say a prayer for me in church. Tell Johnny and the whole family that I am well.
Your loving Son,
Joseph

Bushy kissed the page and sealed it inside the envelope. The address he knew by heart and wrote it on the outside of the envelope with the best handwriting he could muster.
"Hey Joe, how are you feeling today?" Marcy, the nurse, was asking again. She was very considerate toward all of her patients.
"Doing very well, thank you."
"Well, I need to take a look to see how the wound is healing."
Joe laid back on his creaky bed and the nurse came around to remove his bandages.
"I am hoping that we can be done with the Dakins Irrigation treatment and we can get you up and walking again." she said while she worked.
"I am going stir-crazy in here," he said.
"That tends to happen once people start feeling better, so that is a good sign," she said.

"HEY!" A young soldier had entered into the hall and shouted.

"The War Is Over! The Krauts Surrendered!"

"The shooting stops at 11!"

•

Monday November 11th began as a cold and dreary day in Midvale. Since the diner is closed on Sundays, it was always a bit more difficult getting everything ready to service customers. Johnetta was working her first opening on a Monday. She had not even been working a month at Stella's. It was difficult to get acclimated to the six a.m. start time. It reminded her of working on the ranch because they always started early, but it had been a couple years.

The cold morning walk alone from Annie's place was invigorating. As she walked into the diner through the rear entrance at five minutes to six, Marty was already bouncing around the kitchen preparing for another day.

"Morning, Jo Jo," he had been sampling the coffee already.

"Hey Marty," she replied with a smile and a wave, wanting the day to get off to a good start.

"Cold out there this morning!"

"It certainly is."

"I think that we are in for an early winter," he prophesied.

"Is that what your Farmer's Almanac says, Marty?" Johnetta said back over her shoulder as she walked to the front counter.

"Make fun all that you want, Jo Jo, it's real!"

"Okay," it was starting already. At least the lighthearted banter made the day go by quickly.

"Hey, Jo Jo, put the chairs down, then turn on the lights and unlock the door," I will be ready to go in fifteen.

"Are you sure?"

"Yeah. Sometimes we get some smelter guys stopping in before their shift starts at 7."

"Sure," she was somewhat skeptical.

"You have opened before right?" Marty was trying to remember.

"Yes, just not on a Monday," she said while lowering chairs in the dark dining room.

"Okay, it's pretty much the same as any day for you upfront. Get the chairs, set the tables, straighten out the menus, get the order pads out, pencils for you girls, the lights, the door and a smile!"

"Aye mah Captain!" Johnetta said in her Brogue.

"You sound like Annie when you do that Irish thing," Marty said.

"Scottish, not Irish, Marty!"

"Right, it's all about the same," he was sassy this morning.

"Nae even claise," she shot back.

"You Cameron girls are all the same!"

The morning carried on like that until the first time the bell on the front door jingled and four loud men rolled into the diner at 6:15.

"Good morning gentleman," Johnetta said with a smile. She knew that the smelter rats always tipped pretty well in the morning before work when coming in with their guy friends, but not so well in the evening with their wives.

"Good? It is a great morning!" Said one of the burly men in response.

"Really?"

"Absolutely!"

"Why is it so great?" Johnetta wondered.

He flopped the mornings newspaper down onto the table that they were claiming and it fell open to the front page to the large text headline: "World War Over!"

Johnetta could not believe it and stood with her hand on her chest in disbelief. The guys hooted and hugged around the table. Marty came out from the back to see what all the commotion was about. As he walked through the double swinging half doors, he witnessed the strangest sight. Four men hugging and Johnetta sitting and crying at their table.

"What is going on out here?" He said, a little more annoyed than curious.

"The war is over!" Said a couple of the guys in unison.

Marty could not take his eyes off of Jo Jo and walked over to her.

"Jo Jo, are you okay?"

"Why are you crying, Missy?" Joked one of the oblivious men.

Marty shot them all a look as he knelt down in front of Johnetta.

"I am sorry, Johnetta," he said.

"Hey, let's move you guys over to another table," Marty picked up the menus from the floor and stood to lead the guys away from the weeping waitress.

"Why, what did I say?" Asked one of the men to Marty.

"Her husband was killed in France four months ago," he said quietly.

Johnetta got up and went into the bathroom to compose herself.

Five minutes later she was cleaned up and ready to work.

"Sorry about that, gentleman," she said.

"No problem. We are sorry for what happened to you," they all said in different ways.

"Thank You. It has been a difficult few months."

Another twenty minutes the men filed out of the restaurant and headed off to work. They left her almost twenty dollars for a tip and a note on the receipt.

"Thank you for your sacrifice."

That one took ten minutes in the bathroom.

When she came out of hiding Annie had arrived to start working her shift.

"Hey, Sis. I didn't even hear you leave this morning," then noticed that Johnetta had been crying.

"Marty told me about the war," she reached out to hug her.

"I am better now. The guys gave me an eighteen dollar tip!"

"What?"

"Yeah, maybe I should cry more often," she said and everyone laughed.

"It is a good day," Johnetta admitted.

"Hey, we are going to offer half off our French fries today, for the victory," Marty announced.

The girls groaned.

•

To say that the mood in base hospital six improved would have been the understatement of the century. 'The Great War To End All Wars' was over with as many as sixteen million servicemen and women dead on all sides. The elation brought spontaneous cheers, clapping, hugs and crying that went on for hours. Everyone who entered the facility was greeting with renewed enthusiasm. Sometimes too much male enthusiasm toward the female nurses. Only half the amount of pain killers were dispensed on that glorious day compared to during the conflict. The bloody nightmare was over.

Bushy wore a contagious smile the entire afternoon. He let the letter to his mother leave the way that he had written it, hoping that it would quickly make its way the thousand miles to Spinete. He was thankful that the nurse was going to make sure that it got into the French postal system. Otherwise, it would have been sent back to the States first and then forwarded overseas. That would have taken months to accomplish and may well have been returned to Utah for lack of sufficient postage.

With the letter gone on its way, Joe dreamt about what he would do after the war. He hoped that he could get out before Christmas. He knew that he would have to go stateside to collect his final paycheck. What he did not know is where that would be. The Yankee Division was a New England Division originally, but he had trained at Camp Funston in Kansas and caught up with the rest of the YD in France. So, getting back to Utah would take him some time. He knew that he had a job at the smelter when he returned, but was dreaming of some time away fishing a mountain stream, maybe somewhere remote.

One of his highest hopes was to return to Midvale and get back on his motorcycle. Thinking about riding his silver Indian again had occupied many long nights in foxholes. He remembered buying it from the guy who worked the docks at the smelter because he needed money to get married. Bushy would often find himself dreaming about riding along the roads south, retracing the route he took on a camping trip to Mukuntuweap National Monument. Remembering the rugged beauty of the red canyons and peaks that had inspired him to keep fighting to get back home, through the long nights under the constant gas alarms. His heart was racing with anticipation.

"Listen up, Men!" A camp officer was at the front of the long room wanting undivided attention.

The room was very slow in responding to the visitor.

"Attention!" He barked with authority.

"Gentlemen. I have two announcements. I need you to hear both of them. Fighting on the Western Front has ceased. German representatives have signed a cessation of aggression pact effective 1100 hours."

Cheers rose up, again.

"Secondly." He paused for the cheering to stop.

"Secondly this hospital is now under quarantine. There have been several soldiers that have contracted the Spanish Flu. As a result, all personnel are hereby, quarantined to quarters until further notice."

Silence swept over the room.

Death just would not stop knocking.

•

IX.

'Killer'

The elation over the announcement of the end of the war was short lived at Base Hospital
Six, in northern France. While the rest of the world celebrated the long awaited victory
over the Central Powers, the men in Bushy's ward were overcome by the apprehension of
being infected with the dreaded Spanish Flu. There was an overwhelming sense of
helplessness that gripped the weary men. This was not an enemy that could be blown to
bits with an artillery barrage.

The potent strain of Flu sweeping the globe was reaching a climax in Europe, as the war
ended. It was attacking its victims by restricting the ability to cough out the phlegm the
virus caused the lungs to produce. Thus, people would suffocate and die in their own
spittle. The term Spanish was attached by the fact that so many in Spain had been
infected, including the Monarch of that country. In the other warring European nations an
information blackout had been imposed during the war and news agencies were unable to
speak of the outbreak on either side of the conflict. There was no such news blackout in
Spain, being neutral in the war, and reports of the deadly 'Spanish' virus were being
spread all over the globe.

Almost 20% of infected people worldwide died from the outbreak and one third of the
world's population contracted the virus in 1918 and early 1919. The greatest percentage of
Spanish Flu epidemic victims were between the ages of 20-40 years old, which was the
age of most of the men fighting in the Great War. More doughboys were killed by the
Influenza outbreak than by enemy bullets and bombs during the horrific conflict.

During the third day under quarantine at Base Hospital Six the mood was somber, then a
couple of the men began coughing early in the morning after breakfast. As the day

progressed, more of the soldiers joined in the chorus. Nurses donned surgical masks to try and protect themselves from the spread of the deadly virus. Other wards were reporting a few cases of the Flu, soon leadership moved all the infected men into one central location. A couple of men were ushered out of Bushys ward. Four masked orderlies came, picked the bed up and carried the whole thing off with the soldier lying on it, coughing up a lung, while the entourage moved out through the guarded doors.

This new killer triggered even more fear for the wounded men, in that hospital. The irony of surviving the vicious battles in the greatest war known to mankind and then succumbing to some kind of influenza bug, weighed heavily on all of the men. Tension was on high alert during the next few weeks as more and more of the men came down with the illness.

Bushy's cough began on day four of the quarantine. It was innocent enough after breathing in some of the water he was drinking. But the hacking would not quit, then the fever came rushing over him and four others in the ward. Nurses tried to have the men cover their mouths with a mask but every time a coughing fit attacked, it was ripped off. They tried to use isolation curtains around the infected, to seal them off from the healthy. Nothing stopped the rapid spread through the entire ward. All of the medical staff succumbed to the dreaded illness.

By day six there was no one guarding the door of the hospital and some of the men wandered outside to get some fresh air, in their delirious state. Some of the infected died within a few hours of contracting the disease. The coughing fits deprived their organs of oxygen turning large patches of skin blue and black before they suffocated.

The people that survived the flu were sick for at least a week. Fever and coughing fed cycles of dehydration and malnutrition which devastated the already weakened immune system into systemic collapse. The wounded men looked ragged and felt worse.

The yellow flag of quarantine flew above the hospital for the last two long weeks of November. The war was over, but people still were dying in droves. During this time, doughboys returning from Europe brought more than themselves home from the war. Infection rates soared in the eastern U.S. during the last few months of 1918 and would sweep west through early 1919. Over 675,000 Americans would eventually die from the Spanish Flu, before it was done wreaking havoc.

Joseph felt the worst when he lay flat. It was as if he could not breathe, then cough himself to the point where he passed out on his bed, several times. He propped his pillow under himself and tried to sit up with his back against the cool plaster wall. The fever caused him to shiver violently beneath his wool blanket, but sitting up did help with the coughing fits. His vision was blurry and he could not manage to walk himself to the bathroom down the hall, because of his leg wound. The hole from surgery had almost closed up but his leg continued to ache. Soon his bedpan was overflowing and using his crutch, he managed to steal his neighbors pan to pee in during the night.

He stood to urinate into the pan on the side of his bed. A coughing fit ensued and the pan was knocked over onto his feet which he tried to avoid. That motion caused him to lose his footing because of the shooting pain in his right leg. On his way down, he struck his head squarely on the side of the metal frame of his bed and knocked himself out cold. His limp body landed in the mess of the bed pan remains that had splashed across the floor. Blood trickled from the cut on his temple and his nose may have been broken during his face's sudden stop on the tile floor.

•

Dugald truly loved his life on these mornings. He rode Pharaoh behind his property in Cottonwood Canyon. Lone Peak towered in front of him as he made his way south over Cottonwood Creek. The water churned and ran high in the creek that day, so he slowed his horse and they made the crossing at a walk. Just over the creek the land began a swift rise into the foothills of the majestic Lone Peak. From this point, the summit was over three miles away and appeared close enough to reach out and touch with its snow covered cap. The air was clear and crisp, a perfect day for a ride. These were Dugald's treasured thinking times with nothing but him, Pharaoh, and an open frontier.

He turned east toward the unsettled country. The sun was bright and in his eyes as it peered over the towering Wasatch Range. Dugald knew the route well, having lived up in these hills for the last couple of years. He was amazed that he could convince his beautiful city girl wife, Pearl, to live out on the edge of the wilderness, nearly ten miles from town. It had been his dream to live near the mountains, since the first time he laid eyes on them back in 1910. He was hooked, Utah was paradise. It was a promised land of rugged beauty.

Dugald and Pearl bought ten acres of wooded land complete with an old cabin. They were virtually the only homestead on the entire stretch of Cottonwood Canyon Road at that time. He fixed up the cabin and built a small barn for his beloved horse. Emily came along and stole his heart. She was so beautiful, just like her mother and so precious. He was determined to teach both her and their newest little girl, Thelma, to love these mountains the way he did. He was convinced that he could. Dugald dreamt of the day when they would ride these trails together, racing and laughing along.

He also had dreams of having a son. He determined that his son would have a better relationship with his father than what he had with his own dad. Even still, in honor of his father, his little boy would carry forward the same given name.

His father was a quiet man which made the young Dugald feel somewhat isolated and uncertain about many things. His father worked so hard on the farms in Scotland that he rarely saw him. When they came over to Zion, young Dugald was whisked away to

Brother Richie's ranch within two days of arrival. He was not home for his father's sudden illness. The final memory Dugald had of his dad is a half hearted wave as he rode off with Brother Richie. His feelings were ambivalent, but he had been overcome by the excitement in going to live on the big Richie Ranch down in Charleston. He was 15 and in his eyes, ready to become a man. Young Dugald was counting on the old Missionary to make it happen in more ways than one.

"See ya Dad," were the final pathetic words to his father from the horse drawn wagon, eagerly sitting next to his new hero and mentor. He traded his own father for an unknown stranger. And yet, it did seem that his father was somewhat complicit. He could have said something to stop it all, but it would have been in vain because the young lad was determined to leave his childhood behind in Scotland, and his family in Salt Lake.

Oh, how he had wanted those five minutes back a thousand times over these last eight years. Dad died a few weeks later, before he could get up to Tooele to visit him. It was a real punch in the gut hearing the news from his mother near the entrance of the little hospital. It felt like a piece of him stopped growing on that fateful day. Like a father sized hole took up an uninvited residence in his heart.

That was part of the reason that he liked to ride alone up in these foothills. He spent some of the time having conversations with his dad. Trying to discern what he would have said to him if he was here riding next to him, guiding him. These talks managed to take some of the sting of separation away. The imaginary rides helped Dugald deal with a myriad of disappointments and distractions in his complicated life. They helped him keep some perspective on things.

Whenever he made the final turn for home, he would push his cowboy hat down tight, bring Pharaoh up to a gallop and always say, "See ya, Dad," to the wind. Then the quickening breeze would drive a few more tears from his sad blue eyes, while his regretful heart made for home.

•

"How did we manage to both get the same day off?" Johnetta asked her sister.

"I told Marty that we needed the time together," she smiled as the train broke away from the Midvale station.

"Next stop, Salt Lake City," the old man announced across the car.

"Thanks for coming shopping with me," Johnetta said with a somber expression.

"Well, my little sister has been making a killing lately on tips, so I am here to make sure you don't get robbed," Annie said with another smile.

"So what is going on with people wearing Doctor masks around?" Johnetta asked, noticing a few on the train.

"You haven't read about the Spanish Flu in the paper?"

"No, I have been far too busy earning tips," Johnetta replied with her own half smile.

"It's really bad out east right now," she said to her younger sister.

"I guess wearing the mask helps protect you from getting it."

"Great, more death, just what we all need," Johnetta felt a wave of sadness wash ashore. Annie did not know how to respond to Johnetta's depression anymore, so she just tried to stay positive during the frequent emotional storms. Annie knew that seventeen year old's are not supposed to be widows.

"Do you think that I married Neils too young?" Johnetta asked a few minutes later.

"Well, you were young," Annie considered the question further.

"Can I be honest?"

"Yes, of course," Johnetta said.

"Maybe you saw Neils as the answer to the Walter problem in your life," Annie winced a little inside after voicing the truth out loud.

"No. You're right, I did see him as the ticket out of Walterville. Now I feel guilty for having used him for that."

"I didn't know him well enough to get married, Annie," she said, getting a little choked up.

"Well, Johnetta, I walked down that same road with Les," Annie admitted.

"Really?"

"Absolutely. I was determined to not live with that man either and Les was convenient."

"Ouch."

"Yeah. Not one of my prouder moments, or best decisions. I was not very nice to him. We were completely different people. Those two years were miserable for the both of us. We didn't..., we didn't love each other." Annie admitted.

"I was only a week past my eighteenth birthday when we got married," Annie pointed out.

"I certainly didn't want to have his children."

"Sorry, I didn't even notice," Johnetta said.

"You were so young Johnetta."

"When Maggie and Robbie started courting they tried to play matchmaker with Les and me," Annie explained.

"So when mom started courting Walter, at the Bishop's request, I knew that he was going to be trouble and I wanted no part of living under the same roof."

"I didn't have that option," Johnetta said with more than a little self pity.

Silence reigned between them for a few moments.

"Dad's death brought so much suffering to our family," Annie recognized.

"Yes, it did. Eight years later we are still struggling from the ramifications," Johnetta thought out loud.

"You're right Johnetta," Annie said at the new understanding.

"It seems that the only one who isn't distressed is Maggie." Annie said.

"Well remember, she left the family the minute she turned eighteen," Johnetta reminded her.

"Typical, she was the true believer in the whole coming to Zion thing," Annie pointed out.

"And Mother, of course," Annie followed up with that quick logic.

"Well, you left six months after she did," Johnetta indicated.

"I did. Every move in my young life was because Maggie was doing it. I idolized her. My whole life I have done things because Maggie did it. I got baptized because of Maggie. I came to America for the same reason. I married Les." Annie's anger was searching for more examples.

"But you got married before Maggie did," Johnetta realized.

"I had to beat her on something!" Annie and Johnetta laughed out at the sad truth.

"I believe that most of our problems in our family point back to Dad's death," Johnetta stated.

"I think that most of our problems stem from listening to those crazy Missionaries in the first place." Annie said.

Johnetta was stunned by the revelation from her sister. She had her discussions with Mary over the years but had always felt that Annie was marching in lockstep with Joseph Smith and Brigham Young.

"Most of the things that those men promised to us in Scotland, were lies ," Annie said in whispered tones.

"I know that now, but I never considered that you would believe that!" Johnetta said quietly.

"What changed?"

"Get divorced as a L.D.S. woman and you'd find out," Annie said with the bitterness still evident.

"What happened?"

"The Bishop up in Ogden wanted to meet with me after the divorce was final," she said, glancing around.

"I thought that he was going to warn me about Church teaching or console me over the loss."

"What did he do?"

"He was going to claim me Johnetta, like a cow suddenly up for auction," she said as tears tipped over the edge of her enraged eyelids.

"Really?"

"I told him to get lost and he threatened me with sanction." Annie was not holding back.

"Sanction?"

"Yeah. He was going to take my name before the Ward as a reprobate if I didn't comply with his advances and become his third wife."

"You have got to be joking," Johnetta said in disbelief.

"You know what happens to a woman who has been declared apostate?" She was asking Johnetta if she understood the implications.

Johnetta answered by running her index finger across her neck.

"Exactly. 80% of the ritual killings in Utah are done to women. I believe those are the ones who stand up against the old perverts who want to add them to their harems," there was a fire in Annie's eyes that Johnetta had never witnessed before.

"Does mother know?"

"Yes. I ran to her first. They helped me get out of Ogden and move to Midvale away from the Bishop," Annie said.

"They?"

"Yes, Believe it or not, Walter was the first one to offer me money to get away. He grew up with Stella's son Marty. Walter helped me disappear, Johnetta."

"I had no clue," Johnetta said, astonished.

"I have sworn off the Mormon way of life, that's why Maggie and I don't get along anymore."

Johnetta's eyes grew wide in disbelief. The entire episode happened while she was living in Inkom. She was so miserable that she did not even notice her own sister's plight.

"Weren't you afraid that Les would tell the Bishop where you were?"

"No. Les wasn't exactly acting like a good pew sitter himself. He didn't love me Johnetta, but he didn't want me dead either. He moved back to Salt Lake after the divorce to get away from all that mess."

"Who was the Bishop?" Johnetta asked.

Just as she did, a young woman behind them leaned forward and placed her hands on each of the Cameron sister's shoulders and whispered a warning.

"Ladies, there are many itching ears hanging onto every word you two are saying. The killings are real but you have to keep your voices down." She said in a slow, deliberate whisper, then went back to reading.

Johnetta and Annie grabbed each other's hands tightly and glanced around for the first time since the discussion got heated. Straining to see if they had garnered unwarranted attention from fellow passengers.

After a few moments of stunned silence, Annie leaned in close to Johnetta's ear.

"It was Bishop Andersen," she said slowly and looked into Johnetta's shocked eyes.

•

"When you stay out of the wind, it's not too bad up here on deck, for December," the portly man said.

"Exactly, what I was thinking," Joe said.

"Mind if I sit?" The man was speaking of the empty deck chair next to him.

"Go ahead," Joe had been stealing a few moments of quiet in the rare sunshine, as the man took the seat.

"Not seasick are you?" The man asked.

"No. Never had a problem with that."

"I'm Tim."

"Joe."

"Where is home Joe?"

"Utah." He said to the constant roll of the hospital ship.

"Well you are a long way from home."

"Yes, and it feels like I have been gone an entire lifetime," Joe replied.

"Where are you headed?" Joe asked.

"Michigan," Tim said.

"Ah, the Great Lake State," Joe replied, interested.

"Yes, the lakes are beautiful. Not so much in December though, we are more of a winter wonderland this time of year," Tim smiled at the memory.

"So what put you on the hospital transport, combat or the flu?"

"Both. Combat first," Joe said.

"Which did you find to be the most difficult?"

"Well, they each had their own kind of death. Combat was more intense but at least you could shoot back at your enemy."

"Touche, Joe. Well said."

"What division did you fight with?" Tim asked.

"The YD. Ah, the Yankee Division, the 26th."

"Oh, I served in the 28th."

"I think that we fought just west of you guys in the Argonne," Tim said it like he had been an officer, who knew the battlefield map.

"The 28th was the, um, the Keystone Division?" Joe remembered.

"Yes you have a good memory," Tim admitted.

"Well I know the 32nd, the Red Arrow guys fought next to us in the Argonne. They were from Michigan," he was confused by Tim's contradictory comments.

"I was assigned to the 28th as a Chaplain," Tim explained.

"That must be a tough job." Joe was not joking, he meant it.

"Well, not the fighting part like you, just trying to help the men deal with all of the stress of battle," he explained.

"It was the most difficult thing that I have ever done," Joe admitted a minute later.

"I can understand that, it was brutal."

"Brutal is a good word to describe it."

"How are you coping with what you saw?" The Pastor side came out.

"I pray more than I ever have."

"So you're a man of faith then?"

"Yes. I grew up in the Church from a little boy."

"Did that help you in the war?"

"I know that God was the only one that kept me alive out there," Joe was looking right into Tim's eyes.

"Okay," Tim said, listening.

"I never met anyone who outright rejected God during the war."

"Even the most vulgar men would pray before battle," Joe said with a quiet confidence.

"I think that you are right, Joe from Utah."

"So what church did you grow up in?" Tim inquired.

"The only church in my village was a Roman Catholic parish," Joe said.

"Was that back in the old country?" Tim instinctively asked.

"Yes, Spinete, Italy."

"Where is Spinete?" Tim asked.

"About 50 miles north of Napoli, if you could fly like a bird, that is," Joe explained with his hands and his voice.

Tim smiled.

"So, I live in a little village in Michigan that only has one church. It is mostly farms in that part of the state. It may be ninety miles north of Detroit, if you could fly like a bird," repeating Joe's idiom.

"Okay. How close to the big lakes are you?"

"Well if you go about fifty miles due east you would splash into Lake Huron," he explained.

Joe chuckled at the thought.

"Tell me Joe, how hard is it being a Catholic in a Mormon state?" Tim was interested in his response.

"It's not too bad, there is a large Italian population that has immigrated to Utah, from all over Italy. So there are several churches. The largest is St. Mary Magdalene right in downtown Salt Lake. But there is no church like the old country," he said with apparent deep affection for his Italian parish.

"Chaplain Ross!" The young man called out.

"Yes?"

"You need to say the blessing over the food," he was a little desperate. He had been searching for some time.

"Okay, I will be right there," he stood.

"Well Joe, I hope you get healed up, get home safely and have a Merry Christmas," he offered his hand.

"Thanks Padre. Have a Merry Christmas yourself!" The men shook hands without Joe standing on his weak right leg.

"Merry Christmas," he thought about that for a few moments before chow. A Merry Christmas indeed.

•

"What?"

"Yes, Bishop Andersen," Annie repeated in her sister's ear.

"Let's call the Bishop, 'Bill,' while we are on the train, in case someone is listening," Annie suggested.

"Okay."

"It really was Bill?"

"Yes, the same Bill that moved up your way." Annie meant the church in Inkom.

"The same Bill that was invited to my wedding?" Johnetta said.

"That is why I almost didn't come, Johnetta." Annie insisted.

"But it had been over four years and Walter was convinced he had moved on to someone else."

"Is that why you got your hair changed?"

"Yes."

"Oh my goodness!" Johnetta replied astounded.

"Then when he didn't show up, I was so relieved."

"I can only imagine the fear in your heart."

"Walter said that he wouldn't let the man do anything to me," Annie remembered like it was yesterday.

"I have gained so much respect for Walter, today. I can't believe it!" Johnetta said so surprised by the revelation.

"Salt Lake City," the man announced over the heads of the people in the train car.

"Let's let everyone else get off first," Annie whispered.

The train stopped hard at the Salt Lake station. Most of the people were in a hurry to get off and get going with their day. When Annie thought the coast was clear, the two sisters disembarked the train nonchalantly. What they had failed to see was the man two rows behind them, who used his newspaper as a cover. He exited the train and began to follow them at a distance south of Temple Square.

He lost sight of them at an intersection, mistakenly thinking that they had gone into a store. Bounding across the busy street the man went into the Temple complex through a side entrance.

"Hey Bennie," the receptionist greeted her old friend.

"Hey Linda, how are you doing?"

"Real good, thank you."

"Could I use your telephone? It's really important."

"Sure thing. I have to run to the restroom anyway, you can sit right down at my desk," she said and took advantage of the moment. Bennie dialed the memorized number.

"Hey it's Bennie, I am down in Salt Lake and I was riding up from Nephi on the train and you'll never guess who got on in Midvale."

"Not one, but two of the lost Cameron sisters," Bennie was pleased with himself.

•

"Oh my goodness! Look who made it back from his French vacation!" Dugald smiled at his long lost friend as he made his way through the door.

"How are you Dugald Cameron?" Joe sincerely asked his smiling coworker as he extended his hand.

"Better than I deserve Joe. How are you doing?"

"So much better now the war is over."

"What is going on with your limp?"

"I got shot in the leg by a German Aero Plane, no less!"

"You did not!" Dugald couldn't believe it.

"Yes, I did."

"Wow, did they promote you to General of the Italian Army because of that?" Dugald loved teasing his co-workers, especially Joseph Jacobucci.

"I missed you Dugald, but you tease like a little girl," Joe counter punched.

"That's why we didn't want you fighting in the war!" Joe continued.

"Did you smell any French women while you were there?" Dugald asked.

"All of them!" Joe shot back.

Everyone gathered around Joe shaking hands and welcoming him home.

"Hey General, did you earn any medals over there?"

Joe ignored the Scot and shook another hand.

"Joe did you come home a hero, like Pershing riding in on his white stallion?" Dugald got lots of laughs from the other men in the lab.

"Well, my Scottish Cowboy," Joe started.

"Do you still wear your Kilt when you ride old Pharaoh?" Joe quipped.

Everyone had a good laugh and were encouraged to get to work.

"Let's go talk in my office," Dugald said to Joe and they both walked away together.

Dugald Cameron was in management now, which was something new in the nine months that Joe had been gone. He was only 23 but the owner loved the young man. They even attended the same church. Some say that the draft board was influenced by the owner of the United States Smelting, Refining and Mining Company to skip over Dugald's name, if he ever was selected. The boss made it plain that his job was vital to the war effort, so Dugald was never drafted. Terry had been and everyone knew that a non-Mormon was not going to get the position that opened when that happened. Terry was killed in action in the battle of the Somme last summer.

"Sit down," Dugald said.

"Thank You. Big boss now!" Joe said, looking around at the small office.

"No, not quite yet," he smiled.

"So how is your leg, Joe?"

"It is getting better every day." Joe said while looking down at it again.

"When did that happen?"

"October 23rd," Joe said, now a little concerned.

"Well, that was only a little over two months ago," Dugald figured.

"Yes. It was somewhat of a miracle because my gas mask may have saved my life. The bullet went through the rubber on the mask first then missed my bone and my artery," he explained.

"That is welcomed news," he said.

"Yes, it is."

"How was it really over there?" Dugald sat on his desk next to him and wanted to know.

"Imagine the hardest thing that you ever had to do and then let a few thousand guys who hate your guts shoot at you while you do it," he said a little bleary eyed.

"Then add in the foulest smells, the biggest explosions you could ever imagine and the faces of your friends being vaporized in front of you all day long. Then you might begin to have a little picture of that war."

Dugald was speechless.

"I am thankful that I survived when so many men I knew didn't."

"Wow."

"But that time in my life is over now and I have to move forward, Dugald," Joe said, ending all further war talk with someone who had no common point of reference.

"I understand, Joe," Dugald said, but he didn't have a clue. He too, was glad the subject was over.

"So when can you start back at work?" Dugald was giving him permission to set his own day back.

"Monday?"

"Excellent."

•

"Good morning, Stella's."

"Hello Marty?"

"Speaking."

"Hey, Marty, this is Walter."

"Walt! How are you doing?"

"Good, good."

"How is everything up in Pocatello?"

"It's been cold up here lately," he said.

"Still working for the railroad?"

"Yes, it's a good job, Marty. The kind that you retire from. How is the restaurant business?"

"Good. We have been very busy until this Spanish Flu outbreak in Salt Lake," he said, concerned.

"Yeah, Margret has gotten sick but I don't think it's the flu."

"I am sorry to hear that," not knowing where the conversation was heading.

"Hey is Johnetta working today?"

"She doesn't come in for another hour, but Annie is here," he explained.

"Can I speak with her for just a minute?"

"Sure, let me get her for you. It was good talking to you Walt. I hope Margret gets better real soon."

"Thanks Marty. I will have to stop in and catch up when we are down visiting the girls," he said.

"I look forward to it, old friend," Marty said.

"Let me get Annie."

"Thanks."

"Hello Walter?" Annie asked.

"Hello Annie," Walter said.

"Sorry to call you at work," he said.

"That's okay, Marty said mom was sick?" Annie sounded worried.

"She isn't feeling well but we don't believe it is the flu. She doesn't have a fever, just feels rundown. The doc said to let her rest," he was trying to reassure her.

"Well, that's good, I guess?"

"We received a call from Pearl," Walter was trying to break the hard news gently.

"Yes?" Annie was straining to hear over the noise of the crowded restaurant.

"Annie, Dugald has the flu."

"Oh no!"

"We thought that you and Johnetta needed to know," he said.

"Thanks, Walter. Please tell mom to get better real soon."

"Will do," he said.

"Marty will let me call Pearl to check up on Dugald. Tell mom not to worry, he is strong," Annie said reassuringly.

•

"He was only twenty three!" Johnetta was crying hard again.

Annie had no words to share as she sat next to her sister in their cold apartment. Annie had come back from work several hours early after hearing the grim news from her sister in law Pearl, that Dugald had died during the night. He had fought the flu for over eleven days but didn't have enough left at the end. Now, two little girls were left without a father. Emily and Thelma would have to face the rest of their lives without their loving dad to guide them and teach them. Cruel memories drove Annie and Johnetta to tears.

"Marty is going to close Stella's for at least a week," Annie said a few minutes later.

"Because of the quarantine?" Johnetta asked.

"Yes. He just thinks that it is the smart thing to do."

"There won't be any customers anyway," Johnetta said.

"What about the funeral?" Johnetta asked with concern in her eyes.

"It's only going to be a graveside interment," Annie explained.

"I am going," Johnetta was determined.

"Yes, we are," Annie grabbed her sister's arm with her own.

"Pearl said that mom can't travel yet."

"She has to miss Dugald's funeral?"

"Yes," Annie said sadly.

"That is going to be hard for her," Johnetta knew.

"I don't think that there will be many people, with the flu going around."

"All public gatherings have been cancelled including church services," Annie said.

"That's why there is only the graveside service?"

"Yes, it's Monday at 11:00."

The quarantine made the Cameron girls feel like prisoners in their own apartment. Neither slept very well that weekend thinking about their strong brother succumbing to the flu. The unexpected death triggered Johnetta. She was not sure how much more she could handle. All of the pain that she had walked through with Neils came flooding in on top of the latest tragedy.

Dugald had always been a stalwart for Johnetta. Nearly six years her elder they had spent so much time together over the early years playing in Scotland. The grand adventures that Dugald, Mary and Johnetta went on each year to explore the new farms that their father worked, brought memories flooding back. The times spent fishing in ponds, running through rolling fields thick with tall grass and the beautiful purple heather in bloom. Dugald was Mary and Johnetta's protector in those early carefree days. His genuine smile and quiet demeanor gave Johnetta confidence that life was going to work out, and was a window for the big picture.

When they moved to Utah, Johnetta had not known that Dugald was scheduled to go work on the Richie ranch. The day he left, she felt a huge loss. Her big brother was whisked away from her life. At nine, she remembered crying herself to sleep for days, confused by the sudden change. If that had been the only thing to change, things may have been a bit different. Losing Dugald that first time in 1910 was hard, then dad got sick and everything solid fell into a million tiny pieces.

All of those losses piled on top of each other for Johnetta the child. When she was two years old her parents had another son named Hector. He was the last of the Cameron clan. Near his second birthday he came down with a bad case of whooping cough and died a couple of weeks later. Johnetta remembered the tiny casket in their house and the sad gathering of family and friends. It would end up being a watershed moment for the little girl in her formative years. Many of the emotions that welled up inside of her when facing another death were directly related back to her experience with little baby Hector.

The infant's death impacted her parents in dramatic ways, throwing Margret into a tailspin for a couple of years. It made her willing to listen to a missionary from Utah speak about a fanciful new religion sweeping the globe that put her back in control of life. She put up no obstacles to the two older girls becoming involved. Her husband was suspicious from the beginning and told her on many occasions that she was still mourning Hector's passing. But in the end, Margret got her way.

With Dugald's passing Johnetta felt all of the misery together and added the years of living in Inkom, completed by the death of Neils, bringing the overwhelming saga down on her shoulders. Dugald's death prompted not only familiar feelings of loss and insecurity but an avalanche of depression. Life was too hard to handle. It was so devastating that she climbed inside of herself, erecting a large fortress in which to hide, and committed to remain secluded.

Snow fell and the cascading flakes were suspended on the cold mountain air that morning in the Midvale cemetery. The four Cameron girls gathered to bury their beloved brother. Maggie, Annie, Mary and Johnetta stood in foreboding. The Cameron clan had come together despite the statewide quarantine, to say fare thee well. A few other unfamiliar people gathered with them at the graveside to pay their respects to their friend, coworker and boss. Included in the small group was a limping private from the 26th Yankee Division.

From a distance, Annie noticed the man getting out of his car and looked over to Johnetta. Mary was between the two, so Annie nudged Mary with her elbow to get Johnetta's attention. When Johnetta looked up, Annie was pointing with her eyes to the man that was going to be officiating Dugalds funeral. Bishop Andersen made his grand entrance.

•

X.

'Hello Dolly'

"Hey Joe!" Called some of the waving neighborhood kids.

Joe responded to the calls of his admirers with a finger salute from just above his right eye. He headed out for a morning ride on his beloved Indian motorcycle as the v-twin thumped through the middle of their street baseball game. After another few blocks, he veered the bike south onto state highway 89, the main thoroughfare through Midvale. Joe longed for these days and was determined to take full advantage of the beautiful cloudless June morning with an adventure.

He decided the night before that he would head south to explore Utah Lake, wanting to take in the sights and ride the narrow road all the way around the popular destination. Life was too short, and he felt he needed to break out of his everyday rut. Joe had been working extra hours covering for other men for the last few months and knowing work began again at three o'clock he needed the get-away.

Just south of town the road became dusty and the Indian ran like a champ. Later, he was thankful for his goggles, while insects had hit him in the face riding near the water. His leather helmet was hot but still an improvement over the army helmet he wore a year ago. After being drafted and three months of training, June 12th was the day that he had shipped out to France. Having survived the ordeal, he needed a few hours alone to work through the emotions that kept boiling up.

Stopping at a roadside parking area near the western shore of the large lake he went down to the water. He took a little walk through the park that was covered with tall stately pine trees. His butt was sore from the forty mile ride and his legs needed stretching. A hundred feet into the woods, he unexpectedly became overcome with emotion. Whisked back to the war in France. His left eye began twitching from the renewed visitation of the suppressed feelings. Something about the sound of the breeze moving gently through the trees had triggered him back to the war. Faces of his dead friends came marching into his memory to the point that he had to press his back against a tree that was looking out over the water to maintain his balance.

With no other soul as far as he could see, on that Thursday morning, Joe finally let loose and wept over all of the crap he had witnessed in that damn war. Yes, he remembered telling Dugald that he had already turned the page on that part of his life, but sometimes the book is reopened on its own. The trauma was real and keeping it bottled up was not working. He had not slept well, since being back home as vivid dreams would wake him. His eye began to twitch whenever he thought back on the details of the war.

He was living with a couple of distant cousins from the old country and they would find him on the floor in the middle of the night screaming for guys to get their gas masks on. On another occasion his family shook him awake from a dream in which he was calling out Weasel's name at the top of his lungs, hiding beneath a blanket and covered in sweat. There was the time when he was stabbing his dream bayonet into his bed, killing another imaginary Hun. His plan to turn the page on that part of his life was faltering and he tried to attribute some of that to all of the hours that he was putting in, at the smelter.

Joe had been working so much to be able to send more money home to his mother and brother who had struggled through a long, tough winter. But the stress had been building, all the way back to his first action at St. Mihiel, then the utter brutality of the Argonne and all the way through the graveside funeral for Dugald, back in February. Since that time, he had tried to focus on his job to shake off all the death. That seemed to work, for a little while. Now the place deep in his heart, where he had pushed all of the horrors of war, was bursting at the seams, leaking into his life.

"God. Please help me," he prayed in desperation.

Now sitting on that sandy shore it felt as if some of the pressure began to miraculously unravel inside of him. He wept away the better part of an hour in complete isolation. He felt the hand of God restore his broken heart there at that lake. It had taken six long months after he had returned, before he felt like he could try to be himself again.

"Thank you Father," was his simple prayer from his renewed heart.

His mission took him to the opposite side of the lake into Provo to find a gas station so he could get back home and on with life.

•

"There she is, ladies and gentlemen, the birthday girl!" Annie was being ridiculous in front of a restaurant, half full of breakfast customers, who began clapping at the embarrassed young woman.

"How old is she?" Some guy asked from the back.

"Not old enough for you," was Marty's quick response to a hail of laughter.

"Hey, Johnetta, Happy Birthday kid!" Marty said with a large smile.

"Thanks, Marty," she said walking into the kitchen and out of the customers' sight.

That was how the day began for Johnetta. She volunteered to work on her eighteenth birthday for two reasons. First, she knew that she could play the birthday angle all day and her tips would be huge. Second, she knew that remaining home alone would not be good for her. The last few weeks her attitude had improved significantly; she was beginning to turn a corner. Today was her first day as an adult even though she had been dealing with so many adult situations over the last couple of years. It felt like some of the pain of the last year was beginning to subside.

"Happy Birthday, Johnetta!" Another said as they left a two dollar tip on the table.

"Thank you, see you next time!" She said after them.

"Hey, you are making a killing today," Annie whispered to her as they both waited at the kitchen service window.

"I know, I can't believe it!" She flashed a bright smile to her sister.

"It is good to see you smile, Jo Jo," Annie said.

"Thanks, it has been a good day, Sis," Johnetta said as she loaded her arms with a plated order.

After Johnetta delivered her order, she checked on other tables. Then, wiping down one in her area, she looked up as a silver Indian motorcycle thumped its way into the parking lot. The young man parked at the window in front of where Johnetta was finishing the set up of a four-seat dinner table. She was in fact watching the man and his motorcycle. As he turned his bike off, he stepped off and pulled it onto the kickstand. Stretching his back with his arms overhead, he growled out loud. Removing his goggles and leather helmet he placed them on the seat, raked his fingers through his thick curly hair and walked through Stella's door and into Johnetta's life. She had not taken her eyes off of him since he rolled up, and was the first one to eagerly meet him when he walked in.

"Hello, welcome to Stella's," she said, with a full smile and something going on in her belly.

"Afternoon," Joseph replied blind, while his eyes adjusted from the outside brightness.

"Just you today, Sir?"

"Yes, Miss," he said.

"Follow me," she said and turned toward a table in the unoccupied corner of the diner, in her area.

"So where are you riding in from on that two-wheeled beast?" She said with a smirk.

"France," he said slyly. Now that he could see his waitress he was taken, right away, by her bright blue eyes.

"Right. You drove that thing all the way across the pond?"

"No, you're right." He smiled, as he sat down.

"I was down at Utah Lake, have you ever been?"

"I have ridden past it a few times on the train down to Nephi," she said handing him a menu.

"What would you like to drink, Sir?" Asking him the standard question.

"Would you like to go?" He asked with a big grin.

"With you?"

"Sure, why not?"

"I don't even know your name," she blushed and tried to hide it.

"Joseph, pleased to make your acquaintance," he said as he stood and extended his hand.

"Johnetta," she said and took his strong calloused hand into her own and her heart skipped a beat, while she looked into his intense brown eyes.

"Can I still get breakfast, Johnetta?" He had placed his left hand on top of theirs.

"I, I can check for you, Joseph," she said, a little overwhelmed at the attention from such a handsome man.

"Thank you," he said, while removing his grip from her warm hands.

Flustered, Johnetta turned and left for the kitchen with a huge smile on her face. She made eyes at Annie to meet her at the service window just as soon as she could.

"Marty," Johnetta was whispering for Marty to come to the window, so she could be discrete.

"What's up?"

"I need you to do me a favor," she said.

"Okay, only because it's your birthday, what do you need?"

"Anything up to half of my kingdom?" He was smiling and spreading his hands like a king.

"I need you to make my customer breakfast,"

"WHAT? You're a real pain in my neck!" Marty was kidding.

"Sure, what do you need?"

"Not sure yet, I was checking with you first," she said.

"Let me know," Marty said, walking away back to his cooking serfdom.

"Who is the good looking guy?" Annie asked.

"Joseph!" Johnetta said with a little too much enthusiasm for Annie to believe, then walked back to her new favorite table.

"So Joseph, we can make you breakfast if you like," she said with full eye contact.

"Thank you," he said with a smile and started naming off his large order.

"Johnetta, could I get a coffee?" He asked a little quieter.

"Sure can," she whispered back.

Johnetta's other two tables cleared out after a few minutes and she made her way back toward Joseph who was smiling at her. She walked over to him with a smile of her own.

"So how long have you worked at Stella's, Johnetta?"

"About seven months now," she replied.

"Are you from around here?"

"I am now. My sister Annie works here too." She volunteered.

"What about you?"

"Yes, I live in Midvale but I was gone for a while," he said.

"You were in the war, weren't you?" She asked.

"Yes. How did you know that?"

"You said you came from France on your motorcycle," she smiled.

"Right. You listen well," he smiled back.

"So, do you and Annie live close by with your parents?"

"No. And yes," she chuckled.

"Annie and I live together about half a mile from here," She explained.

"But our mother lives up in Idaho."

"Oh," he said, finishing his meal.

"Johnetta, do you need anything?" Annie said while she walked over to check up on her and the handsome young man who had so engrossed her sister.

"Hi, I am Annie," she jumped in and introduced herself to Joseph.

"You two certainly are sisters," Joe said looking at them both.

"So Joseph lives here in Midvale," Johnetta said to Annie.

"Annie, order up," Marty shouted from the kitchen.

"Oh, gotta go," and she was off.

"So what do you do for a living Joseph?"

"I work at the smelter," he said.

"Oh just like half of the town," she quipped.

"Right."

"I have to take care of some other customers, do you need anything right now?"

"No thanks."

A few minutes later Johnetta migrated back into Joseph's orbit.

"I like talking with you, Johnetta," he started.

"So, would you like to go down to the lake with me sometime?" He said boldly.

"Yes, that sounds nice, but we're not going to take that, are we?" She smiled pointing at the motorbike.

"No, not the first time," he winked back.

"You think that there is going to be more than one date luv?" She shot a confident Scottish look his way, with one hand on her hip.

"One can only hope, Johnetta," he said with a smile and another long handshake.

"How about Saturday?"

"Well, I am not working Saturday, what time do you have in mind?"

"10."

"How about we meet here?" He offered.

•

"Morning Bishop."

"Bennie, come in, come in," he said with distracted aloofness. His impressive dark mahogany desk and high backed chair projected the proper amount of authority to all who dared enter.

"Have a seat," he opened his hand toward the chair on the opposite side of the massive desk. That guest chair was small and sat lower in the commanding presence of the Bishop. He had ordered the shorter seat on purpose, a few weeks earlier.

"Nice office. Looks like the promotion is doing quite well for you," Bennie said.

"How can I help you, Bennie?" The Ward Bishop loved the flattery, looking down from the perch of his new throne.

"I have some news regarding the Cameron girls sir," the large man said to his unofficial boss.

"Oh really?"

"Yes, sir. We now know that they are living together in Midvale, which was confirmed by another Bishop."

There was a long pause.

"Is there more?"

"We believe that they may be working at a local restaurant," he said with a bit of apprehension.

"That's it?" The Ward Bishop said with an air of annoyance.

"I saw them both arm in arm at their brothers funeral in Midvale cemetery back in February."

"Three and a half months later and that's all that you have come up with?"

"I wish I had been with you that day," Bennie said.

"Well you were taking care of your sick wife, Bennie. How is she?" Pausing for a moment of humanity.

"She is much better, Bishop, thank you for asking," he said, happy to break the tension.

"Plus we had those other three unfortunate ongoing investigations to handle this spring," Bennie pointed out.

"Yes, you are correct," Ward Bishop Andersen admitted.

"Now getting back to this Cameron project. I think that we need to pressure the oldest daughter Maggie and her husband Robbie Sagers. They will know where we can find them."

"Where does this Robbie Sagers live?" Bennie wrote a note in his little black book that he had removed from his jacket pocket.

"Ask my secretary on your way out. She should be able to find their address. You could accidentally bump into them after a Sunday service," he said, head spinning.

"So, Bishop, if you don't mind me asking, what is the reason for locating these two girls?"

"Let me remind you Bennie, these two have fallen away from the faith and their eternal soul is in jeopardy. I may be willing to have one of them relocated to another private location and under the proper tutelage, rescue their endangered soul."

"Oh, Okay. I thought that we were just going to do the normal apostate thing."

"Not yet Bernard," the Bishop had unwittingly let his anger seep out for an instant.

"Bennie, this is what your special team does. It helps wandering souls find their way home." said the back in control Bishop.

"People are calling us the hit squad," Bennie said bluntly.

"Who says that?" The Bishop was clenching his stomach muscles.

"Just a rumor that I heard through several people around town," he reported.

"That's nonsense Bennie. You are performing God's work. The work that you were called to do," the Bishop was raging inside but hid it well enough to convince the idiot in front of him.

"Now you are going to locate Robbie Sagers, so we can save those two wandering Cameron girls." The Bishop pointed to the door with his eyes and a wry smile.

"Yes, sir," Bennie replied, taking the familiar hint and made a beeline for the office door.

•

"Good morning Johnetta," said a smiling Joseph with a covered basket in his hand and the other hand behind his back.

"Good morning Joe," Johnetta replied with her own smile.

"Wait, can I call you Joe?"

"Sure," he said.

Joseph presented his date with a gift, a large white daisy.

"For you," he said and bowed.

"Thank you, that is very kind," she was blushing a bit.

"Do you have a pocket knife," she asked.

"Of course," Joe said and produced his trusty wooden handled folding knife.

"Thank you," she said, opening it and trimming the stem off halfway down. Johnetta slid the daisy in her hair just over her right ear and handed the closed knife back.

"It looks great," Joe said.

"So what's in the basket?" Johnetta asked.

"That is a secret for later," he smiled.

"Oh, Mr. Mysterious," she exclaimed.

"We have to get going, to catch the train," he said pointing the way toward the station.

"Okay, lets go."

"So, is Annie your only sister?" He asked to start the conversation as they walked away from Stella's. Annie watched from inside the restaurant window, waving and smiling for her little sister.

"No, I have two more all older than me,"

"What about you?"

"I have an older brother, John," he said stepping over a small branch.

"Any brothers?"

"Yes, but they both have passed," she said as emotionless as possible.

"I am sorry to hear that," he said.

"My father passed away over eight years ago, that was hard on my whole family," he continued.

"I don't think that my mother has ever gotten over it," he said walking next to her.

Joseph caught the slight scent of perfume.

"Lilac?" He wondered.

"So, where is your mom now?" she asked.

"She still lives in the family home back in the old country," Joe explained.

"Old country?" Johnetta was uncertain of the meaning.

"In Italy. We are from Italy," he confessed hoping that it would not be a deal breaker for her.

"Oh, that explains your dark complexion," she said smiling, and trying not to look into his captivating eyes.

"My father came over in 1890 to work at the smelter. We followed in 1902 and lived here until the judge closed the plants down. No work, so we went back home and back to farming. My dad returned in 1910 but got sick and came home the next year and died from black lung within a few weeks," Joseph felt like he was talking too much.

"How did your family come to Utah?" He asked.

"Well we came over from Scotland in 1910," she began and they turned the corner into the station.

"Two round trip tickets to Provo," Joseph told the man behind the counter.

"With what return date and time?"

"4 pm. Today, sir," Joseph said to the man with glasses, handing over the money.

The train was already waiting in the station when they stepped onto the boarding platform, so they found a seat in the first car and Joseph placed the basket on the floor by his feet.

"So, you are a Scot then?" He said playfully.

"Aye," she replied in Brogue and laughed.

"I used to work with a guy from Scotland. He was a good guy," Joseph mentioned.

"Where did you go when you arrived?"

"We rented a place east of here, and dad was to work in the smelter. I think he worked four days then he got sick,.... And he died a few weeks later," she admitted.

"Oh, my goodness," he said.

"That had to have been so hard for you?"

"It was the worst thing ever," she said.

"Then nine months later my mother got remarried to a man I could not stand and he moved us up to Idaho to start building his dream of a ranch."

"So you became a farmer?" Joe asked.

"It was the hardest work to build that farm up from nothing. We lived in a dirt house for over two years and Walter was always angry," she explained.

"But my sister Mary and I have many good memories of that place too."

"So you said that your dad died in 1911 when did you come back over?" she asked him.

"I came back in 1913 alone. I was nineteen and I stayed with some cousins in Midvale and got into the smelter right away because the guy hiring knew my dad," he explained.

"That makes you twenty five?" She was counting in her head.

"I will be twenty five in a few weeks," he said.

"How about you Johnetta? How old are you?"

"Well, on Thursday when some random stranger came roaring into my restaurant on a motorcycle, that was my birthday," she said a little sheepishly.

"Really?" Joseph asked.

"Yes. I turned eighteen," she said with eyes sparkling in the sunshine coming through the window.

"Happy Birthday Johnetta, I am sorry I missed it!" He said laughing.

"You didn't, silly," she said laughing in return, not confessing that meeting him was the best part of her day.

"June 12th was the day that I shipped over to France a year ago," he stated.

"Oh, last year?"

"Yes. On Thursday I was out celebrating living through that war," he explained.

"That must have been awful, the war I mean," she shuttered, as Neils entered her mind for the first time in a couple of days.

"That was the hardest thing that I have ever done," he said with a hint of pride.

"I bet you are glad that it is over," she said, changing the subject.

The talk went back and forth for the entire forty five minute ride down to Provo. Laughing and talking about friends, food and favorite places to visit. Joseph was heaping the charm on the pretty Scot. Telling funny stories from work and living with family for the last six years. When the train lurched into the Provo station, the faces of each of the two were sore from the constant smiling and laughing.

They had an unannounced guest, behind them by three rows, hiding in a newspaper, listening intently. Bennie decided that he would wait around until the four o'clock return trip to get more of the story, rather than follow the two through the streets of Provo.

The mile walk west down to the point on the northern side of Provo Bay in Utah Lake was filled with joy for both of them. Which was a first for each in a very long time, and time itself melted beneath the pressure of two young lives sharing their hearts. Nothing else in the entire universe mattered to either of them in those precious moments, on that day without a clock.

"So let's grab a place over here away from the others," Joseph said and moved north along the beach toting his basket. He kept walking for another ten minutes until he happened upon a secluded, sandy place surrounded by thick pine trees, looking west out onto the open water.

"How about this spot?" He asked.

Johnetta just sat down on what felt like enchanted sand.

"Perfect," she said while taking in the scene.

"I brought us some lunch from little Italy," he said.

"Wait! What? You ran all the way into Salt Lake this morning to get us food for our lunch?" Johnetta was astounded by the commitment.

"I went early on my bike," he said.

"For you."

"Wow!" she said.

"I wanted you to taste some real Italian food," he explained.

"Thank you, Joseph," she was even more impressed with her handsome Italian man.

Joe spread out a small blanket for the two of them and put the basket in the middle of the space.

"My lady," he said, offering her his hand to help her up. Johnetta moved over to the makeshift dining table.

"Today we go on a short tour of the tastes of Italy," he announced like a ringmaster in a circus.

"Thank you, sir," she said.

"First some cheese, Parmesan. Right from the old country," he cut her off a little corner of the small block.

"That is very good," she said, enjoying the moment.

"Now some olives," he presented his offering.

"I like the black ones," she said while trying to choke down the bitter green ones.

He laughed at the face she was making.

"Now, for the vino, a simple Lambrusco," he presented the small corked bottle.

"Are you trying to get me drunk?" She laughed, covering a growing nervousness since she had never tasted wine before, Italian or not.

He produced two small glasses from the basket along with a small loaf of crusty Italian bread. Popping the cork he poured each glass only halfway full.

Johnetta started to refuse the offer but decided to throw caution to the wind and took the glass from the charming man. Neils always focused only on the practical things, it seemed that Joseph was immersed in the details of each precious moment in life.

"To our beautiful beginning," Joseph said in a toast. They clinked glasses and Johnetta slammed the entire glass down in a single red faced gulp.

Joseph almost choked on his wine watching Johnetta's facial contortions. He began laughing out loud.

"Lambrusco is a sipping wine," he explained through his lingering laughter.

Johnetta was embarrassed by her own innocence.

"That was the first time I ever had any wine," she admitted to her escort.

"I am sorry for laughing, Johnetta. The face you made was priceless," he explained, not wanting to embarrass her.

The crusty bread followed then some cured Italian meats and to finish off the feast a Cannoli. They ate and talked and watched the small waves roll onto shore. Lying back on the blanket, the two of them tried to identify shapes in the puffy cumulus clouds that lumbered overhead in the blue sky.

"It haes bin a bonny day. Ta." Johnetta said to him while lying on her side and her hand holding up her head.

"Sei una bella donna," Joseph whispered back and touched her on the cheek.

"What did you say?" She asked tenderly.

"What did you say to me? He inquired.

"I said that it has been a beautiful day, thank you," she translated.

"Dugald used to say something like that," he thought out loud.

"Who?" She asked him to clarify what she thought she heard him say.

"My Scottish friend at work," he said a little puzzled.

Johnetta was dumbfounded with the thought and sat upright.

"His name was Dugald," he said, wondering about her sudden facial change.

"Was his last name Cameron?"

"Yes, how did you know that?" He said and sat up with her.

"He was my brother, Joseph," she said, now sad and amazed at the same time.

"I am so sorry. I didn't know."

"He was a good man and my boss."

"I met with him when I got back from the war and he worked with me, because I was wounded." Joseph explained.

"It was the flu," she said from the place in her own head.

"I had heard that. I even went to the graveside funeral. I already had survived the flu in France."

"You were at the cemetery?" Johnetta looked at him intently.

"Yes." He thought back to the scene.

"I must have been standing behind you and your sisters. The four of you were standing arm in arm."

Johnetta began to cry and Joseph felt awkward but settled on moving next to her and placing his arm around her shoulders.

"He was a good man, Johnetta," he whispered in her ear and let her cry.

"I didn't know that you were wounded," she asked while wiping the tears from her face a few moments later.

"Yes, I was shot by a German Aero Plane during the Argonne."

"Really?"

"Yes."

"How do you know what shot you?"

"The airplane was the only thing shooting at us at the time. I was running across an open field for cover at the edge of the woods when the German came over the trees and strafed the company of men I was with," he said, while staring back to France in a long pause.

"You are the first one I have told the details to," he whispered.

Johnetta burst into tears again, this time with both hands up to her face and leaned over on the blanket.

"What is it Johnetta?"

"Did I say something?" Joe was confused. He took a chance and put his hand on her shoulder again.

"Are you okay?"

"If I said yes, would you believe me?" She said, sat back upright and tried to regain her composure through humor.

Joseph did not know how to answer or what to say.

"I have to tell you something Joseph, but I am afraid that you will be disappointed with me," she said.

"Okay," he said in a confused reply.

"I was married to a man that was killed in France," Johnetta waited with tears falling on her shirt.

"I am so sorry to hear that, Johnetta," he began reliving some of the losses he had experienced.

"I lost so many friends over there," he said, with a somber recollection.

After a long pause he looked up at her again.

"Do you know where?" He asked her.

"A place called Chateau Thierry on July 18th."

Reaching back in time he was unsure if he should tell her what he knew.

"My unit went through there a couple of days after the fight. It was brutal." He decided to just be as honest as he could be.

"I am sorry, Johnetta."

She cried more now. A few minutes later she wiped her tears and looked at him.

"One hell of a first date," she said and laughed.

They both laughed for a few moments, then laid back to watch more clouds float over them.

"How did you do that Joseph?"

"Do what?" He asked.

"Face all of that danger, all of that death?" She asked.

"I was afraid all of the time and I prayed more than I ever have," he said.

"Do you think God heard you?"

"Yes. Absolutely. He saw me through that whole war."

"How do you know that?" Johnetta was unconvinced.

"The constant chaos required it."

"The amount of ordinance flying by your head, bullets hitting at your feet, pinging your helmet. The gas attacks, trenches, mortars, artillery, charging Germans. There were a million ways to die everyday, all within an inch of you. The bullet that hit my leg went through both sides of my gas mask that was strapped on near my stomach, before entering my leg. An inch right and it would have shattered my femur and I would have probably died from infection. An inch left and it would have hit my artery and I would have bled out in five minutes."

Johnetta reached down and took his hand into her own.

"Thank you for being so brave," she said while looking at the side of his face.

A tear dropped from his left eye, rolling down his cheek and onto the blanket.

"I never felt brave, Johnetta," he admitted, turning his head to look at her.

"But you were so brave, Joseph," she insisted.

Silence dominated for a few beautiful minutes as the two held hands on their own private beach.

"I think we missed our train," she said as her stomach jumped with laughter at the thought. He joined into the humor.

"Do you care?" He asked.

"Not even a little," she said.

"So what did you say to me in Italian?" She smiled at him.

"Sei una bella donna," he said.

"What does it mean?

"You are a beautiful woman," he said, gripping her hand a little tighter.

•

"Bennie, you lost them?"

"Again?" Andersen was incredulous.

"I know that they bought a return ticket to Midvale for four o'clock and they never showed up, boss," he insisted.

"You stay at that train station all night if you have to! Do you understand me?"

"Yes, sir," Bennie said and hung up feeling even more inadequate than when he had phoned.

"Thanks," he said to the station employee who allowed him to make the call. Of course it was only after he had flashed his Ward Bishop Special Services identification badge.

"Is there anywhere to eat around here?" Bennie asked the ticket guy through the little window.

"Two blocks east there are a few places over there."

"Thanks."

"Hey, when does the last train come through heading north?"

"Ten o'clock."

"Thanks Buddy."

•

The next few weeks the two were inseparable. If Johnetta was working when Joseph was out he was eating at the diner. If Johnetta was home when Joe was working then she was talking about him to Annie, Mary and anyone else that would listen. At first, Annie loved the fact that her sister was moving on from all of the recent death that had infected her life. Then, after a few weeks of hearing about nothing but Joe, Joe, Joe, Annie began to get somewhat jealous. With that emotion wearing on her, she called Maggie one morning, when Johnetta was already at work to chat.

Needless to say, Maggie was not impressed in the least to hear that her sister was dating a Roman Catholic. Maggie knew that she needed to intervene for her sister's spiritual well being. Robbie was informed over dinner that evening of Johnetta's deteriorating condition. Margret was concerned that Johnetta would walk away from her solid Mormon upbringing and become a Catholic. Robbie in his usual calm demeanor reminded Maggie that she had not talked to Johnetta yet, and to not put the cart before the horse. When she met with Johnetta, and found out the truth from her lips, then she could warn her sister, not before, he said.

Maggie went the very next day to Midvale and just happened to stop into Stella's for a late lunch with all of her children.

"Jo Jo!" The three ran to their favorite aunt when they saw her.

"Dorthy! Verne and Ella!"

"What a great surprise!" Johnetta was trying to hug all of them at the same time.

"Hi Maggie!"

"Hey, Jo Jo, can we eat lunch at your restaurant today?" Dorthy asked seriously.

"Why, yes, you may!" Jo Jo answered and picked her up off the floor.

"My shift is over in fifteen minutes, Maggie, what great timing!"

Johnetta sat her family at a table for six and promised to join them in a few minutes. She had a couple of customers to take care of first.

"Hey it's Aunt Annie!" Five and a half year old Verne announced to the table.

"Hi guys! Did you come all the way down the mountain to have lunch with us today?"

Annie knew why Maggie arrived and regretted the decision to call her earlier.

After all of the small talk diminished, and the two aunts joined the table, Maggie did not hesitate.

"A little birdie told me that Johnetta has a new friend!" she said.

"Johnetta has lots of friends, little birdie," Johnetta said to Maggie but glared at Annie, knowing why Maggie suddenly showed up for lunch.

"What's his name?"

"Joseph. He is extremely handsome, charming and a gentleman on top of it."

"He is a Veteran. He was wounded in the war," Johnetta was trying to impress her sister.

Maggie recognized that there was a glimmer in Johnetta's eye when she described the man and her heart sank.

"Where does he work?"

"At the smelter like half of the city," she said.

"He actually works in the lab and Dugald used to be his boss."

"No kidding?" Maggie was surprised by that information.

"Yes, he even came to Dugald's graveside ceremony."

"He did?"

"Yes, he said he stood behind us during the entire service," Johnetta happily reported.

"That was very thoughtful of him," Maggie admitted, wondering if the man may be willing to convert.

"He is very thoughtful," Johnetta agreed.

"Is he a Godly man, Johnetta?"

"Ah, we have gotten to the crux of the matter, the entire reason for Maggie's visit," Johnetta thought.

"Very," is all that she could come up with in the moment.

Maggie was a bit annoyed with her baby sister's answer.

"It was shallow and immature," she thought but resisted the urge to speak.

"He told me some of his experience during the war and how he knew that it was only through God's guiding hand that he made it out alive," Johnetta said.

"Really?" Maggie questioned.

"He told me that it was a miracle that he didn't die when he was shot by the German airplane."

"How does one know what shoots you when a battle is raging all around?"

"Joseph said that the airplane was the only thing shooting at him at the time."

"Sounds like quite the story, Johnetta," Maggie was patronizing the eighteen year old now.

"How old is this Joseph?"

"He is the same age as Neils!" Johnetta was now becoming weary of the inquisition.

"But is he one of us?" Maggie insisted, in her older-sister pretending-to-be-mother, voice.

"What are you asking?"

"Is he a Latter Day Saint, Johnetta?"

"No! Most definitely not!"

"That should make you really think, young lady!" Maggie barked louder than what she intended.

"I think he makes me happy," Johnetta said and left the table.

"Her bishop is not going to be happy about her insolence," Maggie told a stunned Annie.

"You are going to tell her Bishop?"

"It is for her own good Annie!"

"Because she isn't marching in lockstep with you?" Annie was raising her voice now.

"This has nothing to do with me, Annie!" Maggie snapped.

"I wish that I would have never told you any of this Margret," Annie used their mothers name.

"While I am down here I think you need to hear about the condition of your heart too, Annie."

"How long has it been since you have been in church? Since you've tithed?"

"And you are going to tell me about my heart?" Annie was half standing glaring at her arrogant sister.

"Go climb back up to your damn mountain, Maggie!" Annie said and stomped off to find Johnetta.

"Annie! The children!" Maggie was insulted.

"Good bye, kids," she said over her shoulder.

•

XI.

'Love To Death'

"Johnetta! You look lovely, dear," Martina smiled.

"Thank you, Martina," Johnetta said rather shyly, the two shared an embrace with an extra squeeze.

"How was your trip down?" Andy asked and joined the hug.

"It was fine," she said.

"I want to introduce you to my friend, Joseph. He took the day off to escort me on the trip," Johnetta said to her former in-laws.

"Mr. Skeem, Mrs. Skeem," Joseph said and he firmly shook their hands and smiled with admiration.

"Joseph is a Veteran and he was wounded in the war," she was proud of her man.

"Thank you, Joseph, for serving," Andy said and shook his hand again.

Martina wiped a tear and tried to smile.

"He also was in Chateau Thierry the day after Neils was, ah.."

Both of Neils' parents began to cry.

"I am sorry Joseph, I don't know where I keep finding these tears," Andy said, trying to hold them back.

Johnetta and Martina were embracing each other.

"No need to apologize to me, I am sorry for the loss of your son," Joseph said, maintaining his composure.

"It looked like it was a brutal battle on the part of the front where Neils fought." Joseph said further.

"So the memorial is done now?" Johnetta asked, to break some of the tension.

"Let's go have a look together," Martina said and started moving, holding Johnetta's hand, with Andy and Joseph bringing up the rear.

"So what Division did you serve with, Joseph?" Andy was trying to think of something else.

"The Yankee Division, Sir, 101st Infantry," Joe responded.

"And your son?" Joseph knew that talking about his fellow fallen soldier would honor both the man and his parents.

"He served in the Ivy Division, in the 58th Infantry," Andy said proudly.

"You were wounded?" Andy asked.

"Yes, Sir," He began, then told the story of his miracle to his girlfriend's former father in law while they strolled down the narrow lane through the Nephi Cemetery. Martina was in front of them but listened intently as the story unfolded. When they arrived at the new twelve foot tall monolith, dedicated to the five young men from the area that gave their lives in the service of their country during the Great War, a silence descended. They studied the stone carvings of doughboys. One for each of the fallen soldiers and a central plaque with the names of the dead.

There he was, 'Private Neils Skeem, 58 Inf. Chateau Thierry, France. 18-7-1918.' Martina stepped forward and ran her fingers through the carving of her son's name, like she was reaching out through death's veil, and wiping the hair from his forehead or caressing his childhood face. Andy was, by her side, silent for the next few minutes. They were both unsure as to how they had survived the tortuous year, and a renewed sense of loss washed over them. Johnetta stood a step behind and was crying along with them. Joseph was trying to maintain his composure and stood next to Johnetta.

"Okay," she nodded to Joseph.

"Mr and Mrs. Skeem we brought some flowers to lay here. If you would like to have the honor," Johnetta said to them in hushed tones.

Martina and Andy both looked at each other for the briefest of moments.

"Joseph, would you do the honor?"

"Yes, Sir."

Joseph snapped to attention as the other three stepped aside. Placing the bouquet at the foot of the monument then regaining his rigid spine, he carefully lifted his right hand in salute to his comrade and held it for a ten count. Returning the salute he lifted his right foot just enough to spin on it and his left heel at the same time, slapped his feet together and made one stride away.

Andy, Martina, Johnetta and a few onlookers were captivated by Joseph's maneuver that he had obviously done a million times in the Army.

"Thank you for honoring our son today," Martina said and kissed Joseph on the cheek. Andy shook Joseph's hand and the group departed together.

Andy wanted to ask Joe questions about the trenches, tanks, planes and even tactics. It turned out he had spent the last year reading up on the war and the role the Americans played in it. He was curious about the different battles and situations the Yanks found themselves in, during the fighting. Joseph answered every question to the best of his ability, while they walked.

Through that time they spent together that afternoon Andy's broken heart began to mend. Not that the pain would ever go away, but now at least, he felt that he understood it a little better.

"Thank you, Johnetta, for bringing Joseph with you, it meant so much to be able to talk with a man who lived through the war," Andy said.
"It was very nice to meet you. You have found yourself a good woman, Joseph. Take good care of her."
"I will, Sir," Joseph nodded.

"Thank you so much!" Martina wrapped her arms around Joseph and kissed him on the cheek.

"Thank you for making Johnetta happy again," she whispered into his ear and walked away crying.

•

"Who is this Joseph character?" Andersen was intense.

"I haven't looked into him, yet," Bennie added.

"Why not?"

"He wasn't even on the scene a few weeks ago now he is hanging around the youngest sister all of the time."

"Well, find out who this malcontent is!"

"I am running out of patience on this investigation," the Bishop said while dropping his pen and reclining back into his throne with both hands to his face rubbing his eyes.

"We now know where she works and it shouldn't take too much time to figure out where this guy is from. He rides an Indian motorcycle around town," Bennie stated.

"If he is L.D.S. then it could complicate matters," Andersen said from his deep thoughts.

"How so?"

"We can't justify putting an end to the problem as easily, especially if he is connected," Andersen was looking at Bennie again.

"He looks like he may be Italian or something," Bennie reported.

"That could make him a Catholic," the Bishop was thinking that little tidbit through.

"Then, he could be prosecuted as a spiritual hindrance," Bennie said.

"Yes, there have been a few of those types in the past," the more hopeful Bishop responded.

"If he is one of us then we will have to make sure he is in proper standing with his Bishop and not a reprobate of his own measure," Andersen continued his train of thought.

"We could just run him out of the girls lives," Bennie implied a good beating may be in Joseph's future.

"Once we remove the Italian guy from the scene we will make a move on the Cameron's."

"Assuming he is not too connected," Bennie stated.

"Right."

"Which sister?"

"The younger."

"Okay, you are the boss."

"Get on it." Bennie left the plush office, gently closing the door on his way out.

"I am going to finally have that girl!" The sadistic Bishop was thrilled at the prospect.

•

"Hey, little lady!" Joseph said to the surprised Johnetta, coming out of her apartment door.

"You scared the crap out of me!" Johnetta gasped.

"I'm sorry, I didn't mean to startle you!" Joseph felt a little guilty at the prospect.

"Good morning, Mr," Johnetta snipped, happy to see him.

"Did you just get out of work?" Noticing his grubby appearance.

"Yes, I volunteered to cover for someone out sick," he said.

"You worked sixteen hours and came over here, just to see me?" Johnetta drew close.

"Of course I did," he said and kissed her on the lips.

"I missed you," she said as they embraced.

"All the way since yesterday's lunch," she said and kissed him again.

"Do you want a ride to work?" He was smiling at the offer of a ride on the back of his Indian.

"Sure," she said, much to his surprise.

"Really?"

"I trust you Joseph," she was looking into his eyes.

"Let me start it up, then you climb on back and hang on."

As they pulled out onto the side street Joe noticed a familiar green car.

"Where have I seen that car?" He thought while zipping past it's windows.

"I have seen that guy before, too," he said in his brain without turning his head.

His Army situational awareness training kicked in, as he glanced around to see if there were any others.

"Hang on tight!" He yelled against the wind. Johnetta pressed her head against his back to shield herself from the wind. In two minutes they pulled into Stella's parking area.

"That was crazy!" Johnetta said as she dismounted the beast, smiling.

"Crazy fast!" He replied with a grin.

"I gotta go," She said then kissed him and walked to the door.

Joseph was a bit surprised by the kiss out in front of the restaurant for everyone to see. Now he turned and pulled near the street and waited for a moment. He was looking north to see if the green car was in sight. He would need to find out if they were following him or Johnetta.

"There it was!" His heart jumped in his chest.

"Okay buddy," he said to himself, "let's play."

Joseph pulled out onto the street in front of the green car by half a block and watched him in his mirror. The car rolled past the restaurant and kept pace behind the Indian. Joseph knew what he had to do and sped up. A few miles down the road, he signalled with his left arm that he was going to turn left. He turned hard, after a car passed and accelerated. Mr. Green Car did the same.

"The wild goose chase is on," he thought and smiled at the game. He was going in the opposite direction of his house hoping the guy did not know where he lived.

He thought about the fact that he was not carrying a gun, knowing he needed one in this situation.

"Who is this clown following me?" He asked himself, becoming nervous.

Joseph's only plan was to lure him away from Johnetta and to not give away the location of his house, so they would have a fall back position, if necessary. How he was going to lose his tail would take some figuring. Then, he saw the long ore train heading south and his plan appeared in front of him.

He let off of the throttle and began to slow to stop before the tracks. Joseph rolled to a stop and placed one foot on the ground. The man in the green car pulled in behind the Indian as the train's horn pierced the air, announcing it's arrival at the intersection. Joseph's left eye twitched in anticipation.

At the last possible second, Joe gunned his bike, dumped the clutch and raced across the track in front of the train. The man in the car was caught and slammed his steering wheel in frustration. Joseph smiled, looking back at the scene through his mirror, knowing that he had gotten the best of the man that time, but worried for Johnetta and Annie. He needed a plan and a place to hide his motorcycle.

•

"Of course the move was deliberate, you idiot!" the Bishop was fuming through his telephone at his incompetent buffoon.

"Okay, now what do you want me to do?"

"Stake out the diner and grab him there," he said red faced.

"Yes, Sir."

"Take some help along!"

"I will get a couple of the boys to help," he said.

"Good."

"What if he doesn't show up?" Bennie asked.

"He doesn't appear to be a coward, I think he will show up to protect his girlfriend," Andersen reasoned.

"We will get this taken care of boss man," Bennie said and hung up before he was insulted again.

An hour and a half later two cars rolled into Stella's parking lot and backed into a couple of spaces that were the farthest away from the building. Four large armed men waited in the cars with an unobstructed view of the front entrance. Watching the movements of the staff inside through field glasses and waiting for Joseph, the Italian, to appear on his motorcycle.

•

"Thank you for keeping us safe Joseph," Annie said as she brought her large bag in through the front door of the apartment.
"Look at that! Your Indian is inside your house!" Annie said with surprise.
"This is the first time since winter," he said with a smile.
"Come in, Johnetta," Joe said, grabbing for her bag of clothes. He leaned his new Browning semi-automatic shotgun against the wall right next to the door and took the bag.
"Come in, come in," he said.
"Annie, Johnetta, these are my cousins Dominic and Felix," Joe said, and greetings were exchanged.
"You two girls are going to be in the bedroom in the back of the house and I will sleep here on the davenport," Joseph was directing all of the pieces of the plan into place.

After fifteen minutes of the girls settling in, Johnetta made her way to her boyfriend who was sitting on the couch with the shotgun close by while tinkering on his bike.

"Hey you," she said and sat down next to him.
"Bella donna," he said with a smile and they kissed.
"Thanks for keeping us safe Joseph," Johnetta said with her forehead touching his.

"I don't know how dangerous the guy is, and he knows where you live," Joe said.

"That is the reason I bought the Browning today," he said, nodding to the new shotgun.

"Where we used to live," she corrected him.

"Right," Joseph said.

"We will start looking for another place tomorrow," Johnetta reassured him.

"What about another job?" He asked.

"We don't know about that yet. We will have to see if they showed up after you picked us up," she said, trying to be cautious, but not frightened.

Annie joined the two love birds in the sitting room.

"Felix loves to cook and plans on making dinner tonight," Joseph said.

"Thanks, you guys," She was appreciative.

"You haven't had his cooking yet," Dominic said with a laugh.

"I can tell that you two are related," Annie said.

"Just by their laugh," Johnetta finished.

"Right!" Annie smiled.

"So, Joseph, what do you think we ought to do now?" Annie asked the veteran.

"We don't know what this unknown man's intentions are. I need to find that out."

"How are you going to find that out?" Johnetta asked.

"We have the advantage now," Joseph said.

"How so?" Annie asked.

"This guy in the green car has only seen us. As far as I know, he has never seen Felix or Dominic so they are going to be our spies that will feed us intelligence," Joseph explained to the captive crowd.

"That is an advantage," Annie agreed.

"We need to find out as much as we can about him and what he is doing watching us." He continued.

"Then we can decide how to respond."

"I told Marty that I would come back after the restaurant closes and talk to him," Joseph said.

•

"Hey Walter, it's Marty calling."

"Marty how are you doing? Not having trouble with my girls are you?" He asked and laughed.

"The girls are fine," Marty said.

Margret was listening in, right next to Walter in fact, and was relieved to hear the good news.

"But there is someone I am nervous about," Marty said.

"Not this new boyfriend is it?" Walter asked.

"Joe? No, are you kidding? Joe is a good guy. No need to worry about him."

"Then who?"

"There is a guy nosing around Annie and Johnetta's place. Joe spotted him in a green car and he followed them here. Then he was following Joseph on his motorcycle."

"What?"

"Joe came and got the girls out of work early and took them to his place after getting some of their things."

"Why would he do that?"

"Because he was nervous that the green car guy was up to no good."

"Okay,"

"Turns out he was right. The green car thug came with three more guys back to the diner and waited in the parking lot until almost closing time."

"Really?"

"Yeah. They came in and ordered dinner and asked my waitress fifty questions about Johnetta, Annie and Joseph." Marty said.

"No kidding?"

"It's not the police is it?" Walter wondered.

"They never said they were the Police, Walter," he said.

"I think that they need some help," Marty said.

"I will be on the first train down."

After the conversation was over between the two men Margret was chomping at the bit.

"I am going with you," She insisted.

"No, Margret you are not coming along."
"This could be dangerous and having you there will not help me keep those girls safe."

•

"I love you, Joseph Jacobucci," Johnetta whispered from beneath the blanket on the floor with her lover sleeping next to her.
Joseph turned over and looked into her beautiful blue eyes. Her face was glowing even in the early morning light, which made his heart dance.
"I love you Johnetta Whitelaw Cameron. Ever since the first time I laid eyes on you in Stella's restaurant," Joseph said and kissed her.

The passion between them returned, all inhibitions were set aside.
"You are the most handsome man I have ever seen," she said to him between kisses.
They were both hoping no one, in the house, would wake early and walk into the room.
"You make me so happy," she whispered in his ear.

•

Western Union Telegram.
5-8-1919
To: Mr. Joseph Jacobucci
32 West Maple Avenue, Midvale, Utah, U.S.A.

From Giovanni Jacobucci
Spinete, Compobasso, Molise, Italy
Joseph, mother is very ill. Stop.
Doesn't have long to live. Stop.
Please come home now. Stop. End.

•

The news that came that Saturday morning was a tragic surprise for all three of the Italians in that Midvale home. Having just cleaned up from breakfast the little cohort was making plans to expose Mr. Green's intentions. Mr. Green was the name given to the mysterious man who drove the green vehicle and was assigned, by committee during the course of the discussion, right when the first knock came.

"Someone is at the door!" Felix whispered to the group gathered at the table, with his hands thrust outward.

Joseph moved and grabbed the shotgun from its perch leaning against the wall and clicked the safety off. He motioned for the girls to move to the rear of the house, then he took up a firing position, next to the door, as Felix answered.

"Who is it?" Felix asked through the wooden barrier.

"Western Union," said the voice in response.

Felix ripped open the door and stepped to the side all in one motion.

The poor western Union employee almost wet his pants as he looked into a pair of intense brown eyes behind a shotgun pointed at his head. Neither of Joseph's eyes twitched.

"What do you want?" His voice was as intense as his eyes, trigger finger at the ready.

"I just have a telegram!" said the terrified man, trying to do his job.

"Put it down and back off of the porch," instructed Joseph, who did not lower his weapon an inch.

"Okay. Okay. Don't shoot me!" The man's voice cracked under the strain.

Joseph nodded for Felix to retrieve the yellow letter. The Western Union man ran off in a panic toward his truck.

Joseph's foundation was shattered to the core with the news of his mother's illness.

Johnetta came from the back bedroom at the cry, and drew close to him.

"I am so sorry, Joseph," Johnetta whispered.

Marty walked across the gravel lot, with a pie in his hand, toward the green car. The vehicle had returned the next morning.

"Persistent bastards," Marty said under his breath, while maintaining his half smile. What the two men in the car could not see was Marty's Colt .45 1911 tucked in his belt.

"Morning gentlemen," Marty in his white apron said while leaning forward.

"I thought that you might like some chocolate pie, while you wait," he said. Both men glared at him.

At that moment, Walter stepped out from the patch of thick pine trees behind the car and knocked on the passenger window with his .44 revolver, much to the surprise of the two occupants.

Marty dropped the pie when both men reacted to the metallic knocking and drew down on the driver with his .45.

"Easy now, boys," Marty said. He reached in and felt for the drivers gun and found it holstered beneath his left arm inside of his shirt.

Walter yanked open the door and put his gun in the face of the startled second man.

"Now you two have got some explaining to do," Walter said.

"We don't know nothin," the second man shot back and Walter grabbed the man's hair at the top of his head and pulled him out of the car. During his fall toward the gravel Walter's knee smashed the man's nose flat against his face. He felt it snap under the pressure and put an exclamation point on the entire morning with a blow to the back of the man's head with the handle of his .44. He was out cold.

Walter drug the man's limp body back into the pines, searched, located and confiscated his pistol for his own use, then kicked him square in the ribs with his cowboy boots. Something snapped inside the man's unprotected body. Walter tied him up to the tree with a rope from his pocket and stuffed a rag down his throat.

Returning, from hiding the man, he climbed into the rear seat of the car. He pressed the six inch barrel against contestant number one's head.

"Come on, Marty," Walter said.

"Start the car, we are going for a little drive," Walter said while Marty closed the passenger door.

"You guys don't know how big of a mess that you are getting yourself into," Bennie said to his new passengers.

"And neither do you." Walter said from the back.

They had the man drive west for over an hour.

"I think they call this the Great Salt Lake Desert Marty," Walter said. Marty just smiled.

"Pull over mister," Marty said.

The man skidded to a stop on the side of the dusty road.

"Turn off the engine."

"Marty, get out, and cover him," Walter instructed.

"Right," Marty took up his position outside of the man's door with his gun leveled in his chest.

Walter got out of the back and told the man to get out.

"Take off your boots," Walter said.

"What?"

"Take off your boots," Walter said again.

Bennie was getting nervous now, so he kicked off his boots toward the front of the car.

The white sand was already getting hot in the late morning sun.

"Now the socks."

Bennie complied.

Walter gathered them all up and tossed them into the car.

"Now I am going to ask you a couple of questions and I need you to be honest with me," Walter was nose to nose with the man.

"Okay," the barefoot man replied while on the inside he was seething.

"What were you doing watching the restaurant?" Marty asked real slow.

"What are you talking about? I was waiting for a friend," Bennie bluffed.

Walter slammed his boot down onto the man's toes, breaking a couple.

"Ahh," Bennie crumpled to the ground in excruciating pain grabbing his foot.

"You, sir, are not being honest."

"Who were you watching?" Another slow deliberate question.

"No one!"

A swift kick to the ribs brought a low grunt from the man.

"I ask you again, who were you watching?"

"Alright, alright, it is the little Italian kid on the motorcycle," he said hoping to satisfy them with as little information as possible.

"Give me your wallet," Walter insisted.

The man threw it out on the ground, not wanting to have any more ribs bruised. Walter picked it up and tossed it to Marty.

Marty shuffled through the thick black wallet, pausing to read a few different things.

"Bennie here is part of the Ward Bishop special services division," Marty said.

"The Kill Squad?"

"Are you part of the Kill Squad?" Walter directed the question to the man on the ground, who offered no response.

Another kick to the ribs and a punch to the man's head brought more groans.

"You better hope I never find you mister, I will kill you." Bennie threatened Walter.

"What did the Ward Bishop want with that kid?"

Walter was not in the mood to wait for answers. He knew that this was probably the guy who did-in Pete. A few fists and a couple kicks made the man a little more receptive to a discussion.

"The Bishops thinks that the little wop is leading some people astray from the faith and wanted me to send him a message. That's all it is," Bennie was as convincing as he could muster.

"Who is he leading astray?"

"The Cameron girls," the man admitted.

Walter and Marty drove back to the restaurant alone. Thinking that Bennie would have a long hobbled walk from the middle of nowhere before anyone would find out, as long as the guy in the pine tree had not gotten away that is.

Upon returning they found number two still tied up. They ushered him into the back of the car and drove southeast and dropped him off down a little two track road out past Heber City. He was also without boots or socks.

•

"I need to get a passport," Joseph explained to the woman, at the desk.
"I have an emergency, is there any way to get one today?"
"Usually, it takes four to six weeks," She began to say. Joseph cut her off.
"My mom is dying and I need to get to her," he trailed off.
"There are expedited passports that you will have to be interviewed for,"
"Okay, anything," Joseph said with wide eyes.
"The earliest appointment I have is tomorrow at ten," she was reading from a large scheduling calendar.
"Yes, of course."
"Here is a list of the items that you will need to bring with you. And here is the application form."
"Your name?" She asked, pencil ready.
"Joseph J-a-c-o-b-u-c-c-i," he said.
"Alright Joseph, we will see you in the morning and I am sorry to hear about your mother," She said with an affirming smile.
"Thank you Ma'am."

Joseph knew that his next stop needed to be at Stella's. He was driving Felix's well used Model T and planned to pull around back to speak to Marty. Joseph wanted to make sure that the girls had a safe place to live while he was gone. The trip would take about six weeks, he figured fifteen days each way and ten days at home. He was hoping ten days at home would be enough. He was struggling with the thought of his mother's death. "She's not dead yet," he told himself and drove on.

The next three weeks went by like a blur for Joseph. Securing the time off of work, train tickets, passage on an ocean liner. He bought the expensive Stand-By return tickets because he needed to be flexible. They found a discrete little place for the girls to live up in Millcreek and new jobs, not in restaurants. They got settled and Joe left them the Browning, after taking them out to shoot it for themselves. Marty had not seen the two thugs around Stella's anymore, even though he had bought a Browning for his own little welcoming committee, if they should ever bother to reappear.

Joseph was torn between two worlds as he held Johnetta. He didn't want to leave her with the recent trouble. Yet his mother needed him home.

"I am sorry that I have to leave you," he said into her ear.

"You need to be with your mom, Joseph," Johnetta was reassuring him even though inside she wanted to hold him forever.

"We will be fine, don't worry about us Camerons!" Johnetta smiled.

He left through the door without looking back.

•

"Bennie! You look awful, where have you been?" The surprised Bishop came down from his throne to shake the limping man's hand.

"Hello Bishop," he said without showing any emotion.

"Someone jumped me and Peewee at Stella's. Took us from behind and knocked us around."

"Next thing I know and I'm getting the crap kicked out of me out in the desert," Bennie had rehearsed that story for some time.

"The desert?"

"Yes. I had no idea where I was. They took my boots and socks. Had a couple of broken toes and ribs. My face was pounded to a pulp," he weaved the tale with just enough fiction to veil his true intentions.

"Then what happened? You've been gone for four weeks Bennie."

"Well, I couldn't walk very well, and not at all during the day," he explained.

"About the third day, an old Mexican farmer picked me up off the side of the road and took me home on his mule," he said with just enough emotion to be convincing.

"So where is Peewee?" Andersen asked.

"No idea," Bennie said as he sat down. Andersen moved back to his perch on the other side of the desk.

"Who did this to you? I know you have to have some ideas rolling around in that head of yours."

"I wish I knew, boss," he said.

"So how did you get back?"

"The old farmer fixed me up. Then he walked to a neighbor who was twenty miles away and had them give me a ride into Spanish Folk, in a wagon," he said, then looked up. "The ride alone took three days," he finished the tale.

"Quite the story Bennie. Quite the story indeed," Andersen said and was only a bit suspicious considering the man before him looked like half of the mercenary he employed.

"Any news on the Cameron investigation?" Bennie knew that he needed to appear to be concerned about the things that interested his boss.

"They have vanished, along with the Italian."

"What? How is that possible?"

"I think they headed out of the area. Just got on a train and left," He was motioning with his hands as he spoke about his loss.

"What about the sister in Tooele?"

"I will have you pay them a visit," he said reasserting his control.

"I want to do some checking around for Peewee too." Bennie said knowing that he was going to use that search as a cover to find out about Marty and his little helper.

•

"Girls!" Walter was banging on Annie and Johnetta's front door.

The door swung wide open and Annie was staring down the barrel of the Browning pointing at the surprised step dad.

"Walter!"

"You scared the crap out of us!" Johnetta said angrily.

"I am sorry, there was no other way," he said walking into the house and closing the door.

"No other way, I could have killed you!" Annie was furious.

"Listen, you girls have to pack your stuff, we are moving."

"What?

"Why?" Johnetta followed up.

"We have to be quiet and get moving, the short story is," he paused and even choked up a little.

"Walter, what is it?"

"Marty and Stella were found dead and the restaurant was burned to the ground," he peered at the two.

"You have got to be kidding!"

"Oh my God! No!" Annie said.

"Listen girls, we can talk about it on the ride out of town, but it is not safe. That you are here so close to the Temp..," he stopped himself, not wanting any neighbors to hear.

"You cannot stay here," he said flatly.

The two girls were immobilized by the shock of the news. The pair were more than just a boss they were like family.

"Do you know what happened?"

"We can talk about it during the ride," Walter insisted and began to collect their belongings.

"You will have to mourn later, go now and gather your things."

Within two hours the three of them were on the road east crawling up a mountain pass in the sturdy work truck. Walter had somehow been able to borrow the vehicle from the railroad yard in Pocatello, for the midnight move. The women left their large davenport in the abandoned apartment. It was just too big and heavy for the three of them to move. They were able to get everything else into the truck.

"You guys are going to live with Mary over in Roosevelt for a while," Walter said.

"I didn't want anyone overhearing where I was taking you."

"I cannot believe this is happening." Annie said.

"What is going on? Why is this happening?" Johnetta was demanding answers.

"Marty called me and wanted to scare off the people that were watching you and following Joe," he explained.

"What did you do?"

"We met the guys in the parking lot the morning after the incident. They had returned and were staking out Stella's again."

"Marty and I, we roughed them up and dropped them off out in the desert to give you time to get resettled and out of sight," Walter said.

"What do you mean you roughed them up?" Annie fired back.

"Let's say that we made it hard for them to return to their jobs for a few days."

"But they did return Walter and they killed them!!!"

"I know," he said.

"Do you remember Pocatello Pete?"

"Wasn't he found dead?"

"Yes, but not from his criminal enterprise," Walter said.

"You mean the moonshine he was selling you?" Johnetta said coldly.

"Yes Johnetta, the moonshine," he admitted.

"Pete was an old friend of mine and he was the victim of a ritual killing."

"Do you know what those are?"

"Yes."

"I believe the same squad just killed Marty and Stella," he lamented.

"Why? Pete I could somewhat understand, but Stella?"

"Or Marty? He was the nicest man," Annie began crying.

"I think that it was revenge for what we had done. I am sure they were trying to get out of him who I was," he said.

"Did he tell them?" Johnetta wanted to know.

"Never," Walter insisted.

"He would never rat me out to them."

"So, we are moving because if they were willing to kill Marty and poor Stella, they won't stop until they find us."

"I don't think that they are looking for you, I think they have something against your boyfriend," Walter said.

"We move you out to Mary's and do not join the church out in Roosevelt. Use your married names because they know the Cameron name."

"Is Roosevelt far enough away?" Annie asked.

"I believe it is, it's over a hundred miles," Walter said and looked at both of them to reassure them.

"Don't tell John what really happened. Tell him your boyfriend is abusive or something," Walter said.

Johnetta glared back at the irony in the statement and decided to leave it alone, for now.

•

Western Union Telegram.

14-9-1919

To: Miss Johnetta Whitelaw Cameron

67 South Street Apartment B, Millcreek, Utah, U.S.A.

From Guiseppi Jacobucci

Napoli, Campania, Italy

Arrived Naples. Stop.

Home with mom tomorrow. Stop.

Miss you already. Stop. End.

Undeliverable. Residence abandoned.

•

"Thank you, Mary for letting us stay here," Annie said to her sleepy sister, whom she was hugging.

"Anything for you two!" She said and yawned with a full gaping mouth.

"I am going to make some tea for us!" Mary announced.

"Then you can tell me all about it." And she walked away to the kitchen and it's wood stove.

Johnetta was watching through a window as Walter and John unloaded the rest of the furniture into the barn. A dust devil twirled by to greet the newcomers. It had been a long and stressful night driving through the mountains of north east Utah. This place was a high dusty desert town named after Teddy the former President. A farming boom was taking hold and John planted alfalfa for the previous two years with much success. Mary and John married almost a year earlier but did not seem to be getting along. The old farmhouse that John inherited from his parents was large enough to accommodate the sisters and more helping hands around the farm was welcomed by both of them.

"So what is going on?" Mary asked the pair to explain.

A month later, the routine of farm living was once again part of Johnetta's life. With the routine, it had become easy for the old familiar feelings to return. The fighting in the homestead was not Walter and Margret, as it had been so many years before, with her and Mary gathering around the fire each evening in Idaho. Now the rancor was between Mary and John, as their marital bliss had evaporated after a few weeks, beyond the honeymoon. Annie and Johnetta were now the ones huddling for evening talk time after long days of hard farm work.

Annie noticed Johnetta becoming more distant.

"How urr ye daein' Johnetta?" Annie asked her little sister.

"A'm 'ere," she responded in the old familiar.

"This whole arrangement makes me feel just like I did in Inkom, hopeless," She admitted.

"Do you think Joseph has returned yet?"

"I don't know," she began to cry.

"How will he ever find me out here, Annie?"

"I don't know. I guess I haven't considered that."

"Everyone that we were connected by is gone," she pointed out.

"Even Stella's," Annie contributed.

"He probably has moved on, anyway," Johnetta said.

"No way, that guy loves you," Annie asserted.

"He won't anymore," Johnetta mumbled.

"What, like he went home and stayed for some Italian girl?"

"I have thought about that," she admitted.

"He loves you Johnetta," Annie said.

"That is sure to be over now, Annie!" Johnetta voiced.

"What are you talking about? His mother is sick so it could take some time, Johnetta," Annie insisted.

"I am pregnant."

•

XII.
'Buried Treasure'

"Momma, I am home!" Exhausted Joseph was whispering in his mother's ear.

"Momma, I came back to see you, and you waited for me!" Joseph could not hold back his tears any longer and laid his head down on her bed.

"Figlio mio! Finalmente sei tornato da me!" She said in her raspy voice.

"Oh, Momma!"

"Yes, I have come back!"

"Let me have a look at you, my son!"

"You are a beautiful man, Giuseppi! Just look at you!"

"No longer a boy, now you are a man!"

"Look at you!"

"Figlio mio!"

"I have missed you so," she insisted.

"Thank you for working so hard and sending all of the gifts that you do. It means so much to all of us!"

"I am so proud of you," she was caressing his face as she poured out her heart.

"I am so proud of you. Figlio mio!"

"Momma, I have missed you terribly," he said after composing himself enough to be able to speak while hugging the frail woman all over again.

"You are so strong you might break me in half," she cherished the ache.

'Tell me about the war, my American hero," she said smiling.

"Where did you get shot?"

"In the leg, Momma. It was a miracle that it was not any worse," he said to her, not wanting to give too many details.

"I was praying for you all of the time, my boy. Every minute of every single day."

"Thank you Momma, God rescued me, every single day."

"I knew that he would answer my prayers for my son."

"He did, Momma. He did."

"He chose you before the foundations of the world were set to be his very own in Christ," she proclaimed over her son as she had done so many years before.

"Yes Momma, I am his very own creation."

"Momma, what did the Doctor tell you?"

"The Doctors, they know nothing!" She proclaimed.

"Now, that sounds like my Momma!" Joseph said with a big smile.

"They say that I don't have too much longer to live, Giuseppi. But they don't know. God knows. Only God knows when he will bring me home to be with Padre," she said with a glint in her eye.

"Why, Momma, why? You are still so young."

"I am tired, Joseph. So many years without my Benny has made me tired and lonely."

"I die from a broken heart," she proclaimed.

"Now you can stay around. I am home."

"How long are you staying?"

"Don't worry Mother, I am here right now," he said.

"Giovanni said that you have found a girl!"

"Yes Momma, she is a beautiful girl," he had a sparkle when he spoke about Johnetta.

"Is she an Italian girl, Joseph?"

"She is an American girl Momma," he declared.

"Okay, but where was her family from?"

"You forget Joseph, I am an American too!" She said with pride, pointing to her tattered little flag on the window ledge.

"Her family came from Scotland," he said.

"Is she good to you?"

"Yes, Momma, she is very good to me," he said.

"What is her name?"

"Johnetta Whitelaw Cameron."

"That is a good strong name," she thought and said.

"I am going to ask her to marry me when I go back, Momma," he spoke his desire out loud for the first time and hearing it made it more certain in his heart.

"You are a good man Joseph and you will make a good husband to her."

"You bring her here for a visit? I want to meet my new daughter."

"Yes, Momma, of course."

•

"Just what in the Devil were you thinking?" Bishop Andersen was enraged at Bennie again.

"What do you mean sir?"

"You killed those two and torched that restaurant!"

"I know you did it. Your bloody hands are all over this."

"Now the chief of police is up in arms. He says that you guys in the 'hit squad' are out of control and he doesn't know how much longer he can cover for senseless acts like this!" The Bishop used finger quotes around the acrimonious title.

"I cannot confirm or deny the allegations, Bishop," Bennie mentioned the quote out of habit.

"I taught you to say that, you nincompoop!"

"I would think that whoever did this thing may have been searching for information that could help in an ongoing investigation," he stated.

"You would think," with that the Bishop returned to his seat and flipped his pen onto the top of the pile of papers on his desk. Looking at the man for a few minutes he was trying to ascertain his real motives.

"This was a simple payback, wasn't it?"

"Some might say that it was so," Bennie was not advanced in the art of nuance.

"You have said so," the Bishop was correcting the man.

"What?"

"You are trying to quote the Bible," Andersen just shook his head.

"Forget it. You are an idiot."

"So what have we learned about the Cameron's and this Italian kid?"

"Not one thing."

"Did you drop in on the Sager's?"

"Yes, and they don't know where they are either."

"Okay. That is hard to believe."

"I think that they are being honest, sir."

"Alright, I guess that I will have to trust your judgement."

"We have so much more to get done, Bennie."

"On to other cases then?"

"For now."

•

"Mother?"

"Mary, is that you?"

"Hello!"

"Yes, Mary. I can hear you."

"Mother, you should visit. You need to visit."

"What?"

"Come alone."

•

Margret Whitelaw Cameron was not feeling well on the morning of the train ride south from Pocatello. She had been under the weather for a few months and felt like it was something more serious. She was tired all of the time and had little ambition for anything more than caring for seven year old Ethel and her husband Walter. Getting on the train alone taxed her both physically and mentally, but her girls needed her and she would do anything for them. Traveling alone was one thing, but she was attempting to journey almost three hundred miles from home, without being noticed.

Walter had insisted on silence from everyone in the family, so as not to imperil them with knowledge. Innocence cannot be faked for long, by anyone, was his reasoning, making ignorance a superior position. Walter had a knack for the underhanded and illegal, much to Margret's regret. This time however, his gift was beneficial to her precious offspring.

Margret remained on the commuter train all the way to Nephi, where Gordon Skeem picked her up and drove her through the mountains, over to Roosevelt and dropped her off at a park for children. That move gave Gordon plausible deniability. Mary came to the playground and picked Margret up in their old truck. It was an exhausting day for everyone concerned.

After the eleven hour adventure, Margret waited on a small bench for Mary, just yards from a swing set. A truck pulled up with both Mary and Annie aboard.

"Mother!" Annie said jumping down from the faded blue vehicle.
"Annie!" Margret was struggling to get her tired body up from the stiff wooden bench. After the embrace Mary joined in, for her hug.
"Can we talk to you for a few minutes, before we get back to the farm?" Annie asked.
"Why certainly, you can speak to me wherever you need mah Lassie!"
Annie glanced around before she began. As the oldest she was selected to break the horrible news. She needed to be brave.

"It's about Johnetta," she paused.
"What about Johnetta?" Margret was going into momma bear mode.

"Well, she is having a hard time."

"Okay... With Joseph being away?" Margret asked.

"Yes, that too," Annie was afraid to utter the words.

"Annie Cameron, I am tired, just spit it out!"

Annie drew in a long breath and Margret held hers.

"Mother, Johnetta is pregnant."

The raw ugly news hit Margret hard in her empty stomach and she sat down.

"Oh Johnetta, whit hae ye dane?" Margret began to moan.

Both girls sat down, one on each side, comforting their diminished mother.

"Is it Joseph?" Margret finally asked, glancing up at Annie.

"Yes."

"She loves that man."

"Johnetta is so full of shame right now that she is saying that she doesn't want to see him anymore."

"Well, what kind of man is he Annie?"

"Joseph is a kind man. I know that he loves Johnetta."

"Well, he should have respected her as well!" Margret was angry.

"It was both of them, Mother."

"I know it was."

"I just wished she had done it the proper way." Margret lamented.

"And so does she," Mary said with her hand on her mother's shoulder.

"We thought that you should hear the news from us, before Johnetta tells you."

"Does she know that I am coming?"

"No. We were afraid that she might walk off, like she did before." Annie said.

"She is not in a good place, Mother." Mary added.

"Well, she does have a history of doing that, doesn't she?" Margret was thinking out loud.

"Joseph's not a Mormon is he?"

"No."

"All the more reason she must remain hidden. We don't need them to make an example out of her."

"We agree."

"An out of wedlock pregnancy with an outsider, makes one a prime candidate to be made an example. They would want to make her pay for their sins."

"Especially after what those animals did to Marty and Stella," Annie added.

Silence reigned for a good long time while some children played in the background, reminding the women of a better time.

"Well, I guess the exciting part is another little grand baby to care for," Margret was grasping for hope and for grace.

•

"Mother, you are out of your bed!" Giovanni could not believe his eyes.

"Yes, I have a guest," she said with a confident smile.

"Momma, I am hardly a guest," Joseph said while he ate more of his breakfast.

"Your brother worries too much," Maria said to Joseph.

"Momma, you haven't been out of your bed in a week," John exclaimed while embracing her from the side.

"I think that I would like to take a bath today," she was requesting warm water.

"Okay, we can do that!" John made a face of wonder at his little brother.

"So how is Utah?" Maria turned to Joseph, wanting an update on the place she lived for five years.

"Utah is good. It is growing so much since you have been there. The smog is almost all gone now with only one smelter running, so the farmers are happy."

"So, you can actually see the mountains?" Maria was laughing.

"Yes!"

"Tell me about your Johnetta," she asked.

"I brought a picture of her and two of her sisters," he said moving toward his travel bag.

"Wonderful."

"I knew that you would ask to see her," he replied, finding the photo.

"Here she is Momma, she is the one on the right. Mary is seated on the left and Annie is standing behind them both."

"Beautiful! They sure look like sisters!" Maria was smiling.

"That is so true," Joseph showed Johnny the photo next.

"Very pretty, what is she doing with you?" John was smiling at his kid brother.

"You haven't lost your sense of humor, brother!"

"You've been losing your hair though!" Joseph was laughing now.

Joseph wanted to wrestle around with his brother, but John wasn't having any of it, perhaps because little Joseph was now much thicker than John.

"I am so blessed to have both of my sons near me," Maria said to herself and to Jesus.

•

"Johnetta, my love!" Margret began crying.

"Mother. Mother, I am so sorry that I have disappointed you again," Johnetta was crying as well.

"This is a difficult time for you," she said looking into her eyes.

"Tell me about your Joseph."

"He is a good man, Mother."

"Does he know about the baby?"

"No. He left for Italy before I even knew. His mother is dying," Johnetta explained.

"Is he ever coming back?" Margret was letting worry win for a brief instant.

"Mother, he is a good man. I know that he is coming back because he bought a Stand-By return passage," Johnetta said.

"I just don't think that I should tell him about the baby."

"Why in the world not?"

"Would he feel like he was stuck with me for the rest of his life? And all of the responsibility of raising a child."

"I am afraid that he would just run away from me," Johnetta admitted.

"He is not that kind of man, Johnetta," Annie said, joining the conversation.

"Plus he is responsible for his actions," Mary chimed in.

"He moved you two out of Midvale when he thought you were in danger."

"You are just afraid, Johnetta," Margret said.

"I am afraid of what he will think of me. I am afraid that he would hate me or leave me. Fear follows me everywhere I go, Mother."

"Do you love him?" Margret asked.

"Yes. More than anyone I have ever known."

"Then you must tell him."

•

Maria rallied during Joseph's visit. The time that she spent with her son was a soothing balm for her soul. She decided that leaving him while he was in Italy would be a waste of their precious time together. They spent many hours talking about memories, life, dreams and even regrets. They marvelled at all of the conversations the walls of that old house had witnessed. The years of laughter, hordes of people, times of celebration and tears.

Maria held her boys up on pedestals, like all Italian mothers, and she saw hers' as a connection to the future. The investment of her life's work; raising her boys into good men, was worth all of the years of effort and struggle in her mind. Maria would have gladly given a hundred lifetimes to fulfill that holy calling, but she only had the one to offer and God had made it more than adequate.

The time for Joseph to depart arrived too rapidly for Maria. Her mother's instinct sought to protect her sons from the inevitability of her demise. During her entire life she had acted as a shield to them, a protector. The boys had a difficult time without their father's presence for most of their childhood and Maria wanted to do everything within her power to counteract that negative force, but that time had long passed. She was coming to her end on this earth and she needed to be at peace. Rare is the gift that she had received. To be able to look both of her children in the eye and say without regret, that she had fought the fight, finished the race and kept the faith.

"Joseph, come here," Maria called from her place sitting up in her bed.

"Yes, Momma, what is it?"

"Sit down next to me," she said while patting the old mattress.

"Okay," he was a little puzzled.

"You have to leave tomorrow, no?"

"Yes, I have stayed longer than my boss wanted me to," he said.

"You need to go, my son."

"I give you my blessing."

"I don't want to leave you," he said to her.

"Momma, I don't want our visit to end," he was tearing up.

"I know Joseph, but you have to go on with your life," in her mind she spoke the final word.

"Go and marry young Johnetta. Start a family," she smiled through a portal of time, seeing his future before he could.

"I don't know if she is ready to be married again," Joe said.

"God has a plan, my son. Trust him. Johnetta will be ready in his time."

She held onto his hands, feeling the pulse through his veins knowing that this entire life had been a gift to her and she was eternally grateful.

"Maybe you'll have a little girl one day and you can name her after me," she was chuckling at the thought of a little baby girl.

"If we do, I will, Momma. I will name her after you."

"Look at me Joseph." She took his face in her hands.

"God has blessed me with you, always remember that."

"You have shown me the love of God all of my life," Joseph said in tears.

"You are a good man and God will take care of you when I go home."

"Travel well."

Joseph held his mother and Maria kissed him a few dozen more times before she fell off to sleep.

•

"You have to remain in hiding, Johnetta," Margret said with a short cough.

"At least until Joseph comes home and makes this right," she said while clearing her throat.

"If he even wants to," Johnetta said below her breath, from her place of despair.

"Walter says that these men, who were watching you, are paid killers," Margret said.

"Paid for by the Mormon Church," Mary proclaimed.

"They can get away with anything in this state," Annie chimed in.

"How does Walter know?" Johnetta asked.

"Lets just say that Marty and Walter paid them a little visit to try and convince them to move along."

"Then they killed Marty and Stella in retribution?"

"We don't know who did that," Margret said.

"What about Walter? Is he next?" Annie wanted to know.

"That means that you are in danger too, Mother!" Mary proclaimed.

"No. Listen, Walter said that the men did not know who he was and his name was never mentioned. He felt that if they knew who he was they would have already made their statement."

"What did they do to those men?" Johnetta asked.

"He said that they didn't kill them, just taught them a lesson." Margret reported.

"I have already said too much, it is better if you don't know anything."

"The plausible deniability," Mary said, thinking out loud.

The weight of the conversation hung heavy in the air of the farm house.

"How will Joseph even know where we are?" Annie asked the obvious question.

"You're right Annie! Everyone that connected the two of them has died, or is in hiding," Mary pointed out while making eyes toward Johnetta.

"I do want him to find me, but I could never risk his life to do it. I feel trapped," Johnetta was distraught over the entire situation.

"Give him some credit, he survived the Great War, I think he is smart enough to fight his way through this," Mary said.

"I know the men that execute people in the name of religion must be ruthless killers and Joseph isn't a murderer," Johnetta said.

"No one is suggesting he is, Johnetta," Annie said to reassure her.

"Pregnancy is just making me crazy!" Johnetta exclaimed.

Her sympathetic sisters laughed at the proclamation.

"It will certainly do that my dear," Margret said as the bright morning sun broke over the mountains and flooded into the room.

"Mother you don't look so well," Annie noticed in the early morning light.

"Are you feeling alright?"

"I have been feeling a bit off, as of late," she admitted.

"You should lie down and rest from your travels," Mary said to her.

"I am just so happy to be here visiting with three of my darling girls."

"Yes, we remember the old Scottish saying, mother," Annie, the eldest daughter in the room acknowledged.

"Be happy while you're living for you're a long time dead!" They all repeated it.

•

"Joseph! You have returned," Dominic said, welcoming his cousin.

"How is your mother?"

"It was a good visit, she was up eating and laughing the entire time," he reported with a travel weary smile.

"We have some disturbing news, Joseph," Felix piped up.

"What is it?"

"Where is Johnetta?"

"Sit down Joseph."

"After you left for the old country, Stella's was burned to the ground."

"Marty and Stella both died in the fire."

"What?"

"You have got to be joking, right?" Joseph's eyes grew wide.

"Where is Johnetta?" He was determined to know.

"We drove up to their apartment the day after the fire just to check on them like you said to do," Felix said and looked down at the floor.

"What?" Joseph was standing now eyeing his Indian still in the living room.

"The place is abandoned Joseph," Dominic said.

"What happened to them?"

"We don't know. No one knows where they went. All of their belongings and the two girls just vanished. Poof! Into thin air in the middle of the night."

"I have to go see for myself," he said walking over to the motorcycle.

"Joseph, won't they be watching for you?" Felix warned.

"I don't care!"

"Why didn't you contact me?" He demanded from his roommates.

"We didn't want to worry you Joseph."

"I went home to say farewell to my mother and now I have come back here to lose my lover as well?"

"Take Felix's car," Dominic pleaded.

Joseph would have none of it. Dragging the motorcycle outside through the front door it fired on the first kick. Joe put his goggles and helmet on as it warmed in the waning light of the late October sky. He had traveled seventeen days to get home to his new life and now it felt like it was falling apart in front of his eyes. Anger spurred on by exhaustion pushed him all the way to the abandoned Millcreek apartment. Despair was waiting for his embrace.

•

Western Union Telegram.
3-11-1919
To: Mr. Joseph Jacobucci
32 West Maple Avenue, Midvale, Utah, U.S.A.

From Giovanni Jacobucci
Spinete, Compobasso, Molise, Italy
Momma left for home on All Saints Day. Stop.
It was peaceful in her sleep. Stop.
I am coming over soon. Need Work. Stop.

•

The news was too much for Joseph. He sat down and cried right in the middle of the sitting room of their crappy little house. Darkness tore at his heart. He felt that now both his past and his future was lost. On some levels, he was prepared for his mother's inevitable departure, but he was not at all prepared for the apparent loss of Johnetta.

Events merged like the massive hurricane that had hit the Florida Keys at the beginning of his final journey to Italy. It ravaged Florida, the gulf coast and Texas before dying out, over New Mexico and southern Utah.

This storm in Joseph's heart was raging and appeared not to have an end. Everywhere he searched, he came to another dead end. The more recent attempts rested on his ability to find Johnetta's sister who lived up in Tooele. He knew her maiden name was Maggie Cameron but few women are known by their maiden names. Her married name remained a mystery. Over the course of a week he asked around the smelter and the thousands of people that worked there, if they knew anything about Dugald's family. The dead ends were driving him mad.

He even went so far as to search the newspapers' obituaries, in the library, for the seven weeks that he had been away. Nothing, thank God. There was, however, a long story about the suspicious fire at Stella's, but few clues.

That morning's telegram had come and put him on the couch in a desperate state. Curling up under a blanket he soon fell asleep and into a dreamworld. He was ushered back to the war in France, lying in the bottom of a filthy trench with blue chlorine gas all around him. He was talking with Weasel about dying and neither of the armed men wore a mask. Many strange people made their way past them in the trench waving as they traveled. His father walked by, passing without a word. Some Germans that he had killed slushed through, dragging their rifles. Then a few of the men from Company D told him to get up and get back into the fight, then they ran off.

Weasel was resting his back against the wall of sandbags just listening to Joseph ramble on about nothing coherent. Looking closer, Weasel's face was detached from his skull. Joseph's mother entered the trench and rubbed his hair on the top of his helmet-less head. She dropped some bread into his lap and left, skipping like a schoolgirl. Then Johnetta appeared walking toward him for a few steps and instantly vanished, which pushed Joseph out of his dream world; sweating on the floor of his home.

By the middle of December, Joseph still had not found Johnetta and was growing despondent. He had lost weight and often neglected even routine hygiene. Everything was consumed with finding his lost lover. Nothing else mattered. His work suffered in the process. He missed days without excuse or concern. He pushed his boss to the edge of tolerance, in spite of his recent plight.

"Pull yourself together," were words said to him on more than one occasion.

Relief came for Joe's desperate heart when his big brother showed up at the Midvale house. The reunion was sweet, feeling to Joseph like a victory in a long trail of defeat. To celebrate John's arrival, the four members of the house took Felix's car up to Salt Lake to visit a western part of the city referred to by locals as 'Little Italy.' A few Italian restaurants on the same stretch of road had garnered the name. Knowing the popular destination well, they parked a block south, away from the congested streets and walked over to their favorite place.

As the four jovial men were seated at a table over in the corner of the dimly lit diner, an adjacent table took a keen interest in the group. One of the men in particular looked familiar to the duo from the Bishop Special Services group.

"I knew it was just a matter of time and you would come back to me, Joseph," Bennie smiled wide at the gift God had granted him. He contemplated that dessert had been served, a lucious ending to a bitter story.

•

Johnetta's fear was renewed and compounded with the news in her mother's recent letter. The note was tucked into a larger envelope addressed to John and Mary. Using the legitimate address, Walter was driving the twenty miles over to American Falls just to mail the monthly correspondence, to avoid any notice and possibilities of giving away the girls' location.

Johnetta read the small letter while touching her growing belly. She felt life move around inside of her for a couple of weeks and was even more committed to remaining hidden for the safety of her child. Margret had warned them not to have any contact with Maggie because someone was nosing around, trying to get a read on where the girls were held up. Maggie was in on the scheme and was not going to let the man anywhere close to her sisters. She did not like the situation in which Joseph and Johnetta found themselves, but would never give them up to the secret ritual group. Johnetta was thankful. She feared that her mother was not feeling any better since her long journey back in September, and wondered how forthright she was being in the correspondence.

Her heart longed to hear from Joseph and wished there was a way to send him a signal of her whereabouts. Fear countered her longings and she kept out of sight from the entire world as winter progressed.

•

The meal had proved to be fantastic as the men shared loud and long over a few bottles of wine and several courses of dinner. The food was top notch, even for the men straight from the old country because the cooks were the real deal.

"It is good Giovanni that you have come to America again," Felix said lifting his glass. "Salute!"

"It has been a difficult couple of years for farming," John admitted to the men.

"It seems like the ground is all used up," he continued.

"Let it rest, Johnny," Dominic said, repeating old farmer wisdom.

"How was mother's passing?" Joseph had been waiting all evening to ask his brother.

"You know, brother, she so enjoyed your visit. She talked non-stop about it for the next few weeks, then she was ready to leave. Like she had decided to stay for you and made up her mind to be finished," he said somberly.

"Joseph, before she died she told me not to ring the bell for her."

"Why would she say such a thing Johnny?"

"She wanted us to ring the bell together," he said.

"She made me promise, Joseph."

"Don't ring the bell for me until my son comes home again."

•

XIII.

'Running Rabbit'

"Joe, did you notice the two guys sitting across from us?" John said to his brother on the way out of Antonio's Italian Eatery.

"The big guys."

"No, why?"

"They were behind you watching every move we made and I think they were trying to hear us."

"Where are they?" Joe turned around to have a look through the glass.

"Johnny show me."

"They were sitting right by us," John said while trying to locate them through the dimly lit diner window.

"I don't see them!"

"You meatballs looking for somebody?" Bennie was walking up the sidewalk toward the group of four Italian men.

The four fanned out in response to the perceived threat from the two thugs.

"What do you want?" Joseph asked the larger of the two men.

"Well, Joseph, we want to talk to you for a few minutes, that's all," Bennie said with both of his hands spread open.

"How do you know my name?" Joe shot back.

"That's not important right now. What I need is for you to come with me," he said.

"You're dreaming if you think that I'm going anywhere with you."

"Well, I have to say that I am a little disappointed by your attitude," Bennie cracked.

"You are that son-of-a-bitch who burnt down Stella's, aren't you?" Joe guessed.

"I don't have any knowledge about that," Bennie lied, but slowed his approach.

"You look like the creep that was stalking a couple of girls I know."

"In the green car?"

Bennie opened his coat just enough to reveal his gun in it's holster.

"You two-bit punks are going to shoot us here on a crowded street," Joseph spoke loudly enough to be heard by others, and heads turned. He was challenging the man to his face. He lived through enough death already in his short life and was not going to be intimidated by this guy.

John, Felix and Dominic were shaking.

"Let's ditch these losers," Joe said and the four of them turned and ran.

"Don't run to the car yet," Joseph said in Italian and a low enough voice not to be overheard by their pursuers.

"We are going to try to out flank them," Joe said.

Bennie and his large partner took off running after the men, knocking a few others out of the way. They knew they were not going to catch anyone with speed they did not possess.

"Get the car," Bennie barked and the other thug broke away and crossed the street.

The four men split into two groups and went in opposite directions.

Bennie did not know which group to follow, so he circled back toward the car, as well.

"One day, Joseph! One day we will meet again real soon!" Bennie called out through his panting breath.

•

"Hey, Robbie, how are you doing?" Bennie reached out his hand and grabbed the shift leaders hand in greeting.

"Hello, Bennie. Surprised to see you here in the smelter," Robbie said in all honesty.

"Well, as it turns out I know lots of the guys around here, Robbie," he smiled.

"Imagine that. Small world I guess," Robbie said nonchalantly.

"Any word on your wife's missing sisters?" Bennie was pressing. Robbie sensed it.

"Strangest thing, my wife is distraught about the whole situation," Robbie was embellishing his wife's reaction, just a bit.

"Any idea who an Italian guy named Joe would be? I know that he works here."

"Are you serious? An Italian guy named Joe is like half of the Italians guys that work here," Robbie said with a smile.

"I imagine that you are right," Bennie admitted, not allowing his internal frustration to leak out.

"I will talk to you later Bennie," he said.

"Okay, Robbie, thanks,"

·

Robbie walked into the lab, in mid February during the afternoon shift, he stayed over, since he was a day shift supervisor. He was searching for a motor man named Joseph. He asked his friend Larry if he knew a guy that fit the description.

"That's gotta be Bush-man," he responded over the noise of the shop.

"Was he wounded in the war in France?"

"Yes."

"Where is he now?" Robbie asked.

"I think he is working in the back today," Larry said, sensing that it was important.

"Do you want me to get him for you, Robbie?"

"Yes. Send him into the lab office," the taller man said.

"Will do," Larry turned and left to find the Bush man.

Five minutes later Joseph Jacobucci walked wide-eyed into Dugald's old office looking for someone named Robbie. He had not been inside the office since his last meeting with Dugald.

"Robbie?" He gently knocked on the inner office door.

"Are you Robbie? Larry sent me up. He said that you wanted to see me?"

"Shut the door please," the tall thin Robbie Sagers said.

"Okay," Joe was wondering if this was due to his crappy work record as of late. The last thing he needed was to lose his job. He shut the door behind him.

"Have a seat, Joe," he said.

"I have something to tell you that cannot be repeated."

This opening statement got Joseph's attention.

"I'm listening."

"I hear that you fought in France?"

"Yes, a lot of people did."

"You are right, there was almost thirty from the smelter alone," he said.

"My brother in law was killed over there."

"I am sorry to hear that, Sir. Too many good men didn't make it home from that war."

Robbie paused for a few moments just looking at the young man before him.

"I think you knew him, Joe," Robbie said.

"Really?"

"His name was Neils Skeem," Robbie said.

Joe stood up.

"Neils Skeem was your brother in law?" Joe asked.

"Yes. My wife Margret, who is known as Maggie has a sister, Johnetta, who married Neils at the beginning of the war," he stated plainly.

"Do you know where your sister in law is right now, Robbie?" Joseph asked, looking the man squarely in the eye.

"Why would you want that information, Joe?"

"Because, I love her and have been looking for her for months."

"What do you mean?"

"At the end of August I went home to Italy, my mother was on her deathbed and when I returned Johnetta was nowhere to be found. I have searched everywhere, for four months, and I still cannot find her."

"Please tell me where I can find her," the young man was desperate.

"Sit down, Joseph," Robbie said.

"Johnetta is in hiding. I personally don't know where she is, but I can send you to a place that could help you, if you are the right Joe that is."

"I am the right Joe. I will do anything to find her, Robbie," he said.

•

"Any news on the Joe front?" Andersen asked his subordinate.

"It won't be long, he works at the smelter and it's just a matter of time now."

"Have you alerted management?"

"I have personally talked to almost every manager in the plant," Bennie reported.

"Good."

"I am going to get this arrogant little meatball, if it's the last thing I do, sir."

"Well, he is only half of the issue, right?"

"Yes, and the other half has been silent for months. Not a peep. Even the girl's oldest sister has no clue where they have gotten off to," Bennie said with confidence.

"So strange," the Bishop said while another thought hit him.

"Now that you mention it, I think that there were four Cameron girls, Bennie, not three," he said like a light switch had been flipped on.

"Maggie, Annie and Johnetta are all that I know about, boss."

"There was a fourth. Older than Johnetta but younger than the other two," he was racking his brain now, trying to look back into his Inkom days.

"She had a funny name, if I remember," it was on the tip of his tongue.

"Mary Robina! That's it! I remember that she didn't much like me and was often sassy."

"I bet if you find her, you will find the rest of the clan," the Bishop was impressed with himself once again. He looked at Bennie and smiled with his sardonic edge.

•

"Joe, you need to make a trip to Pocatello and look up someone named Adamson. He lives by the old schoolhouse on the east side of the city, Elm Street," Robbie had said the night before.

Joe drove Felix's car all the way north to the Pocatello city limits. When he drove over the rough set of railroad tracks, his rear tire exploded and the car came to a grinding halt. Joseph had to strong arm the little car around the corner onto a local neighborhood on a street with no name.

Flat tires were not uncommon, for anyone that owned a vehicle. Joe had repaired many of them over the years. The spare tire was on the back of this car and was without the one thing most needed in a spare tire, air. Joe had to decide if the tire or the information about Johnetta was more important.

"Not even close," Joe said to himself and walked down the cold avenue without a marker. He was hoping to find someone outside that he could ask about the Adamson home.

Near the end of the block a little girl was out playing in the snow making an ice man out of large rolled balls of wet snow.

"Excuse me," Joe said.

"Yes?"

"I am looking for Adamson's place. Do you know where they live?"

The girl ran off onto her porch and called out for her mother.

"Mother, mother, there is a man outside," yelled the girl.

Joseph didn't know if he should move any closer to the house and decided to stand his ground.

It was a good decision because an angry woman with a shotgun came out onto the front porch and racked a round into the chamber.

"What do you want?"

"I, I was just asking your daughter where I could find a house, that's all," he said while taking a few steps back.

"Who wants to know?"

"Just me, honestly Ma'am." He was nervous that he had overstepped some unknown Idahoan boundary.

"What is your name?"

"Joseph," he said with his hands up.

"Who are you looking for?"

"The Adamson home," he said.

"Who sent you?"

"No one, Ma'am."

"How did you find out about the Adamson's"

"Robbie Sagers at the smelter down in Midvale." Joe sure hoped this woman wasn't connected to the big lugs he had run into in Salt Lake, because he had just told her everything he knew.

"Get up here," she said to him.

"What?"

"Come on a little closer," she said now with a smile that Joseph was not able to read.

"I think that I will stay out here," he said with a puzzled look.

"You are looking for a Cameron girl right?" Margret said in a lowered voice.

"How,... What?"

"Relax. I am Margret Cameron. I won't shoot you, just yet anyway," she said lowering the barrel.

"Umm. Okay," Joe relented and walked forward with a few cautious steps.

That had been the weirdest and most difficult introduction of his life. He still was not convinced he was safe, as he walked inside of the house and sat at the dining room table. Margret placed the gun on the old table, within reach.

It was at that point that the real interrogation began. Every question imaginable, Joseph answered to the best of his ability and memory. He noticed that Margret began to relax as he explained his answers in detail to her.

"So you are Joseph from Italy?"

"Yes."

"The Joseph!"

"I hope so!"

"My daughter was very fond of a handsome young Italian man with the same name."

"She was?"

"Don't you know?"

"Of course I know, I just don't know if you were aware of that yet."

"So where were you in the month of September?"

"I had received a telegram from my brother that our mother was gravely ill and that I needed to go home."

"Where is home?"

"Italy, Spinete Italy," Joseph explained.

"My family immigrated from there," he explained.

"I am so glad to finally meet you Joseph!"

Joseph Jacobucci took a free breath.

Margret relented, and explained everything that had happened from the time that he had left to the present. She only left out one minor, but growing detail, she figured that was up to Johnetta to explain.

"There is something that I need to ask you Ma'am," he said.

"What is it?"

"I love your daughter and have planned to ask her to marry me the moment I returned from Italy, but I wanted to ask you first."

"That is very honorable of you."

Margret stood and hugged Joseph.

"Yes you have my permission," she said, now looking into his eyes.

"But you have to promise something Joseph," Margret was serious again.

"Okay," he cringed a little inside.

"You must take her away from Utah," she insisted.

"Yes, you are right," he admitted.

The whole entangled affair had become unmanageable and unsafe for both of them. Margret knew that the greatest gift she could give her girls was the freedom and her permission to leave with that blessing.

"I want to marry as soon as we are able. You should come. You, and all the sisters," he said.

"Me too?" Ethel said, poking her little head around the corner.

"I am a sister!"

"Yes, you too!" Joseph announced.

•

"Mary? Is that you?" Johnetta was asking the figure sitting on the davenport in the darkness.

"Yes, Johnetta," She replied.

"Is everything okay?"

"No." She was sobbing.

Johnetta made her way to her sister's side and sat in the darkness while she cried on her shoulder.

"What is it luv?"

"John didn't come home again last night. I know he is with that girl."

"I thought he was done with her?"

"So did I."

"What are you going to do?"

"My marriage is over, Johnetta."

"I am so sorry, Mary," she said while stroking her hair.

Suddenly, a vehicle with one headlight came crashing up the rough driveway to the farmhouse. The two sisters were peering out into the darkness trying to decipher who it was when the car squealed to a stop. The driver's door opened and a young woman with a long blonde ponytail jumped into the dim light that the one headlight was providing. She was running toward the porch. Mary jumped from the couch and met her at the front door.

"Suzanne?"

"Mary, thank God you are here!"

"What is it?"

"I saw John last night out with his,..." she hesitated.

"Girlfriend?"

"Yes."

"But that's not why I am here," she was frightened.

"What is it?"

"There were three men, big men, asking around the restaurant if anyone knew where the Cameron girls lived."

"John asked them what they wanted with the sisters," Suzanne continued.

"They said that had come from Salt Lake and were doing an investigation and needed to ask the girls some questions so they could clear up some pressing matters."

"When was this?" Mary asked.

"About eleven last night," she said.

"It gets worse," she blurted out.

"John said that he would lead the men out to his farm in the morning!"

"A friend of mine was there at the little gathering with me and told me that those men were a part of that 'hit squad' everyone is talking about."

Annie came downstairs to the sitting room during the commotion and could not believe what she heard.

"We have to run girls," Annie said with wide eyes.

"Yes, we need to get you three out of here, right now," Suzanne insisted.

"Where will we go?" Mary asked no one in particular and everyone in general.

"My parents have a remote place, near Vernal. I am going to take you there," Suzanne said.

"We get you out of the immediate danger and then you can figure out your next move," she had thought about this during the drive out to the farm.

"Do you think it's really the same guys that were watching us in Midvale?" Johnetta asked.

"Who else would it be Johnetta?" Annie said nervously.

"Makes sense," Mary interjected.

"My parents are devout Christians and I know they will protect you from the squad," Suzanne said.

"Hurry, pack your things. We have to get going."

•

The ride over to Roosevelt was difficult with a snow storm up in the mountain pass for Joseph and John. They managed to get behind a truck and rode his tracks through the thirty miles of treacherous switchbacks; pulling into the small city early in the morning. The skies had cleared and the roads were slushy. The trip that should have taken four hours had cost them eight, battling the elements.

The map Walter had made for them was clear. First they would fill up the nearly empty car, with gas, and then make their way to Johnetta. Joseph did not want to stop for anything, but knew that Felix's car would be empty in less than ten miles. Within a few minutes, they were back on the road. Only another five miles north and he would be united to his long lost love. The anticipation grew inside of his chest as his gut filled with butterflies.

The farm was on the left, on Poor Farm Road, about a half a mile west of Willis Road. They made the final turn through a wooded section, then down a hill and over a creek. The road climbed out of the valley and opened up to farmland on both sides of the street. The white farmhouse came up on the left.
"Wait!" Joseph said to his brother in the driver's seat.
"The green car!"
"Go past the house," Joe said pointing the way.
Two men stood out next to the car while another man, a very familiar man, walked out onto the porch, down the steps and toward the mysterious green vehicle. There was another vehicle, a truck, off to the side with a younger man.
"That was the gorilla from little Italy," Joe said.
"Slow down a little," he told his brother while he strained to see what he could.
"Looks like the young guy is arguing with the leader guy," Joseph said.

"I don't think the girls are there."

"How do you know that?"

"The men would be gone already if they had what they came for," John reasoned.

"Go down the road and turn around so we can drive past again," Joe instructed his brother.

"Joe, we are not going to do anything stupid."

"Just drive by again," he said.

"They don't have the girls, there was nobody in the car," John said.

"I know, but I need to see what is going on," Joe argued.

"Right now you hold the advantage Joseph, if you go back you take a chance on giving that up," he rationalized with his little brother.

"Okay, but we need to talk with the other guy. That was probably Mary's husband John," he explained.

"He would have to know where they are."

"Maybe he is hiding them from the hit squad?" Joe wondered aloud.

•

"How far along are you," Suzanne asked Johnetta.

"As near as I can figure I'm about 30 weeks," Johnetta said, trying to cover her obvious shame.

"These roads are terrible this time of year," Mary said from the back seat as they bounced along.

"So why are you doing this, Suzanne?" Annie wanted to know.

"Aren't you John's sister?" Johnetta asked.

"No, I am married to John's older brother Mark," she said.

"We don't really get along with John all that well. No offense Mary, this has nothing to do with you," she explained.

"None taken," Mary said from behind her.

"I had a cousin that had gotten pregnant out of wedlock and the man she was with left her. Then she, not the man, was made an example of," Suzanne was still disturbed by the thought.

"Her throat was slit?" Mary asked.

"Yes, like a pig you would cook for dinner," she said and a tear dropped into the dimness of the interior of the car.

"So, I wanted to help you get away," she said.

"Thank you, Suzanne," Johnetta said.

"I don't really know anything at all about you, Johnetta, but you don't deserve to die."

With that thought, silence reigned for several long moments.

"Just a few more miles." Suzanne said.

•

"Bush!"

"Larry?" Joseph said into the relative darkness of the little hallway janitor closet.

"Hey, you've got a visitor, actually two," Larry said to the man just inside the entry door.

"Who?" Joe walked toward him, looking around.

"The one that told me to come and get you. He says for you to go out back through the furnace room. He will meet you in the warehouse by the old crane."

"Okay. Who is the other visitor?"

"The other guy has been asking around here, if we knew any Italians named Joe, like he had been searching for you or something. His name is Bennie and he is a big fella who works for some big shot Bishop up in Salt Lake."

"Who is out at the old crane, Larry?"

"Can't tell you, on a promise," he said to the nervous employee.

"Don't clock in," he was not suggesting.

"I will personally write your time in later, now go."

Joseph left and within five minutes was standing by the old faded yellow crane in the dark part of the ancient plant. This area had not been in use for production, since they switched over to lead smelting, even though they stored some old equipment in the cavernous space. His heart was pounding inside his chest. Even though he had always trusted Larry, had he set him up for some unforeseen reason? The question was trying to grab his attention, but his situational awareness training had him instead focusing on escape routes and possible weapons to be used for his defense, if needed. Then out of the shadows a vaguely familiar voice called to him.

"Joseph!"

•

"My parents aren't home," Suzanne revealed when they pulled to a stop in front of the dark log residence. The long narrow driveway had snaked a quarter of a mile through a thickly wooded lot.

"What?"

"Where are they?"

"They had to travel back east to visit my Uncle, who has taken ill," she explained.

"You will be safe here, it is remote and no neighbors live close," she deduced.

"They have a telephone, but it is a party line with about ten other houses connected," Suzanne warned them to keep off, if at all possible.

"So what are we going to do now?" Annie asked, carrying her and Johnetta's bag, banging into the base of a thick aspen tree.

"You are going to make a plan and in two days I will come back and help you," Suzanne explained with a smile.

"There is plenty of food, please make yourself at home," Suzanne said, opening the door and reaching for a light.

"This is really amazing, Suzanne," Annie said.

"Thank you so much," Mary said.

"Is there a washroom?" Asked Johnetta.

"I have to pee so bad. The baby has been dancing on my bladder for half an hour."

•

"Robbie?"

"Yes," he said, and then Joseph allowed himself to breathe.

"What is going on?"

"The men that were watching you and the girls are here, waiting for you. Supposedly to ask you questions," he said just above a whisper.

"I think they want more than just that," Joe said in response.

"I believe you are right," Robbie said.

"Larry said that I had visitors," Joe explained, as he found him in the darkness.

"Where is Johnetta?" Joe asked right away.

"You didn't find her?" Robbie asked.

"No. The thugs that had chased us in Little Italy were at the Roosevelt house and the girls were nowhere to be found," he explained.

"What?"

"I don't know what has happened to any of them," Joseph said, visiting the edge of his emotions.

"I will call Walter Adamson to ask if he has heard anything."

"Mr Green, doesn't know either," Joe said.

"Mr. Green?" Robbie was confused.

"I am certain that the man called Bennie is the guy in the green car. My cousins and I have just been calling him Mr. Green," Joseph explained.

"Bennie works for the Ward Bishop's Office."

"He knows a lot of people," Robbie warned.

"Meet me up in Tooele at Don's Service Station on the south end of town, tomorrow morning at 6 am."

"Now get out of here!"

•

"Ask Johnetta if she remembers where we went to my sister's wedding," Walter instructed Mary.

"Tell her not to say the name out loud over the phone," he continued.

"Okay," Mary covered the phone to ask her sister.

"She said that she does," Mary replied.

"Good, in two days I will meet you there at four o'clock," he said.

"Where?"

"On the road at the edge of that town on the same side as your old fire pit in Inkom," he said, being intentionally vague, in case someone was listening.

"Okay, got it. Thank you, Walter!"

"Be careful!" Click.

Ten minutes later Mary phoned Suzanne to inform her that they needed a ride into Salt Lake City the day after tomorrow and they needed to leave early in the morning. The escape plan for the three Cameron sisters was set.

•

Robbie sat down in the car, closing the door.

"Morning, Joseph," he said and shook the man's hand.

"Morning, Robbie," Joe returned.

"Walter is going to try to get the girls out of hiding tomorrow," Robbie revealed.

"I will get them," Joe claimed with wide, eager eyes.

"You can't Joseph. They are watching for you. They will have your address by this afternoon, I am sure of it," he warned.

"You have to get your affairs in order and get out of town," he said.

"I have a plan. I am selling my motorcycle today to a guy from work and buying two tickets to Kansas City for Johnetta and I," he said.

"Okay, that is a start," Robbie replied.

"I thought that I would have more time," Joseph lamented.

"We all do, but time is exactly what you don't have," Robbie said.

"Do you know anyone at the courthouse that could perform a quick wedding?"

"Yes, I do. An old friend of mine is a judge in the Davis County court over in Bountiful," Robbie revealed.

"I would like the family to witness our wedding," Joe said.

"I'm not sure that you are going to have that much time Joseph," Robbie said.

"I know and I don't even know if Johnetta will say yes," he admitted.

"There is that," Robbie agreed.

"I am going to Pocatello and wait for Walter to return with Johnetta," he said.

"After I sell the bike I will gather my things and go."

"That is a good idea. Best of luck to you, Joseph," Robbie offered his hand and exited the car.

"Thank you Robbie, for all of your help," Joseph said before the door latched.

•

"Are you girls ready to go to Salt Lake?" Suzanne asked, with a smile.

"Well, we are ready, but we are not going to Salt Lake City, Suzanne," Annie said.

"What? Why not?"

"We will be headed north this morning," Mary said.

"There were people listening in on our discussion, so we lied to throw them off our track." Mary said in a more calm matter-of-fact manner.

"We wanted you to know that we needed to travel a long distance," Annie said.

"Okay, whatever you need, I am glad to help," she said brimming with renewed confidence.

"We really appreciate all that you are doing for us," Johnetta said.

"It's my pleasure," Suzanne said.

•

"It's me."

"Yes?"

"Got information on the three blind mice."

"And?"

"They are coming into Salt Lake, today."

"Good news." Andersen said to his deputy.

"Was told they will be arriving late in the day from Vernal."

"Excellent!"

"Looking forward to the reunion at last!"

"Also, one of them is pregnant," he said.

"What? Which one?"

"The young one."

"She had the Wop boyfriend?"

"Yes."

"We will definitely have to cut off that tail as soon as he shows his greasy little Italian head again."

"Yes, sir. I should have him today."

"How is that?"

"Finally I.D.'d the mangy meatball."

"Good news all around today, Bennie!"

"Going over to the smelter to get his address and then we will pick him up."

"Drop him in the soup."

"During the day shift at the smelter, you're kidding right?"

"No, you're right. Put him on ice until midnight shift, then do it."

"Gotcha boss."

•

"Walter, I have got to go pee," Johnetta said.

"Five minutes," concealing his smirk was getting harder with each mile.

Five minutes later they arrived at the house. Johnetta raced from the car across the now semi-frozen brown lawn, up the steps and inside. In her haste she did not realize that her mother had not greeted her at the door. Ethel was not around, either. The only thing on Johnetta's mind was her bulging bladder. Walter, in the meantime, took the car with the two sisters for a long ride around the block to pick up his wife and daughter, who were waiting at a friend's home.

After relieving herself and washing her hands Johnetta exited the water closet into the sitting room, tugging on her flowered print shirt. Standing in front of her was Joseph Jacobucci with a bouquet of flowers.

"Johnetta!"

"Joseph, oh my Joseph!" She ran to him and him to her. Joseph's eyes grew wide as he noticed Johnetta's protruding belly. Shame washed over Johnetta like an ocean wave, before they embraced. Joseph was stopped in his tracks by the mind-bending reality. Johnetta covered her face and cried out loud.

"I was so afraid that if you found out about the baby, you would want to run away from me!"

"Johnetta. I love you!"

"I had no idea that you were pregnant!"

"I love you and want to marry you! I would never run away from you."

"Why would you ever want to do that?" She did not believe what he said.

"Johnetta, I have searched for you for months!"

"I was afraid for so long that you ran away from me."

"I was convinced that you found out that I was pregnant and didn't want anything to do with me," she said.

Joseph closed the final two steps that separated them and gently embraced the love of his life, trying not to smash his baby in the process.

"Johnetta, I have loved you from the first time that I laid eyes on you. I want to marry you."

"Will you marry me, Johnetta?"

"Yes. I will marry you, Joseph."

"Thank you. I thought that I had lost you," Joe whispered into her ear.

"Feel this," Johnetta grabbed his hand and placed it on her belly just as a strong push came from the baby inside.

"Wow!"

"If it is a girl can we name her Maria?"

"Of course."

"You are going to be a good father Joseph Jacobucci," Johnetta said to him, smiling through her tear stained face.

•

"Bennie, I thought that you were going to have both of them taken care of today?" Bishop Andersen was beside himself. He was standing and berating the man with his office door wide open, not caring who heard.

"You snivelling idiot! They were handed to you on a platter and you managed to screw that up," his face was red with rage at this point.

"Don't forget Bishop, who found them, I did!" Bennie stood, face to face with the man and not giving an inch, this time.

"I'm just gonna close this," Andersen's secretary said without looking at either of the men and shut the door to keep the argument from bouncing further down the granite hallway.

"Now what?" Andersen asked and sat on top of his desk trying to deescalate the situation.

"There are only a few places left that they could go," Bennie suggested.

"That you know of," Andersen corrected the man again.

"Right."

"If the two of them are reunited then they probably went to Idaho where mom is located," he said, thinking out loud.

"Then go get them."

"If they get married, it becomes much more complicated."

•

"Do you, Joseph Jacobucci take Johnetta Whitelaw Cameron, to be your lawfully wedded wife?" Asked the judge in his distinguished long black robe.

"I do," Joseph said with a smile, looking into Johnetta's eyes.

"Do you, Johnetta Whitelaw Cameron, take Joseph Jacobucci to be your lawfully wedded husband?" The Judge was smiling now too.

"Yes, I do, your Honor."

"Then by the power vested in me by Davis County Utah, I have the distinct pleasure of proclaiming you husband and wife. You may kiss your bride."

Joseph and Johnetta kissed and the visitors in the courtroom celebrated.

"This is always my favorite duty as a Judge," he said while signing the official Marriage License with the newlyweds.

"Thanks Judge for doing this on short notice," Robbie shook the man's hand and smiled.

"My pleasure, Robbie, it is good to see you again."

The joyous celebration was shared by all of the Cameron girls, Margret, Walter and Ethel. Along with John, Dominic and Felix.

"Momma would be so proud Joseph," John declared to his brother.

"We are all meeting at Antonio's in Little Italy." John was informing the family of the plans for dinner. The gathering place had been kept confidential to protect everyone, just in case.

"We should go," Walter said out loud knowing that they were not safe standing outside of the court house.

•

"The Adamson house is empty sir," Bennie knew he had been foiled again and waited for the Bishop's anger to flow.

"Bennie, listen, just got word that Judge Morton up in Davis County has scheduled a last minute wedding today at the courthouse.

"Okay! We finally caught a break."

"Can you make it before the court closes?"

"It will be tight."

"Go!"

Three hours later the two cars came flying into the courthouse locking up their brakes. The four men piled out and ran up the twenty steps for the double doors. They were locked.

"Let's check around back," Bennie said to his gang of thugs.

Leaving the cars running they jogged around to the rear entrance of the building just as someone was coming out.

"Excuse me!"

"Yes?" The elderly man said.

"I am from the Ward Bishop's Office and I am in need of some information." Bennie was panting.

"Well, I am Judge Morton, how can I help you?"

•

"Ting, ting, ting, ting, ting, ting," the glasses in the crowded Italian Eatery erupted with the jubilant noise, encouraging the newlyweds to kiss again. Many of the patrons and employees, who were not part of the celebration, enjoyed the innocent scene.

Joe and Johnetta enthusiastically complied with the tradition.

"Gross!" Said Mary in jest.

Margret was overjoyed that things had worked out for Johnetta, even though there was still an undercurrent of fear for her until they got out of the state, away from the reach of the evil forces. She was reassured by Walter's presence, knowing that he was armed and somewhat dangerous.

In the pit of Margret's stomach she knew that this gathering was the last time that they would be all together, in one place. Call it a mother's intuition, if you must. She tried to devour every single precious moment, glancing from daughter to daughter and smiling at the memories that came to the front of her heart. By Margret, Annie, Mary, Johnetta and young Ethel, she was truly a blessed woman, in spite of all of the pain over the years. In that very moment, she missed both of her Dugald's, terribly and tiny Hector, knowing how much they would have enjoyed the celebration.

"Contentment is always a developing thing," she thought to herself.

"Just when you think that you have it, life brings more challenges and you question your heart's grasp on peace," she reasoned.

Margret walked over to her Johnetta and new son Joseph and whispered to them both at the same time.

"I love you, please care for each other."

And with those exact words Bennie and his crew walked through Antonio's Italian Eatery front doors.

Walter had positioned himself with a good view of the entryway, knowing that danger was at hand. He took in the celebration with one eye, and the other in search mode. Losing a friend had brought his commitment for his family's security up a notch.

Walter witnessed Bennie's entrance into the restaurant. The man's eyes scanned back and forth, before he asked the hostess a question. It was at that precise moment that Walter bolted from his chair to Johnetta and Joe, taking them by their arms; instructing them to move. They went toward the kitchen in the rear of the restaurant. He pushed the two through the swinging doors and turned.

The oblivious hostess pointed out the wedding party to Bennie and his crew. They had taken several steps in their direction, when Walter turned to look. That is when Felix and Dominic got out of their chairs to challenge the men, who were twice their size.

"Get out of my way meatball," Bennie growled, grabbing Felix by the arms and tossing him aside. His partner pushed Dominic in the chest and sent him sprawling over another table, crashing over the stunned diners, slamming into the floor.

Walter caught up to Joseph getting into Felix's car, while Johnetta opened the passenger door. Walter jumped on the running board and drew his pistol while watching the back door of the restaurant and hanging on with his left hand to the window frame.

Joe fired the car and began backing out of the parking spot when the rear door burst open. Two of Bennie's crew walked out drawing their weapons. That is when Walters .44 exploded into the evening air. The first round hit the thug on the right center mass, spraying the closing door behind him with blood and body parts. The second man was so shocked by the gun being fired at them, that he flinched and recoiled away from his collapsing partner.

Walter's second round blew a hole in the block wall behind the cringing hooligan, causing him to waver and scurry even more. Joseph jammed the car into first gear and dumped the clutch spinning the tires and lurching Walters' mass toward the back fender of the Ford. He was able to catch himself before he fell off of the moving vehicle and stand back up when Joe hit second gear. Walter sent another round erupting from the barrel of his gun to pin the man down.

Inside Antonio's after Bennie sent Felix flying and his partner crashed Dominic, three sisters stood and threw their water glasses at the two goons while screaming out that these intruders wanted to kill the bride and groom. This caused several men to rise to the newlyweds defense. Both of the men were wrestled to the ground with John holding onto Bennie's legs. Felix and Dominic piled on top throwing hay-makers. The second pair of assassins went around the melee and through the swinging doors in pursuit of the targets. They were momentarily slowed by a waitress trying to exit the kitchen with a tray full of food.

Robbie hastily led all of the women out of the restaurant's front door and down to the parked cars before the group released Bennie and his accomplice. Once Bennie produced his badge everyone fell away from the fight and the chaos subsided.

Everyone got away except the one lone Italian holding onto Bennie's legs.
"Alright little man," Bennie said, as he drove his thumb into the man's collarbone, bringing instant submission.

"We are going to have a short discussion," Bennie's partner took John's right arm and wrapped it around his back by the grip on his thumb. John groaned in pain as Bennie looked around the diner for any more threats. He had a small cut on his forehead from the impact of a glass and the blood trickled down onto his eyebrow.

They marched John outside and threw him against their idling green car with a thud.
"What's your name, grease ball?"

John just glared at the mountain of a man in front of him.
Bennie gave him a quick punch to the midsection which doubled the man over.
"I said, what's your name, meatball?" He demanded again.
"John," he coughed out between gasps for air.
"Progress."

The lone living thug from the back of the restaurant, Dave, came into the scene, white as a ghost.

"Tim's gone," he announced.

"What?"

"Shot dead by one of them," he said nodding in John's direction.

"Well John, where is Joseph going tonight?"

"I don't know," he tried to lie.

"You look just like Joseph, is he your brother?"

"No."

"You are lying to me, John, and I don't put up with people lying to me, do you understand?"

Four hard punches and John was planted face down on the ground.

"Pick him up," Bennie said to his partners.

Bennie slapped John awake with several hard smacks to the face.

"You with us Johnny?" Bennie relished this part of his job.

•

Robbie and the girls caught up with Joseph, Johnetta and Walter fifteen minutes later at the downtown Salt Lake train station.

"You have to go," Robbie was anything but calm.

"We are leaving on a train to Kansas City," Joseph announced to the group.

The girls were all huddled together hugging and saying their farewells.

"Did you see my brother or Felix and Dominic?" Joseph asked Robbie.

"No, they were piling on the big guys so you could get away," he deflected, ashamed.

"Please go back to look for them," he pleaded.

"Okay, but you two have to get on that train."

"We will."

Margret hugged her new son in law and kissed him on the cheek with a tear in the corner of her eye. She embraced Johnetta for a good long time, not wanting it to ever end, with a full stream of tears flowing down her face.

Ah wull aye loue ye, Johnetta," She said looking into her daughters crying eyes.

"Dinnae ever keek back."

"A loue ye, Mither." Johnetta managed to say with her face buried in her mother's shoulder.

"Fare thee weel, mah lassie. Fare thee weel."

"Lang may yer lum reek."

•

XIV.

'Making The Straights'

Walter grabbed the newlyweds and turned them toward the station's main entrance. "We have ten minutes until the train leaves, let's get you in your room," he whispered. The three of them took the two bags out of the car, waved to the group of family and stepped into the terminal.

Johnetta held Joseph's hand as they searched for their private room. Her head was swirling with different emotions that ranged from elated to confused. In the matter of just a few days, she had gone from alone, pregnant and on the run to married, leaving her family and beginning a new life somewhere in Missouri. The insanity of her wedding reception, Walter shooting that hand cannon of his while riding on the running board, again finding the love of her life, dealing with all of the shame of the out-of-wedlock pregnancy that she had to keep hidden for the last seven months, was all quite daunting. She felt like she had said her final farewell to her mother and maybe even her sisters, whom she loved her entire life.

Those complex emotions were rising inside of her, spinning and bringing her crippling uncertainty, like traveling on sponges with nothing firm beneath her feet, while they walked down the narrow passageway looking for suite A-14.

"You two stay put. Draw all of your blinds, keep the lights off and do not come out," Walter said.
"Okay," Joseph replied.
"I will knock five times, and five times only, when I return."
"Five times," Joe repeated the order back, like the Army.
"I am riding the train with you for awhile just to make sure that you are safe," Walter said

as he slipped his large knife behind the room marker and popped it off of the passageway wall, next to the door.

"Thank you, Walter, we appreciate all that you are doing," Johnetta smiled.

"You two are going to be fine, I am just being extra cautious," he said.

Joseph offered his hand in gratitude.

"I will say my goodbye before I leave," Walter told them.

Joseph slid the door shut and locked it, as Walter popped off more of the room identifiers from the passageway wall with his knife.

While the light was on, Joe reached into his travel bag and pulled out the Browning shotgun and installed the barrel, slid five rounds in and racked one round into the chamber.

"Just in case," he said to his nervous bride while releasing the gun's safety.

"Okay," she said, sat on the bed, and began to cry.

Joseph sat next to her and wrapped his arm around her shoulder.

"We are going to be okay, Johnetta," he whispered.

"I am the luckiest man in the world, do you know that?"

"Don't forget the light," she said afraid.

Joseph stood and flicked the switch, ushering in darkness to the tiny cabin.

•

"Leave him," Bennie said to his men. Dave gave the unconscious John a swift kick to the ribs as a parting gift and the trio loaded into their vehicles.

The ride to the Salt Lake station only took twelve minutes.

They left their cars running at the curb and bounded up the steps. Bennie was winded when they made the double doors. Upon reaching the ticket counter, Bennie produced his badge and pushed his way to the front of the small line.

"Which track is the train to Kansas City?" He demanded.

"The eight o'clock train?"

"Yes!"

"Three East."

"Where is that?"

"All the way down the concourse then left in the East Corridor."

"Thanks."

"It departs in four minutes!"

•

Walter managed to break off ten markers from the wall before another group of riders entered the car searching for their cabin. He entered the rest room at the front of the car and tossed the badges in the trash. Stepping into a stall he reloaded his gun and tucked it back in it's snug holster beneath his left arm. Exiting the restroom he went right and made the jog to exit the car. Sliding the door he stepped outside on the platform and crossed over to the next car, slid its door open and entered.

The next car forward was an open general seating car, with rows of wooden benches on each side of the aisleway. About thirty people were in the car now, double from when he had walked through with Johnetta and Joe, about eight minutes prior. People boarding the train that held private cabin tickets would all have to make their way back through this car. This is where he established his lookout position and took a seat in the final row closest to the exit. These two sets of doors would have to be his Alamo. The final exit door, the transition platform and the entry door to the cabin car is where he would make his last stand.

•

"All aboard!" The conductor announced just as the three men from the squad entered the loading platform.

"Hold that train!" Bennie screamed.

Fifteen seconds later out of breath he showed the conductor his badge.

"The train is leaving the station, sir!" The conductor proclaimed.

"Well then leave if you have to, we are coming aboard searching for a fugitive!"

"All right," he conceded.

"But don't be scaring the passengers!" The old man demanded, wagging his finger.

"Listen up," Bennie said before they entered the car.

"One each way, maintain eye contact, I will stay in the middle waiting for your signal.

Slow and thorough with big friendly smiles," Bennie instructed.

"Lift your hat off your head as a signal if you find them, then wait for us."

"Don't exit your car without turning around."

"Gotcha boss."

"If we come up empty we will search the cabin car together. Do you understand?"

"Yes."

"Yes."

•

Joe and Johnetta were lying down in their cabin bed together sharing with each other their memories and experiences from the last several months. Just trying to get a sense as to what had happened.

The time started out with them lying down next to each other both on their backs looking up into the darkness of the cabin and chatting. Joseph's right hand was on top of the Browning that was lying next to him. The awkward first few minutes gave way to a distant familiarity that they both had been desperately missing. It wasn't long before Joe was lying on his back and Johnetta's head was on his chest telling the details of her long story. They had both missed each other's company but still needed time to reestablish their connectedness. A warming calm began to enter the cabin as they talked. Bits of quiet laughter were making their way into their conversation.

Then the train jumped beneath them, pulling away from Salt Lake City, at last, and in the shadows they smiled.

•

Walter recognized the big thug from the back doors of the restaurant the instant he entered the car at the front. It was the man that he had tried to shoot but missed. Walter crossed his arms in front of him sliding his right hand onto the pistol's grip beneath his shirt. He was trying to appear like he was a tired passenger settling in for a long ride.

The goon walked as the train lurched forward, from the station. Walter saw right through his fake smile and small talk while he made his way to the back. The man hung onto each seat for stability as he passed. Walter knew he was in search mode.

"They don't know that Johnetta has a cabin," Walter realized and looked past the man through the glass window in the door and into the next car. There was Bennie. He watched the guy in Walter's car for a few moments, who then turned and peered forward, apparently watching another of his stooges. Walter knew at that moment that there had to be three men on the train.

Assassin number one was about halfway back through the car now, still walking the aisle like a creepy politician working a crowd. Walter pulled his cowboy hat down a little and prepared to enact his plan. He needed to see Bennie turn his head away toward the forward car before he could move. As the man got closer Walters' heart began to pound in his chest. The guy was now blocking his line to Bennie, in the next car.

As the goon took another step, he leaned slightly away to grab for the next seat and Walter saw that Bennie was looking away. Walter stood to his feet which drew the goon's gaze, he winked and exited through the door toward the cabin car. The man lunged for Walter but missed and was off balance when he reached for the sliding door.

Walter grabbed the man's hand and pulled him through the doorway onto the empty transition platform between the cars and buried his six inch knife into the man's throat while the door closed. He collapsed into a heap onto the steel grate. Walter looked up through the door window to see Bennie entering the general seating car in pursuit. Walter stepped through the next door into the dimly lit cabin car and broke the bulb inside of the light fixture on the wall, which covered the entry area with dark shadows.

Bennie was more than halfway through the car, moving with authority, as Walter thrust his knife through another light bulb just outside the entry door on the platform causing complete darkness to envelop the area, giving Walter the advantage he needed.

Bennie's partner caught up to him as they made it to the rear door of the car. They opened the sliding door and light illuminated the fate of their comrade. They stepped onto the platform and Dave bent down to feel for a pulse on the man's neck and was greeted by a river of sticky warm blood. Bennie looked down in horror at his fallen friend and instinctively drew his pistol from its hidden holster. The first door of the general seating car closed and shut off most of the light to the platform. The chugging train picked up speed.

In that brief hesitation, Walter made his move. Throwing his door open he landed a boot hard on the side of Bennie's right knee, dislocating it and sending him down in pain. Walter's left hand knocked Bennie's gun to the side and slashed Dave across the face with his knife. He reared back and kicked Dave in the chest sending him sprawling backward into the sliding door, grabbing for his cheek in a bloody panic.

Bennie's .38 revolver exploded next to Walter's ear as the man fell hard onto the steel platform. Walter lost grip on his knife in reaction to the gun being fired. He lunged toward the big man and brought his boot down on Bennie's fat chin and knocked him out cold with the one blow. He turned back to Dave and pulled him off of the door.

"Get up!" Walter said to the bleeding man as the train was gaining momentum. Dave tripped on his partner's dead body and almost fell on his face.

"If you jump now, you may not die," Walter made the generous offer while he put the cold barrel of his gun to the man's forehead. Without hesitation, the man jumped off of the train and into the night.

Walter knew that moving Bennie's limp body was going to take some effort. He reached the lever for the safety gate on the right side of the platform and opened it, swinging it out away from the hulking man. Walter had to sit on the platform, grab through the steel grates and push Bennie's body off with his legs. The unconscious man flipped off of the moving train bouncing away into the darkness.

Fortunately, the dead guy was not as big as the other two, so Walter grabbed him up from behind and dragged him to the side and rolled him off of the platform; closing the safety gate, he put both of his hands on his knees and drew in some deep breaths. "That could not have gone any better," he said to himself.

"What are you doing out here?" The elderly conductor was looking at Walter bent over.
"It is dark out here and I fell down," Walter lied.
"A passenger said that they heard some loud noises coming from back here," the man justified his questioning.
"That was me hitting the steel," he replied.
"Are you okay? The man asking was concerned and helped Walter stand upright.
"It looks like you are bleeding!" The conductor pointed to Walter's face.
"I cut my hand when I fell," he said.
"I am going to rinse it in the washroom," he just wanted to escape.
"You've got some blood on your face too," the man was pointing.
"Thanks. You should have someone fix these broken lights, you can't see anything out

here," Walter exited the noisy platform into the cabin car.

"I will get a maintenance guy on it right away, sir."

"Let me know if you need anything else."

The sliding door closed itself.

•

Bennie was badly bruised and his left arm was fractured from the fall off of the train. He had been outsmarted by the guy in the cowboy hat, again. He was embarrassed and angry as he limped back down the track back toward Salt Lake City. He figured that he was only a few miles east and could see many lights ahead of him, but his pace was excruciatingly slow. Every part of his body hurt and he just wanted the day to be over, but he had one thing left to do before that could happen. He had to find a phone.

An hour later he was close to a road that ran parallel to the tracks so he made his way down the embankment and onto the empty street. Another fifteen minutes and he was riding in the back of a truck heading toward the train station. Upon arrival, he waved at the generous driver and walked into the building looking for a telephone.

Showing the man his badge, a janitor let Bennie into an empty office.

"Thanks," he said.

"Do you want me to get you some help, you look terrible," asked the man.

"That's what I am doing, but thank you." Bennie responded.

He sat at the only desk in the room and picked up the phone.

Ten numbers later the line clicked a few times as operators connected the long distance call.

"Hello?" The man answered on the other end.

"Sam?"

"Bennie, is that you?"

"Yeah."

"How are you doing?"

"Not very well, Sam,"

"What's the problem?"

"My problem is on a train that will get to Kansas City Sunday morning."

"Okay. What do you need me to do?"

"End it."

•

XV.
'Peace Is'
An Epilogue.

The evening in bed talking had returned much of what had been lost over the last six and a half months of pure frustration. Johnetta and Joe shared their dreams. They agreed to try to settle in a house in the country, with enough land to have a big garden and a bunch of kids running around, as many as God would bless them with.

A simple life of family and friends, work and home, love and loss, God and country. Getting rich, becoming famous or even being noticed by anyone else was never a motivating factor for either of them. Their desire was to have a life based in love and lived in honesty. Those desires began in both of them before they knew each other. It was what they had fought for, strove toward and demanded from themselves long before that night on an eastbound passenger train.

"We are not going to Kansas City," Joe admitted.

"Why not?"

"I had to tell everyone that we were going to Kansas City to keep them safe and to keep us safe," he explained.

"The only information that they would be able to honestly communicate to anyone else would be that we were going to Kansas City."

"But we are not?" Johnetta said, still confused.

"Right. We are going to get off the train in Topeka and catch a north bound to Lincoln. From Lincoln we go to Detroit."

"So Detroit, Michigan is our final destination?"

"Yes, I can get a job working for Henry Ford."

"Ford, the car brand?"

"Yes, in a Ford factory where they build cars in Highland Park," he responded.

"Highland Park?"

"It is just north of Detroit."

"Why Ford?" She asked, somewhat surprised that he had researched the subject so thoroughly.

"Ford pays really well and he seems to care about his employees," Joe explained.

"Okay, as long as we are together and away from all of the craziness, I will be happy," she smiled at him. She was impressed.

"That's why we are switching trains," he said.

"But don't mention it to Walter," he hoped she understood his reasoning.

"To keep him safe?" She asked.

"Yes."

"Thank you for having a plan," she said to him.

"And for being so brave," she kissed him.

"I love you Johnetta."

"I love you, too."

"I could not believe the lengths that Bishop Andersen went to, and for what?" Joseph said a few moments later.

"It was Bishop Andersen?"

"That is what Robbie told me, I never have met the man." Joe stated.

"He is a creep. He was trying to control you."

"Really?"

"I think that he wanted to claim me or Annie," Johnetta said with disgust.

"Claim you? What does that mean?"

Johnetta sat up to explain.

"Because I was a young widow the church took care of me. But they also try to marry all the widows off to someone else in the church so they don't have to take care of you for very long. That is what happened to my mother after my dad died. Sometimes the older men want younger women so they can keep having more children, so they take more wives which, in Mormonism, increases their celestial status."

"Oh," Joseph was shaking his head.

"So Andersen was always trying to maneuver his way into taking a Cameron girl for his own."

"Like you were a piece of meat or something," Joe said.

"They hold life and death over their wives and even eternal life," she said.

"That's the teaching that husbands are the ones to call their wives into heaven by their secret name?"

"Yes, they teach that husbands have that authority over their wives' eternal life. I think it was set up to keep women as second class humans." Johnetta declared.

"The longer that I have lived around Mormons the more confused I become about what they believe," Joseph was shaking his head in disbelief.

"I don't," Johnetta said.

"The longer I lived around Mormon's the clearer it all became. I have lived in this lie for far too long. They lied to us to get us over here from Scotland, wanting more workers in the promised land. They lied to us to get my mom married off to Walter. They lied to us about the need for us to work to earn God's love instead of believing that Jesus' love was enough. They told us more lies so we would give more money to secure a better place in heaven. It was all lies and manipulation, for their own benefit," Johnetta had finished composing her declaration of spiritual independence.

"The Mormon mess continues," Joe said, half under his breath.

That statement triggered Johnetta's memory all the way back to a discussion that Uncle Angus and her father were having around a fire, before they left Scotland. Angus had used that exact phrase, the 'Mormon mess,' in his description of the movement. Johnetta shook her head and let out a puff of air in grave chagrin.

"That is what my uncle Angus said to my father," she confessed to Joe.

"It is so true," Joseph agreed.

"I know that now," she admitted, while feeling duped she fell into Joseph's embrace.

"You should have been to Mass back in Spinete," he said to her smiling, while reaching back in time.

"It was as if Angels visited us every time we gathered."

"That is where I truly experienced the presence of God," he proclaimed to her.

"There is nowhere like it."

"I don't think that I have ever felt that, Joseph. Now, I feel lied to," she said.

"Jesus is what we really need, Johnetta. I learned that during the war and it changed me," he told her.

"Jesus is the Savior of the world, he died for me and rose from the dead, Joseph. Joseph Smith is a fraud, who lived only for himself, and used innocent people to build his own earthly kingdom."

•

The five firm knocks to their cabin door came just past midnight. Joe gripped the Browning just in case Walter had been compromised in some fashion. Slowly opening the door, Walter was grinning on the other side.

"Is it safe to come in?" He asked with a smile.

"Yes. Of course," Joe said. Johnetta sat up in the bed as the door clicked shut.

"The problem is gone," Walter said.

"So, there was a threat?" Joe asked.

"Yes, three men. Bennie and two of his goons."

"Where are they now, Walter?" Johnetta asked.

"Well, let's just say they got off the train a few hours ago," he said.

"Thank you, Walter," she said.

"I am getting off in Denver, but I wanted to bid you farewell now so you two can get a good night's sleep."

"We appreciate everything that you have done for us," Joseph said.

Johnetta walked over and hugged her step dad.

"Walter, I just wanted to tell you how sorry I am for the way that I treated you over the years," she was looking into the man's eyes.

"That is water under the bridge, Johnetta."

"Honestly, I was so angry at my father's passing that I never gave you a chance. All of my anger got wrung out onto you and for that, I am sorry."

"I appreciate that, Johnetta."

"I wasn't much of a man back in those days and I deserved what I got. I am sorry that I wasn't a better father figure to you and your sisters," Walter confessed.

She hugged him around the neck.

"Thank you for telling me that," she said.

"Give my love to everyone."

"One more thing," Walter said and handed an envelope to Joseph.

"Congratulations on the wedding, take care of these two precious people, Joseph."

"I will Walter," is all that Joseph Jacobucci could manage to say.

The two men shook hands and Walter left their honeymoon suite. The envelope contained almost five hundred dollars from their family and friends. A contribution to their new beginning together, away from the madness of Utah.

Ten minutes after midnight on Saturday March 13, 1920, the eastbound Union Pacific train pulled into the Denver, Colorado station. Walter Adamson stepped off onto the platform and out of their lives, he caught the next train back to Salt Lake City.

Unbeknownst to any of them it would be their final meeting in this life.

Margret Whitelaw Cameron and Walter K. Adamson continued to live together in Pocatello, Idaho with young Ethel. Margret died just two months later, May 21, 1920 from cancer of the Uterus. Margret was 48. Walter remarried about a year later. To everyone's surprise nine year old Ethel died suddenly from a ruptured appendix June 8, 1921. She was laid to rest next to her mother, Margret.

Margret Cameron Sagers returned with Robbie to their quiet life in Tooele, raising their six children.

Annie Cameron took a job in the southern part of the state and fell in love with a man named John Schulston. They ran off to Jacksonville, Florida later that year and married in January 1921.

Mary Robina Cameron took a job in Pocatello and lived with her mother Margret, Walter and young Ethel. She remained living with Walter after her mother had passed away to care for Ethel. She married Bonner Shane in July 1921.

Giovanni Jacobucci recovered from the savage restaurant beating and returned to Spinete, Italy. He resided in the family home with his wife and children.

Bishop Andersen fired his wounded enforcer Bennie after three of his men ended up dead on the simple mission. Bennie slipped away into the Montana wilderness. Andersen never discovered what happened to Joseph and Johnetta Jacobucci. The Bishop's reign of terror would continue for a few more years before he came up missing. Some say that the molten lead of a smelter burned him to a fine dust.

Joseph and Johnetta Jacobucci waited over thirty three years before returning to visit family and friends in Salt Lake City, Utah. They had turned the page on their old life that had been filled with so much death, deception and destruction. They stepped together into their future and from the shadows into the light, the moment they disembarked the train at the regal Michigan Central Station in Detroit. This unexplored promiseland birthed hope in their hearts, breathed new life inside their souls, and launched another chapter in their extraordinary journey.

> "7 And he will swallow up on this mountain
> the covering that is cast over all peoples,
> the veil that is spread over all nations.
>
> 8 He will swallow up death forever;
> and the Lord God will wipe away tears from all faces,
> and the reproach of his people
> he will take away from all the earth,
> for the Lord has spoken.
>
> 9 It will be said on that day,
> "Behold, this is our God,
> we have waited for him that he might save us.
> This is the Lord; we have waited for him;
> let us be glad and rejoice in his salvation."
> Isaiah 25:7-9 ESV.

•

Bibliography
Books.

Belmonte, Peter L., "*Days Of Perfect Hell. October - November 1918. the 26th Infantry Regiment in the Meuse-Argonne Offensive,*" Atglen, Pennsylvania, Schiffer Publishing, 2015.

O'Donnell, Patrick K., "*The Unknowns, The Untold Story Of America's Unknown Soldier And WWI's Most Decorated Heroes Who Brought Him Home,*" New York, New York, Atlantic Monthly Press 2018.

Fax, Gene, "*With Their Bare Hands, General Pershing, the 79th Division, And The Battle For Montfaucon,*" New York, New York, Osprey Publishing 2017.

Yockelson, Mitchell, "*Forty-Seven Days. How Pershing's Warriors Came Of Age To Defeat The German Army In World War I*" New York, New York, New American Library, 2016.

Swanson, Ella Sagers, "*Valiant Hearts. The Life and Times of Margret Cameron Sagers and Bruce Robert Sagers, Jr.*" Tuscon Arizona, Privately Published, 1987

Smithsonian, "*World War I, The Definitive Visual History,*" New York, New York, DK Publishing, 2014. Janet Mohun, Senior Editor.

Reader's Digest, "The Story Of America" Pleasantville, New York, Reader's Digest Association, Inc, 1975.

ESV Study Bible, "Psalm 121, Isaiah 25:7-9," English Standard Version, Wheaton, Illinois, Crossway Bibles, 2008.

Martin, Walter Ralston, "*Kingdom Of The Cults,*" *Revised, Updated, and Expanded Anniversary Edition*, Minneapolis, Minnesota, Bethany House Publishers, 1997.

Organizations.

A special thank you to Director of Archives, Mr. Johnathon Casey and his dedicated team of researchers at the Edward Jones Research Center located in the National World War I Museum. 2 Memorial Drive Kansas City, Missouri.

VFW Post 1669 Royal Oak, Michigan.

Websites.

Britannica.com

Exmormon.org

Historyonthenet.com

Inkomcity.org

Lds.org

Libertyellisfoundation.org

Nps.gov

Theworldwar.org

Scotranslate.com

Scotlandwelcomesyou.com

Utah.gov

About The Author

Craig Matthews has been married for nearly four decades to his high school sweetheart. They live surrounded by woods in rural Michigan at the end of a dead end road. They have three married adult children, seven grandchildren and currently nine chickens. Craig has always been an American history buff. He enjoys his speaking engagements, reading at the beach, backpacking, writing, baseball, kayaking, playing with his grand kids, storytelling and many forms of creative expression.

Craig Matthews (on the right, complete with his 'writing beard') with his late brother Jeffery Cameron (in the cool shades) on the grounds of the National World War One Memorial in Kansas City, Missouri, January 2020. Jeff lost his twenty-seven month fight with stage four colon cancer on July 8th, 2020. Craig was present and praying for Jeff as he crossed over from death to life.

Rest in Peace, my Brother.